DOWN TO THE SEA

A Novel of The Lost Regiment

William R. Forstchen

D0126660

A ROC BOOK

ROC
Published by New American Library, a division of
Penguin Putnam Inc., 375 Hudson Street,
New York, New York 10014, U.S.A.
Penguin Books Ltd, 27 Wrights Lane,
London W8 5TZ, England
Penguin Books Australia Ltd, Ringwood,
Victoria, Australia
Penguin Books Canada Ltd, 10 Alcorn Avenue,
Toronto, Ontario, Canada M4V 3B2
Penguin Books (N.Z.) Ltd, 182–190 Wairau Road,
Auckland 10, New Zealand

Penguin Books Ltd, Registered Offices:
Harmondsworth, Middlesex, England

First published by Roc, an imprint of New American Library,
a division of Penguin Putnam Inc.

First Printing, December 2000
10 9 8 7 6 5 4 3 2 1

 REGISTERED TRADEMARK—MARCA REGISTRADA

Printed in the United States of America

PUBLISHER'S NOTE
This is a work of fiction. Names, characters, places, and incidents either are
the product of the author's imagination or are used fictitiously, and any
resemblance to actual persons, living or dead, business establishments, events,
or locales is entirely coincidental.

BOOKS ARE AVAILABLE AT QUANTITY DISCOUNTS WHEN USED TO PROMOTE
PRODUCTS OR SERVICES. FOR INFORMATION PLEASE WRITE TO PREMIUM
MARKETING DIVISION, PENGUIN PUTNAM INC., 375 HUDSON STREET, NEW YORK,
NEW YORK 10014.

If you purchased this book without a cover you should be aware that this
book is stolen property. It was reported as "unsold and destroyed" to
the publisher and neither the author nor the publisher has received any
payment for this "stripped book."

For Clayton Stokes, who, with a letter at the right moment, helped set things on the proper path; the fire control guys on the Web who awe me with their technical knowledge; Gus, who gave me a whole new perspective on the "adventure" of life; and, finally for a little friend, Adam Rose, a young man filled with courage.

PROLOGUE

"As I look upon you today, I see not just the promise of the future, but also the spirits of all those who gave the last full measure of devotion so that we could be here to celebrate this day."

President of the Republic, Andrew Lawrence Keane, paused for a moment. His gaze swept the audience, the ranks of the new cadets graduating from the academies, their families, and the thousands who had gathered to celebrate with them.

In the crowds, he could see the few who had survived, old comrades of so many hard-fought battles. Some nodded in recognition, others stiffened to attention, several of them saluting as their old commander looked their way.

God, have we really grown old? he wondered. Wasn't it just yesterday that we came to this world? Wasn't it just yesterday that on these very plains beyond the city of Suzdal we drilled our new army, preparing for our first battle?

His comrades of youth had slipped away, and it was hard to accept that he was drifting with them as well. Already they were the stories of yesterday, memories fading, turning to gray and then to hazy white.

He caught a glimpse of old Pat O'Donald, barrel chest long ago slipping to his belt line, retired from the army, now a popular senator. He was sitting with the other dignitaries: William Webster, yet again secretary of the treasury; Chief Justice of the Supreme Court Casmir; Gates, publisher of a chain of papers; Varinnia Ferguson, president of the technical college—all of them growing old. Others were gone forever, crossing over the river to join comrades who had made that final journey long years before. Kal was gone, as was Emil, who had seemed like he would live forever, but had drifted into the final sleep only the winter before.

Yet, at this moment, he could see them as it was so long ago, the men of his army, Mina, Ferguson, Malady, Showalter, Whatley, and Kindred. And behind them the hundreds of thousands who had died to create the Republic, to give them the blessed days of peace that had lasted for twenty years.

He was suddenly aware that he had not continued with his speech, but his audience was patient. They knew what he was feeling at this moment, and he saw more than one lower his head, wiping tears from his eyes.

The boys graduating from the naval and army academies—and they did still seem like boys—waited patiently, looking up at him, and he smiled.

"I have but two things to say to you today." He paused, a rhetorical flourish this time, as he stepped out from behind the podium and indicated the flag of the Republic with his one arm.

"Love freedom. Love it more than anything else on this world. There is but one of two conditions in this life: you are either free, or you are a slave. We, your parents, fought a war unlike any other. It was not to conquer. It was not for power. It had but one purpose, and that was to set us free, to set free you, our children who were yet unborn.

"So love that freedom as you would your mothers, your fathers, and the families you shall one day have. Do that, and this Republic will endure.

"The second thing is about the concept of the Republic and the relationship between government and free citizens, who must remain eternally vigilant, and will take at least an hour to explain."

He could see more than one cadet shift uncomfortably, struggling to remain polite, as the day was hot and their dress uniforms made it even worse. He smiled.

"But your families await you for a final farewell before you leave for your postings, and, frankly, during all my years I've heard too many long-winded speeches and given more than one myself. So, I'm letting you off. Let's close this ceremony and have some fun."

Polite chuckles erupted, and a few of the old veterans shouted for him to go ahead and talk as long as he wanted. He held up his hand and waved them off, then stepped away from the podium. A cheer erupted from the graduating cadets, and a thunderous ovation rose from the entire audience. The band sitting on a raised platform behind him stood up and started to play the national anthem, "The

Battle Hymn of the Republic." Within seconds the thousands gathered joined in.

Andrew looked over at Kathleen and took her hand in his and squeezed it. The words, no matter how many times they were sung, always cut into his soul. . . .

"I have seen Him in the watchfires of a hundred circling camps . . ."

Watchfires . . . the Tugar watchfires; encamped on this very spot outside the city, he thought, remembering the bitter cold of that winter and the siege.

"In rows of burnished steel . . ."

The charge at Hispania, sweeping down from the heights, bayonets fixed, the final, desperate lunge that swept us to victory.

He lowered his head. The final stanza always moved him to tears.

"As He died to make men holy, let us die to make men free . . ."

The last refrain echoed, and though the official language of the Republic was now English, many sang the words in their native tongues: Rus, Latin, Chinese, Japanese, Greek, Welsh, Gaelic, old Norse, and a dozen other languages spoken in the fifteen states of the Republic.

As tradition demanded, when the last words drifted away, the cadets broke into a cheer, hats flying into the air; the black campaign hats of the infantry, the white caps of the navy, and the sky blue of the aerosteamer corps.

He looked over at Kathleen. Unashamed tears flowed from both of them, for this was not just another ceremony of state for them. She leaned against his shoulder.

"The house will be empty tonight," she whispered.

"It has been ever since he went off to the academy."

"Not really, Andrew. He was home on vacations, weekend passes. We knew where he was. . . ." Her voice trailed off.

"We have to let go sometime."

She said nothing, and he pulled her closer.

Madison, their oldest daughter, was married now, living in Roum, where her husband was stationed with the railroad engineering corps. The others—he tried not to think too much about them. The twins had died seven years ago in the typhoid fever epidemic, and young Hans had been taken the following spring by consumption.

Abraham was the last of their children, born the autumn after the end of the war, and he had grown up far too quickly. Andrew saw him coming through the crowd, which was swarming up around the speaker's platform. His arm was thrown around his closest friend, Sean O'Donald, wearing the sky blue uniform of a newly commissioned pilot.

Andrew quickly wiped away his tears, and Kathleen, forcing a smile, went up to embrace him. The boys stopped, both of them grinning, and snapped off their salutes to the president. Andrew, putting on his stovepipe hat, returned the salute. The hat, in fact the entire ceremonial outfit of the presidency on this world, made him feel more than a bit self-conscious. Old Kal was the first to adopt the stovepipe hat, black morning coat, and chin whiskers of the legendary Lincoln, and forever impressed in the mind of the populace that this was what a president was supposed to wear. In his first term as president, Andrew had reluctantly adopted it.

As the Constitution demanded, a president could serve only one six-year term, and for twelve years he had been out of office, though he had accepted a seat on the Supreme Court and, at the same time, had returned to his first profession, that of a college professor.

The Chin crisis, however, had forced his return to the political arena. The Chin had created something he had always hoped to avoid, a political party based on power for one ethnic group, a disastrous development for a nation he had dreamed could somehow merge itself together into a single entity that ignored national origin and race.

In writing the Constitution he had (and would admit to no one that it was deliberate) left out any restriction against nonconsecutive terms and thus ran for president again. The Chin had mounted an opposition, but all the other states rallied to Keane and it had been a landside. In the first hundred days of office he rammed through dozens of bills and several constitutional amendments, the key ones being that English would forever be the official language of the state. The argument was simple: of all the fighting units, the men of the 35th Maine and the 44th New York, who represented no particular group, had fought to free all people. English was the compromise that favored no one state of the Republic over the others.

He had carried it off, cooled the crisis, and, combined with an explosion of economic growth, the Republic was now flourishing.

Kathleen stepped past him, sweeping Abraham into her arms. The boy looked over at Andrew, smiling indulgently. He knew his mother would never accept the fact that he had already grown up.

He could see Kathleen in the boy's fair complexion, the wisp of reddish hue to his hair, but he saw his own eyes in the boy, pale blue, but deep and filled with intensity.

Sean O'Donald stood behind him, so unlike his father, so much his Roum mother; tall, slender, dark eyes, jet black hair. So like his mother as well in spirit: quiet, introspective, stunning in intellect. It was hard to believe that here was the son of the brawling artilleryman Pat O'Donald.

Pat came up behind the two boys and clapped both of them on the shoulders. "Congratulations, me boys," he said, his voice filled with emotion.

He was breathing hard, florid features bright red from the noonday heat, and undoubtedly from the "nip of the cruel," as he put it, that increasingly controlled his life. Throughout the war Pat had reveled in the shock of combat, but after the death of Hans, something seemed to slip away. Like so many veterans, he was haunted by having seen more than any one man should bear and having carried one too many burdens.

Sean stiffened and turned to face his father. "Good morning, sir, and thank you."

Pat's gaze caught Andrew's for a second. He seemed to want to hug the boy, but instead just extended his beefy hand, which Sean took, held for a second, and let drop.

Abraham, at last free of his mother's tearful embrace, stepped back and smiled.

Two more newly commissioned officers came up to join them, and Andrew turned to acknowledge them.

"Father," Abraham announced, "may I introduce two of my friends, Flight Officer Adam Rosovich and Flight Officer Richard Cromwell."

The two snapped to attention and saluted. Andrew returned the salute, his old military bearing still with him, then extended his hand.

Adam he vaguely knew by sight, Cromwell by the controversy that had surrounded his admission to the Naval Academy. His father was, after all, the arch traitor of the war; the overplayed villain in more than one of the melodramas so popular now in the playhouses. He was five years older than most of the cadets, his mother a Merki slave who had survived the slaughter pits and annihilation that had destroyed most of Cartha when the wars ended.

When Cromwell had presented himself to the admissions board, claiming the right of the son of a veteran of the original Yankees who had come to this world, it had triggered outrage and, at first, a denial. Then Andrew had directly intervened, making a special ruling that any son of a Yankee could claim admission if he passed the boards.

He looked into Cromwell's eyes, never having met him, and in that instant judged his decision to be a sound one. Cromwell returned his gaze unswervingly, and he sensed that the bitter years of survival as a slave had bred a toughness in the young man that few of this generation now had, having grown up in a world of peace.

He was almost as tall as Andrew at six foot four and slender to the point of looking gaunt, a clear sign of the malnourishment he had suffered as a child growing up a slave in the enemy camps. But it was evident that he was hard, his wiry frame taut and strong. His left cheek was marked with a pale scar that cut from the ear to the corner of his mouth, most likely a blow from a whip or dagger, and Andrew suspected that if this young man took his dress uniform off, a body cut by such scars would be revealed.

Millions of Chin and Cartha had suffered thus when the Hordes had stopped in their migrations to fight the Republic, turning the people of those two nations into slaves and a source of food. That any of the children of that generation had survived was a miracle. When the Merki had abandoned the Cartha realm, they had systematically slaughtered more than a million people. Cromwell was but one of a few thousand children to survive the nightmare.

His grip was firm. He hesitated for a second, then finally spoke.

"Mr. President, thank you for intervening on my behalf."

"Don't thank me, Cromwell. Though some do not care for the name you carry, I will say that I knew your father and believe the reports that in his last seconds he had a change of heart and died serving the Republic. I think we've made a good bet on you, son. Just prove us right."

Cromwell solemnly nodded his thanks, his dark features again revealing a toughness that Andrew sensed could be dangerous in a fight.

"Father, we got our orders. We head out this evening and, well, we sort of want to . . ." Abraham's voice trailed off.

Andrew looked back at his son. Such a contrast, he thought, between his own boy and Cromwell. Abraham, born after the war, had known only peace and saw the old conflict in a hazy, romantic light. Cromwell was old enough to know different and had been shaped by that knowledge. Andrew wondered how his boy would look a year from now and felt a sudden stab of fear.

Things were happening, out in their adopted world, and all his old instincts told him that there was a storm on the horizon. He feared it would soon wash over them and perhaps sweep his son away.

Abraham was waiting for an answer, and Andrew forced a smile. "I know, head down to the Mouse for a few."

The Roaring Mouse was a tavern run by one of former president Kal's nephews, a legendary haunt amongst the cadets. The place was supposedly strictly off limits while they were in the academy, but it would go out of business if that rule was observed.

"Your assignments?" Andrew asked.

"You know where I'm heading, and, sir, it bothers me," Abraham announced.

"Orders are to be obeyed whether you like them or not," Andrew said with mock severity. "The fact that you are assigned to General Hawthorne's staff has nothing to do with politics. You scored in the top five of your class, that's the usual slot, so not another word on it."

It was an outright lie, but after all the years of service, he felt he had the right to ensure that his only surviving son was safe for a while.

Abraham looked around at his friends, obviously a bit relieved by his father's statement, which showed that he had not tried to pull for such a plum assignment.

"And the rest of you?" Andrew asked.

"Air reconnaissance officer on the *Gettysburg*," Cromwell replied.

"Naval Ordnance Development Board," Rosovich replied, a slight note of disappointment in his voice.

"You don't sound happy, lieutenant," Andrew said with a smile.

"Ah, yes, sir, I am."

It was an obvious lie.

"He wanted a field assignment," Abraham interjected, and Andrew could sense that his son was playing a little game. Most likely Adam had pressed him to try for a last-minute change of assignments.

"Mr. Rosovich, if you were selected for the Development Board, it was undoubtedly because Professor Ferguson asked for you. I'd guess you scored in the top of your class in flight engineering."

Adam reluctantly nodded his head. "Yes, sir, I did."

"Then the finest service you could perform for the Republic is to take this assignment. Don't worry, you'll have plenty of chances later for a flight squadron."

Adam smiled politely, his gambit an obvious failure.

Sean O'Donald, who had been standing quietly to one side, finally spoke up. "Air reconnaissance officer on the *Gettysburg* as well, sir," he announced.

Pat looked over anxiously at Andrew, and in that flicker was a subtle indication that Pat would have preferred something far safer.

"They must think highly of your ability to put you with our navy's newest armored cruiser."

"I asked for it, sir."

Andrew nodded, saying nothing.

He looked at the four young officers, all of them filled with such hopes and enthusiasm this day, all looking so proper and elegant in their dress uniforms. In the crowd gathered below the platform, he saw more than one young lady waiting patiently, gazes fixed on their chosen beaus. He smiled inwardly, wondering how long the comrades would actually stay together at the Mouse before secretly heading off for a final, brief rendezvous. They were all shipping out today. That was another tradition of the service, to send out the new cadets on their graduation day, and he suspected that more than one would make a promise of marriage once their first six-month tour of duty was up. He silently prayed that they'd still be alive to keep those promises.

"Go on, boys. Abraham, your mother and I will see you off later at the station."

Again the smiling salutes and the four comrades turned, leaping off the platform to disappear into the crowd. Andrew's thoughts turned toward his own affairs. Other burdens now awaited him. a congressman from Constantine, corrupt as the summer day was long, was looking for yet another government job for a "nephew." And Father Casmir, now a member of the Supreme Court, wanted to argue yet again about the Ming Proposal. Behind them, Andrew could picture all the other seekers, flesh pressers, hangers-on, critics, and false praisers.

So now I look like Lincoln, he thought, absently reaching up to touch the gray chin whiskers, which Kathleen, in private, kept threatening to cut while he was asleep. As he looked over at her, a flash of pride and love swept through him, for already she had composed herself. She was turning to sidetrack a senator whom she knew was a gadfly to Andrew, charming the man with compliments about his far too young wife.

Pat pressed in closer. "Times I wish we could erase all these years, be back at our tent at the front, sharing a bottle with Emil and Hans."

"The old days are gone, Pat. It's a new age now."

"Ah, I know, Andrew darlin', I know. It's just hard to believe how quickly it changed."

"Your boy looks fit. He'll do well."

Pat lowered his head, and an audible sigh escaped him. "He never cared for me, you could see that today. I've tried to make amends, I have."

Andrew was silent—for what could be said? The boy, like Abraham, has been born the autumn after the end of the war, his mother of Roum aristocracy, a niece of old Proconsul Marius. And Pat had never married her. Andrew, Emil, all of Pat's friends, had tried to push him on the issue, but he would laugh, then sigh and say he could never be tied down, and Livia, the darling, understood that.

And yet she gave the boy his father's name, raised him with love, and waited for the soldier she loved to one day

acknowledge the truth of their union. She had died waiting.
Only then had Pat realized his mistake, but by then it was
far too late. Though the boy accepted his father's recognition now, there was no love.

Pat wistfully watched as his boy fell in with the others,
disappearing into the crowd.

"Pat, we do have to talk later."

"What?"

"I don't want word of this getting out, but I want your
opinion on recent events."

Three events, unrelated on the surface, had occurred in
the last month, and he alone was privy to all of them. Hawthorne had brought the first news, an anomaly noticed a
week ago at an obscure outpost named Tamira's Bridge,
where a skirmish had erupted between the cavalry and a
rogue gang of Bantag riders. One of the dead Bantag was
carrying a revolver. It was not an old remnant of the Great
War, but a modern weapon; in fact, better than anything
the Republic could manufacture.

The second was political: yet another flare-up by the
Xing Sha movement in the state of Chin, calling for separa-
tion from the Republic and renouncing the treaty with the
Bantag. The annoying madness would consume yet more
time and struggle to try and hold the expanding Republic
together and keep it from fragmenting apart into rival
states.

The third one, though, worried him the most. It had
preyed on his thoughts even while giving his speech on
what was supposed to be a day of happiness and pride. A
courier bearing a sealed dispatch from Admiral Bullfinch,
headquartered down in Constantine, the main base of the
Republic's fleet on the Great Southern Sea, had arrived
only minutes before he left the White House this morning.

A merchant ship, thought lost in a storm two months
ago, had limped into the harbor the night before last. Its
report was chilling.

Driven farther south by the storm than anyone had pre-
viously gone and returned to tell the tale, the captain of
the ship reported making landfall on an island of the dead.
They had found a human city there, one that obviously had
been annihilated within the previous year.

It was a city of thousands and had not fallen prey to the

Malacca Pirates, which had been the main concern of the fleet in recent years. The city had been flattened, and some of the remains of the dead showed that they had been eaten. One of the sailors, a veteran of the Great War, said it looked like Roum after the siege. Buildings had been blown apart by shelling and the streets were still littered with fragments, shell casings—and the wreckage of an airship.

The city, however, was over five hundred miles south of the treaty line drawn with the Kazan embassy. The ship's presence in those waters was a direct violation of the treaty and thus no inquiry could be made officially at the twice yearly meeting with the ambassador of Kazan, which took place at a neutral island on the boundary line. If more was to be learned, it would have to be done by other means.

Pat, looking at Andrew, could sense his uneasiness, and he drew closer. "It's the Kazan, isn't it? Something's been found at last."

The flicker of the old light in Pat's eyes was disturbing to Andrew, for somehow it rekindled something is his own soul as well, something he would prefer remained forever buried.

"How did you know?" Andrew whispered.

"Andrew, darlin', I can smell a war from a thousand miles off. I've told you for years there'd be another, and I can see it in your eyes."

Andrew looked at him closely. He was holding something back.

"All right," Pat chuckled, "one of my staffers saw the courier and asked around the train crew this morning. They say the docks and rail yards are already buzzing with word about it. Something's coming, Andrew, something big, something beyond anything we've ever known. You can sense it the same way you can feel a storm coming long before you see it."

Andrew nodded, looking at the happy crowd, enjoying this day of peace; the eager boyish faces of the new officers, the proud gazes of parents, many of them veterans like himself.

We were that young, Andrew realized, when we fought our war. Boys really, going off to see the elephant, never dreaming that it would bring us to this mad, terrible world, and though we were boys, we quickly became men of war.

He caught a glimpse of his son at the edge of the crowd, following a stream of cadets heading to their traditional watering place for one last round before shipping out.

"If what happened to that city is any indication of who the Kazan are, there will be war. But it will be their war, Pat," he whispered, nodding to the young cadets, "and God help them."

ONE

Hanaga tu Zartak, the Qarth of the Blue Banner of the Kazan, left his stateroom and strode onto the foredeck of his flagship, the great battle cruiser *Halanaga*. A triumphal roar, echoing from half a thousand of his followers, greeted his appearance; clenched fists raised heavenward in salute.

His gaze swept the assembly, and then he lifted his eyes to the fleet of nearly a hundred ships, which even now was steaming out to sea. Fast-moving frigates plowed through the curling waves, spray soaring up, catching the early morning sun in what seemed to be showers of bright red rubies cascading across the decks. Billowing clouds of black smoke coiled from stacks, whipping out to windward, and water foamed up from astern as the frigates leapt forward to take position at the van of the armada.

Behind them rode the armored cruisers, several of the older ships still sporting masts, which this morning were stripped of sails. And finally came his ship and the five other great battle cruisers of the fleet of the Blue Banner.

Crevaga Harbor, known to the human cattle who inhabited it as Crete, already lay astern, the smoking ruins of their city a beacon that he knew would draw the fleet of the Red Banner as surely as the scent of rotten carrion drew the eaters of the dead. The human city had been under the direct control of his brother since its coal mines were a precious source of fuel for his fleet. The maneuvers of the last six months, the sweeping of the Cretan Isles, the destruction of his brother's base of supplies and human slaves, had changed the course of the war, shifting the balance back to his favor. The long-anticipated final confrontation would be today, deciding whether he would hold the throne or his brother, Yasim the Usurper, would gain ascendancy.

The roaring cheers of his faithful echoed and reechoed, picked up by the other ships cruising nearby. A light frigate, racing at full steam, cut across the stern of his ship, plowing through the wake, bow shooting high into the air to come crashing down in an explosion of spray. The Shiv warriors, humans bred by the Holy Order of the Shiv, lined the deck with raised fists, their distant cries echoing.

He acknowledged their salutes, but his heart turned cold at the sight of them. The Order had been the one winner throughout this conflict, which had pitted the family of Zartak against itself. Five brothers had turned against one another, and now there were only two, Yasim and himself. But always the cult of the Shiv had been there, claiming holy neutrality and slowly gaining in power.

He had paid handsomely for their services, draining his coffers for warriors and for the assassins who had dispatched two of his brothers and various cousins. Once today was finished, there would be the reckoning with the Shiv. It was already planned, and he would see it through to its bloody conclusion.

He looked over his shoulder at the temple room, located just aft of the forward bridge. Hazin, his personal priest from the Order, had stepped on to the bridge, trailed by a steaming cloud of sweet-smelling incense. In his hands was the Holy Gir, the text of the Prophet Vishta, He who had walked between the stars.

As Hazin held the book aloft, all fell silent. Many fell to their knees and lowered their heads as Hazin, in the ancient tongue, called for the blessing. Hanaga endured the ritual. It was, after all, part of the game of power. The prayer finished, he stood back up and lowered his head to kiss the sacred text then turned to face the assembly.

"Today is the day we will claim victory!" he cried, and lusty cheers greeted his words.

"Today is the day we have striven for, the day that shall end the bitter strife caused by all those of my clan who wish to claim the empire. After today, my comrades, there shall be an end to it. We shall go home and again know peace."

"Signal from frigate *Cinuvia,* my lord."

One of the signal commanders stood respectfully at his side, hesitant to interrupt. Hanaga nodded for him to continue, even while cheer after cheer echoed up from the foredeck.

"Enemy fleet of seven battle cruisers in sight."

Hanaga turned and looked at the assembly of staff officers gathered around him. "Was it not as I said it would be? The fleet of the Red Banner has taken our bait. Today, my comrades, we shall see my brother defeated—"

"Sire, there's more," the signal officer interrupted.

Hanaga looked over at the aging, gray-pelted officer, a loyal warrior who had stayed by his side when so many others had gone to the Usurper. He could sense the tension in his voice.

"Go on."

"Sire, frigate *Cinuvia* also signals a report, a message dropped from a scout airship. Behind the fleet of the Red Banner, the White Banner fleet of your cousin Sar approaches as well, and is fifteen leagues to the southeast behind the Red fleet."

Stunned, Hanaga said nothing. A lifetime of intrigue had taught him to make his face a mirror of indifference, and yet, those who knew him noticed the intake of breath, saw the nervous flicker of his eyes as he struggled for control.

He nodded, looking away, wondering how many other ships' captains were, at this very instant, reading the same signal flags. When this day was finished, if she still lived, he'd gut *Cinuvia*'s captain for being either a fool or a traitor bent on shattering morale.

"It doesn't matter now," Hanaga finally replied in a soft whisper. "Let my cousin join my brother. Fifteen leagues gives us three hours before they come in range. We will smash my brother before they arrive. We will settle it today." He scanned those gathered about him. "Settled here, now!"

All were silent.

"To your stations my *andu,* my brothers of blood. Not a word to those beneath you that Sar has betrayed us."

The officers silently departed the bridge while pipers sounded the call to battle stations. The lower ranks, still ignorant of the news, cheered lustily as they ran to their stations.

Hanaga raised his glasses, training them forward. Yes, he could see the lead ships of his brother's fleet on the horizon, which was dark with smoke. They were coming on fast. He wondered if their coal bunkers were nearly empty.

The voice of prudence whispered to him to pull back. The island behind him lay in smoking ruins. The vast stockpile of coal, hundreds of thousands of tons, enough to fuel the entire fleet for a month, was a raging inferno. The column of smoke was a beacon visible from a hundred miles away.

Pull back, draw him out. His troops occupied the hills above the town and would prevent any attempt at mining. But if his cousin had indeed betrayed him and switched sides, he could not hesitate. He had to destroy his brother today.

Damn Sar. Chances were that he would switch sides yet again, going over to the winner of this fight. To pull back now would show fear, and Sar would then join Yasim for certain.

An aerosteamer swept through his view for a second, trailing smoke. The air battle, which had been raging since before dawn, continued above the fleet. He lowered his glasses. The airship was several miles off, flame licking along its portside wing. Several Red Banner planes trailed it, weaving back and forth, flashes of light flickering from their forward and topside gunners. The burning ship's portside wing folded in, and the plane spiraled down, smacking into the sea. The Red planes broke off, dodging outside the range of a frigate's guns, water spraying up several hundred yards short. The planes spiraled upward, gaining altitude.

Annoying flies, Hanaga thought, rarely capable of damaging a battle cruiser but bothersome nevertheless. He trained his glasses back on the horizon. It was difficult to discern, but he thought he could see the observation tower of a battle cruiser, a dot between sea and sky. The horizon, for the breath of a hand span, was black with smoke that continued to spread, sign enough that the entire fleet was approaching.

His frigates, storming forward at nearly fifteen knots, were now more than a league ahead and spreading out, while the cruiser squadron moved to windward, staying in formation, line abreast.

Walking to the railing he looked aft, back toward Crevaga. The human city was in flames, marking the immolation of a hundred thousand, a city which had been part of his traitorous brother's original fiefdom. So much for Yasim's protection. It had fed the warriors of his fleet in an orgy of feasting that had lasted three days and nights.

The bridge around him was cleared, all having respectfully withdrawn, and he saw the priest of the Holy Order. He beckoned Hazin to come to his side.

"You assured me that the Grand Master had taken care of Sar," he snarled, keeping his voice low so no one would hear the exchange.

"I did, Your Highness."

"I emptied my treasury to your Order. Yesterday, when we assaulted this city, your precious Shiv warriors failed to arrive as promised."

"Sire, you know a storm swept south of here. It delayed the transports."

"And now Sar has joined my brother? To many coincidences, priest. Too many."

"Sire, I can assure you that the Order honors its contracts."

"Hanaga sniffed derisively. "If I believed all you told me, Hazin, I'd have died years ago. I do not believe in coincidences. I paid more than thirty million to the Grand Master to use the Shiv and thus spare my troops, and another thirty to assure that Sar either joined me or was killed."

"And I can promise you he has joined you. Yes, his fleet sails behind your brother's. And why? Wait until battle is well joined and you will see."

Hanaga turned and caught the eye of his officer of the guard, motioning him to come over as well. "I have been assured by this priest that Sar is on our side."

The guard, well understanding the tone of his master, said nothing, waiting for what came next.

"If Sar's ships open fire on us, I want you to cut his heart out."

Hazin's gaze did not waver. "I can assure you, sire," he whispered, "such theatrical statements are a waste of time for both of us. You will see the truth soon enough."

Ignoring him, Hanaga turned away, raising his telescope to scan the approaching fleet.

The smoke on the horizon continued to expand outward. The observation tower of a battle cruiser now rose well above the horizon, and he saw more tops as well. The range had to be less than seven leagues.

Hanaga turned to an aide and told him to pass the word

to the master gunner to be certain to lay on the lead battle cruiser.

Speed dropped off slightly as steam was diverted from
the engines to power the six armored turrets, two forward,
two amidships and two aft. The ponderous turrets slowly
began to turn to port, then back to starboard, testing their
traverse. As they did, the single heavy gun in each turret
rose, then lowered. The lighter turrets, lined up below on
the lower gun deck, did the same, but these were powered
by the muscle of a half dozen crew turning the traverse
cranks.

Atop the main turrets, gunners handling the steam-powered
multiple-barrel guns were busy loading clips of ammunition.
Spotters were scanning the skies overhead, watching as
aerosteamers dodged in and out, skirmishing, jockeying
for position.

Another one came spiraling down, this one with the distinctive fork-tailed stern and single main wing of a Red
Banner plane.

"Sire, may I point out that if Sar was not fulfilling his
obligation, he'd be sailing with your brother. Instead, he is
farther back," Hazin whispered, daring to come to Hanaga's side.

Hanaga felt a cool uneasiness that the priest stood so
close to him. The Order of the Shiv, once just another cult,
was now a power to be feared even by those of the Golden
Family of the Throne. After all, it was he who had first
used them to murder his elder brother for control of the
throne. Hazin had been the instrument behind that first
arrangement and during the last twenty years of conflict
Hazin had stayed by his side.

"I would interpret this as meaning that Sar is coming on
at full steam," Hazin continued, whispering softly. "Your
brother is trying to avoid action with him and close with us
first. This is not betrayal, it is fulfillment of an agreement."

Hanaga looked over. Yes, the priest did have the
"sense," the at times unnerving ability to read minds. It
was why he made such an excellent truth sayer, one who
could read the thoughts of the unwary, who were not aware
that a Master Priest of the Order often hid behind the
throne at audiences.

He could sense the priest's eyes looking at him, piercing,

as if gazing straight into his soul. He knew the priest was trying to gain an advantage, and he held his gaze for a moment, then threw back his head and laughed.

"There is a game within a game, priest, and at this moment I shall simply carve straight in and see if Tenga"—as he said the word of the Immortal, he briefly lowered his head—"is with me or not."

The priest smiled. "I never knew you across all these years to be religious. You use me as you use anyone else."

"Yet I once called you a friend."

He allowed himself to smile when he spoke the word *friend*. It had indeed been true. They were of the same age. Hazin, of a minor family, had been sent to be a playmate and companion before going off to join the Order. The Order had returned him, ten years later, to serve as adviser and liaison to a brother who would murder a brother and thus start the bloody civil war that had consumed the Empire.

"Once?"

"You have your path, I mine. Besides, did you not once tell me that only fools have friends, and emperors who are fools do not live long?"

"No, you still have friends, My Emperor. The difference is, at least with your friends, if you should decide to dispose of them, you give them a painless death."

Hazin smiled. "Your offer to have my heart cut out rather than consign me to the amphitheater, is that a mark of friendship in our world?"

"If I want to be emperor, I need first of all to be ruthless, even to friends if need be. You told me that as well more than once. 'The greater the power you seek, the fewer you should allow yourself to love. For ultimate power, let no one into your heart.' Thus it was written by Batula the Prophet."

Hazin smiled. "I taught you that, you know."

"Yes, I know."

The emperor continued to stare at Hazin for a moment, as if trying to judge something, and then he turned away, deliberately focusing his attention on his brother's fleet, drawing closer. The hulls of the battle cruisers, and even of the frigates, were clearly in view. The range was less than four leagues.

Behind him, the bridge crew was at work. The master gunner was quietly communicating via a speaking tube with the range finders perched inside the observation platform, which soared a hundred feet above the bridge. Receiving the report, he then pulled open another tube and passed the information on to the turrets, where gun elevations were being set. Technically, the two fleets were already within range. The heaviest guns were easily capable of reaching across four leagues. But no one had yet to master the two problems of long-range gunnery: firing weapons from the unstable platform of a ship's deck and hitting a moving target.

Hazin left Hanaga's side and went into his small temple. He emerged a minute later leading a human male—one of the Shiv.

Hanaga looked at him warily, as all of his race did, for the Shiv, though of the human cattle species, were not quite of them. The Order had experimented for ten generations to breed humans into the ultimate warriors of the Empire; the ultimate sacrifice to please the desires of Tenga. There were rumors that, on the island headquarters of the Shiv, the breeding of the race had been expanded to those of the ancient blood as well.

This human stood far taller than the unbred cattle, though not as tall as those of the blood of the Hordes. His face a pale olive, the skin an amalgamation of all the various subspecies of cattle since the breeders of the Order sought from all the human races the prime examples of physical strength and endurance, which they then bred. This specimen was, even for the Shiv, perfection: muscles clearly defined, powerful as it stood naked, a light sheen of sweat covering its body.

It stood motionless, showing not the slightest trace of fear.

Hazin stepped before him, drawing a razor sharp blade, which glinted in the sunlight, and held it before the Shiv's eyes.

"Do you see what I hold?"

"My liberation," it whispered in reply.

Hazin nodded and started his ritual chant in the ancient tongue, the Shiv joining him in the prayer. Many of those on the bridge looked over with a mixture of curiosity and awe.

The prayer finished, Hazin handed the dagger to the Shiv and stepped back. Without hesitation, it reversed the blade and cut its own throat, slashing with such force that Hanaga could hear the grinding of the honed steel against backbone.

Amazingly the sacrifice stood motionless, barely flinching as blood sprayed out, striking Hazin, spattering across the deck.

The Shiv continued to stare at Hazin, and he actually showed the flicker of a smile as the priest extended his hand and covered the victim's eyes.

Finally, its legs buckled and the body fell, the dagger falling from its hand. A murmur of approval arose from the bridge crew; the sacrifice had been a good sign.

A halyard was looped around its feet by two novitiates of the Order who scurried out of the small temple, features cloaked by their robes. Grabbing the other end of the rope, they hoisted the body up, wind blowing the spray of blood out across the deck, stopping at last beneath the gunnery control tower where it hung limp, swaying as the ship cut through the foaming seas. The same ritual was being performed on every other ship of the fleet.

"Lead enemy ship has opened fire!" One of the bridge crew, glasses still raised, was pointing directly forward. Hanaga raised his glasses and caught the puff of smoke drifting from the forward deck of the lead ship of the Red Banner fleet.

Long seconds passed, and then he heard the low shrieking moan as the first shell winged in. From the sound he could tell it was off to windward. A tremendous geyser of water lifted up a quarter mile to starboard. Jeering laughter erupted from the topside deck crew.

It was meant as a challenge, nothing more.

His own battleships were ranging line abreast, half a mile separating each, leaving them plenty of room to maneuver while the armored cruisers continued to angle out to port, moving forward of the main battle van.

Ahead, the frigates were beginning to engage, and splashes of water rose from the first salvos. A lucky shot from the Red fleet caught one of his frigates amidships. A dirty gray plume of smoke erupted, followed a second later by a burst of steam exploding from the ship's single stack.

"Master gunner announces we are within range, sire."

Hanaga looked back into the armored bridge. The eyes of the helmsman, pilot, and chief communications officer were barely visible through the narrow slit cut in the foot-thick cupola of iron. He looked forward. The distance was two leagues, but the sea was nearly calm. There just might be a chance.

He nodded approval. Stepping back from the railing, he opened his mouth and covered his ears.

A steam whistle blasted, signaling the ship's crew that the heavy guns were about to fire. A second later the four guns forward opened up, each launching a shell weighing over a quarter of a ton. The entire foredeck was instantly cloaked in a boiling yellow-gray cloud of smoke from the three hundred pounds of black powder that set each shell on its way. The entire ship seemed to freeze in position for a second, even to surge backward. The blast of fire tore the hood from Hazin's head and swept over the jet black mane of Hanaga. He gloried in the sensation of the raw power as the most powerful weapon his race had forged on this world in a thousand generations unleashed its strength.

Screams of incoming shells tore overhead. Four of them impacted several hundred yards astern. Another exploded as it struck the water a quarter mile forward and slightly to port. Following the signal from the flagship, his other battle ships opened fire as well.

"Strikes forward of flagship," a spotter shouted, eyes still glued to the oversize glasses mounted to the forward railing. "Three impacts spotted, two hundred paces short, can't see the fourth. Enemy battle ships returning fire."

"My lord, perhaps we should move inside," Hazin announced, and Hanaga readily agreed. It was one thing to make the heroic display at the very start, but in seconds half a hundred shells would come raining down around his ships.

He stepped into the iron cupola, and even though the afternoon was not uncomfortable, the inside of the cupola was stifling hot.

The tension was tangible as the seconds dragged out. Even inside the cupola he could hear the scream of a shell passing overhead and then another. A towering fountain of water exploded just a hundred paces ahead, sending a shock through the entire ship. The iron grating beneath his feet lurched. More geysers soared, some three hundred or more feet into the air, one so close that a cascade of water showered the deck, dropping bits of coral from the ocean floor.

Everyone was blinded for long seconds amid the confusion of sea water and smoke. Then they were clear, afternoon sunlight flooding into the cupola through the narrow view port.

Directly ahead, less than a mile off, the swarming battle of frigates was in full swing. One of Hanaga's ships was heeled hard over to port, deck already awash, survivors leaping into the foaming sea. Seconds later another simply exploded, magazine detonating, lifting the entire foredeck straight up and peeling it back from the hull, which blossomed outward. Fragments of iron and broken bodies tumbled hundreds of feet into the air.

Finished with the laborious task of reloading, the first forward gun fired again, followed seconds later by the second turret. Below deck, he could hear the secondary batteries opening up, pouring their shot into the frigate battle.

The frigate action was starting to get close, and several of the topside steam-powered machine guns opened up.

It was time to shift into battle-line formation, and he passed the order. Seconds later he felt the ship heeling beneath his feet. Forward, the massive turrets swung in the opposite direction, ready to fire a broadside. A cheer echoed up from below as the gunners amidships and astern finally saw something to shoot, the long closing to range finished at last.

"All primary guns, fire on the Red flagship," the gunnery master cried. "Secondaries concentrate on the closest enemy frigates."

The ship erupted in an inferno of noise. Steam hissed from turrets and the light machine guns. The thunder of the great engines below pounded rhythmically, secondary guns firing with sharp reports, and every few minutes one of the guns in the heavy turrets exploding with a thunderous roar that shook the entire ship.

"*Asaga*'s in trouble, sire!"

Two of the enemy frigates were bearing straight down on the battle cruiser, which was the sister ship of his own vessel. Chances were, they were mistaking it for the flagship. Hanaga braced, fists clenched, a silent curse on his lips.

Asaga's main guns were fully depressed, slowly turning to bear. Its secondaries raked the frigates. Explosions detonated across the armored foredeck of the lead enemy ship, blowing its forward turret clean off. A thunderclap of light ignited, and the enemy frigate lurched, explosions ripping across its decks. The ship then shuddered, turning away.

The second frigate, however, emerged out of the smoke and confusion. Racing in without hesitation, it slammed into the starboard bow of the *Asaga*. A huge mine set in the frigate's ram below the waterline blew.

The two ships actually leapt out of the water from the detonation, the entire forward half of the frigate disappearing. *Asaga*'s bow seemed to hang in the air for a second, and then it mushroomed outward. The explosion had snapped through its lower decks, penetrating into the forward magazines, which held nearly four hundred tons of shells and black powder.

The force of the explosion, even from half a mile away, stunned Hanaga. The men in the armored cupola staggered backward from the force of the blow. The forward hundred feet of the *Asaga* disappeared. The barrel of a five-inch gun, weighing several tons, came spinning out of the cloud of debris, slamming across the deck of the flagship, punching clean through the armor until it stuck out like a broken bone.

The aft end of the dying battle cruiser rose, then came crashing back down. Its forward momentum drove the ship forward ramming hundreds of tons of water through shattered decks and dragging the ship under. The stern lifted up, propellers still spinning, even as the boilers filled with water, exploding.

More detonations convulsed the ship as it corkscrewed. Aft turrets popped from their mounts. A hundred tons of iron and steel dropped, crashing into the water. The crews, if still alive inside, undoubtedly had been smashed to bloody pulps by the blow.

What was left of the ship went straight down. Air, raw

steam, and flotsam jetted out of the broken armor plates and the open turret mounts. The stern disappeared beneath the boiling waves, and then, several seconds later, another explosion erupted, blasting part of the stern back out of the water as the aft magazines blew. The shock of the explosion raced through the water, sending a thunderbolt shock through the decks of the flagship.

The *Asaga* was gone. From the time of the ramming till all was destroyed had been less than thirty seconds . . . and a thousand of Hanaga's finest sea warriors were lost.

The flagship had continued to turn, and the disaster was now astern. Five of Hanaga's six turrets were engaged. The enemy van steamed in the same direction less than six thousand yards off while the insane swirl of the frigate battle raged between them. Both sides tried to block the other from closing while wanting, at the same time, to dash through and make their suicidal runs on the enemy battle cruisers. The light armored cruisers had joined the struggle as well. Both of the fleets having run to windward now turned in on each other.

He saw his first clear hit on an enemy battle cruiser, not the flagship, but still a deadly strike, lifting a forward turret clean off. Massive geysers rose hundreds of feet high, churning the turquoise water into a foaming maelstrom of dark sand, coral, and thousands of dead fish.

The two fleets raced on for several leagues, gradually angling in closer, leaving the frigate battle astern.

"Our flyers, my lord!"

Hanaga ran to the starboard side and peeked out through the open viewing slit. He had kept hidden a hundred aerosteamers, based on land and far heavier than the flimsy handful of planes launched from the rocking deck of a ship.

The airships swept in, hugging the water, several passing dangerously close to his own ship. When his forward turret fired, the shock of the passing shell tore a wing off of a plane. It flipped over, spiraling out of control and crashed into the sea.

The air fleet pressed forward, spreading out.

"Damn! They are not concentrating!" Hanaga cried, looking over at his signals officer. "Can't you order them to concentrate on the flagship!"

"My lord, in all this confusion, they'll never see the signal flags!"

"Try, damn it, try!"

Ignoring the danger, he stepped out of the aft hatch of the cupola and came around to the forward bridge. Part of the railing was gone, scorched black, and he noticed a greasy smear, what appeared to be the charred remnant of a leg that had slammed into the side of the cupola and lay broken and flattened on the deck.

The aerosteamers continued forward and then, to his stunned disbelief, the first airship dropped its bomb a good mile short of the enemy fleet. It pulled up sharply and banked away. One after another the aerosteamers unloaded. Forming up after their leader, the airships started to climb, moving clear of the battle.

Only a handful of the airships pressed in, and all of them were torn apart by the firepower of the Red fleet's steam machine guns.

Hanaga stood silent, glasses trained on the lead airship. He thought he could almost see the pilot, the master of his air fleet, and wondered if he was laughing.

"Your brother most likely got to him," Hazin sighed. "I tried to warn you about that."

"Masterful," Hanaga whispered. "He must have reached him moons ago. A plan within a plan."

"You would have done the same."

Hanaga nodded, and then, letting his glasses drop, he slammed a fist against the side of the cupola. "But those were my airships!" he cried. "I'll have the air master's head on a spike for this!"

"If we survive," Hazin whispered. "My lord, we are already outnumbered by the Red fleet alone. The air strike was your main hope. That is finished."

Hanaga waved him to silence. If they had turned traitor, why not bomb his own ships? That was curious. Most likely the air master could not get the pilots to agree to a full betrayal and instead simply went for neutrality. Damn them all.

"Signals officer. Order all battle cruisers to turn straight into the enemy line!"

He looked back toward the armored cupola. The officer stood within, wide eyed. All had seen the betrayal of the air fleet and, with it, the dashing of their hopes for this day. With *Asaga* gone, the odds were now three to two against them, and on the distant horizon to the southeast the dark smudge of smoke, marking the advance of Sar's fleet, was spreading out. Most likely the fleet was already in view from the upper gunnery control tower.

The officer still hesitated.

"Do it!" Hanaga roared.

The terrified face of the signals officer disappeared. Seconds later, a small top hatch on the cupola opened and the flags raced up on a halyard, catching the breeze, snapping out as they reached the base of the gunnery tower a hundred feet above the bridge.

A heavy shell came screaming in, the wind of it nearly knocking Hanaga over. It slammed into the water barely a hundred yards off the starboard rail. The shock of the explosion washed over him. He ignored it, his glasses trained on the enemy battle line.

The helm, responding to his command, sent the eighteen thousand tons of ship into a sharp, graceful turn, water slicing up from the bow, deck heeling over. As they straightened out, the forward turrets fired, the smoke temporarily blinding him.

Yellow gray clouds whipped past, and looking to port, he saw that all but one of his surviving battle cruisers had followed orders and were turning straight into the enemy fleet.

The maneuver had cut his effective strength nearly in half for now only the forward and middle turrets could bear on a target, while his enemy's stern turrets could continue to fire. The maneuver had, at least for the moment, thrown their aim off, for the next salvo of shells arced high overhead, crashing down a half mile astern, and hitting where the fleet would have been if they had continued on their parallel course.

The battle of the light cruisers was almost directly ahead. The ships were slashing at one another at ranges of less than a thousand yards. A Red fleet cruiser disappeared in a monumental explosion. One of Hanaga's frigates rammed another, blowing off the ship's stern. The frigate actually survived the blow, backing off, its secondary bow intact.

A high shriek came roaring down from above.

Hanaga flung himself to the deck. The shell struck the flagship just aft of the bridge, detonating on top of the portside, amidships turret, blowing it apart. A shower of debris and choking black smoke blew forward. The only thing that saved his life was the heavy bulk of the cupola between him and the explosion.

He felt something hard slamming against the inside of the cupola.

He staggered to his feet and looked inside it. Wisps of smoke coiled out of the view ports and then cleared. He felt a shiver of fear. A fragment from the explosion must have cut through the narrow access porthole aft—either that or up through the deck below. The red-hot metal then slashed around inside like a pebble tossed back and forth inside a shaken bottle. Everyone inside was smashed to a bloody pulp.

Another shell arced in, detonating just aft of the stern. The force of the blow raised the back end of the ship, then slapped it down. He sensed immediately that something was wrong, most likely a propeller torn off by the force of the blow or a drive shaft bent.

"My lord, we've lost the fighting bridge!" Hazin shouted, trying to be heard above the explosions, firing guns and steam venting from a broken line with the shrill roar of an undead spirit.

Hanaga nodded, still in shock from the force of the blow and the carnage that had been wrought where he had been standing only seconds before.

"The ship will have to be steered from the engine room!"

Hanaga still could not reply. His forward guns fired again, and, looking up, he saw that the enemy fleet was frightfully close, now less than a league away. Gunners were lowering their barrels. Soon they would be firing over open sights, and nearly every shot would tell.

The enemy fleet was holding its line, not breaking off to run. They were accepting the challenge of the suicidal charge.

"Your orders, sire?" Hazin cried.

Another shell screamed in, and he ducked low, flinching as the bolt struck the bow deck. But it hit at such a low angle that its percussion head failed to strike. He saw the massive bolt skid up off the deck and go tearing out across the ocean, tumbling end over end, disappearing into the smoke.

For twenty years I struggled to reach this moment, he thought. How many of my kin have I slain, how many assassinations, how many knives in the back and feasting cups of poison? How many treaties made to be broken, how many hundreds of thousands dead? All for the power of the Golden Throne, holding it against so many of my kin, my own brothers, till only Yasim was left to challenge me. Yasim, of all of them the weakest in moral strength, but also the most cunning. He held back until I had eliminated nearly every other rival, and then he struck.

In a mere glimmer of a moment all had changed. The dreams of dawn were now sinking like the bloodred sun into a bloodred sea.

And my brother will win this day. Damn his soul, he will win.

Hanaga looked back to the southeast. Or will it be Sar, the bastard? He had to smile. Damn, in a way we are all bastards. It does not matter if our fathers took the vow of mating or not. We exist to kill or be killed, to seek the power of the throne of the Kazan Empire and, once there, to slaughter any who might dream to replace us. Birth blood is but an excuse to reach for it. All that mattered in the end was seizing the power and holding it.

Another shell screamed in, this one striking astern, the force of the blow lifting the deck beneath his feet then slamming it down. He raised his glasses and focused it on his brother's flagship.

No strikes yet. Then he saw what appeared to be a hit, bits of deck soaring up . . . but no explosion. Why no explosion?

We should have made a dozen hits by now. He saw one fire on an enemy battle cruiser, and that was all.

Why no explosions? Half their ships should be aflame or sinking by now. I have some of the best gunners in the Empire.

"Should we signal the fleet to break off?" Hazin asked.

Hanaga looked around. All was confusion. Several of his battle cruisers were still pressing straight in. One of them was on fire from halfway behind the bridge all the way astern, but its forward guns were still firing.

A brilliant flash of light erupted from the enemy line. A light cruiser exploded, tearing apart from stem to stern, magazines blowing, but the ships of the main van, all of them were still in action. A feeble cheer went up from the topside gunners of his own ship. Their cries were soon drowned out as another shell tore in.

An officer came up and saluted. "Sire, thank Tenga you are alive. Assistant gunner Sutana sent me to find you. He claims that none of our shells are exploding."

"I know that. I have eyes, damn it."

"Sire. Assistant gunner Sutana begs to report that he ordered a shell fuse to be opened, and he discovered that the primer was bent."

"What?"

The officer lowered his head. "Sire, the primer for the shell was bent so that it would not strike the detonator on impact."

Hanaga looked at him, unable to speak.

More shells thundered in, a number of them the sharp, whining cracks of the enemy fleet's secondary batteries. One of them struck the gunnery control tower, and, with a rending crash, the tower tottered and fell to starboard. The shrieks of its crew were cut short as the tower crashed onto the deck astern, piling in with all the other battle wreckage.

"Tell Sutana to install new fuses on all shells as they are brought up from the magazine."

"Sire, that will delay firing."

"Don't you think I know that? Are you suggesting we fire shells that don't explode instead?"

"No, my lord."

The officer quickly withdrew, obviously terrified.

An enemy frigate emerged from its confusing battle, which had drifted astern, but was now catching up again with the main fleets. The frigates drove straight at the flagship. The secondary guns below deck trained on this new threat. Topside machine gunners opened up, tracers snaking out across the water, aiming for the bridge.

Hanaga stood silent, oblivious to the slaughter.

Hazin drew close to his side. "Sire, abandon ship."

"What?"

"Sire, we have been betrayed," Hazin said forcefully, looking straight into Hanaga's eyes.

"Yes, betrayed."

Without waiting for comment, Hazin stepped over to the starboard railing, leaned over and, drawing a red pennant from beneath his tunic, he started to wave it at a frigate that had swung out of the main battle and was now running parallel and slightly astern of the flagship. Within seconds the frigate started to speed up and draw closer.

Hanaga, barely noticing Hazin's activities, stood silent. Always he had mastered the crisis of the moment, but this was beyond mastery. He had fallen into an elaborate trap. He finally looked over at Hazin, ready to give the order to have his heart cut out, but saw that the executioner he would have assigned was dead, his head blown off.

Another shell detonated astern. He could feel its blast ripping below deck, screams echoing up through the ventilation shafts, followed by bursts of steam.

Guns on both sides were fully depressed, shots angled so low that shells, when striking the water, skipped back up and screamed on. He caught a glimpse of one of his battle cruisers steaming between two of the enemy ships, all guns firing, and then it disappeared again behind the veil of smoke.

The frigate coming in on the starboard side reversed its engines, slowing to match the speed of the dying flagship.

Hazin was again by his side. "Follow me, my lord. Staying here now is suicide. You have to rebuild. There is still the army ashore, which can hold for weeks if need be. And remember, my Shiv will be landing on the opposite side of the island. We can hold, then negotiate with Sar or your brother later. Staying here, you die."

Hanaga could feel the listing of the ship beneath his feet. It was taking on water astern.

No one was on the bridge other than he and Hazin. A forward hatch popped open, and sailors poured out, some of them horribly scalded, fur and flesh peeling off.

He looked back again at Hazin. "I was betrayed."

"We have been betrayed, sire," Hazin replied sharply. "Now, in the name of Tenga, come with me while there is still time. I can save you!"

As he spoke, he pointed at the frigate alongside, barely a dozen feet separating the two ships. A line snaked out from the frigate, and Hazin grabbed it, securing it to the railing.

"Sire!"

A couple of crew members of the frigate had hold of the other end of the rope and were shouting for them to come down.

"There will always be a tomorrow, Hanaga," the priest said calmly. "Your legend must be rebuilt. The struggle must go on. Sar and your brother will have their reckoning, and you must position yourself to pick up the pieces afterward. Today is but a moment."

Even as he spoke, the priest grabbed hold of the rope and swung himself over the side. Hand over hand he went down the rope, alighting on the deck, then motioned for Hanaga to follow.

Hanaga hesitated, but then went over the side, slipping down, burning his hands. Even as he reached the deck, the frigate turned off sharply and started to race away.

Hanaga, stunned, looked back at his once proud flagship, victor of a dozen actions, listing heavily, explosions tearing it apart.

Hazin put a comforting hand on Hanaga's shoulder. "Sire, let's retire to the captain's cabin. You need a drink."

Hanaga nodded, humiliated that he had abandoned his ship, leaving loyal sailors and comrades there to die. He tried to justify it as an action any emperor would take, and yet still it cut into his soul.

Hazin pointed at the hatchway leading into the captain's cabin.

"You go after me. It would seem unfitting for me to go first."

Hanaga nodded and stepped through.

And there, on the other side, he saw half a dozen of the Order.

There was a momentary flash of recognition, a realization of how all the pieces of this moment, laid out across years, had finally come to this.

The blow from behind staggered him, propelled him forward into the cabin. He gasped, clumsily reaching toward his back, feeling Hazin's dagger in it.

Then those of the Order closed in to finish the ritual.

"I trusted you once," he gasped, looking at Hazin, friend of his youth, Second Master of the Order.

"And that, sire, was always your mistake," Hazin sighed, an almost wistful note in his voice.

The blows came, one after another, daggers cutting deep, driving in.

He no longer resisted. Weariness with life, with all its treachery, forced him to yield.

Hazin pulled the dagger from Hanaga's back, held it as if testing the balance, and looked down at the dying emperor.

"The Empire," Hanaga gasped.

Hazin smiled. It was the last thing Emperor Hanaga of the Kazan saw—someone he had once called friend knelt down to finish the job.

TWO

"Sir, what the hell is it?"

Lieutenant Richard Cromwell scrambled up through the lubber hole and out onto the fighting foretop. Squatting next to the lookout, he raised his glasses.

The fog, which had rolled in at nightfall, was breaking up. Occasional stars and one of the two moons winked through the overcast. But that was not what interested him. It was the glow on the horizon, a dull red light that flared, waned, and flared again. Occasional flashes, like heat lightning on a summer's night, snapped around the edge of the burning glow.

Just before sunset the lookouts had reported a smudge of smoke on the horizon. They had taken a bearing and sailed toward it throughout the night. Now at last they had something.

"When did you first notice this?" Richard asked.

"Just a couple of minutes ago, sir. I called you as soon as I was certain it was not my eyes playing tricks," the lookout, a young Rus sailor, replied slowing, stumbling over his English.

Richard nodded. The glow of one of the rising moons had more than once tricked an old hand into thinking something was out there.

There was another flash, this one a brilliant white flare that reflected off the low-hanging clouds.

"Good work, Vasiliy. I think I better wake the captain."

Richard stood, a bit unsteady. The rising seas, which had been blowing up since late afternoon, had finally laid him low. Coming up to the foretop, where the roll of the ship was accentuated, made it infinitely worse. Only a novice went down from the foretop through the lubber hole. Experienced sailors climbed out onto the shrouds and momentarily hung suspended, nearly upside down, before reaching the ratlines, then going down hand over hand. Some of the top men would simply grab hold of a sheet or halyard and, if wearing leather gloves, slide down to the deck.

Ignominious or not, he gingerly went feet first through the lubber hole, reached the ratlines underneath, and carefully went back down to the deck, hanging on tight for a moment when a wave out of rhythm with the eight to ten foot rollers, raised the bow up high, before sending it crashing down.

Knees wobbly, he hit the deck and made his way up to the bridge. Making sure that all buttons were properly snapped and that his collar was straight, he approached the door to the inner sanctum, the captain's cabin, and knocked.

"Come."

He stepped into the darkened cabin. "Cromwell, sir, senior officer on watch. There's light on the horizon. Foretop lookout spotted it about ten minutes ago. I think you better come up and see it, sir."

The dimmed coal-oil lamp by the captain's bunk flared to life.

With a weary sigh, Captain Claudius Gracchi swung out of the bunk, feet going into his carpet slippers. Nightshirt barely covering his knees, he stood up, fumbling for the spectacles on the night table.

Putting the glasses on, he looked at Cromwell. In spite of the spectacles and rumpled nightshirt, Claudius still had the bearing of a Roman patrician: hair silvery gray and cut short, shoulders broad despite his sixty-five years of age. Long ago, before the Republic, he had actually commanded a galley, but he had adapted well to the new world created by the Yankees and was as adept in commanding a steam cruiser as he had been commanding a ship powered by sail and oars. His stern bearing was simply a bluff. He was a favorite with the sailors of the fleet, known as a man who was just and always willing to hear someone out. Command of the Republic's newest cruiser was seen by everyone as a fitting capstone to an illustrious career.

"What kind of light is it, Mr. Cromwell?"

"Sir, a red glow, like a fire, but there are flashes, something like heat lightning, but it's different somehow."

Captain Gracchi nodded, running fingers through what was left of his thinning mane. "Come on, lad, let's look at your fire."

Even when awakened in the middle of the night, Gracchi always had a calm, fatherly manner. It was usually then as well that he lapsed into calling Cromwell, and a few chosen others, *lad*. He shuffled out of the cabin and onto the bridge, Cromwell respectfully following.

Picking up a set of glasses hanging next to his chair, he braced his elbows on the railing and scanned forward. After the light of the cabin, Cromwell had to squint for a moment, letting his eyes adjust again to the darkness before he could see the glowing patch of red on the horizon.

"Current position?" Gracchi asked, and Cromwell, anticipating the captain's request, had the chart up, the latest hourly passage marked off.

He nodded, eyeing the chart. They were five hundred miles beyond "the line," the division created by treaty with the Kazan nearly fifteen years ago. There were no markers, islands, or territory to define it, simply a line traced across a map beyond which both sides had agreed not to tread.

The agreement had come after President Keane's first term in office. Keane had vehemently argued against it, declaring that if the Kazan were so insistent that no one venture farther out, that must clearly indicate that they had something to hide, or worse, to conceal until such time as they wished to reveal it.

Opinion in the navy was divided. Some, including Admiral Bullfinch, had declared that until such time as the Republic could truly muster a significant fleet, it was best to observe the agreement and to quietly build. But the building had been slow. The entire fleet still only numbered nine armored cruisers. *Gettysburg* was the newest, and three more sister ships were ready to be fully commissioned by the end of the summer.

Thus it had come as a surprise to everyone on board when Gracchi announced, as soon as they had put to sea, that they had been issued secret orders directly from President Keane to sail beyond the line and, as he put it, "poke around a bit."

Gracchi lowered the glasses for a moment, examined the chart, grunted, then raised the glasses back up.

A minute or more passed, Gracchi muttered to himself, as was his habit. Some in the crew thought it a clear sign that the old veteran was slipping. Cromwell had no opinion about it. A man of intelligence never passed opinions on captains, they simply obeyed and survived. Gracchi was the captain, and if he wished to mutter that was his right.

Compared to some of the others in command, muttering was an idiosyncrasy Cromwell could deal with. He had heard the stories about Captain Feodor, who had been quietly removed from command after his crew reported that he had taken to climbing the rigging at night in order to talk to the saints. Then there was the infamous case of Captain Xing, who, after six months of cruising on a survey mission, without once hailing another ship or sighting land, had simply pulled out a revolver, blew out the brains of his first lieutenant and chief petty officer, then flung himself over the railing, where the sharks which always trailed the ships, made quick work of him.

Command created a certain level of madness at times in the fleet, and Gracchi's muttering, if it went no further, was nothing. Besides, Gracchi was one of the survivors of the Great War, and for that alone he deserved respect.

"That's a city burning," Gracchi finally announced, lowering his glasses to look at Cromwell. "Seen it more than once back in the war." He sighed, shaking his head. "The other flashes . . . I'd say it's a fight, one hell of a fight."

Cromwell, having learned from the beginning of life that when unsure it was best not to speak, remained silent.

Gracchi looked off absently. "We've come out here to scout around a bit, Mr. Cromwell, and I think we've found something. I take it you've heard the rumors about what that merchant ship, the *Saint Gregorius,* claimed it found."

"Yes, sir."

Everyone had heard. It had been the hottest topic of conversation ever since Gracchi had spoken to the crew about their mission.

"Well, son, I think we've found another city getting sacked. I can feel it. You can almost smell it.

"I think we've stumbled into a war. After all these years we've finally found them.

"Mr. Cromwell, I suggest we beat to quarters. Roust out the chief engineer yourself and tell him to fire up the boilers. I want a full head of steam if we need to maneuver. Get the sailing master while you're at it. Have him draw in all sails. We'll run on steam alone."

Gracchi began heading back to his cabin, then turned. "And damn it, boy, have someone get me some tea."

Cromwell saluted.

The armored cruiser *Gettysburg* was a sleeping ship on this, the midnight watch. The only ones topside were the bridge crew, lookouts, and the watch officer.

Within seconds all that changed. Cromwell shouted for the petty officer to pass the word to beat to quarters. The petty officer raced aft, leaping down the gangway to the main gun deck below, while Cromwell went forward, gaining the open hatch to the fo'c'sle, officer territory.

Gracchi had told him that only a short generation ago the domain of officers had been aft, where the following breeze was still fresh and the open quarterdeck a place for the high and mighty to take the morning air. All that was gone on this long-ranging armored cruiser. Though it still might sport sails, twin engines were mounted just aft of the midships, massive boilers and pistons, over seven hundred tons of ironworks to power the twin propellers. Aft was now a place of steam, coal bunkers, grease, and heat, and forward was where fresh breezes and relative quiet reigned.

Taking the steps two at a time, he landed on the main deck, and raced past the tiny cubbyhole cabins of the eight midshipmen, four ensigns, and his superiors. Pausing at Chief Engineer Svenson's cubicle, he pound on the door, shouted the captain's orders, and moved on to the sailing master, then down the corridor for good measure, making sure the rest were up as well.

Within seconds Svenson was out of his cabin, trailed by a faint scent of brandy and a couple of ensigns, one of them very unsteady. Gaming dice were on Svenson's bunk. One by one the midshipmen piled out, filled with questions. Cromwell simply pointed them topside, shouting for them to move smartly and get up there ahead of the men they commanded.

Stopping at his own cabin, he popped the door open, leaned in, and shoved his sleeping roommate, Sean O'Donald. "Come on, Irish, we're wanted topside."

Sean rolled over, sat up groggily and rubbed his eyes. "What? What time is it?"

"Move it!"

Richard raced back out the door and joined the rush of men pounding up the stairs. Aft he could hear pipes shrieking, echoing down the corridor. The crew was coming awake.

It always amazed him how a ship could be so quiet one moment and absolute bedlam the next, then within minutes the bedlam would give way to a steady, disciplined silence as men reached their stations and set to work.

Though he longed to be on the bridge, to hear what Gracchi was saying about the light, Cromwell went forward. His battle station was the lone scout aerosteamer, positioned at the bow. There had been two of them, but poor Sean, flying the second plane, had snapped off a pontoon on a bad landing. It was a common enough occurrence, especially when the seas were running high, but the accident had shorted them one of two precious planes, and the normally placid Gracchi had been none too kind to O'Donald when they had finally fished him out of the drink.

Flying a scout plane off of a cruiser was an extremely hazardous job. Flying itself was nearly suicidal, even without trying to take off from a ship at sea and then survive the landing.

Launched by a steam catapult, the plane could scout two hundred miles or more and return—that is, if the pilot could navigate his way back to his ship. Navigating, though, was only the start of the problem. The real challenge was the lack of anyplace to land.

There had been talk of transforming the older cruiser *Antietam* into an aerosteamer carrier, razing the masts and converting it solely to steam power. With a cleared deck aerosteamers could not only take off but also land. One of the old monitors on the Inland Sea had even been converted as an experiment, but nothing had progressed beyond that.

The problem was that without the masts, the ship lacked the range. On engine power alone a ship could cruise only a thousand miles from port and then had to head straight back. In the vastness of the Southern Sea, the hybrid design of sails and steam seemed to be the only answer for the distances that needed to be covered.

Therefore, once launched, the pilot had a most interesting task. On return he had to bring the fragile plane in and land it alongside the cruiser, hoping that the ungainly pontoons underneath endured the shock of landing. The cruiser would then swing out a hoist and pull the scout plane, which was based on the air corps' reliable Falcon design, back up on board.

More often than not the landing on the rolling seas ended in disaster, and it was lucky if the pilot and his gunner were fished out alive. Even if they survived, not uncommonly a wing would be stove in or the canvas hydrogen bags amidships on the plane would be punctured while being hoisted back on board. Thus, on most voyages, an aerosteamer would be sent aloft only in the direst of circumstances, or when close to port, and the plane could safely make it to land with dispatches.

Gracchi, acting more aggressively, had been launching both Sean and Richard ever since they had crossed the line, and yesterday the result had been Sean's near death and the loss of a plane.

In the darkness, Richard went forward, stepping aside as half a dozen foretop men raced past, leaping onto the rigging and scrambling aloft into the night. Strange, he was a pilot, but the thought of dangling two hundred feet up, straddling a yardarm in the darkness, was absolutely terrifying to him. Most of the crew thought him mad for being a flyer. He thought them mad for going aloft. They were utterly without fear and on a bet would dance a jig atop the tallest mast.

As he approached his airship, its faint outline was visible in the starlight of the Great Wheel overhead. The frame was covered with canvas, the wings folded back. His launch crew of four came up, reported, and within seconds were at work. At times the drill seemed a futile gesture. Gunners at least fired blanks on a regular basis and even engaged in some live target practice; a barrel tossed overboard and then shot at from a thousand yards out, the crew coming the closest getting an extra ration of vodka.

There were competitions as well between the mast crews for speed of taking canvas in and spreading it. Even the engineering crew had the satisfaction of racing to bring the boilers up to steam and, on rare occasions, especially when they were coming back into port and could waste the preciously hoarded fuel, of unleashing the pent-up steam and bringing the great cruiser up to flank speed.

But for the men of the aerosteamer crew, launch and recovery seamen Bugarin, Yashima, Zhin, and Alexandrovich, the drill was always the same. Pull off the canvas cover, set the wings, then set the burners for the caloric hot-air engine, check steam power to the catapult, but don't open the line. Every pound of steam was precious and filling the two hundred feet of hose from the boilers was a waste of energy if there was no launch. Then, if given the order to actually launch, pour the five-gallon glass jugs filled with sulphuric acid into the lead-lined vat containing zinc shavings and wait the fifteen minutes for the resulting hydrogen to fill the midships gas bags.

The last two steps were merely simulated and had never actually been done as part of a battle drill. The men had been delighted with the activity of the previous three days, but the crash had dampened their enthusiasm and they expected tonight to be another drill with no results.

Alexi arrived first. He was always enthusiastic, and Richard already knew his words of greeting.

"Well, sire, perhaps this time we fly!"

Alexi's family had lived in the great woods north of Suzdal, and despite having moved over twenty years ago to the Republic, he had grown up accustomed to the old way of address.

"Perhaps, Alexi, something is up."

"What, sire?"

Cromwell pointed to the southeast, and Alexi, with his catlike eyes, immediately spotted the flickering glow on the horizon, which Richard could now just barely discern.

"Ahh, a fire at sea? Perhaps there'll be some fun then for us."

Bugarin, Yashima, and Zhin joined them, gossiping amongst themselves as they cleared the tarpaulin and struggled to swing the wings forward. Richard checked carefully as the team set the locking pins and fastened the bi-level wings into place. Pins not properly set were the most common kind of accidents. The wing would snap back at launch, and the plane would dive straight down. Their comrades on the starboard-side catapult stood around glumly. There was nothing to do now that their plane was gone. Cromwell's command leveled a few good-natured jibes about their now being drafted to go shovel coal.

The rest of the ship was a flurry of activity. The bow gunner crew was clearing the tarps from the twin-mounted steam gatling guns, uncasing the ammunition drums and slapping them into place. Fire crews connected hoses to pumps and tore the lids off buckets of sand hung from the railings.

The single turret forward, containing a massive fourteen-inch muzzle-loading gun, slowly turned, steam wheezing from the vent ports. From inside, Richard could hear the gunnery master shouting orders, preparing the weapon to be loaded if the captain should decide to go to full alert. The problem was that once loaded, the gun could not be unloaded other than by firing it, and ammunition was too expensive to waste whenever an alert was sounded.

Below, on the main fighting deck, Richard could hear firing ports on the starboard and port side being cleared. Armament below was a six-inch rifled breechloader forward, and another aft, with two ten-inch muzzle loaders amidships. The guns could swing to either starboard or port, then be run out and fired. Farther down, below the waterline in the forward and aft magazines, the steam hoists were tested and the first shells and powder bags loaded in, ready to be sent up through brass-lined tubes to the main gunnery deck.

Secondary guns lined the topside deck, the lighter three-inch weapons maneuvered by the muscle power of their crews.

Overhead, in the three masts, more than a hundred men swarmed, awaiting the command to take in and let out sail. If an enemy was sighted, sails would be furled. All motive power would shift to the steam engines that were still powering up as stokers tore into the coal bunkers, trundling out wheelbarrow loads of the precious black rock, upending the barrels into the open maws of the furnaces, which, with every passing second, glowed hotter and hotter. Rakers spread the hot coals out, the burning heat coiling around the hundreds of feet of piping that fed cold water through the boiler. The water flashed to steam that thundered into the pistons and hundreds of yards of piping that fed power to the turrets, gatling guns, hoists, pumps, pulleys, and Cromwell's catapult launch.

Richard felt a rumble pass through the ship. The propellers, turning over, dug in. The command then went up for all sails to be furled.

The drill had been done a hundred times since they had set sail, less than a week after his graduation from the academy, but this time Richard could feel the tension. He could see the glow on the horizon from the main deck without aid of field glasses. It reflected off distant clouds, shimmering, then dying down, punctuated by sharp flashes.

"Lieutenant Cromwell, you're wanted on the bridge."

Richard followed the messenger, dodging around fire crews laying out buckets of sand and ammunition carriers bringing up three-inch rounds to the topside guns. Gaining the bridge ladder, he scrambled up. The deck was illuminated only by starlight, and the dim glow of the helmsman's lamp had an unworldly feeling to it. Gracchi barely looked up at him, just a sidelong glance.

"You ready to fly, son?"

Startled, Richard did not respond.

"Well?"

"Ah, yes, sir."

Gracchi, putting down his mug of tea, came up to Richard and placed a hand on his shoulder. "I want you to be cautious, son. Get up, use the clouds. I want you to get a good look at what is up ahead. Two things: what is burning, and who the hell is fighting. Don't let yourself be seen, then hightail it back here before dawn.

"We're in dangerous waters, Richard. I expect you to find out what the danger is and get back alive."

Richard, stunned, said nothing. A night launch was rare enough. A night landing, except for some practice runs on the Inland Sea, had never been done.

To his surprise, Gracchi offered his oversize mug of tea to him. Cromwell's knees instantly turned to jelly. Yet he was even more afraid that Gracchi would see his fear, and he struggled to still his hands. He accepted the mug and took a long drink. He detected a hint of vodka in the drink.

In the dim light he could see Gracchi smile at him in a fatherly way.

"Sorry, lad, but it's got to be done. Get your bearing from the helmsman. We'll hold our course steady at five knots. Don't do anything foolish, just get a good look, then come straight back. We'll pluck you out of the water, you can count on it."

Richard simply nodded. Enlisting in the naval flying corps had presented a certain challenge. Why he had joined a service where his name was despised was tied up in his anger toward the race that had turned his father and then destroyed him. He had no real love for the Republic, but at least it had offered him a goal, a chance to rise above the ghastly poverty of those few who had survived slavery and now lived in a desolate land that would never recover from the occupation by the Merki. Now had come the moment to prove something, not only to those around him, but also to himself.

"Take Mr. O'Donald as your navigator and spotter. The boy needs to go back up, shake some of the fear out of him after that crash."

"Yes, sir."

Putting the mug down, Cromwell saluted even as Gracchi turned away to other tasks. Getting the heading and location, which was, as usual, just a fair guess, Richard jotted the numbers down and went forward to where his crew waited.

"Alexi, light the engines."

"Sire?"

"Damn it, Alexi," Richard snapped, "it's 'sir,' nor 'sire.' Light the engines. Yashima, make sure the fuel is topped off and ammunition is aboard. Zhin, open the line to the steam piston."

He spotted Sean standing next to his empty catapult, launch crew gathered listlessly around him, watching Cromwell's team at work. He casually walked over.

"Sean, would you mind going below and getting my flight gear and yours?"

"Mine?"

"The old man says you're going up with me."

"I'm flying?"

Richard nodded, and in the starlight he could see the look of confusion mixed in with excitement at the realization that they were about to do a night launch.

"Richard, we've never done this before. I mean, a night launch and recovery."

"You're telling me?"

Sean forced a smile and took off, returning several minutes later with flight overalls. Richard slipped into his and buttoned it halfway up. The night was still warm, but aloft it would cool down a bit. He strapped a revolver around his waist, then pulled on a leather cap, goggles up on his forehead. Sean did the same, and the two waited as his crew continued preparations. Alexi, who normally would have gone up as his gunner and spotter, was obviously glad to be relieved of the assignment and said nothing.

"Top off the airbags?" Bugarin asked.

Richard nodded, unable to speak for a moment. Bugarin broke open the hydrogen generator box, carefully put on gloves, leather apron, and face covering, lifted out the five-gallon glass jar of sulphuric acid, and poured the contents into the lead-lined box filled with zinc shavings. Sealing the box, he connected the gas hose to the aft air bag, which was built into the tail assembly of the ship. It would provide just enough additional lift to get the scout plane aloft.

Richard started to pace back and forth nervously as his crew sprang to work. Then, chiding himself, he stopped, and put his hands behind his back, though he was still clenching and unclenching his hands.

The hissing of the caloric engines, which took only a few minutes to generate power, caught the attention of the gun crews. A chief petty officer came over to Richard.

"Going up, sir?"

Richard, not sure if he'd have control of his voice, simply nodded.

"Well, good luck."

Again, only a nod.

The petty officer backed off.

The minutes slowly passed. Richard, finally breaking free from his statuelike pose, moved slowly around his airship; careful to avoid the single propeller aft, which was beginning to windmill. Alexi was up in the nose hatch, pulling the canvas hood off the forward gatling, which would be controlled by Richard once they were aloft. Zhin, carefully closing off the gas, then joined Bugarin on the traverse gear, which pointed the launch ramp off at a ten-degree angle from the bow so that the plane would not snag on the jib bow at launch.

It was time.

His crew, finished with their tasks, stepped back, staring at Richard and Sean, illuminated only by the dim starlight.

"She's all set, sir," Zhin announced, his English soft and precise.

Richard nodded stoically and, without comment, clambered up the ladder hanging from the side of the launch ramp and into the forward cab. Sean, following, climbed up past Richard into the observer/gunner's position amidships. Richard handed back the paper with their coordinates, and Sean slipped it onto the clipboard holding his navigation chart.

The instruments were all but invisible in the darkness. He knew the bearing, but seeing the compass was all but impossible . . . damn.

Get a bearing on the Southern Triangle once aloft, he realized, then reverse it on the way back. He passed the suggestion back to Sean, who announced he had already thought of it.

Richard tapped his rudder pedals, looking back over his shoulder to glimpse the tail, then checked his stick. Next came the throttle. The engine hummed up smoothly. No way to check the gauges—he had to do it by sound and feel alone.

"All ready, sir."

Alexi—Cromwell could sense his excitement—was standing up on the side of the plane.

"Ready."

"I'll get you off on the uproll, I promise it, sir."

Richard, annoyed by Alexi's fussing, said nothing.

There was no way to delay longer, though he had a sudden longing to get out of the plane and let Sean do the whole thing by himself.

He raised his right hand out of the cockpit, clenched fist held up, signaling down the crew that he was ready.

What happened next came as a shock. Alexi, misreading the signal in the darkness, hit the steam release valve, slamming the launch piston forward.

Cursing silently, vision jarred by the unexpected blow, Richard clutched the stick with his left hand, pulled back too far and pitched the plane into the edge of a stall; propeller howling, the plane hung above the waves. He shoved the stick forward. For a gut-wrenching second nothing happened, and then the nose finally slipped down, leveling out.

He caught a glimpse of the jib boom to his right, then it was gone. His heart still thumping, he leveled off, putting the plane into a shallow banking turn.

Gettysburg stood out faintly in the starlight, her sails drawn in, her mast bare. He swung around her, mainsail yardarms at wing level. Something caught his attention. The wake of the ship glowed with a rich phosphorescent green that stretched back for a mile or more. The sight was stunning and revealing, as well; a clue as to how to spot a ship at night.

He swung out behind *Gettysburg* more than half a mile, then gingerly circled back in, lining up on the wake of the ship, and started to climb. He flew straight up the line, taking his bearing on the Triangle, which was off the starboard wing, bisected by a forward strut.

Directly ahead the glow of fire drew him as he winged up over *Gettysburg,* mast tops now a hundred feet below. Figuring it was best to gain altitude, he continued on his slow climb, pushing forward at nearly fifty miles an hour, climbing at two hundred feet a minute.

As the long minutes passed, wind slipped past his windscreen, heavy with tropical warmth and rich with salt scent. The glow on the horizon began to spread out, a clear indicator that it was close, not more than forty or fifty miles.

An errant breeze caused the plane to buck, rise up, then steady back out.

"Smell that?" Sean shouted.

Richard raised his head up . . . smoke.

He pressed on. They slipped into a wisp of cloud, the temperature instantly dropping, then came back out. He descended slightly, leveling out, or at least tried to level. With less than twenty hours of flight time on scout planes, half of it gained over the last three days, he was still amazed that he had survived the launch. The thought of landing was more than he wanted to contemplate at the moment.

Bracing the rudder with his knees, he raised his field glasses, tried to find the fire, then gave up.

"Sean, use your glasses. Tell me what you see," Richard shouted.

"Already on it."

Richard looked back over his shoulder and, in the starlight, saw the outline of Sean above him, elbows braced on the upper wing.

"Damn big fire. Can see buildings. Damn big. It's a harbor."

They flew on for several minutes. Sean remained silent, half standing, elbows braced on the upper wing, scanning forward. He lowered his glasses and slipped back into his seat.

"Ships!" he cried. "I see ships burning, there's shooting . . . there, a gun flash, you could see the ship."

Richard, peering forward, wondered how Sean did it. He could see the flashes, the fire, but only as pinpricks of light.

"Richard, I don't like this."

"What is it?"

"Those aren't pirates or raiders. Those ships are too big."

"We better get in closer."

Richard edged the plane up, taking it into the bottom of the clouds; dodging out, slipping back in again. Soon he could pick out individual flashes of light, forward of the city. Rippling lights erupted, flashes of fire that climbed heavenward, then winked out. Seconds later splashes of silent fire detonated, brilliant yellow lights that winked out as quickly as they ignited.

"You see that?" Richard cried. "Like rockets."

"Hundreds of them," Sean shouted excitedly.

More and more flashes were visible, spread out for what he estimated to be miles to either side of the burning city and forward of it.

He tried to brace the rudder again and raised his glasses. This time he caught glimpses, startling glimpses of fire, explosions that danced and weaved in his vision, one so brilliant that he was temporarily blinded.

"Richard, may I ask that you just fly? I'll look."

Richard, surprised by Sean's commanding tone, almost fired a quick retort, but then realized that his observer was right. His job was to fly, O'Donald's was to look.

He reset the glasses in their rack. He had a momentary shock when he realized that he had drifted from what he had hoped was an arrow-straight course. The Triangle was directly off his starboard wing.

He banked over sharply, embarrassed and a bit frightened by his lapse. How long had they flown thus? Would he be able to find *Gettysburg* now?

A brilliant flash erupted, towering upward, expanding out.

"By all the gods," Sean gasped. "I think an entire ship went with that."

Several minutes later, a dull rumble washed over them.

Watching the pattern of lights, Richard sensed that this was not an attack by some alien fleet on a city. Rather, it was a battle between two fleets. The burning city was merely a backdrop.

The dull distant rumble of the battle grew in intensity. Another detonation, as brilliant as the first one; the flash so bright that it lit up the sea as bright as day, and Richard could actually see other ships.

"Never seen anything like them," Sean cried. "No masts, round things on top instead."

"Turrets, like monitors?"

"Like giant monitors, four round turrets on one. Damn, did you see that one shoot?"

Richard had caught the flash of the guns, but in the confusion and distance he wasn't sure.

"Just hold her steady, Richard, take us straight on in."

The sound of gunfire was continuous, the shock waves rippling over them with sharp intensity.

There was no longer any doubt in his mind that two fleets were in action. He caught glimpses of sparkling shells arcing upward, disappearing into the darkness, then seconds later causing flashes on the water as the shells exploded. The only question left now was who, and in his mind there was no doubt.

It was the Kazan.

He had to make a decision. Continue to press in, get a close-up look, or come about and carry the precious information back. The Kazan had been found at last, and, given the similarity of the ships engaged, they were at war with one another.

"Damn!"

Richard saw it a second later, flashing by underneath, illuminated by the flash of an explosion . . . a flyer.

Startled, he pulled up, looking back over his shoulder. Behind him Sean had unfastened the lock holding his gatling in place and started to swing it around.

"Don't shoot!" Richard shouted. "He might not have seen us."

"We suspected they could fly, but did you see the size of that thing?"

Richard wasn't sure. It was hard to judge in the darkness. He headed upward, but there were no clouds nearby.

Three more flyers slipped underneath. Watching carefully, he judged them to be five hundred or more feet below. Then one of them started to turn.

O'Donald shouted a warning even as Richard pulled into a sharp climb.

"It's lining up on us!"

Height or speed? He hung on to the stick for several seconds, frozen with indecision, and spared a quick glance back. He spotted a flicker of movement, starlight illuminating the white wings. It was hard to judge the distance, but a guess told him it was several hundred yards back. The plane was within range if they had machine guns, and given the carnage going on straight ahead, it was idiotic to assume otherwise.

He nosed over, going into a steep dive that in seconds put the scout plane up to its maximum speed of ninety miles an hour. The ocean, though several thousand feet below, seemed to rush up, and the raging battle seemed perilously close.

"Where is he?" Richard cried.

"I can't tell, lost him when you dived. Next time warn me!"

A flash of light snapped past.

Time seemed to freeze. He remembered lectures at the academy, talking with old sailors, veterans of the Great War, about what it was like. The shock of realization that for the first time someone was shooting at you, trying to kill you . . . and that in another instant the world would continue to spin on in its grim course, and you would not be part of it.

Another flash shot past. Sean cursed, steam hissing as he opened the cock. The gatling spun to life, spitting flame, the vibration blurring vision. Richard wondered if the chocks that shut the gun down would work if Sean should happen to swing it due aft, where his shots would shred the propeller.

He still couldn't see the instruments in the darkness. Sense alone told him that he was pushing the plane beyond any speed he had ever flown before. Chopping back the throttle, he pulled up sharply, the control stick shaking a violent tattoo, wires humming, one parting with a riflelike crack.

"Where the hell is he?"

There was no reply.

Richard spared a quick glance back over his shoulder and was stunned by the sight of Sean hanging half out of the plane, arms locked around the breech of his gun.

Richard leveled out, and Sean swore wildly, swinging his legs back into the plane.

"Damn it, why aren't you strapped in?" Richard screamed.

In the starlight, he could see Sean's terrified grimace.

"Where is he?"

"How am I supposed to know?" Sean gasped.

Completely disoriented, Richard looked around. There was a flash directly below him, a mushrooming cloud of fire spreading out across the sea, the explosion soaring up, the shock of it rocking his plane. He felt a shuddering shriek, the nearby passage of a shell sounding like an out-of-control train rushing past.

He nosed his plane over, banking sharply, putting the fire of the city directly behind him.

"We're getting the hell out of here."

He continued to dive, the wind shrieking, pushing the plane. He looked aft, caught a glimpse of the Triangle.

Looking forward, he saw Gavala, the star that was the point of the Hunter's Spear, low on the horizon, and two points off to port.

He raced back out for the open sea, pulling up to clear a ship that suddenly appeared out of the darkness and in seconds disappeared astern. It was a ship without masts, he realized, turrets mounted fore and aft.

The ocean seemed to spread out to either side, and with a start he realized that he was only feet above the water.

"Five more degrees to port," Sean cried.

"What?"

"You're about five degrees off."

Sean had always scored highest in their navigation classes, so Richard followed his order without comment.

But after a few minutes something else caught his attention.

A fire glowed on the horizon, not as big as the one he had been approaching less than half an hour ago. It was simply a pinpoint, flashes of light that popped, flared, and disappeared.

A thought crossed his mind. From the position of the Great Wheel, which showed intermittently through the scattering of clouds, he judged it was little more than half-way through the first watch. Less than three hours ago he had come awake and wandered to the galley for a cup of tea and biscuits before going on watch. Three hours ago he would have had no idea of what it was he was now seeing, or how to judge it.

Ahead there was another fight, ship to ship, and someone was burning. Was it his ship dying? Were they now alone a thousand miles from home?

THREE

"My lord."

Hazin stirred, momentarily disoriented. He had always hated ships, the constant movement, the stenches coming up from below.

"My lord, there's a ship."

Hazin sat up, nodding, wearily rubbing the back of his

neck. The captain's bunk was far too small for his towering frame. At nine feet he was tall even for one of his
race.

He stretched, nearly losing his balance as the deck beneath his feet dropped and rolled. He looked over at the
messenger, a novitiate of his order, but one obviously accustomed to the sea; he balanced easily, shifting com-
fortably.

Though the sea was the theater upon which the game of
physical power was played out, it was an environment he
secretly feared. It was an environment one could not control, the way one could so easily control the minds of
others.

Once aboard a ship, one's fate was in the hands of too
many unknown variables. In spite of all the elaborate plans,
the games within games, there was always the possibility
that an hour hence a storm could send one to the bottom.
Or a raider of the Orange Banner, who acknowledged no
power, could take and hold them for ransom. Or a raider
of the Orange Banner, who acknowledged no power, could
take and hold them for ransom. Or a rival with a fleet of
a hundred vessels might suddenly appear where he was not
supposed to appear.

He fumbled to brush the wrinkles out of his bloodstained
robes. Hanaga's blood—dried flecks of it dropped off. He
felt nothing, though it was the blood of an emperor he had
supposedly served since early youth.

Poor fool, he should have seen it coming. Everything was
but part of "The Plan," the concealed reality. For all in
this world was but a shadow of a deeper reality. Hanaga
should have sensed that. His brother Yasim, knew it. That
is why he was now the emperor, at least for the moment,
and Hanaga was dead.

The novitiate—the red stripe on his left sleeve marking
him as a *summa* of the second order—waited patiently, but
Hazin could sense the young one's agitation.

"The ship, our captain does not know what it is," Hazin
guessed.

"Yes, my lord, he asks your presence on the deck."

"Lead the way, then."

Hazin followed him out of the stateroom and up onto
the deck.

The total darkness at sea was always a bit unnerving, and it took him a moment to adjust, half feeling his way along as he weaved through the maze of ladders that took him up to the bridge. As his eyes adjusted to the dark, he could pick out the glow of fire astern, flashes of light, a star shell hovering on the horizon; sinking, disappearing. Beyond the naval battle glowed the human city's consumption by flame.

"My lord, Hazin."

The captain bowed at his approach. Though nominally a ship of the Blue Banner of Hanaga, in fact it was crewed by his order, or at least those of his order loyal to him, yet another wheel within wheels. It had been his safety net, something the Grand Master of the Order had not anticipated. Yes, he had been ordered to kill Hanaga because the Order had decided to switch sides, but Hazin's own survival would not be expected.

"Lookouts reported sighting a ship," the captain announced. "It's off our starboard bow, range less than a league."

"The emperor's?"

The captain shook his head, and Hazin remembered that the term no longer applied to the individual associated with that title.

"Hanaga's or Yasim's?"

"Neither, I suspect." The captain motioned to the night glasses mounted on the bridge railing.

Hazin bent over, seeing nothing for a moment. Finally he caught a glimpse of something, a darker shadow on the dark horizon. A strange silhouette, masts . . . the ship had masts.

"Human?"

"I think so."

"Not like anything we've seen before, is it?" Hazin whispered.

"Not one of the island traders or their renegades. Too big for that, and you'll see sparks trailing. It has engines as well."

Hazin slowly moved the glasses back, trying to compensate for the roll of the ship, acquiring the shadow again. The ship looked foreshortened, angling on almost a direct intercept.

"I don't think it's seen us," the captain said. "It hasn't changed course since we've sighted it. It's already in range."

What is it? Hazin wondered. It was definitely not the emperor's or any other ship of the fleets of the Banners. No sailing merchant ship, human or of the Kazan, would be within a hundred leagues this day. Only an idiot would wander anywhere near this confrontation between claimants of the throne.

So, either it was a blind idiot . . . or it was the humans known to reside on the north shore. The Yankees, who had so easily been frightened off with a treaty while the Empire settled its internal differences.

They would have to be contended with, in due course, especially now that they had reached the sea and ventured upon it. But here, now?

He weighed the possibilities. Behind him a plan had been completed . . . and ruined. Hanaga, the fool, was dead. The new emperor had paid the Order well for the betrayal, but he would never know that it was, in fact, but part of a power struggle within the Order itself, an attempt by the Grand Master to eliminate not just Hanaga, but his own lieutenant as well.

Hazin grinned, wondering how much time should pass before he allowed the Grand Master to know that he had not died on Hanaga's flagship as intended and all but ordered to do.

"Have we been followed?" Hazin asked.

"We were, your holiness. From the Red Banner."

Hazin smiled. What would they think? That Hanaga had indeed escaped? A puzzle for them to ponder. The Red Banner would sweep the seas come dawn, but they would be empty, except for wreckage and the few defiant ships of Hanaga that had somehow survived the night. "And now?"

The captain paused, looking aft where the fire glow of the battle shimmered on the horizon. "Not now. This ship is the fastest of its class."

He detected the pride in the warrior's voice. Pride and attachment in one of his station bore watching.

"We'll be silhouetted by the fire in another minute," the captain warned, looking at his master.

Hazin leaned over, training the glasses on the intruder's outline, barely distinguishable against the starlight. They could turn aside, run ahead and across its bow and be gone. He wondered if they had spotted him as well. . . . No, for if they had, he knew he would sense it. Something would warn him, as it always had.

Though he did not believe in fate, a concept alien to his order, to the essence of what he was, he could not help but wonder why, at this moment, such a random thing had unfolded.

As always, the decision came without hesitation.

"Take it."

"Master?"

"You heard me. Take it."

"May I caution you on two things?"

Hazin turned.

"Gunfire might reveal us to pursuit."

"I know that."

"Whatever that ship is, it is an unknown. Unknowns are the gray path."

Hazin smiled. "Precisely why we take it."

The ship had been cleared for action throughout the night, and a single command from its captain rippled through the ship, bringing it to the highest state of readiness.

Hazin could feel the increased tempo of the engines. The deck canting beneath his feet as the helm was put over. There was no sense in making some sort of foolish display of bravado on a pitch-black night, and besides, the crew was of his order and such stupidity would cause doubts.

He stepped into the armored bridge, standing in the middle. Only a novice would make the mistake of touching—or leaning against—the plating when action was imminent.

A rush of steam from the bow signaled that the frigate's forward guns were swinging into position.

"Captain. Signal from foretop lookout."

Captain Gracchi lowered his glasses, which had been trained on the flickering glow and looked over at his signals officer.

"Ship sighted off the starboard bow."

He started to turn, raising his glasses again, when the shocking glare of a salvo ignited. The flash blinded him, the ocean flaring up as bright as day.

Cursing, he closed his eyes, turning away. Seconds later he felt the deck heave. Knocked off his feet, he slammed against a railing. Gasping, he staggered back, holding his side.

"Signals!"

Another flash, this time he was turned away, and in the glare he saw the signals officer sprawled half over the railing, decapitated. Forward, the main mast leaned drunkenly, stays snapping, sounding like rifle cracks.

Another salvo, this time he clearly saw the ship lying not a thousand yards off, bow wake standing out a brilliant white in the glare.

He felt the thunderclap snap of a gun belowdecks firing, the glare flashing out, lighting up the sea. Topside, several of the steam-powered gatlings were firing, their staccato roar joining the confusion. Tracers skipped out over the sea, winking out as they hit the water.

"Helm! Hard aport!"

He looked back at the armored cupola. Illuminated by the flashes of light, the helmsman inside was staring at him, wide-eyed in panic.

"Damn you! Hard over! Get us the hell out of here!"

Another flash lit up the sea again, followed seconds later by a geyser of water erupting astern, *Gettysburg* lifting with it, a shudder running through the ship.

All was madness. Flashes of light, the screaming roar of shells coming in, the forward mast finally letting go, tumbling overboard, sailors trapped in the rigging screaming as they fell to their doom.

Their tormentor was now directly abeam. It presented a strange silhouette: no masts, squat, low, moving with impossible speed, knifing through the water. Tracers snapped back and forth; gatling rounds, three-inch shells, the air heavy with the rotten-egg stench of black powder.

"Captain, aft magazine reports fire!

He started to turn, gaze locked on the midshipman who was standing before him, shaking with fear."

There was a momentary flash, time seemed to stretch

out, a fireball of light soaring up from an open hatch.
Strange, so many thoughts tumbled together. The war of
so long ago. . . .

The terrified boy looked back, saw the explosion mushrooming, deck plates rupturing, peeling back like rotten
wood punched by a giant. Claudius Gracchi barely had time
to put a reassuring hand on the boy's shoulder before the
explosion engulfed them.

"My God, was that ours?" Sean gasped.

Stunned, Richard did not know. The fireball spread out,
color shifting from brilliant white, through yellow, to deep
red. Expanding, it grew dark, disappearing except for flickering embers, which winked out as they hit the sea.

"It was ours," Sean groaned. "I know it was ours."

"Shut up, damn it," Richard snapped. "You're not sure."

"I saw her, it was the *Gettysburg.*"

"It could have been the other one."

Sean, stifling a sob, began to pray.

Richard strained to catch a glimpse of the other ship,
hoping that he'd see the familiar outline of the *Gettysburg.*
Mist and smoke clung to the surface of the ocean. For a
moment he debated the idea of pulling up, turning away,
and then circling until dawn.

But then what? If *Gettysburg* was gone, they were
doomed and would have wasted most of their precious fuel
as well.

And if it was gone, then what? It was nearly a thousand
miles back to the nearest outpost of the Republic. There
was a scattering of islands dotting the seas, most of them
uninhabited, or worse the hiding places of pirates, who
would make short work of them.

His stomach knotted with fear.

"We're finding out now," Richard shouted. "I'll come in
low, keep a sharp watch. If it's the *Gettysburg,* we'll pull
back up and circle until they signal for us to land."

"Let's leave this place now!"

"And go where?" Richard cried, looking back over his
shoulder.

Sean fell silent.

Richard edged the throttle up, dropping low, leveling off

as they plunged into a low-hanging bank of fog, coming out, racing between the overhanging darkness and the black ocean. Another cloud was ahead. He pulled up slightly, raced into it. The air suddenly turned heavy with the sulphurous smell of coal smoke and burnt powder.

They popped through and starlight appeared directly overhead.

"There it is!" Sean cried.

Richard didn't need to be told. He caught the glimmer of the ship's phosphorescent wake. Tracing the glowing blue-green glow back to the stern of the ship, he had a chilling realization.

It wasn't the *Gettysburg.*

Now what? Keep on going? Turn back to the chaos of the island, or just head out to the open sea?

He felt a sense of utter futility and abandonment. The *Gettysburg* was gone. Captain Gracchi was dead, all his comrades dead. That explosion had been her magazines going up. Anyone still alive had most likely been blown into the shark-infested sea.

A blind rage seized him. Leaning forward, he grabbed the breech of his gatling, spun open the steam cock, and pressed the trigger.

A snap of light shot out, the barrel spinning to life, spitting out five hundred rounds a minute. The tracers snaked down, weaving, then cutting across the bow of the ship.

Sean opened up as well, cursing wildly.

Within seconds snaps of light arced back.

A violent shudder slapped their plane. An instant later the engine seized. One of the propeller blades tore loose, spinning off into the darkness.

He was tempted to simply point at the ship and end it. Pulling back on the stick, Richard tried to stretch out the glide, but within seconds he could feel the airspeed bleeding off, the controls going mushy. They were going into a stall. Panicking, he pushed the stick forward. Momentarily he regained control.

Still the tracers followed them, swinging back and forth. Dimly he heard Sean scream that they were burning. The ocean rushed up to meet them.

* * *

"There, that's what we want!" Hazin cried, pointing at the burning aerosteamer as it plunged into the sea. "Mark the spot!"

The frigate continued to turn, sweeping through the wreckage.

He had wanted an intact ship, prisoners, a chance to evaluate how this new piece fit into his game. All that had disappeared in a blinding flash.

"Fire a flare."

"Master, if we light a flare shell, anyone within ten leagues will see it."

"Anyone within twenty leagues saw that ship blow up."

"It will give them a clearer bearing on us. For all we know, there's a ship of the Blue Banner closing at this very minute. They know the silhouette of this ship, and they won't take the time to ask questions about our surrendering or not."

"Light it," Hazin replied sharply.

The captain nodded, passing the order.

The gun on the forward turret elevated and fired. The shell streaked upward, arcing, and then ignited with a brilliant flash, the flare swinging on its parachute. The ocean beneath it was illuminated as brilliantly as if both moons were full.

Lookouts forward shouted the bearing. The strange aerosteamer was clearly visible, one bi-wing and forward cab sticking out of the water.

He watched intently, waiting, and then saw movement.

"I want them alive!" Hazin shouted. "No matter what it takes, I want them alive."

Gagging, Richard struggled to the surface. Blindly he lashed out with his knife, cutting through the fabric of a wing that had crumpled over the forward cab, trapping him as the plane had settled and started to slip under.

He broke to the surface, shrieking for air. Then something grabbed hold of his leg, pulling him down. He went back under. For a second of blind panic he thought it was a shark snagging his leg.

No, he had seen sharks attack. Both his legs, his entire lower body, would already be gone if it were that. They were out there, and soon enough they would close, but not yet.

He surfaced again, fighting for air, then went under. Sean was clutching him.

Richard grabbed him, pulling him up, his comrade clawing at him wildly. He tried to push him back, and both of them got tangled in canvas, and wires; the wreckage of an airship that was rapidly going under.

Richard kicked violently, gaining the surface yet again, Sean by his side.

"Richard! I thought I'd lost you!" Sean gasped, still clinging to him.

"Just grab a spar, anything but me," Richard sputtered.

Fumbling in the dark, Richard grasped one of the half-submerged float pontoons, which had snapped off on impact. Grabbing Sean by the collar, he pulled him over.

"The sharks, how soon?" Sean whispered, panic causing his voice to break.

Richard didn't answer. Soon enough. If either of them was bleeding, it'd be only a matter of minutes before a pack of them latched on to the trail and closed in. He reached down to the holster on his hip . . . the revolver was gone.

Damn.

In spite of the warmth of the tropical sea, he began to shiver.

A sun seemed to explode directly overhead, casting a hellish blue-white light. A wave lifted them up, and he saw the ship bearing down on them. It was hard to judge distance, but the vessel seemed only a few hundred yards off, and for a second he thought it just might be the *Gettysburg* after all, this entire affair a tragic mistake.

But it wasn't the *Gettysburg*. The ship was smaller, sleeker, a blocklike turret on the forward bow where the *Gettysburg* had its aerosteamer catapult. The ship was reversing its engines, knifing straight toward them.

The sea around him was littered with debris: bits of wreckage, a broken spar, flame-scorched canvas trailing behind it, part of a table sliced in half, chairs, bits of cloth, cable and rope, a deck grating, and, scattered here and there, bodies and parts of bodies.

Neither of them moved. The ocean was silent except for

the engines of the approaching ship. The effect was frightful. "Richard," Sean hissed, pointing at a body floating atop
a cresting wave. A fin, rising half a dozen feet out of the
water, slashed in, cutting a razor wake through the water.
The body jerked, then abruptly disappeared beneath the
waves.

"Don't move," Richard whispered.

The ship was still closing in. A boat was being lowered
from amidships, already half lowered. He could see dark
forms illuminated by the flare, running along the deck.

"The Kazan," Sean gasped.

Richard looked over at his gunner. "Your revolver, you
still have it?"

Sean fumbled with one hand, and shook his head. "I
lost it."

Richard groaned. "A hell of a choice," he said, his voice
shaking. "We can start swimming, but that will draw attention from down below. It'd be over in a minute."

Sean shook his head violently. "If the Kazan are anything
like what we've heard, you know what will happen."

Richard suddenly felt a strange detachment from it all.
They were facing death either way. He looked over at Sean.
His companion's teeth were chattering with fear.

The away boat was in the water, oars flashing, coming
straight at him. In the bow he saw one of them, rifle in
hand.

An unintelligible, guttural voice was shouting. The Kazan
had a weapon raised, was pointing it.

Richard looked back and forth from Sean to the Kazan.
Two choices of death. . . .

He saw a body lift out of the water less than a dozen
yards away; the open mouth of a shark, the flash of teeth.
The terror of it was too much, and he started to swim the
last few feet to the boat, Sean following.

"My lord, if he is alive, we will find him."

Emperor Yasim tu Zartak was silent, icy gaze sweeping
the sea. A flyer hummed past, skimming low across the
water, heading into the darkness.

Yasim lowered his head. He was exhausted. A moon ago
all would have thought him dead and his brother's star
in its final ascendancy to zenith. And then everything had

changed. In the end, all it had taken was a bribe—a bribe that had emptied his coffers and indebted him for life to the Order. It was that or defeat, and though one was barely preferable to the other, still it *was* a victory.

He looked back at his bridge crew. All stood silent, respectful . . . and in awe of what had transpired this day; the climax of a generation of war.

The fleet of the Blue Banner, what was left of it, was burning. As for the Yellow, a blade in Sar's back had settled that issue—yet another bribe. Half the Yellow had lowered their flags, switching colors to the Red. The other half had fled into the darkness.

It had all seemed so effortless, and none knew its true cost: The pledges made to the Grand Master. He smiled sadly, the cost, perhaps the throne itself; a price that would empty the imperial coffers for a hundred years, all that just for two blades in two backs. Granted, a few hundred others had died, or would die in the days to come. It would all be so seamless; done with a certain elegance.

Would the Grand Master rest with this victory? Would he be content, or would he now reach for the throne as well? Surely he would not sit back and expect nothing; not after the price exacted.

With the riches paid, the estates transferred, what force could the Grand Master marshal? An entire fleet perhaps? There were mercenaries enough out there. Half of his fleet was hired through the Shiv, and they could change sides again tomorrow.

No. The war was far from over, he realized. The Banners of the Green, the White, the Black—they might pledge to the throne for the moment, but what was the game behind them?

The flare on the distant horizon winked out.

"I wonder why they fired a star shell?" someone on the bridge whispered.

The emperor ignored the breach of etiquette. Time enough later to find out who had dared to raise a question in his presence and punish him accordingly.

They wondered if Hanaga had escaped after all. Unlikely; it was the second to the Grand Master himself who had been assigned the task of killing. An interesting choice. Undoubtedly the Grand Master wished as well to eliminate a rival to his own power. Yet someone had indeed transferred from the flagship of his brother. It was not his brother. His inner sense told him that his brother was dead.

With a sharp clarity of insight, a clarity that had saved him more than once, the new emperor of the Kazan understood at least part of the puzzle, and smiled.

FOUR

General of the Armies Vincent Hawthorne shifted uncomfortably in his saddle, absently rubbing his left hip, which always troubled him when he rode.

"You wish to take a break, sir?"

Vincent looked over at his adjutant, Lieutenant Abraham Keane, and smiled. The boy was shaping up just fine, still a bit too eager to please, but, then again, young lieutenants fresh out of the academy tended to be like that.

He had his father's lanky frame, long-limbed, narrow chest, high cheekbones, full lips, and, unfortunately, his father's weak eyes, which required thick glasses. But he had inherited as well his mother's Irish red hair. To look at him was somehow a reminder of himself of thirty years ago, when the world was new, the wars had yet to come, and youth seemed eternal.

"Not much farther, Lieutenant. The Bantag have spotted us, so we might as well press on in."

Abraham nodded, removing his campaign hat to wipe the sweat from his brow. Vincent knew the boy's canteen was empty, and he was tempted to offer a sip from his own, but decided against it. Good to let him suffer a bit and learn. The old veterans behind them expected their officers, no matter how young, to be as tough as they were.

Vincent looked back over his shoulder at the regiment following him, riding in columns of four. It was a grand sight, trailing back across the open steppes, hot dry wind whipping the guidons, dust boiling away from the column, sweeping off to the distant horizon.

Their dark blue sack coats, khaki trousers, and black knee-high boots were obscured by the thick layer of dust.

Most of the men had their bandannas covering their mouths so that only their eyes were visible.

He had a flash memory of the final battle of the war; the vast open ground, the limitless sky overhead and the thundering charge of the Bantag Horde.

A few of the men behind him had been there, though most were like Abraham, new to the ranks, enduring military service at one of the isolated outposts ringing the Hordelands. For twenty years it had been thus, twenty-five outposts ringing the million and a half square miles assigned to the defeated Hordes at the end of the Great War. The duty was tough: patrolling the range, ensuring that the Horde stayed within its territory, maintaining an uneasy peace between two races that had known nothing but hatred and conflict for thousands of years.

Those who had once been the masters of this world had finally tasted bitter defeat, and only a fool would assume that they did not harbor a dream of returning the world to what it had once been.

A distant hum caught his attention. Shading his eyes against the noonday sun, Vincent caught a glimpse of an aerosteamer lazily circling. Signaling for the column to change direction, he headed toward the steamer, knowing that it marked the destination of this, his annual trek into the Bantag Range.

Eager anticipation showed on young Keane's face, and Vincent smiled.

"This is your first ride out here, isn't it?" he asked.

"Yes, sir. I've never seen a Horde encampment before, just a few hunting parties."

"During the first battle of Suzdal, the Tugars camped all along the hills east of town where the new city now is. The golden yurt of old Muzta—now, there was a sight—must have been fifty yards across. Their tents stretched as far as the eye could see. It was a grand and terrible sight."

He looked over at Abraham. God, how the years have passed. That seemed just like yesterday. It was colored, though, by the haze of memory. It was hard to remember the sheer terror; the umens drawn up, the thundering chants, the rhythmic pounding of scimitars on shields that so strangely sounded like the approach of a freight train.

And the terror of the charge. The way they came on like a hurricane, oblivious to loss.

Abraham knew none of that. All he would know would be the legends, the memories, the Decoration Day and Victory Day parades, where aging veterans gathered with his father, the Colonel, to remember the fallen and march in review, then retire to the nearest tavern to expand upon the stories and memories of old.

The losers, though, what did they now remember? Vincent wondered. Like Prometheus, they were chained to the rock of memory, tormented by the dream of greatness lost.

He looked back again at the column. Only a couple of them, mostly the older NCOs, had fought at Suzdal, Hispania, Rocky Hill, or the Liberation of the Chin. Some had seen a few minor skirmishes, really nothing more than shoot-outs with an occasional drunken band of Bantags, where two or three were killed on either side and then a flurry of protests and accusations would follow. He wondered how these boys would fare if they suddenly faced not a few drunks, but instead a tidal wave; a full umen filling the horizon ahead, sunlight flickering on drawn blades, the sky overhead turning black as night as volleys of arrows, hissing like snakes, rained down upon them.

Riding through a dried riverbed, he urged his mount up a steep embankment, grunting with pain as he leaned forward. His old wound had never really healed, and even after twenty years he still had to change the protective pad that covered the hole drilled into him by a Bantag bullet. Splinters of bone still worked their way out and only last month Kathleen had been forced to operate yet again to withdraw a particularly painful fragment.

He knew she had most likely told her boy to keep a careful watch on him, and Abraham was doing his part, riding beside him, close enough to offer a supportive hand if he should start to lose his grip on the saddle.

He waved the boy off.

As he crested the riverbank he felt more than heard a distant thunder. The sound instantly sent a cold shiver down his back. It was unmistakable, a deep resonant rumble. His mount pricked up her ears, slowing, tossing her head up to catch the scent of the wind. He'd caught it as well; a mingling of horse, leather, and the musky stench unique to those of the Horde.

He reined about, looking back at his column. The tail of it was still on the far side of the dust-filled riverbed. Some of the men were looking up, a few reaching down to unsnap the holster covers for their carbines.

Looking back at the rise of ground ahead he saw them. Visible first were the horsetail standards held aloft. Within seconds, across a front of half a mile they had appeared, a line of Horde riders advancing at a steady trot, silent, silhouetted against the yellow-blue horizon.

"My God," Abraham whispered.

Vincent looked over at him and smiled. "Only a regiment. Just a little show, nothing more. Ride back, tell the troop commanders that all weapons are to remain holstered. We don't want any mistakes. Order the regiment to remain on this side of the riverbank and deploy. Then report back to me."

Abraham hesitated for a second, gaze locked forward, mouth gaping at the display.

"Go on, boy, see to your duty. There's not going to be a war today. If there was, it'd be a full umen coming at us at a gallop."

Abraham, recovering, snapped off a proper salute and reined about.

Vincent continued forward, ordering his guidon bearer and bugler to follow, urging his mount to a slow trot. The Bantag came to a stop at the crest of the ridge, the wind whipping the horsetails of the Qar Qarth's standard. He had learned some of their ways over the years and identified the banner as that of the first regiment of the umen of the white horse, the elite personal guard of their Qar Qarth. Here were the best of them, the victors at Port Lincoln and Capua, bled out in the siege of Roum, defiant, however, to the bitter end. Their ranks, like his, were now filled with the sons of those who had survived the war.

Lieutenant Keane rode up to join him. Like an eager child, he was hoping to be invited along. Vincent hesitated for a second. This was, after all, the only surviving son of Andrew Lawrence Keane.

Political considerations however, swayed him. The one he was going to meet had a grudging respect for Andrew, and it wouldn't hurt to have the boy along. He nodded his consent. Abraham broke into a boyish grin, but then, remembering that he was a newly minted officer out of the academy, instantly assumed the proper look of stern forthrightness.

"Abraham, you can carry my guidon."

Vincent looked over at his bugler.

"Ruffles and flourishes, Sergeant."

The high piercing call sent a chill down his spine. Looking up at the line of Bantags, he half wished it was the call for charge instead. He smiled inwardly. Old memories, old hatreds, and passions, die hard. He had been seasoned by war, bitterly scarred by it, and yet after all these years the dark coiled longing for it lingered in his soul.

The words of Robert E. Lee whispered to him: "It is good war is so terrible, else we would grow too fond of it."

The deep, throaty rumble of a *narga,* the Horde battle trumpet, echoed back in reply. He saw two figures separate from the Bantag line, a rider followed by a standard bearer.

With a gentle nudge he urged his mount to a canter and started up the hill to meet Jurak, Qar Qarth of the vanquished Horde of the Bantag.

Qar Qarth Jurak reined in for a moment, his gaze sweeping across the steppes, focusing on the antlike column deploying across the streambed below. They glanced at the flyer circling overhead.

"Damn them," he whispered softly.

"My Qarth?"

He looked over at his son, who today was serving as his aide, and smiled. "Nothing, Garva. Just remember, stay silent and observe."

The lad nodded eagerly, and Jurak felt a stab inside. The boy's mother had died during the winter of the breathing sickness, which had swept through the impovished camps, killing thousands. He had her eyes, the set of her jaw, the proud visage, and to look at him triggered memories that were still too painful to recall.

"Is that their Qarth?" Garva asked, nodding toward the two that were approaching.

"General of their armies, Vincent Hawthorne."

"He is tiny. How can that be a general?"

"He's one of their best. Remember, he defeated us. Never judge an enemy by physical strength. Always consider the mind. Now, be silent."

Over a year passed since he had last seen Hawthorne. Hawthorne's hair was showing wisps of gray, and by the way he rode it was obvious that he was in pain. He looked even smaller on his diminutive mount. The humans had been breeding their mounts for a size that fit them better. Their horses now looked almost toylike.

Vincent reined in a dozen feet away, stiffened, and formally saluted. "Qar Qarth Jurak, you are well?"

His command of the language was good. It was obvious he had been studying.

"I am well, General Hawthorne, and you?"

Vincent smiled. "A reminder of the old days troubles me." He absently patted his hip. "I heard the sad news of your mate's passing and bring the regrets of Colonel Keane."

"Thousands died," Jurak replied. "Some see it as a sign of the displeasure of the ancestors."

Vincent nodded. He stiffly swung his leg over the saddle and dismounted. It was an interesting gesture, Jurak thought, for the first to dismount was acknowledging subservience, and he wondered if Vincent knew that.

There was a slight grunt of amusement from Garva, but a quick glance stilled him.

Jurak dismounted as well and came forward. For an awkward moment, the two gazed at each other, the small general of the humans, who were the victors in the Great War, the towering Qar Qarth of the Bantag Horde looking down. He let the moment draw out. Humans tended to be frightened when a Horde rider stood close, and they were forced to gaze up at dark, impenetrable eyes. Hawthorne did not flinch. His gaze was steady, and a flicker of a smile creased his mouth.

He finally broke the silence. "We can stand here all day and play this game, Jurak, or we can sit down and talk like two civilized leaders."

Jurak laughed softly and looked back at his son. "Something to eat and drink, Garva."

Without ceremony, Jurak sat down on the hard ground.

The scent of crushed sage washed up around him, a pleasant smell: crisp, warm, ladened with memories.

Hawthorne's aide dismounted as well, unclipping a folding camp chair from behind Vincent's saddle and bringing it up.

"Hope you don't mind that I use a chair," Vincent asked. "At least then we can see eye to eye, and it's a bit easier on me."

Jurak nodded, realizing that Vincent was aware of the implications of sitting higher in the presence of the Qar Qarth.

Garva brought forward a jar filled with kumiss and two earthen mugs. Pouring the drinks, he handed them over. Jurak dipped his finger into the mug and flicked droplets to the four winds and then to the earth before drinking.

As he did so, his gaze fell on Vincent's aide. The boy was watching him, fascinated. There was something vaguely familiar to Jurak.

"Jurak, may I introduce Lieutenant Abraham Keane, who is serving as my adjutant."

"Your sire, then, is Andrew Keane?"

"Yes, sir."

"You come from good blood. How is your father?"

"Well, sir. He asked that I convey to you his personal respects, and his regrets as well for the passing of your mate."

Jurak nodded his thanks. "We both know pain, your sire and I. You are his only surviving son, are you not?"

"Yes, Qar Qarth Jurak."

"Interesting that he became your—how do you call it— your president yet again. Does he enjoy such power?"

"No, sir. It was never his desire to hold that rank."

Jurak smiled. "All of ability desire power."

"And I assume your aide is your son?" Vincent interrupted.

Garva stiffened, and then formally nodded with head slightly bowed.

Jurak, caught by surprise, said nothing.

"I could see your blood in him. Tell me, do you desire power, son of the Qar Qarth?"

"Of course," Garva replied stiffly. "When my sire goes to our ancestors, I shall rule as he did."

"And how shall that be?" Vincent asked. "How shall you rule?"

Jurak looked over at his son, eyes filled with warning.

"Justly," Garva replied coolly.

"Yes, your father has been just."

"To whom?" Jurak asked. "Just to your people or to mine?"

"There has been no war for twenty years. I think that is a worthy accomplishment."

"No war. Define war, Vincent Hawthorne."

"I don't need to do that for you. We both know what it is."

"Let us get, as you humans say, 'down to business.' "

Vincent nodded.

"I received your listing of complaints—the incident at Tamira's Bridge, the refusal of passage to the Nippon settlers, the supposed raids, the disappearance of two flyers, the rumors of raids to take prisoners for the moon feast, and all the other allegations."

"You may call them allegations. I attended the funeral of the thirty-two men killed at Tamira, and their dead bodies were not allegation but fact. As to the incident where a dozen Chin settlers disappeared, by God, if they were sacrificed, I will have one hell of a problem restraining Congress from ordering a punitive expedition. Remember, the Chin are the single largest voting block, and they are screaming bloody murder over this rumor."

"Fifty-three of my riders died at Tamira," Jurak replied, choosing to ignore the issue of the Chin, "and the question is who shot first. We both have our own answers to that."

"It could have sparked a war."

"And you have yet to define war to me, Hawthorne. Remember, I am not of this world. I came here from another place, as did you. I was educated on a world where there are things you cannot imagine or dream of."

Vincent stiffened slightly. "Such as weapons you might dream of?"

"Perhaps, yes. And in my education, I studied the writings of Ju ta Vina, who stated, 'War is the eternal process, and peace is but the preparation for the renewal of conflict.' "

"Do you believe that?"

"You do, otherwise you would not be here, in uniform,

in command of the tens of thousands of troops that ring us in on what you call the Bantag Range and which many of my people define as nothing more than a prison."

"What, then, was the alternative?" Vincent asked sharply. "My God, we could have slaughtered you after the Chin rebelled. Remember, it was Hans that offered the compromise and saved your life as well."

Jurak lowered his head. "I owe him blood debt," he acknowledged, "and yes, you could have slaughtered us."

"We are drifting onto dangerous ground here," Vincent interjected. "Refighting the past is meaningless."

"Yet history is the foundation of the future."

Vincent said nothing, taking a sip of kumiss, then setting the cup down.

"The reason for this meeting is that we are dying here. The herds of the great hairy giants are all but gone after twenty years of hunting. In a few more years what food we can gather will be gone forever. More and more of our horse herds are being devoured. Riders who once owned a dozen mounts now rarely have more than two or three. We once ranged around the entire world. Now we are confined to but one small corner of it, and the land is used up."

"We survive on less land with far more people."

"You are farmers, and you have the machines that you have denied us the right to make or to own." As he spoke he nodded to the flyer, which continued to circle overhead.

"Then be farmers."

Garva barked a defiant laugh, and Jurak did not look back.

"Go suggest that to my warriors up there," Jurak replied sharply, pointing at the regiment deployed on the ridge behind them. "See how long you or I would live. The Ancestors would scoff at us, would be ashamed and deny any who did thus the right to join them on the Everlasting Ride through eternity."

"You are not of this world. Do you honestly believe that?"

Jurak stiffened, knowing that his son was standing but half a dozen feet away, hearing everything.

"Of course," he said hurriedly, "but what I believe does not matter. It is what my people believe that is important. I convinced them to give up the ride, for it was either that or the war continued. I convinced them to forswear the moon feast, to become hunters of other creatures instead."

Vincent's gaze went icy.

"I mean no offense, Hawthorne, but remember, that is how you were viewed."

"I know, and that is why I wonder what it is you and your warriors are now truly thinking."

"You must acknowledge that the way it now is cannot last. Do you honestly expect my people to quietly sit on this empty land and starve to death? The lung sickness of last winter was but the start. They will grow weaker, ask your doctors of it. It is called malnutrition, and as they grow weaker they will become susceptible to a whole host of diseases.

"You have your medicines, inoculations, a wealth of food. We do not."

"Then make them."

Jurak laughed. "How? Where in the name of the Gods do I start? Build a school? Who will teach? What will we teach? I am but one from another world. You Yankees had hundreds of minds to start with. To do what you suggest will take a hundred years, which I don't have. I am worried about what will happen when winter comes again."

"So what are you asking for?"

"To leave this place, to resume the ride."

Vincent shook his head. "You can't ride west. The Chin will never stand for it. You mix your people in with mine, and there will be a slaughter on both sides, and we both know it. If you go east, Congress will never accept that. There are people there. They are not yet part of the Republic, but soon will be. It is their land, and we are sworn to protect it."

"So, you are telling me that we are stuck here."

Hawthorne looked down at the ground, absently kicking an anthill with the toe of his boot.

"The Merki are all but dead. They tried to continue on. Wherever they went, there was rebellion and slaughter, hundreds of thousands of humans, and riders have died far to the west across the last twenty years. The Tugars have settled into the great forest and are surviving."

"Surviving?"

There was a snort of disdain from Garva, and again Jurak let the youth have his way. The humans fully understood that the Tugars were held in contempt for their betrayal of the Merki at the Battle of Hispania. If ever the two Hordes should meet, no matter what the humans threatened, there would be a war of vengeance.

"We are two aging warriors," Vincent said, his gaze again fixed on Jurak. "We can speak bluntly. I am ordered by Congress and by the president of the Republic to inform you that the boundaries of your lands are permanently fixed by the treaty that you yourself signed. Any attempt to move beyond them will be construed as an act of war, and we both know what that would mean."

"You will slaughter us," Jurak replied, his voice cold. "If I had a thousand of those things"—he pointed at the flyer circling overhead—"not those primitive machines but the kind I knew on my world, you would not speak so lightly of war. You do so now because you know that with your land ironclads, your trains, and your flyers, it would not be war, it would be extermination."

Vincent nodded. "I speak to you now as someone who has come to respect you. I came to this world a stranger. At first I hated your race and everything associated with it. I killed as you did."

"Yes, I know. You are a legend, Vincent Hawthorne, when it comes to killing."

Vincent was silent for a moment, features gone pale as if a dark dream had seized him. He lowered his head, the slightest of tremors flickering across his face.

"Yes, I killed on a level that even the oldest of your warriors would admire. I don't want any more of it. Fighting in the field as we once did, line facing line, there was at least some honor to that butchery. This is different. How long could your warriors stand against our land ironclads, our gatlings, the firebombs dropping from our flyers?"

"You made sure in the treaty that we could not. Remember, we are denied the ability to make such weapons."

"What the hell else were we supposed to do? If the roles were reversed, I daresay you would have not been so generous. It would have been all of us to the slaughter pits."

As he spoke his face turned red, anger rising to the surface.

"Yes," Jurak replied quietly. "My people would have demanded such a thing, for both of us realize a fundamental point now. Only one race will survive on this world."

"Sir, it does not have to be that way."

Both of them looked at Abraham Keane, who throughout the conversation had stood in respectful silence behind Vincent.

Vincent started to make an angry remark, but Jurak extended his hand. "Indulge him. Besides, he is the son of Keane. Go on, boy, speak."

Abraham blushed. "Sir, my father has often said that his hope was that somehow we could finally learn to coexist, side by side."

"And you believe this?"

"I want to."

"I know enough of your father to believe him and you, at least as to what you might wish."

"It is what many of us wish," Vincent interjected.

"Wishes, always wishes," Jurak replied sharply. "I must deal this winter with facts."

"We could send food to you."

"Ahh, so now we are reduced to beggary. Should we come to the depot and bow in thanks? Suggest that to my warriors up on the ridge and see what they say. They would choose one of two things in reply to that: either cut their own throats or cut yours. The Ancestors would spit upon them for such an infamy."

"You are telling me, then, that there will be war?" Vincent asked.

Jurak leaned back and closed his eyes, then finally shook his head.

"No. But I am telling you that unless something changes, no matter what we desire, things will become impossible. Either we are allowed to expand our range to new lands, or we starve. No other alternative you suggest can work."

"And that is what I am to carry back to Congress?"

"Tell your Congress to come to our encampments and see the starvation. Then ask them what is to be done."

"Jurak, I hope you know enough about me to know that I will honestly tell them the truth regarding your situation."

Jurak nodded. "Yes, I believe you will."

"But I promise nothing. I will suggest expansion to the north. It is land belonging to the Nippon, which is still open range. They are very testy about such issues, but if we could give you access to the Great Northern Forest, there is game aplenty there. Perhaps that might help."

"For the present at least." Jurak's voice was cool, distant.

Vincent shifted uncomfortably, and Jurak could sense that he wanted to talk about something else.

He nodded to his son, who refilled his goblet with kumiss.

"We've had reports," Vincent continued.

"Of what?"

"The Kazan."

Jurak looked straight ahead, wondering how his son was reacting. His gaze focused on Keane's son, standing behind Hawthorne. The boy was staring straight at him, penetrating pale blue eyes that, if of the Bantag, would mark him as a spirit walker.

Somehow he sensed that the boy knew, and it was disquieting.

Hawthorne looked back over his shoulder at Keane. "Abraham, could you fetch that item you're carrying for me?"

The boy stirred and turned away.

Abraham Keane opened the saddlebag on his mount. As he reached inside, he looked back at Jurak, who was still staring at him.

Something is bothering him, Abraham thought. All of the Qar Qarth's attention was focused on him.

Why?

He pulled out the package, wrapped in an oil-soaked wrap, and brought it up to Vincent, who motioned for him to open it. Untying the binding, Abraham laid the cloth open. He picked up the revolver, the bulk of it so large that he felt he should hold it with two hands.

The steel was burnished to an almost silver gleam, and the grips were made of ivory. It was not an old cap and ball weapon from the war, but a cartridge-loaded weapon, the cylinder holding eight rounds of a heavy caliber. As he held it forth, he looked again at Jurak.

Abraham wondered what it would be like to do what his father had done. More than once his father had leveled a revolver into the face of one of the Horde riders and fired, so close, he had heard veterans say, that their manes had burst into flames.

What was it like to kill? he wondered.

Jurak stared at him, the flicker of a smile crossing his features. "Ever been in battle, boy?"

The words were a deep grumble, spoken in the slave dialect, which was taught at the academy to young cadets who would be assigned to the cavalry on the frontier.

"No, sir."

"Your father killed scores of my warriors with his own hands."

"I know."

"Does that make you proud of him?"

Abraham hesitated.

"Speak with truth."

Abraham nodded. "It was war. Your race would have destroyed, devoured mine. He's told me he fought so that I would grow up safe, which I have."

Jurak laughed softly. "He did it for more than that. He did it because he loved it."

Abraham shifted uncomfortably, gun still in his hands, pointed not quite at Jurak but in his general direction.

What does this one know of me, of my father? Abraham wondered. Is it true that my father did love it, that he gloried in it? He thought of Pat O'Donald, of William Webster, who was now secretary of the treasury and holder of the Medal of Honor for leading a charge. And he thought of the few others of the old 35th Maine and 44th New York who were still alive, who would come to the house in the evening and never did a night pass when they did not talk of "the old days." Always there'd be that gleam in their eye, the sad smiles, the brotherhood that no one else could possibly share. Is that what they love, the memories of it? Or was this leader of a fallen race correct, that they loved it for the killing?

"Did you love it as well?" Abraham asked. "I heard it said that after you defeated us at Capua, you rode before your warriors carrying one of our battle standards, standing tall in your stirrups, acknowledging the cheers of your warriors. Did you love that moment?"

Jurak, caught off guard, let his gaze drop for a second.

Hawthorne, who had been watching the exchange, reached out and took the heavy revolver from Abraham's grasp and inverted it, holding the stock toward Jurak.

"Go ahead, take it."

Jurak, smiling, accepted the revolver, hefted it, half cocked the weapon and spun the cylinder. He raised it up, pointing it toward the flyer, which still buzzed overhead.

"A gift?" Jurak asked.

"No, a return."

Jurak laughed softly. "You speak in riddles, Hawthorne."

"I think you know what I mean, Qar Qarth Jurak."

"Then enlighten me."

"This weapon was taken from one of your dead after the fight at Tamira. You can see it's of the finest craftsmanship. Its precision, according to my designer of armaments, exceeds anything we could now make. It is obvious it is not an old weapon left over from our war."

"So?"

"Where did it come from?"

"You said it was looted from one of my dead."

"A commander of ten thousand as near as we could figure out from his uniform and standard."

Jurak was silent.

"It is either one of two things, Jurak. First, if you are now making such things, it is in violation of our treaty."

"You, however, can make whatever machines that please you," Garva interjected, voiced filled with anger. He stepped up to his father's side. Nearly as tall as his sire, he looked down menacingly at Abraham.

Abraham struggled for control, not willing to let this one see fear, and yet he suddenly did feel afraid. It had a primal edge, as if he were confronting a terrifying predator in the dark. He suddenly wondered if this one had ever tasted human flesh, and he knew with a frightful certainty that if given the chance, Garva would do such a thing without hesitation.

He forced himself to stare up at Garva and not back down.

Jurak extended his hand. "Go on, Hawthorne."

"Did you make this weapon?"

Jurak shook his head. "The machinery required, the lathes, to cut the cylinder to such perfection, even the refining of the steel—you know we couldn't do that and keep it hidden for long."

"Then if you did not make it, how did one of your warriors come to possess it? It's not sized to a human. It does, however, fit your hand perfectly."

Jurak looked straight at Vincent, but did not answer. "The Kazan. Is that it?"

There was a long silence. Abraham turned his gaze away from Garva, again focusing on Jurak. He wondered how one learned to read them, to understand the nuances of gesture, and found it impossible. Always there was that impenetrability he had heard his father speak of so often.

"They are fifteen hundred leagues or more from here," Jurak finally replied, waving vaguely toward the south.

"And twelve hundred of those leagues are ocean, which they know how to sail. Have you been in contact with them?"

Jurak actually smiled, but said nothing.

"Is that from the Kazan?" Vincent pressed, and though Abraham's command of the Bantag slave dialect was far from good, he could clearly catch the tone of anger and even of threat in Vincent's voice.

"Given how this conversation is progressing, I'd certainly take pleasure in meeting these Kazan," Jurak replied, leaning forward menacingly, the revolver in his hand now almost pointed at Vincent.

Abraham looked up to the riders who, throughout the meeting, had remained motionless on the ridgeline behind them. He could see that they were intently watching the exchange, and more than one was shifting. Several had old rifles from the war out of their saddle sheaths. He could sense their eagerness, their hope that something was about to explode.

"The possession of that weapon. . . ." Vincent continued, ignoring the implied threat in Jurak's gesture. "If there is contact between you and the Kazan, I must urge you to step back."

"Why? Is there something about to happen between you and them?" Jurak replied, the slightest of mocking tones in his voice. "If so, it could prove most interesting for the Bantag."

"Don't get involved in it, Jurak," Vincent replied. He sounded almost as if pleading, which Abraham found uncomfortable, but then he realized that it was a heartfelt warning.

"I don't want another war with you. We fought our fight. We don't need another such bloodletting, because if there is, we both know the end result."

Jurak grunted and shook his head. As if bowed under with weariness, he slowly stood up and stretched, then stepped closer to Vincent.

Abraham realized that at last he was seeing anger—the flat nostrils dilating, mane bristling slightly along the neck, the brown wrinkled skin shifting in color to a brighter hue.

"Human, we are not slaves. We are not cattle."

He said the last word in the old tongue, the meaning of it quite clear.

Vincent stood up as well, though the effect simply made the difference in their size more pronounced. Hawthorne barely came up to the Qar Qarth's chest.

"If they are out there," Vincent said, "stay out of it. If we do find them, and there is a war, stay out of it. I tell you this not just as a representative of my government, but as a soldier who once faced you in battle. We do not want another war with you. You have nothing to gain by it except slaughter."

"We have our pride," Garva interjected.

"Silence!" Jurak shifted, gaze locked on his son for a brief instant, and yet Abraham wondered if he was indeed angry, if the son had not spoken what Jurak felt.

Jurak pointed the gun straight at Vincent. "This weapon proves nothing to me other than your fears. Your fear of a Horde you cannot even find; a fear of us, a fear of yourselves." He laughed darkly. "You are afraid of becoming like we once were, aren't you? Your pity stayed your hand, and now you are afraid."

"Pity?" Vincent cried. "In the name of God, we were all sick of the killing. Remember, it was a human, a cattle who saved your life from that insane animal, the Qar Qarth of the Merki."

There was a flicker of doubt, of sadness, on Jurak's face. "Yes, Hans," he said quietly.

"Then in his name, stay out of this. I'll see what I can do about expanding your territory, perhaps even easing the restrictions on making machinery, as long as it can't be used for weapons. I'll do that in the name of Hans and on my honor as a soldier."

"You would do that, Hawthorne. I have heard of this religion you once believed in, this thing called Quaker. Tell me, do you still have nightmares over all whom you've killed?"

Vincent stiffened and then stepped back. "I'll forget that question," he said, his voice filled with icy menace.

Jurak nodded. "I offer apology."

Vincent, struggling for control, could only give a jerky nod of reply.

"There is nothing else to be said here today," Jurak announced. "We understand each other. I have begged, and you have threatened, and now we understand."

"I have not threatened," Vincent finally replied, his voice strained. "I have tried to explain things as they are."

"As have I."

"My adjutant will deliver a written statement to your camp tomorrow, detailing our understanding of what transpired today. Let us ponder what we've discussed and agree to meet again tomorrow or the day after."

"You have such a love of things in writing, you humans. My old world was like that, too. It is one of the few things about it I don't really miss."

"If there is anything else you wish to communicate, I'll remain camped here for a while."

Jurak looked at him warily.

"By the treaty signed between us, I and an appropriate escort have the right to traverse your territory, though I would prefer if I did so as an invited guest who has received your permission."

"My permission?" Jurak laughed softly.

"This is, after all, your land."

"By your sufferance."

"I wish you saw it differently."

"How can I?" There was an audible sigh. "You humans, how can you know what I think? You know nothing of the world I came from, where we were the sole masters. The things I knew there, about the history of our greatness, the half-formed knowledge I still carry of weapons that could sweep you away in a single day, but which I do not understand how to make. Tell me, on your old world, did you not have nations that subjugated and annihilated others solely because they could?"

Vincent did not answer.

"I see that here now. No matter what your intentions,

your sense of honor, as you call it—the fact that you and I can in some way respect each other as two former enemies—will not change the inevitable. I know how such things must always end."

Vincent sadly shook his head. "The better angels of our nature," he whispered.

"What?"

"A saying by our president back home, the one this young officer"—he nodded toward Abraham—"was named after. He once said that. I wish we could be touched by that now, Jurak."

But then he pointed at the revolver still in the Qar Qarth's hand.

"If that, and what it implies, does not unravel everything."

Without waiting for a reply, he turned away and walked to his mount.

Abraham remained where he was for a few seconds longer, looking at the two.

Garva was rigid, gaze fixed on Hawthorne's back, and he sensed that if the revolver had been in this one's hand, Vincent might very well be dead. Garva, realizing he was being watched, looked over at Abraham.

"There will be a day," he hissed, and then turned away.

Vincent looked next at Jurak, but could not read him. Wondering how to withdraw, he hesitated for an instant, then simply came to attention and saluted.

Jurak, a flicker of a smile again on his face, nodded. "At least I will say this," he said slowly, "your General Hawthorne has the spirit of a warrior, and I believe that in his heart, he knows us and sees the tragedy of all that was and all that shall be."

"And what, sir, will you do in reply?" Abraham asked.

"Do? Survive, human, survive." Jurak turned and walked away.

Abraham came up to Vincent's side and gently helped him to mount, then swung into his own saddle.

"There's going to be a war, isn't there, sir?" he asked.

Vincent, saying nothing, rode back to where the regiment was digging in for the night's encampment.

Abraham looked toward the bloodred setting sun that hung low on the horizon, the vast, empty steppes bathed in its bloody light. Strange, it was such a beautiful sight, even though it was filled with foreboding.

A random thought came to him. He wondered where his friends Richard and Sean were. Perhaps, out on the vast open sea, such a sunset was indeed a sailor's delight; a portent of at least one more day of peace.

FIVE

He awoke to hell.

As consciousness returned, he could hear Sean O'Donald's low rasping breath. Good, he was still alive.

Or was it good? No. Death was the only way out now, better if Sean had died from the last beating.

Eyes swollen nearly shut, Richard turned his head to look at his comrade, chains around their wrists, hanging suspended from the ceiling of the darkened cabin.

As the ship rose and fell, they slowly swung back and forth, Sean groaning as he brushed against the cabin wall, then swung away.

The only illumination came from a narrow slit of light through a slightly ajar wooden porthole cover.

Richard Cromwell wished that the room were completely dark so that he could not see the table across from them. Knives, pincers, and whips were laid upon the table, the only furnishing in the narrow room other than the chains that bound them.

How long had it been? He wasn't sure. Definitely a day. Had there been a night? If so, he couldn't remember now. His universe was focused on the pain; the racking thirst that was nearly as terrible; the realization that there was no way out, that they were the prisoners of the Kazan and death was the ultimate outcome.

He tried to become detached, to remember how it once was. He had a vague memory—or was it just what his mother had told him?—of a time when they had been spared the full horror of the Merki occupation of Cartha. She, as the mistress of Tobias Cromwell, was allowed a place to live, decent food, deliverance from the feasts and from the mines.

But then Cromwell had died, and the Merki had sent them into the mines. Even children of two and three had crawled into the narrow seams and retrieved loose rock.

Thus he had lived and grown until the end of the war. He had learned toughness, to look with cold eyes upon unspeakable horror, to watch as others died the most horrible of deaths and to feel nothing.

He wondered how it could be that he was not like so many others who had survived that time; the drifters, the beggars, the drinkers and murderers who had infested the city of Cartha after the war and the coming of the Yankees.

It was his mother's love that had shielded him from that fate. He could remember her soft touch, her stories of her family, rulers of Cartha before the Great War. Her love had formed a shield around him and somehow kept a kernel within his heart alive and warm.

She had died on the final day the Merki fled from the Yankee gunboats on the coast, the liberation within sight. The Merki had massacred nearly everyone. But even among that dreaded race there could be acts of pity. Their master, ordered to slay everyone, had granted her a clean death, a single blow. Then he had looked down, blade drawn, and hesitated.

"Hide beneath your mother, little one," he whispered, and left.

So he had hidden, feeling the warmth that covered him growing cold.

A Rus soldier had found him thus, taken him in and raised him. The old man had been kindly enough, a fisherman living alone, who had taught him to sail, to work, to read and write. The old man seldom spoke, for a wound to the throat from a Tugar arrow had made his speech all but unintelligible, but concealed within was a sharp mind and a gentle strength. They would take their small boat out upon the Inland Sea, and often for days not a word would be exchanged, but Richard had, at least with this lonely old man, learned the strength of silence and patience.

He had died when Richard was eighteen, and only then did Richard learn that this quiet, lonely man had been a hero in the Great War, a war of which the old man had never spoken other than to say that his entire family had died in the great siege of Suzdal and that Perm had sent Richard to replace those he had lost.

Several veterans came to the funeral, one of them the Yankee general Hawthorne. He was the one that suggested Richard attend the academy and offered to give a letter of recommendation, never realizing who Richard's father had really been.

Old Vasiliy had often suggested that Richard take his name, but something within had always stopped him, a defiance toward the world, an unwillingness to concede this one final point. It had caused nothing short of an explosion when he had appeared before the review board to take the exams and placed his true name on the form.

The matter had gone all the way to Andrew Keane, who was not president at the time, but did sit on the Supreme Court. The four years at the academy had been, because of his defiance, less than pleasant. More than one instructor had denounced his father as a traitor and openly mocked his name. And yet his quiet defiance had, in the end, gained him a certain grudging respect.

Vasiliy had taught him never to admit that anything was impossible. Once their net had become tangled in some wreckage, and the old man had told him to dive down and loosen it. The net was too precious to cut away or abandon. He had tried and could not reach it, and Vasiliy simply sat back, lit his pipe and told him they had days if need be, but he would untangle the net.

It had taken a day, he had almost drowned doing it, but he had learned.

And now it is time to die, he thought. I should have died nearly twenty years past. Every day since had been but an extra drawing of breath. At times he half believed in a God, Perm, and Kesus as old Vasiliy called them. At other times, in the face of all the cruelty he had witnessed, it was impossible to believe in any sense or order to the universe, for surely if there was a God he had to be mad to allow such a world as this.

The ship rose on a wave and corkscrewed back down, slamming both of them against the bulkhead. Sean groaned, a shuddering sob racking his body.

"Richard?"

"I'm here."

Sean looked over at him, face contorted with agony. "I can't take it again."

Richard said nothing. He had learned how to block out beatings. In the mines they were the primary way to force children of four and five to work, or simply to amuse a bored Merki master. He had once seen a child slowly beaten to death across an entire day in the same way human children would torment a fly.

The beating of the previous day, however, had not been done for amusement, but for the simple purpose of breaking him down. He understood the method well enough, to push the agony to the limit of endurance, made even more maddening because no questions were asked, nothing demanded as of yet. Pain was simply inflicted, the lash snaking out against their naked bodies until both of them were bloody masses of peeling flesh.

He knew the questioning would come next. They'd be offered yet more torture or a quick release from the pain if they talked.

He looked over again at Sean and saw the terror in his eyes. He wondered if Sean, in turn, could sense the fear within his own soul as well.

"Listen to me," he gasped, pausing to lick his split and bloodied lips. He swallowed to clear his throat. "Lie to them. We'll have to talk, but we can lie." He whispered softly, suspecting that just behind the half closed shutter and porthole a guard was listening. That's why he spoke in English, doubting that any of their captors knew the language.

"Our ship, the *Gettysburg*, its an old ship. We have ships three, four times as big. Let's say, twenty of them. We saw them pulling the wreckage of our flyer in, so tell them the truth about that, but say it's our smallest aerosteamer. Tell them our army has half a million men under arms and can call up another half million. We have to agree on this now. They most likely will separate us soon."

Sean, eyes glazed, stared at Richard. "Why?" Sean whispered.

Why? He was so incredulous, he couldn't respond for a moment.

"It's our duty, that's why," he finally replied.

"Duty? Duty got us into this. I joined because I had to. I was the son of damnable Senator O'Donald. Now look at us."

A shuddering sob escaped him, and he lowered his head.

"Damn it, Sean, we have to agree on this. It will make it easier for both of us."

"Easier?"

"I know how these creatures think. They respect strength. Show weakness, and they'll drag out the agony for their own amusement.

"When they start in again, try to hang on as long as possible. When you simply can't take it anymore, act as if you're breaking, then spill it out quickly."

He looked over at the table where the implements of torture were neatly lined up.

"They get careless sometimes. If you have a chance, throw yourself on one of their blades."

He had seen that done often enough, and though it was easy to say, he wondered if he would have the courage to do so if the chance should arise.

"Then what?"

If we're lucky, they just might cut our throats, Richard thought, but looking at Sean, he realized he'd better not say it.

"The moon feast. That's what they are planning for us, isn't it?"

Richard shook his head. "They only do that to fresh victims."

Sean groaned as another wave rolled the boat, swinging them back against the bulkhead.

A burst of light flooded into the room, and, startled, he looked up. The door was open. Two of them were standing there, both in white robes, unlike their tormentors of earlier, who were stripped to the waist and wore black trousers.

The two entered, the second one far taller than normal for one of the Horde, head inclined low even though the ceiling was over eight feet from the deck.

Richard gazed at him warily. He was thin, almost cadaverous for a Bantag, eyes a strange pale blue, a rarity amongst that race. His gaze was penetrating, cutting directly into the soul.

Richard knew that some were able to do this. The terrifying Tamuka, the fallen Qar Qarth of the Merki, had been one, although those with the power usually stood behind a Qarth or even the Qar Qarth as their adviser.

This one, he sensed, had cultivated the ability to see within beyond anything the Hordes of the north knew or comprehended.

As the blue-eyed one gazed at him, Richard fought to show indifference; the look of a slave who was beyond caring and beyond fear.

There was the flicker of a smile, and then he turned to look at Sean.

Richard watched the silent interplay. Sean gasped for breath, eyes drooping. Again the flicker of a smile.

The blue-eyed one said something unintelligible, and his companion pulled a drinking flask out from under his robe, uncorked it, and held it so that Richard could drink.

He gulped it down. The taste was strange, tinged with a slight bitterness, like a strong herb. The flask was withdrawn and offered to Sean, who drank as well.

The second one drew back and then left the cabin. At first Richard felt some of his strength returning, but then he sensed something else, a strange drifting. The pain was still there, but somehow he felt as if he were floating.

The blue-eyed one smiled.

"Yes, it was drugged."

Richard was startled. The words were in English.

"I seek answers to a few questions. That is all, and then this will end."

Richard wanted to make a defiant reply, but decided that silence was still the best path.

"Just end it," Sean cried, his voice near to breaking.

"It will end." His attention turned to focus on Sean. "Tell me, are you the son of Senator O'Donald of the Republic."

Richard could not help but betray his shock. The blue-eyed one smiled. "We know quite a bit about you." As he spoke he snapped his fingers.

A man came through the door, a human wearing a white robe, the same as the blue-eyed one. And yet something about him made Richard uneasy, even frightened. The man was tall, matching Richard's height, but beneath the robe he could sense a physique that was perfection. The man moved catlike. There seemed to be a coiled and deadly power to him, his gaze cool, almost mocking.

"Years ago I sent a dozen like Machu here north, to learn a few things. Your Yankee language was one of the things he returned with. My Shiv learn such things quickly."

"Shiv?" Sean asked.

He smiled. "My name is Hazin, and you, Sean O'Donald, will learn soon enough who the Shiv truly are."

"I doubt that," Richard snapped.

The gaze turned, fixing on him. Yet again he felt the sense of uncovering, of staring within.

At a subtle gesture, Machu stepped forward. The back-handed blow was delivered in almost a casual manner, but the force of it stunned Richard. For a moment he thought his jaw had been shattered, and he gagged on the blood, which nearly choked him.

The man turned on Sean, and the beating began. Within less than a minute O'Donald was sobbing, begging for it to stop. The whole time Hazin ignored Sean, all attention focused on Richard.

He could feel the drug taking hold, the strange floating, the sudden awareness of the finest nuances of the narrow universe of the cabin, the way motes of dust floated, the scent of salt air drifting in, such a pleasant relief washing away the fetid stench.

He heard the sharp rasping snick of a knife being drawn, and the Shiv held it up before Sean's eyes. As Sean rocked back and forth, suspended from his chains, the Shiv remained motionless, the point of the blade raised so that with each forward swing it barely touched Sean's skin, drawing blood from his arms and chest.

Hazin, meanwhile, continued to stare at Richard.

Not you, he seemed to whisper. The other one is the one I know will break.

"What is it you want?" Richard gasped.

"You know," Hazin whispered.

"No, I don't."

Sean was crying, beginning to beg. Richard froze, closing his eyes, trying to block out the sound, and yet still he felt as if Hazin was looking at him, probing within, seeking for something that could not be described by words.

"No, not that, God no."

Richard opened his eyes and saw with horror that the Shiv had lowered his blade and was preparing to make the most cruel of cuts with it.

Sean was shaking his head back and forth, feebly kicking, his cries drawn out into a long pitiful moan.

Richard looked back at Hazin. "Stop it," he gasped. "I'll tell you what you want, just leave him alone."

"No, you would lie, Cromwell. You would try to save your friend, but still you would lie."

"I'll tell you anything," Sean begged, "just not that."

Richard lowered his head, and in spite of himself tears welled up. He had never had room for pity in his life. There was no room for pity in slavery, it could only lead to death. Yet now he felt it for a comrade who had been pushed beyond the limits of endurance. He wondered as well if he would have broken with such a threat. He wondered if Hazin, who somehow seemed to be inside his very thoughts, knew the answer to that question.

He heard the snick of a lock opening. The Shiv had unsnapped one of the manacles holding Sean and then unlocked the other. O'Donald fell to the deck, sagging down onto his knees. The Shiv effortlessly picked him up and carried him out of the room.

But Hazin did not follow. Another Shiv came in, this one almost identical to the first. He had the same muscular build, the same sharklike eyes devoid of emotion. Richard wondered if the torture was to continue.

Instead there was a blessed relief as the manacles around his wrists were unfastened. He tried to remain on his feet as he dropped to the deck, but his knees gave way. The Shiv pulled him back up and roughly tossed a cloak over his shoulders, covering his nakedness, then pointed at the door.

Legs wobbly, Richard did as ordered. It was difficult to walk. The pain was beginning to float away, replaced by a strange warmth, and yet his mind still seemed focused on his awareness of Hazin.

Stepping into the sunlight, he breathed deeply. The ship was strange, its lines sleeker than the *Gettysburg,* no masts; its deck painted a dull gray and scorched here and there with battle damage. Part of the deck forward had been split apart.

The ocean was a vast expanse of a deep, lush blue, sparkling with whitecaps driven before a warm, tropical breeze. He felt, at that moment, as if it were the most beautiful experience he had ever known—the ocean, the scent of the wind, the rocking of the ship beneath his feet as it plowed through the gently rolling sea.

Hazin stepped past him, motioning to him to follow, and Richard went up a ladder and through an open door. The light inside was muted. What appeared to be an altar of black stone rose at the far end of the room, which was filled with the sweet scent of incense.

Silk curtains over the portholes were drawn shut, but a soft, diffused light filtered through, giving the room a gentle, comfortable feel. Hazin motioned to a chair set by a table. On it was an open decanter and a single crystal goblet beside it.

"Have something to drink, Cromwell."

"Is it drugged as well?"

Hazin smiled. "Of course. You can refuse, but in the end thirst will compel you, and you will drink. So why endure the wait?"

Richard looked at the decanter and hesitated.

"Your friend is drinking even now."

Richard looked bitterly over at Hazin. But his back was turned, facing the altar, holding a burning taper to light a candle.

"Cromwell, we can play this game for the rest of the day. You can even try and kill yourself by not drinking. But I can assure you that you will be forced to drink."

Hazin turned and smiled. "O'Donald is telling us everything—the size of your fleet, your army, types of weapons, he'll tell us all."

"Your spies told you already, so why torture him?" Richard snapped.

"Interesting. You seem more worried about him than yourself."

"I know what to expect."

"I understand your body was covered with lash scars even before the current unpleasant treatment. Were you a slave of the Bantag?"

"The Merki."

"Even crueler. A primitive people, the Merki. It shows a certain toughness on your part."

Richard continued to eye the decanter. It contained a swirl of color, a rainbow sparkle of light that was infinitely pleasing.

"The information we have on your Republic is old. Half a dozen or more years. After the treaty we of course sent spies in, but recent events caused my order to shift its attention elsewhere. Frankly, the appearance of your ship was a bit of a surprise for me, but in the web of things I feel there might be a use for it—and you."

Hazin drew closer, and, pulling out a chair on the other side of the table, he sat down. Richard looked at him warily, gaze flickering to his belt, hoping to see a knife. Though all of this race had an overwhelming physical strength, they were usually slower, even a bit clumsy, and a human moving quickly could at times snatch a blade or weapon.

"I'm not armed, at least not with the type of weapons you seek," Hazin announced dryly, as if bored with Richard's intentions.

"What the hell do you want, then?" Richard snapped. "If poor Sean is breaking, you have what you need. I'll just lie, and you know that. So finish it, damn you."

Hazin chuckled softly. "Spirit. That's why you are sitting here with me while 'poor Sean,' as you call him, is being questioned in a slightly different manner."

Richard bristled, and Hazin held up his hand.

"No. The torture is finished. That was just a way of making one of the two of you pliable. You intrigue me, Cromwell. I just want to talk."

"How did you know our names?"

"Foolish question. I expected better. Your names were written on the seams of your clothing, and both of you had your commission papers in your wallets. Poor security, flyers should never be allowed out like that. One of my Shiv recognized the name O'Donald, and I of course had heard of your father."

Richard stiffened and lowered his eyes.

"Yes, the traitor of your Great War. Did you know him?"

"No. My mother was a Merki slave. He died when I was an infant."

"Yet you kept his name. A certain pride there. I approve of that in anyone, of my race or of yours."

"The Shiv?" Richard asked.

Hazin stood up and returned to the altar, then leaned against it, looking back at Richard. "The future for this world."

"The Republic is the future. If you come after us, you will never win."

"A loyal answer, but then, you only know of your Republic. You know nothing of us, of what we are and shall be."

Richard thought of the ship he was now on, how easily it had smashed the *Gettysburg,* of the man with the cold eyes who Richard sensed could kill with effortless efficiency.

"The Shiv are your future, Cromwell. Across ten generations we of my Order have been breeding humans, seeking the traits desired: physical strength, intellect, and cunning. Those who pass such traits on to the next generation are allowed to continue to breed. The others," and he smiled, "well, they have their uses as well."

Richard looked at him, incredulous. He knew he should feel outrage and disgust, but the damnable drug was making itself felt. The room was drifting, floating. The way the light shone through the porthole, catching Hazin's strange blue eyes, held his attention.

"Imagine what fifty thousand such warriors could do to your army. But there does not have to be a fight. It could instead be a compromise, an understanding without needless bloodshed."

"The Republic will never surrender, as long as Keane and those who think like him are alive."

Hazin nodded. "Yes, I know. Just a dream of mine." He sighed.

Strangely, Richard felt a sympathy, almost a desire to somehow please, to understand. He fought against it, trying to stay focused, to find something, anything in the room that he could fight with, to kill, to go down fighting.

"You have a remarkable strength, Cromwell. I admire that. Everyone else is far too transparent and malleable. It is actually rather boring at times."

Hazin drew closer and remained standing, looking down at Richard.

"I could force you, I want you to know that. The Shiv

are bred to the needs of my order. At five they are taken from their mothers, who offer them up gladly, and for the next fifteen years are trained mainly by those of their own race. Half die in that training for war, or for other work, or for our special purposes."

"Special purposes?"

"We can discuss that later."

"I give them something to believe." He nodded to the black altar. "Combine such strength with religious belief, and you have a force that is terrifying to behold. You, unfortunately, would never believe. Always there would be the memory of childhood, of other things. I could deaden you with what is in that decanter, make you pliable for a while, but you could never be fully of them."

"Why are you telling me this?"

"Because I've never had the opportunity before," Hazin replied. "It intrigues me. You are not of the Shiv, not of the millions of other humans who live among us as slaves. Being different, there must be a use for you. Focusing on that will be an interesting experiment for me."

Richard struggled for control, to somehow avoid the eyes, the sudden thirst, the desire to let the power of the drug expand. After the war, in the rare times that he and Vasiliy had gone to Suzdal, he had seen more than one crippled veteran who had become addicted to the morphine given to them in the hospital. They would sit in a shady corner, oblivious to their squalor, drifting in dreams. Is that what they are doing to me now?

He looked back at the decanter and then, with a slow deliberate gesture, knocked it over. As the decanter fell off the table, it seemed to hang suspended. Fascinated, he watched as it ever so slowly fell, the golden container upending, crystal blue liquid gurgling out onto the dark wooden floor.

His gaze shifted to Hazin.

"No," he whispered. "I suggest that you find your entertainment elsewhere."

"I could make it far more painful that you could ever imagine. We could slowly cut your friend apart in front of you for starters, then turn on you."

"Go ahead. We're dead anyhow." The brave words spilled out of him, even as the thought of what was to come terrified him. He knew far too well what they were capable of. He wasn't sure if his thoughts were fully his own or induced by the drug, but he felt that any pain to come would be brief. Beyond it would be release, to where he did not know, perhaps to see old Vasiliy again, or to sit by his mother's side and feel her warm embrace. To live otherwise, to succumb—he knew that in the end he would take his own life in ignominious shame. He would not make the mistake his father had made, to give way to fear.

He could not bring himself to trade in his reason for living, proving that he was not a slave and not the son of a traitor. "Finish it and be damned," he said, keeping his voice cool and even.

"I like that," Hazin replied, and Richard sensed a genuine admiration in his voice, or was it yet again the drug?

"Believe what you hear, Cromwell. Your gesture just might have saved your life."

He tried not to believe, but he looked up at Hazin with open surprise.

"Yes. There is always some hidden purpose in the overall web, and I think a path just revealed itself for you."

Hazin went to the door and opened it. The late afternoon light streamed in behind Hazin creating a strange halolike effect around him.

"I'll send someone to clean you up, to tend to your unfortunate injuries. Eat, Cromwell, and I can assure you that the food and drink offered will be untainted. I want to talk with you again when your mind is clear."

"Yet the question remains unanswered, is my brother still alive?"

Yasim stood on the Jade Balcony, which overlooked the grand concourse of procession. He had entered the Imperial City at dawn. There had been no fighting. His fleet and that of his late, lamented cousin Sar had been enough to overawe any resistance.

The populace, pragmatic after twenty years of civil war, had accepted his triumphal return without demur. The houses adorned with the blue banner of Hanaga had quickly switched colors to show their undying support of the victor.

Of course, he had proclaimed the usual amnesty, even praising those of the court who had so loyally served his brother. Once settled in, he could begin the quiet process of elimination and vengeance.

And yet the question of Hanaga's survival still lingered. A survivor from Hanaga's flagship had been fished out of the water and claimed to have seen him abandoning ship just before it had exploded.

It would be like him to survive," Yasim muttered, looking over at the slight diminutive form wrapped in the white and gold robe of the Grand Master.

"And which ship did he flee to?"

"The sailor did not know."

"Undoubtedly one of ours."

"One of yours?"

The Grand Master chuckled. "But of course. Don't you think there is more than one captain of a ship who is secretly a member of our order?"

Yasim looked over nervously at the Grand Master. "You said that Hazin was reliable, that he would fulfill the contract."

"Yes I know."

"I sense uncertainty in your voice, Grand Master."

There was no reply.

SIX

"I never realized how beautiful it could be out here," Abraham Keane said, hands clasped around a warming cup of tea to ward off the early morning chill.

Sergeant Kasumi Togo laughed, shaking his head. "You're a romantic, Keane. You should have grown up out here as I did. The steppes can be deadly."

Abe did not reply, looking past Togo, soaking in every detail and reveling in it.

The eastern horizon was showing the first glow of impending dawn, a band of dark purple that was expanding outward, the core of light a golden red. He turned to look to the western horizon. The twin moons, Hasadran and

Baka, old Horde names that had stuck with the human race, were dipping low.

Togo was squatting by the campfire, made of dried horse and mammoth dung. Looking at him, Abe wondered if it had been the same between his father and Hans Schuder, the older sergeant taking the young officer under his wing.

Togo had been with the cavalry ever since Nippon joined the Republic after the end of the war, serving as sergeant in command of scouts attached to the 3rd cavalry. Abe had been naturally drawn to him, sensing that here was a man who could teach him the ways of the steppe and of the Bantag, and the sergeant had been more than indulgent and patient.

"So how is it with the general?" Togo asked, nodding toward Hawthorne's tent.

"What do you mean?"

"With them bastards over there." As he spoke he indicated the encampment of the Bantag, which filled the plains to the east.

"Nothing's changed."

"I heard rumor we're to stay on for a while, keep an eye on them."

Abe stiffened slightly, and Togo laughed.

"Don't get upset, Lieutenant. It's my job, in a way, to know what generals are thinking."

"Well, you didn't hear anything from me."

"Relax, Lieutenant. You're the model of a proper officer, you are."

Abe wasn't sure if Togo was being sarcastic or just having a little fun with him. He knew he was still too stiff and formal, typical of the academy with its spit and polish and every button buffed to a shine. Out here on the frontier it was a different world; of dirty blue and khaki, muddy water, and glaring heat.

"In the old days, they marked the time of dread," Togo said, pointing at the twin moons. "Tomorrow they'll be full, signaling the moon feast."

Abe nodded. God, what a world his parents had known. He could hardly imagine the terror of it. Looking back to the east, he could see the early morning glow silhouetting the golden yurt of Jurak Qar Qarth.

It had been a subject in class more than once, the primal

terror that the mere presence of a Horde rider engendered in all humans, and yet somehow he could almost feel a pity for them now in spite of all that his father, Hawthorne, and others had endured in the Great War. What was it like to lose, to see one's greatness shattered, to live at the whim of another race? A generation ago they had bestrode the earth, riding where they pleased, living as their ancestors had for thousands of years.

In the negotiations of the last week he had sensed that and developed a begrudging respect for Jurak, wondering how his own father would react to the reality of what was happening out here.

He had seen the poverty of their camps, the thin bodies of their young, the scramble for food when the carcass of a mammoth was brought in, more than a little ripe after two days of hauling it from the place where it had been killed and butchered.

"My father, brothers, and sisters all died at their hands," Togo announced, gaze fixed, like Abraham's, on the yurt.

Abe turned. "You never told me that."

"No reason to talk about it." He shrugged, taking another sip of tea.

"Do you hate them?"

Togo smiled. "Of course. Don't you?"

"I'm not sure."

Togo looked at him with surprise. "You, the son of Andrew Keane?"

"I don't know at times. From all that I've heard, my father in battle became another person. But he always said that hatred makes you vulnerable. It clouds your judgment. It closes off being able to think as your opponent does and through that defeating him.

"I do know he hated the leader of the Merki, I think in part because of Hans Schuder. But those over there"—he pointed toward the yurts—"I can't say."

Abe sat down, stretching out his long legs. The ground was cool, and the wetness of the morning dew soaked through his wool trousers. The scent of sage wafted up around him, a pleasant smell, dry and pungent.

He looked around the encampment, a full regiment of cavalry, and he felt a chill of delight. He knew he was romanticizing, and yet he could not help it. The last of the

fires had flickered down, wispy coils of smoke rising straight
up in the still night air. Like spokes on a cartwheel, still
forms lay around each of the fires, curled up asleep. At
times one or two would sit up, then settle back down for
a few final moments of rest.

He caught a glimpse of a sentry, riding picket, slowly
circling the encampment, whispering a song, a lovely tune
popular with the Celts, who so eagerly volunteered for service with the cavalry.

A few night birds sang, and the first of the morning birds
were stirring as well, strange chirping and warbling calls. A
shadowy ghost drifted past, an owl swooping into a stand
of grass, then rising back up, carrying off its struggling prey.

"That's the steppes," Togo said, "beautiful but deadly.
It's where I grew up. My uncle settled a thousand or more
square miles abandoned during the wars. It's part of the
land that the general was talking about with them yesterday."

"I'm sorry, I didn't know."

Togo plucked up a stem of grass and slowly twirled it
into a knot.

"It is always that way, Lieutenant. It is about power and
survival. The world is not big enough for us all. One side
or the other must give way. Their mistake was, they didn't
realize that by enslaving us, they had sown the seeds of
their doom. They should have slain our ancestors on the
spot the moment any of us came through the Portals. If
they had, they would have owned this world forever and
could live on it as they pleased."

"But they didn't."

"And so now they will lose all. And frankly, I hope they
all go to the devil, where they belong."

"General Hawthorne says that we must find a way to
settle this without fighting."

"If you doubt me, go to that yurt that looks so exotic,
and listen to what is being said within. Then you will no
longer doubt."

They know something is happening, Jurak Qar Qarth
thought, staring into his golden chalice of kumiss, which
had been stirred with fresh blood.

His gaze swept the yurt, which had been his home now

for more than twenty passings of the year. Strange, it was hard to remember anything else, of a world of homes that did not move, of cities, gleaming cities, books, quiet places, sweet scents, and peace.

Like the Yankees, I am a stranger here, but unlike them, I knew of wars in which entire cities burned from the flash of a single bomb, of fleets of planes darkening the sky, of ten thousand armored landships advancing into battles that covered a front of a hundred leagues. No, they do not know war as I know, as I could dream of it here if I but had the means.

And that, he knew, was how this world had changed him. When he had come here he'd felt almost a sense of relief of having escaped alive from the War of the False Pretender, a war that was annihilating his world, turning it into radioactive ruin. At first, when his companion had seized the Qar Qarth's throne of this primitive tribe, he had stood to one side, observing, almost detached from it all as if he were a student sent to watch.

All that had changed, however, when it was evident that the new Qar Qarth had gone mad with his power and was leading the Bantag to doom. Plus, if he had not acted decisively, these primitives would have killed him as well.

He had accepted peace to save them, and for a while he had even harbored a dream that somehow he could find a way to preserve them. He knew now that was folly.

He looked over at his son, asleep in a side alcove of the yurt, and his chosen companion of the moment curled up by his side.

My son is of them now, and I am but a stranger in this terrible land. My son dreams of glory, of the ride, of the return to what was.

He looked down at the goblet, the foaming drink stained pink, and took another sip.

And I have become like them as well, he realized. I have learned to hunt, the joy of the ride, even though the land is now limited, to listen to the chant singers, to gaze at the stars and tell tales of what lay beyond the stars while the fire crackled, the scent of roasted meat filling the air. And I have learned to eat of the flesh of cattle.

If Hawthorne but knew of that, what would be the reaction? Their meal tonight, a lone prisoner snatched in a bor-

der skirmish, had been led in and sacrificed even though
the true moon feast was not until tomorrow, but such nice-
ties were no longer observed.

They had slowly roasted the limbs while he was still alive,
his mouth gagged so that his cries might not carry to the
Yankees encamped nearby. Then the shamans had cracked
the skull open, poured in the sacred oil, and roasted the
brains while the victim still breathed, listening to his final
strange utterances for signs from the gods and ancestors.
The blood had been drawn off to flavor the drinks of the
Qars and the Qar Qarth, a now precious brew that not so
long ago even the youngest of cubs had savored.

"The night is passing, Qar Qarth Jurak."

An envoy stood at the entryway to the yurt, the first
glow of sunrise behind him. The guards of the Qar Qarth
flanked him, ready to allow admittance, or, if ordered, instant death for any who dared to disturb him.

He motioned for Velamak of the Kazan to enter.

The envoy offered the ceremonial bow to the purifying
fires glowing in their braziers to either side of the entryway
and came forward, again inclining his head as he approached.

"Stop the bowing and take a drink," Jurak said, beckoning to the half empty bowl.

The envoy picked up a goblet, poured a drink, and sat
down on a cushion across from the Qar Qarth. Then he
raised the cup in salute, following the ritual of dipping a
finger in and flicking droplets to the four winds and the
earth.

"You've learned our customs well, Velamak," Jurak said.

"As an envoy such things are important"—he smiled
knowingly—"in the same way you had to learn when first
you came here."

Jurak stirred, not sure if there was some sort of hidden
meaning here, but then let it pass.

"I am curious," Velamak continued, "about your world."

"Yes?"

"The fire weapon."

"Atomics."

"Yes, that."

Jurak smiled. "And you want to know its secret."

"Think what you could do with such a thing."

"What we could do, or should I say, what the Kazan could do," Jurak replied, his voice cool.

"We do have some skills."

"That my people do not."

Velamak shifted, taking another sip, his gaze drifting to where Garva and his consort slept. "You must admit that when it comes to machines, your people are limited, whereas mine are not."

"I think, Velamak, that even for you such a weapon is beyond all of us," he hesitated for a moment, "and I pray it always shall be."

"Even if our race is finally annihilated by the Yankees?"

Jurak barked a laugh and sipped his drink. Before him was perhaps the answer to all his bitter prayers. Or was it a curse? he asked himself, remembering the old saying to never beg too hard of the gods, or they just might grant you your wish.

Here was an envoy of the Kazan Empire, a realm across the Great Ocean that dwarfed anything imagined by the Horde riders or their human opponents. Here lay the true balance of power to this world.

Here was the possible redemption of his people, a path to survival. Up until the meeting with Hawthorne he had harbored a thought that perhaps there was another way, to move north, and by so doing avoid completely what was coming. If there was to be war between the unsuspecting humans and the Kazan, let it come.

Surprisingly, he did trust Hawthorne and his word. Twenty years of dealing with him had taught him that. Hawthorne believed in honor, even to a hated foe. He was haunted as well by a guilt that made him easier to maneuver. Yes, Hawthorne would go back to their Senate, would plead his case. There would be arguing, the Chin would cry yet again for final vengeance, the Nippon would refuse, and six months from now, when the grass of the steppes was brown, he'd return with a vague promise that he would try again next year.

Equally evident was what Velamak was offering.

"This half-life of radiation that you mentioned in our last conversation, what is it?"

Jurak smiled. "The rate of radioactive decay. Do you understand what I speak of?"

Velamak smiled and shook his head. "Perhaps those of my people who study such things do. Remember, I am just a messenger of the emperor."

"And a priest of your order," Jurak added.

Velamak said nothing.

"Tell your people they need to achieve a fissionable mass through a controlled and uniform implosion."

He smiled as he spoke, knowing that the words were meaningless to the envoy but would be faithfully reported. Perhaps someone back in their capital would vaguely grasp the concept, but to make it a reality, would take far more than a nation that still used steam power to propel its ships and weapons.

"Achieve that, and you can burn a city, a hundred thousand die in an instant, a hundred thousand more die later from poisoning of the air. And no one can return to that place until the half-life of the fissionable material has resulted in a drop below fatal levels of radiation. Does that explain it?"

Velamak gave him a cagey smile. "You talk in riddles."

"Not on my old world. Every student learned it. The question was how to make it. We were in the eighteenth year of the war of the Pretender before it was achieved by the False One's side. A spy stole the secret and gave it to our side. On the day I left my world, eleven years later, more than five hundred such weapons had been made and exploded. Entire continents were wastelands. I got dosed at the Battle of Alamaka."

He rolled up his sleeve to show a burn scar on his arm where the hair did not grow.

"The warriors to either side of me were looking in the direction of the blast and were struck blind."

"A weapon that blinds, how fascinating."

"Not if you were there," Jurak whispered.

He remembered the way his tent companions had thrashed in their trench, eyes scorched to bloody pulps, while the blast and shock wave thundered over them. He recalled the terror of wondering if he had been fatally dosed. He had been ordered to shoot his blinded companions, since they would be a burden if allowed to live.

Jurak sighed and took another drink. "I suspect someday

I'll find a lump or start coughing up blood and it will kill me at last."

"I suspect that even if you did know how to make this thing, you would keep it hidden from us."

Jurak smiled. "You can be certain of it."

"Even at the cost of the people you now lead?"

"Believe me, Velamak, everyone dies in the end from it. Stick to the weapons you already know."

"Yet part of the reason I was sent here was to gain information so that we might have weapons to defeat the Yankees when the time came."

"And what time is that?"

"When we are ready."

Again Jurak laughed. "We have been playing this game of words for months. You are torn apart by war. How many contenders to the throne are there?"

"That doesn't matter. In the end, the Kazan shall be reunited. We will destroy them with ease."

"Who is 'we'? I suspect that this order of yours is far more concerned with its own advancement than any unity of the Kazan Empire or who is upon the throne at the moment. For all I know, you represent only your order and serve this distant emperor only with the left hand."

Velamak shook his head and laughed. "Very adroit."

"Don't patronize me. I might be the ruler of a fallen clan, but I am the Qar Qarth, who can still field thirty umens of the finest cavalry in the world."

"We know that. It is one of the reasons we sought you out."

"And, oh, how we shall pay if war does come. There are forty million humans in the Republic. A million of them can be mobilized in a week. And we shall be the first target."

"The emperor never asked for you to sacrifice yourself."

"Nor would I. The emperor is how far away? Two hundred or more leagues by land to the sea. Then how far, a thousand leagues? Two thousand?"

"Something like that. Remember, we knew of your defeat within months of its happening. If we had known your danger earlier, we would have sent aid. We have had twenty years to ponder this question and to prepare."

"And to fight amongst yourselves, thereby diverting your

strength. Velamak, you have been here for months. Over the last week you have seen one of their leaders from a distance, their finest general."

"Small even for them."

"Call him that when he is leading a charge, as I once saw him do."

"I think you almost like him."

"I do, damn it," he growled, and he poured another drink. "He has the ka, the warrior soul. It's told among us how he alone killed more than thirty thousand Tugars in one night, breaking a dam that flooded their camp, sweeping away their elite umens. Some of us believe as well that he has the tu, the ability to read the souls of others."

"And that is why you forbid me to ride escort and reduced me to watching from a distance?"

"Precisely."

Velamak nodded. "We know the tu and the ka. But I doubt if the humans have mastered it, at least their humans."

"Their humans?"

"Ah, so I have piqued your interest."

"What do you mean?"

"Just that there is much of the Kazan I have still not told you."

"We've talked endlessly of this before, and it always seems that I learn precious little of you and your empire in reply."

"The less you know, the less you will reveal to the humans."

"Oh, yes, such as your foolishness in giving a revolver as a present to Ogadi of the White Taie clan."

Velamak stiffened. "I noticed it was missing shortly after I arrived in your camp. Ogadi was the one who escorted me here from the coast. He demanded a present for his efforts. I gave him a few gold trinkets, nothing that could be identified as not being of your Horde. I had hoped the revolver had been lost when fording a stream. Now I know different. He stole it."

He had never trusted Ogadi. Then again, he rarely trusted any of his Qarths. The damn fool.

"They know of you, Velamak."

"Only a rumor."

"I think they know more. I could sense it from Hawthorne. The revolver was enough to cause concern, but he has seemed pressed these last few days, anxious, as if bearing more information than he would ever share with me. Perhaps one of their ships has finally located where you are."

"As I have already told you, we've met three of their ships. Primitive things, actually. They were defeated with ease, their crews annihilated."

"The humans are incessant, Velamak. You can't stop every leak, every hole in that invisible wall you try to maintain while settling your own differences."

Velamak shook his head. "Only rumors. Remember, the ocean is as vast as your steppe, dotted with a thousand islands, archipelagos, and then our homelands. Yes, there are humans out there, some we have never located. They spread widely across the last twelve thousand years since the Portal to their world mysteriously opened up after being asleep since the Downfall. We have set them to our purpose when necessary, slain them when they didn't fit, but never did we allow ourselves to become enslaved to our slaves as you did."

"Not I, those who came before me," Jurak replied coldly.

"Whatever. What I am saying is that in the years since we have learned of the rise of this human nation, we have maintained a zone of destruction on the islands where they might venture, leaving no trace."

"And again, why did you not just attack?"

"To what gain at that moment? When the blow is to be struck, it must be annihilating, not a half measure. We knew we had gained a small edge on machines thanks to those from your world who had come through the portal nearly a hundred years back.

"Our ships outgun them, our flyers are larger, our artillery is superior in all respects, as are our explosives. Still, what I have learned from you is so damn tantalizing. You speak of wireless telegraphs, these engines you call internal, the creation of light through wires, chemicals that kill, gases that kill, the making of diseases. By all the gods, what we would give for such knowledge."

"And yet I know of it but not how to make it happen," Jurak said.

"Precisely. Ten years of working on such things and no threat of the humans could ever matter to us."

"You have the edge you have, and that is it."

"Damn."

It was a curse not directed at him, but nevertheless he stiffened, sensing an insult. After twenty years as a Qar Qarth, his pride would brook no insult, either real or imagined.

"No, you misunderstand," Velamak said hurriedly. "I understand why. I know that our ship designers are working on this mechanism called firing control, being able to judge a target from a great distance and aim correctly. The advice you gave us years ago on that still bears fruit. Our guns can shoot three leagues or more, yet at sea they are useless beyond two thousand paces. I understand that such a thing is being studied, but ask me to explain and I am useless. I understand that it is the same with you."

"I was but twenty years old when I became a soldier. Prior to that, I was a scholar interested in the writings of the ancients and their philosophies," Jurak replied. "I knew to turn a knob and the light would come on so that I could read, but ask me to explain why the light came on and I had no idea."

"Still, what you have said we shall try to work upon."

"You arouse my curiosity about something."

"And that is?"

"Your humans. I know you feel disdain for the moon feast. I watched you closely this evening."

Velamak waved his hands indifferently. "Primitive, but interesting. I suspect you were far more disturbed than I would ever be."

Again Jurak bristled slightly, but then let it pass. "There is something different about your humans. I have heard rumors of it."

Velamak smiled. "Yes, they are different."

"And what is that difference?"

"They are on our side."

"But you said you slaughtered those on the islands."

"Inferior ones. No, we are talking about those who have lived inside the empire, some of them for a hundred generations or more."

"And are they slaves? Do you feed upon them?"

"At times, but that is inconsequential, and of no concern to them."

"Then what is this difference?"

Velamak smiled. "The Shiv. We breed them. We breed them to match what it is we desire of them."

"And that is?"

"A race of warriors. Bred the way you breed your horses. Those we do not select we slaughter or geld. Only the best continue on, generation after generation."

"By the gods. They could be the seeds of your own destruction."

Velamak smiled. "No. For it is the Order that controls them, and they have something you never gave your humans."

"Which is?"

"Faith. A faith in a god of our creation. They are the Shiv, the elite of the elite, and when the Republic faces their Shiv legions, they will die."

"And what of us, then?" Jurak asked, a cold shiver of fear coursing through him when the full enormity of what he had just heard struck him.

Velamak smiled. "He of my order, who I suspect even now is moving toward final control, he will guide the way."

Jurak lowered his head. For the first time since meeting this envoy he felt at last that he understood what was hidden beneath. This man wasn't just an envoy, he was a fanatic, a believer, who had come to prepare the way for the madness to come.

"So you survived after all, Hazin."

Hazin smiled, bowing low before the Grand Master of his order. He could see the wary gaze, the shift of the Grand Master's weight as he leaned forward ever so slightly, ready to spring if Hazin should make a threatening move.

"My master, I must protest the indignity of a personal search before entering your quarters," Hazin replied. "I would not be so disloyal as to strike you now."

There was a sarcastic grunt of bemusement. "The whole city has been in turmoil since your ship docked, wondering what news you bring."

Hazin chuckled. So they weren't sure. Good.

"Hanaga is dead, as you ordered."

There was an exhale of relief.

Ah, so he did fear the plot within a plot. Fine, that would have diverted his thinking for the moment. "There was no sense in keeping the news hidden. I've already sent one of our acolytes to the palace to give his most exalted highness the good news. I thought it best, however, to report to you personally."

The Grand Master stirred. "Are you certain he is dead?" His voice was filled now with menace.

"If you doubt, fetch the Shiv who were aboard the ship and put to them the question. They disposed of the body after we were done."

"You should have kept some proof for the satisfaction of Yasim."

"The acolyte bears a basket containing Hanaga's head. Is that proof enough, my master?"

There was a chuckle of bemusement. "He'll most likely vomit at the sight of it."

"And vomit again when you press for payment," Hazin replied.

The Grand Master nodded, picking up a dagger resting on his desk to examine the blade.

"He'll pay. He knows the result if he doesn't."

"Yasim might appear a weakling on the surface. But is he?"

"He's a fool. Hanaga was different. Once the civil war was decided, we all knew he would turn on us. We were the one threat left to the Golden Throne. Yasim will be too afraid of us to strike. That, besides the wealth offered, was good enough reason to switch sides and support him."

"The war, however, is all but finished now," Hazin replied. "Playing one against the other was our own path to power. The remaining Banners will submit. And then what?"

"We consolidate our hold. With the payment offered we can expand our temples, gather more recruits. In ten years the cycle of struggle for the throne will start again, and yet again we shall play the game. This new emperor is morally a weakling, but he is lusty enough in his private chambers. Soon enough he will breed the next generation for us to play with."

Hazin nodded, though he did not agree. The Master was

old, the fire was going out of him. He was thinking now like an old one, seeking security, warmth, a comfortable seat by the side of Yasim at the banquet table and amphitheater.

He did not know the full measure of the one he had just placed on the throne. For that reason alone he should die, and for the simple fact that he was in the way.

"The journey has been a tiring one," Hazin replied. "May I have your permission to withdraw?"

The Master nodded, then held up his hand just before Hazin backed out of the door, motioning for him to close it.

"One question."

Hazin kept his features expressionless.

"Your order was to kill Hanaga. It is rare indeed for one to survive such an assignment."

"Yes, it is."

"Yet you obviously arranged it so you would."

"Yes."

The moment has come, Hazin thought. If he has any wisdom, he should kill me now, this very instant.

"You knew my intent in assigning you."

"Yes, to ensure that I would die as well, but I did not."

"And?"

"You could kill me now and find out the result, or let me live and find out the result."

There was a long moment of silence, the master holding the dagger in his hand. At one time, long ago, this one had been his first mentor in the order. Hazin had loyally followed him, because that loyalty had been properly rewarded with advancement. Now he had only one step left to achieve—the final rank within the order, and the master knew it.

Hazin finally looked straight at him. "Better the threat you know than the one you don't," Hazin whispered. "For someone else to get at you, they will still have to contend with me."

There was a subtle nod of agreement.

"The dynamic between us will keep the balance. If there is another rival within the order, such as Grishna or Ulva, they know that if they strike you down I will still take revenge, and if I should be stricken, then you will mete out revenge. As long as we are careful, we can both survive."

"Are you pleading for your life, Hazin? I always thought better of you than to sink so low."

"No, rather suggesting that we both can live or we both will die. I know why you assigned me to kill Hanaga. That was the business of our order, and I could accept it."

He pitched his voice carefully. The master had trained him in the reading of the finest nuances of expression, the slightest change in tone, the flicker of an eyelid, the ever so subtle glancing away when a lie was spoken. That was yet another power of the Order, the training to be a truth sayer, one who could detect a lie in another, no matter how carefully crafted.

He thought of the human Cromwell for an instant, the sharp honesty that was so easy to read, and yet so difficult to penetrate. Then he pushed the thought aside. He had to remain focused.

"I assigned you to Hanaga to get rid of you. The needs of the Order are changing now that the civil war is ending. You, Hazin, thrive on conflict and manipulate it to your own advantage. I am not sure if you can survive now that it is ending."

"We must still contend with the human rebellion to the north."

The master snorted. "Time enough later."

"I don't think so."

"Why?"

"We encountered a ship of theirs." He briefly explained the battle with the *Gettysburg,* but left out the detail of taking the two prisoners.

"Trivial."

"An opportunity. We know that the Golden Throne is increasingly suspicious of the Shiv. The fact that we breed thousands more than will ever be needed for sacrifice, that we have trained them in war, and that they have fought to victory in every engagement makes the emperor nervous. Unleashing them against the human Republic will give us millions to rule and can perhaps reveal as well the location of a Portal."

The Grand Master openly laughed. "You and that mad dream of leaving this place. Is not scheming for one empire enough?"

Hazin could see that the true focus of the conversation had wandered. His own life still hung by a thread.

"I want to ensure the survival of the Order, of our own personal survival."

"Our survival or yours, Hazin?"

"My staying alive guarantees yours as well, Master."

"Is there a threat in those words?"

"A statement of reality," Hazin said quietly, his voice cool, even, without a hint of emotion.

The master stared at him and then ever so slowly put the dagger back down.

"For the moment, then, we shall leave things at that."

Hazin bowed and turned to open the door, using his left hand, which he had kept concealed in the folds of his robe.

Leaving the master's chamber, he hurriedly went down the open flagstone corridor, past one of the pleasure gardens where several of the new initiates loitered, drifting in their hazy drug-induced visions, and entered his chamber, sweeping past the Shiv guards, careful to open and close the door to his room with his right hand.

Once alone he gingerly put a glove on his right hand, careful not to touch anything with his left. When his right was safely covered, he peeled off the dark, flesh-colored glove on his left hand and threw it into a charcoal brazier. Then went through the same ritual again, putting another glove on the opposite hand before using it to remove the other.

Finally he peeled off the robe he had been wearing, careful to not let the folds around the cuffs touch any skin.

The Grand Master was alone in his study. The ceremony for the ending of day would occur within the hour, and he would, as required, go to attend. The poison on Hazin's left glove, placed on the door handle, would still be damp and should penetrate the skin of the palm. It was subtle. He would not even notice it against the cool metal.

Death would take awhile, a day perhaps, but then the convulsions would come, mimicking a brain seizure. Of course, he would carefully avoid going anywhere near him. No one would suspect, or if they did, they would never dare to speak without definite proof.

Hazin realized he was shaking for the first time in years,

and he felt a surge of anger against himself for such lack of control.

The old one had sealed his fate on two points. First, he had been foolish not to kill Hazin immediately once he was in the room. Having sent him once to his death, he should have seen it through to the conclusion. That was a sign of hesitation, perhaps even of sentiment, a feeling unworthy of a Grand Master. Second, he had not seen the true danger that came with peace. If Yasim, who had masterfully engineered his plot over years of conflict, no longer had someone to plot against, he would now turn on the Order. He would do it subtly, cautiously, and then strike with blinding fury.

A diversion would have to be offered, one that would refocus the attention of Yasim, and all the others of the Golden Family, and Hazin realized that fate, if such a thing existed, had dealt him the perfect choice.

It was paradise.

A voice whispered to him that it was all illusion, drugs in his drink and food, but the sensations were so intoxicating that he no longer cared.

Occasionally the one with the blue eyes would come, smiling, speaking softly, reasonably, explaining how clear and simple his course; to submit fully to the Order, to become one of the Shiv and, most tantalizing of all, to one day return home to rule, to no longer be the forgotten son.

How Hazin knew these things Sean was not sure. It was hard to tell what he had actually said, what Hazin already knew, and what he could somehow sense, for he now knew that Hazin's powers were beyond that of anyone he'd ever met, human or Horde.

Someone touched his shoulder and, half rolling over, he looked up at her and smiled. He didn't know her name, he wasn't even sure if she was the one who had come to him the night before, but it didn't matter.

What she said was unintelligible, but that didn't matter either. She was above any dream of loveliness he had ever hoped to know, almost inhuman in her perfection. He wondered if she, like him, had tasted of the lotus.

The land of the lotus eaters, he remembered his mother telling him of that myth.

Perhaps that is where I am now. He looked past the compelling green eyes of the woman to the garden. The riotous bloom of flowers had an iridescent quality to them. They actually seemed to glow with their own inner light. The sight of them made him laugh, and she laughed with him.

She stood up and walked ever so slowly—to his eyes she seemed to float. She plucked a flower and returned, offering it to him. He almost wept with the beauty of the precious violet and red blossom. She leaned over and peeled off a petal, holding it up, brushing his lips with it, then slowly ate it.

He smiled and did the same. She went to fetch another, and he waited with anticipation, feeling a stirring of desire, dreaming of what he would do next with her even as she floated across the garden.

A gentle whisper of a voice, and she seemed to disappear into a cloud, replaced by Hazin.

For a moment he wasn't sure if he had drifted off to sleep, whether he and the green-eyed girl had made love or not. It was hard to remember now.

"I could send you away from here," Hazin said, sitting down by Sean's side.

He felt a flash of panic, but then, looking into those impenetrable blue eyes, he knew that Hazin would not be so cruel. Why would he grant such a gift only to take it away?

"But you know I would not, don't you?"

"Yes."

"You can leave at any time. In fact, I give you your freedom, O'Donald. You can awake in the hour after dusk. I will give you an airship and you can wing off to home, to your people, to the land ruled by your father and his friends."

The way he said it made the mere contemplation of it revolting. Sean felt light-headed, his stomach knotting.

"That choice would always haunt you, though, wouldn't it? To know that this paradise is here, to be tasted at any time. Instead you would live in a land of barrenness, where those who passed behind you would cover their mouths and whisper, 'There goes the son of the drunkard, the senator who is only thus because he hangs on to the power of others. There goes the son of the uncouth, the loud mouth, the braggart, and fool. And he shall one day be the same'."

Sean lowered his head and began to openly weep.

"Your mother endured that, you know, and you were powerless to stop her from feeling that pain, weren't you?"

Sean could not even answer. He merely shook his head as the tears continued to flow.

"Stay with me," Hazin whispered. "Stay with me, and I promise that you can one day return to right such wrongs, but do so on your own terms."

Sean looked up at him.

Hazin reached out and lightly touched Sean's shoulder, tracing a finger along a still open wound from the torture.

"Unfortunate, that, and I apologize."

"Apologize?" Sean was confused. It was as if this one before him now was someone else, not someone to be feared, but to be trusted, followed, even to be loved.

"A mistake. As soon as I realized who you were, I had to make amends, which I am now doing."

Sean could not reply, overwhelmed with gratitude.

Hazin offered him a cup, and he drank the golden liquid, which was sweet but laced with a touch of bitterness.

"That should ease any unfortunate pains you still might have. Soon you will awake, but you will remember. Do you know where you are, Sean O'Donald?"

Sean struggled to focus his thoughts. What did the question actually mean? Here, was that the question? He remembered coming off the boat, the vastness of the city, its gleaming temples, spires, arches, and columned buildings. It reminded him somehow of the stories of how Roum might have looked before the destruction of the Great War, a destruction that his own father had taken part in.

Was that what the question was?

"Kazan. We are in the Imperial City of Kazan," he finally replied, even as the world about him began to drift in a soft, diffused light.

Hazin laughed softly. "So literal in your thoughts, even now. A sharp intellect, which is good at certain moments.

"No, I mean here, now." He extended his hand, gesturing to the garden, the walls embedded with precious gems that caught and bent the sunlight, the fluttering curtains of silk, the lush green grass upon which they sat, and the bubbling fountains that splashed and played a soft musical chant.

"Paradise," Sean finally replied, and Hazin smiled approvingly.

"Yes. You are enjoying paradise and I hold the key to it."

"You?"

"Yes. I can open the gate wide to any who so desire it, or close it forever and cast those who fail into the fire of eternal suffering."

As he spoke, he extended his hand, almost covering Sean's eyes. Terrifyingly, a vision seemed to be concealed within that open hand—of fire, of agony, of eternal longing for bliss never again to be tasted.

Sean cried out and turned his head away.

"Do you believe what I just told you?"

"Yes."

"Look back at me."

Sean turned to look back and was startled, for Hazin was gone, disappeared, a swirling cloud of sweet-scented smoke obscuring all around.

The smoke drifted and curled, slowly parting, and someone else appeared before him. He had never seen such eyes, the palest of amber, her skin a milky white, hair raven black, coiling in a long, wavy cascade that covered the nakedness of her breasts.

"Her name is Karinia."

It was Hazin's voice, but where he was Sean could not say.

"I have chosen her for you, Sean O'Donald. Look into her eyes and see paradise. Fail and know that you will never see such love again."

Sean could not turn away from her gaze. Her features were flushed, and he sensed that somehow she was afraid. He reached out and lightly touched her cheek.

"You will stay and serve?" Hazin asked.

Sean could not answer. Some voice whispered to him that here was the moment that would forever define his life, who he was, what he would live for. But all he could see were her eyes and the actual feel of the garden of paradise, as if all of it had merged into his body and soul and would be part of it in pleasure, or torment, forever.

"I will serve," he whispered.

"Then she, all of this, is yours forever."

He heard a soft laugh, a rustling, and knew that Hazin was gone.

"I'm of the Shiv," she whispered, "and though not born to it, you are now of us."

Startled, he realized that she was speaking English, though her words were halting.

"Is this what you desire?" he asked.

She laughed softly and, leaning over, kissed him.

SEVEN

Throughout the day and into the night an inner sense told Richard Cromwell that something unusual was going on. In the week of his captivity he had grasped a sense of the language of the Kazan, realizing that there were some similarities to the Bantag dialect he had learned as a child.

He had been taken off the ship blindfolded, but the sounds and smells had told him that he was in a city, a city of the race of the Horde, for their musky scent was overpowering. Loaded into an enclosed cart, he had noticed that the ride was smooth, the road well paved, and an ocean of noise surrounded him, echoing in the confines of city streets until they had passed through a gate. The doors clanged shut behind him with an ominous boom.

They had finally removed his blindfold once he was in his cell. He had known places far worse. The cell was even comfortable. He had a cot and a straw-filled mattress, and a thin shaft of light coming from a vent in the ceiling let him know the passage of days.

Hazin had come to visit him, and what he'd had to say was surprising. Throughout Richard tried to reveal nothing that could be of worth, and Hazin had even complimented him on his tact. At the same time, Hazin had seemed to be almost too revealing, telling him of the civil war, their learning of technology from a "prophet" and his companions who had come through a Portal more than two hundred years ago. This had given the Kazan, a minor clan on the island chains that spanned a million square miles of ocean, their first advantage in the endless warfare between a dozen rival clans.

They had made the leap to steam power, to flight, to the weapons they now possessed, and in the process they had defeated their rivals one by one, until finally the Kazan were supreme. Then had come the civil war to decide amongst themselves who should rule.

Of these subjects he had spoken without hesitation, even answering questions Richard had posed. Especially intriguing and frightful was the story of the rise of the Order of Alamut, which had been but one of the numerous cults and secret societies that the Kazan seemed to revel in. It was the prophets who suggested the breeding of humans, first for simple labor, but then for sacrifice as well, and finally for what Hazin called the fulfillment. A topic on which he would not elaborate.

Richard had expressed no reaction to this, assuming all along that the Kazan would be no different that the Bantag or Merki, and Hazin had stepped past the issue as if sensing that there was no purpose in elaborating.

During the years of the civil war, the Order, as it was simply known, had served as assassins for all sides. Once there had been an attempt to wipe them out, an effort led by the grandsire of the current emperor, and he had paid the price, his death an object lesson. From the way Hazin had talked, Richard guessed that the Shiv numbered in the tens of thousands, and he wondered why the Kazan would allow such a strength, which could perhaps turn against them the way the Chin had against the Bantag in the last days of the Great War.

The conversations were strange, perplexing, as if Hazin was educating him to some purpose Richard could not divine.

They had talked thus for days, but today was different. Hazin had not come. Richard remained alone, wondering if something had changed.

In the evening he heard anxious whispered comments in the corridor outside his bolted door, then the swift scurrying of feet. From beyond the vent opening he soon heard someone speaking slowly, as if giving a speech. He made out the Bantag word for dead, "sata," spoken solemnly, followed by an outcry, the high keening wail of their race when mourning.

Shortly afterward, he heard other angry voices, shouts, and then the sounds of fighting, grunts of pain, and the crack of gunfire. In the corridor outside he heard more voices, the sound of someone struggling, as if being forced or dragged down the corridor, and a door slamming shut. He had drifted off to sleep then and was startled awake by the sharp report of a gunshot followed by laughter.

When the door to his cell swung open, he wasn't sure what to expect. Had Hazin merely been toying with him? Was someone coming with a gun to finish it?

He was surprised, and relieved, to see that it was Hazin. An entourage of half a dozen Shiv and several of Hazin's own race followed behind him. Hazin motioned for them to wait and then closed the door so that the two were alone.

"You are intelligent enough to realize that something is happening here," Hazin said, and Richard saw a look in his eyes of excitement, of satisfaction.

"It is kind of hard to sleep when there is shooting going on in the room next to you."

Hazin laughed. "His name was Dalmata. A rival, or should I say, a former rival."

Again the satisfaction was evident.

"My congratulations, then," Richard offered. "Was it ordered by the Grand Master?"

Hazin smiled. "I am the Grand Master now."

You killed him, didn't you? Richard thought.

"Yes. I, shall we say, arranged it," he said in English.

"Why are you telling me this?" Richard asked, and he realized that there was a touch of fear in his heart.

Hazin laughed. "Perhaps because I have to tell someone, and it might as well be you. That is the problem with such triumphs. There can never be an audience, never someone to share the moment with. In my world such victories are achieved alone and celebrated alone."

At that instant Richard found an answer to a question that had bedeviled him ever since he had met Hazin. Why was he being spared? Was it just sadistic amusement or was there another purpose?

Hazin went over to the single chair in the room. A chair sized for a human, so he seemed almost absurd sitting in it. "I was born of the lowest caste," Hazin said. "Every step has been a clawing upward. You, Cromwell, understand that better than most, saddled as you are with the name of a traitor. When I was first told who you were I was intrigued. Why would the son of a traitor wear the uniform of the nation his father had turned against? Why as well would such a nation trust you? It was an interesting skein to unravel, a diversion, even, from the more weighty concerns I was struggling with."

Richard bristled slightly at being referred to as "a diversion," but said nothing, curious to hear what Hazin would reveal.

"I sensed that you more than some might actually be worthy of conversation, and you've proven that. In fact, Richard Cromwell, you even have, as best as I can offer it, my respect."

Startled, Richard said nothing. He had learned enough of Hazin to loathe him. Hazin was remorseless, cunning, casually brutal in the way he spoke of assassinating an emperor he had served for nearly twenty years. Yet what was disturbing was that Richard found him interesting, almost appealing. His intellect, his curiosity to know more about the world, and even, no matter how twisted, his dream of ending the conflict between humans and the Horde.

"The guards outside are waiting for you, Cromwell."

"For what? My execution?"

"No. Your escape."

Richard shook his head and laughed. "I try to escape and then they kill me. Even if I did escape, where would I go? How far am I from Republic territory?"

"One of my navigators will discuss that with you."

"I'm not sure I understand you."

"I'm letting you go, Cromwell, so that you can go back to your Republic."

Richard was tempted to scoff, but a look at Hazin's eyes made him realize that the new Grand Master was in deadly earnest.

Stunned, Richard stood up from his cot. "I don't understand. Why?"

"Call it a gesture."

"For what? Am I to go back with some message? Is that it?"

"No. I have no message for your Republic." Hazin shook his head. "Oh, if they should decide to offer submission, removal of their government to be replaced by those whom I choose to rule, that would be acceptable."

"You know that will never happen."

"Don't be so sure."

"After what my people went through in the last war, they will not tamely submit, especially to one of your race."

"Your forthrightness is a trait I find interesting in a world where such things usually bring an untimely end. Your words might actually have just changed my mind. I could have you killed instead."

Richard stared at him coldly.

"Actually, Cromwell, what I might offer could be the only way out in the end. Is your race ready to fight a genocidal war? To hunt down every last one of mine and kill them? I don't think you have the stomach for it. Your Keane showed charity against a hated foe. I heard the story of how Schuder saved the Bantag Qar Qarth's life. You realize that you would have to slaughter every last one of the Bantag, even the abject Tugars, though I daresay that you might actually derive a certain pleasure from seeing all the Merki put to death."

Richard shifted uncomfortably, for there was a kernel of truth in Hazin's words. His observations always seemed to reach straight to the heart of the matter.

"If you are letting me go, there must be a reason. I don't suspect that you have any feelings of friendship, especially to one of my race."

"No. I've never had a friend, Cromwell, I've never touched love, I never had desire for a mate. Always my focus was elsewhere. Some might think that a pity, but I can at times be moved to a certain admiration, and that you have earned. It wasn't just the foolish sentimental display of trying to protect your hapless friend. Rather, it was the coldness when faced with pain and death.

"You were born to that and learned to shield yourself with it, yet ultimately it never fully hardened you. You could, in fact, be noble, purely for the reason that you feel that it is right and proper to be that way."

Looking at Hazin, Richard almost felt a brief instant of pity. His voice held a note of loneliness that was disturbing.

"The old Grand Master of your order. He was your teacher, your instructor, wasn't he?"

"Yes."

"And you felt nothing at his passing?"

Hazin smiled. "Nothing."

Richard slowly nodded his head. "And this is the final fulfillment of what you sought?"

The smile did not change. "Only a start, Cromwell, and I will admit your leaving is a part in that game within a game."

"Can I take Sean with me?" Richard asked abruptly.

"If he wants to go, but I doubt he will agree. In fact, he is in a cell just down the corridor. Go ask him yourself when you leave here."

Hazin shook his head. "I know he won't agree. Even if he did, it would make things difficult. I'm giving you a flyer. It's been stripped down. I hope you are a good pilot, Cromwell. My master navigator says there isn't enough fuel on board to get you all the way back, but that will no longer be my concern, only yours. For your sake I hope you find good winds aloft otherwise you will ultimately die alone at sea, though the creatures beneath should make short work of you."

Richard felt a shiver of fear, again the primal terror of being devoured alive.

"There's something you want me to do once I return home, isn't there?"

"Just tell what you've seen."

Richard shook his head. "I don't understand. You know I will tell everything, alert my government, warn them of what you are, the threat you pose."

"Oh, yes. Add in that in fairly short order you can expect our fleet off your coast. I have an audience with the new emperor later tonight and shall advise him to do just that, to attack immediately. I would say that by the next month we shall be off your coast. I can be persuasive when necessary, and I can assure you that he will agree."

Richard turned away for a moment, utterly confused. "I don't see any logic to this. If you struck by surprise. . . ." He fell silent, not wishing to let Hazin hear his thoughts.

"Oh, yes, quite. I'll tell you why, even. The civil war has ended, but we still need war. That is why I shall urge the emperor forward. Otherwise he shall have a fleet of eight battle cruisers, a hundred thousand sailors, fifty thousand assault troops, and they will have nothing to do but sit in their barracks and aboard their ships and ponder the new emptiness of their existence. Peace is death, Cromwell. It is war that is the creator.

"I can tell you now I will defeat your Republic."

"Then why let me escape to your enemy?"

"Because it fits what I want. Don't press any further. Tell me, Cromwell, do you take any glory from the killing of a defenseless pup, the crushing of an insect? No, that is forgotten in an instant. It is when the foe has steel that you find yourself, and hone your steel as well. My Shiv will thus be honed for greater tasks to come afterward. I want your Keane to see what is coming, to offer his best, and then to be defeated. That will crush his legend and build mine at the same time. It will even be said that I was fair in such things, noble even for offering an opponent a fair warning rather than striking stealthily with a knife in the back. After the first defeat in such a fight your side will then listen to reason rather than thrash on blindly and in defiant rage. Never corner an opponent, Cromwell. In their terror and rage they just might kill you even as they die. That was the mistake the Hordes of the north made, and that is why they were defeated while I shall win."

Richard lowered his head. "Suppose I refuse to go."

"You'll go."

Richard knew that Hazin was right. His desire for freedom would drive him forward regardless of whether it fit some plan of Hazin's or not.

Hazin stood up and started for the door. "We'll meet again someday, Cromwell. I suspect, if you survive the coming conflict, that you will rise quickly. In fact, I hope you do survive, for I would like to talk again someday."

Richard was stunned when Hazin, in a gesture that was uniquely human, extended his hand. Before Richard even knew what he was doing, he took it. The grip was dry, firm. Hazin released his hand and without a backward glance left the room, the door open.

A Shiv guard stood in the corridor, motioning for Richard to follow. Looking down at the floor, he saw streaks of blood, the type left when a bleeding body is dragged away.

The faint rotten-eggs smell of black powder smoke hung in the air, and as he walked down the corridor he saw a room with a door open. Inside, two humans, emaciated, dressed only in loincloths, were mopping up a pool of blood. At the end of the corridor the Shiv led Richard to another room. Opening it, he was surprised by the comfort within. Tapestries of silk covered the wall, a comfortable bed covered with cushions was in the center of the room, and he detected a feminine scent in the air.

Sean O'Donald lay on the bed, eyes closed, features peaceful.

Richard rushed into the room and shook him awake. Sean looked up dreamily and then with a look of surprise. "Richard. Hazin said you would visit me."

"Come on, O'Donald. We've been freed. We're getting out now. Tonight."

Sean smiled, and Richard instantly realized that he was either drunk or drugged. "You go. I'm staying."

Richard looked back at the door. "Damn it, Sean, we don't have time for this," he hissed. "Hazin's letting us go, at least I think he is. Get dressed and let's get the hell out of here."

Sean sat up and stretched, and Richard suddenly realized that concealed beneath the covers was someone else. Wisps of black hair spread out on the pillow. She half rolled over, the cover slipping away from her shoulder, revealing her beauty. Her amber-colored eyes met his, and he felt a cold shiver.

He forced his attention away, focusing back on Sean. "Now, O'Donald. We're getting out of here."

"And like I said before, I'm staying."

"Because of her?"

"In part."

"How long have you known her, a day? Three days? Damn it, Sean, you can't give up everything just for a girl you met three days ago."

Sean's features darkened. "Give up what, Cromwell? Tell me, what does the Republic have to offer me after what I have found here?"

"Honor," Richard snapped.

Sean leaned back and laughed, turning to look at the girl, who smiled at his amusement.

"Honor? How many millions died on both sides in the last war, a war created by Keane and my father? Was that honor? And they'll do it again. No, thank you. I tried their path. A country run by someone like my father can go to hell."

Sean reached forward and grabbed Richard by the arm. "Stay here. You don't understand Hazin as I do. What he offers to all of us who join him."

"And what is that?" Richard asked bitterly.

"Order. He could unify us all, Richard, Horde and human. We would sweep the world without the type of bloodshed my father helped to create. He offers a dream, and I am willing to be part of it."

Richard pulled his hand away and stood up. "Get on your feet, Lieutenant," he snarled, trying desperately to somehow break through and reach him. "I've got an aerosteamer waiting."

He looked over defiantly at the woman, who had sat up in the bed. Her smile was almost bemused, as if Richard was just a minor interruption.

Richard reached over to grab Sean and pull him out of bed.

"I wouldn't try it," Sean hissed. "You might be able to beat me, but I think the Shiv out there would not go along with it."

Richard looked back at the open door, where half a dozen Shiv waited.

"They aren't human," Richard whispered. "They're bred like horses, like cattle."

He said the last word deliberately, for it was the darkest of insults left over from the war.

"She's of the Shiv," Sean said, anger darkening his features.

"All the more reason to leave her."

"Get out." Her words were soft, but filled with confidence. She slowly stood up, and Richard had difficulty concealing his shocked embarrassment at her nakedness. Yet he was fascinated as well by her beauty, and by her calm, casual ease.

The fact that he and Sean had been talking in English and she had spoken in the same language caught him completely off guard.

How stupid, he realized. If Hazin knew English, he

should not have been surprised that a woman sent to O'Donald knew it as well.

He looked back to the Shiv who stood in the doorway. For the first time he detected an emotion on their part. It was amusement.

He slowly turned back to face Sean. "You'll regret this the rest of your life, Lieutenant O'Donald."

Sean seemed to stir from his hazy distant world, and for a brief moment, Richard saw an old friend from the academy, the cadet who was always so quiet, studious, even withdrawn, and yet sharply capable in any task he set himself to. He tried to smile, to somehow reach that friend and roommate, to remind him of his duty, of who he was, an officer of the Republic.

"It won't work, Cromwell. I'm past such appeals," Sean whispered and turned away.

The airfield was dark, and a light, hazy mist was drifting in from the midnight tropical sea. Richard suddenly realized just how tired he was, and now he faced a flight of unknown distance across an unknown sea.

He slowly walked around the airship. The design was not unlike some of the machines from the last war, bulkier in the fuselage to contain the hydrogen gas bags, a broad, single mono-wing rather than the bi-wings of the Republic's airships. It was three engined, two on the wings and one forward.

He could see where there had been gun emplacements at the tail, above and under the belly. All had been stripped out, as was the gun forward.

No one spoke to him, and somehow the entire scene seemed like a dream. He looked at the rough chart that had been thrust into his hand. It was precious short on details, including only the coastline of the island they were now on and a sketch of where he assumed the *Gettysburg* had been lost, which was off to the northwest.

From that point he knew where he was. That was over thirteen hundred miles from the Republic's main base on the coast at Constantine. The question was, how far was it from where the *Gettysburg* was lost to here? Four hundred miles, six hundred? He believed they had sailed four days after he was captured. That could make the distance just a few miles away, on the other side of a long island, or more than a thousand miles.

Yet he knew as well that Hazin would not send him out unless he had a reasonably good chance of succeeding.

No one spoke to him, but by the way the ground crew turned to look at him, he knew they were waiting. He scrambled up the outside ladder and into the forward cockpit. One of the Shiv followed and, without saying a word, waited while Richard strapped himself into the oversize chair. Stretching his legs out, he could barely reach the pedals. Pressing down on them, he could tell when he looked aft, worked the rudder.

The controls were basically the same: a stick for banking and climbing. The Shiv simply took hold of three knobs mounted side by side on the forward console, and pulled them back. The engines then began to turn over faster. The Shiv leaned back out of the cockpit and climbed down the ladder.

"Thanks, you son of a bitch," Richard grumbled.

Straight ahead he could see two distant bonfires, undoubtedly marking the end of the landing strip. Without any hesitation he pulled the throttles full out. The ship lurched forward and clumsily gained speed.

It was far slower on takeoff than the planes he knew, and he sweated out the final seconds, the bonfires racing past before he felt the wings lifting and he edged back on the stick.

The airship seemed to hang in the air, and he nosed it over slightly, hoping that there were no hills ahead. Then ever so gradually he pulled back, trying to master the feel of the machine, wondering if it would give the telltale vibration through the stick just before going into a stall. He flew on for several minutes, heading due south before he finally ventured a turn, carefully banking the machine to port, watching the stars as they wheeled.

The Southern Triangle seemed higher in the sky by a good hand span, and he tried to work out the calculation, a rough estimate of just how much father south he was. Sean could have done it.

Damn him. He tried to feel pity for his friend, to understand. Hazin had seduced him first through terror, then the drugs, and finally the woman. Could I have resisted? he wondered.

He tried to believe he could have, that Hazin had seen that and decided to use him instead for another purpose. This thought also angered him. I'm escaping, but in escaping I am somehow serving his purpose as well. He toyed with the random thought of somehow trying to find the temple of Hazin's Order, or the imperial palace, and crash the plane into it; a final defiant act that just might throw them all off balance.

And yet if I do that, he realized, the Republic will never know what is coming.

Why do I even care? he wondered. What has the Republic given me? The Yankees speak of it almost as if it were a religion, yet for millions of us it has brought nothing but anguish. If the Yankees had never come, the Hordes would have ridden on. Far fewer would have died, my mother would have never been a slave, and I of course never would have been born.

What does it offer me now? He could predict the reaction when he returned alone, the son of a traitor, bearing a fantastic tale of an empire, a race of humans bred to serve it, of Hazin, and of the betrayal by the son of a legend.

Worry about that later, he thought as he leveled out, trying to gain a fix that would guide him due north. He was distracted, though, by the sight off his starboard wing. A vast gleaming city spread out in a moon-shaped crescent around a dark bay.

He banked over slightly. In training he had flown over Roum twice, and he could tell that the largest city of the Republic would fit into but one corner of what lay below him. A sparkling pavilion, covering acres of ground, was terraced up the side of a steeply rising hill. Its columned boulevard shone from the light of a thousand torches and bonfires, and he knew that this must be the imperial residence. This single dwelling place was nearly as big as all of old Suzdal.

He was tempted to circle but decided against it, for every gallon of fuel was precious. The city slipped by beneath him, and he was still low enough to detect the smell of the fires that illuminated it.

Out in the bay, by the dim light of the Great Wheel of

stars and the first of the two moons rising to the east, he
could see the silhouettes of the battle fleet. The sight of it
filled him with awe. He leveled out and even dropped down
a few hundred feet, throttling back slightly. He counted eight
great ships. Each of them, he had judged, to be three times,
perhaps even four times greater than the *Gettysburg*. They
rode the anchor, deck lights fore and aft marking them in
two lines abreast. Bright, almost festive looking lanterns
hung suspended from the pagoda towers. Surrounding them
were dozens of other ships, smaller and yet still a match
for anything the Republic could offer. The sight chilled his
heart. He banked over, circling twice, trying to count the
ships, to judge their size, the weapons on board.

This was the reason he had to return home. It had nothing to do with Hazin and his game of power. Here was a
threat that could annihilate the service to which he had
given his oath and that had given him a home in spite of
his blood.

Below was a fleet that could destroy the Republic, and
he alone could bring warning of it.

He finally pulled back on the stick, sending his aerosteamer up toward the clouds. He could only hope for a
fair wind that would help to carry him home.

EIGHT

The night was fetid with the oppressive heat of summer.
The poor quarter of the city, as always, stank of unwashed
bodies, rotting food, refuse, excrement, and a moldy, musty
smell that seemed to cling to poverty no matter what the
race, be they human or Kazan.

Hazin, flanked by his escort, negotiated the narrow twisting alleyways that led from his temple to the base of the
Qutiva, the hill of the Imperial presence. The temples of
his order, at least those in the cities of the empire, were
always built in the poorest quarters, for it was thence that
so many novitiates came. Desperation guided them to seek
salvation, no matter what price was required.

The Green Gate, so named for its sheathing of pale green

marble, came into view. The alleyway spilled into the Processional Way, the great boulevard that was the main axis of the city, running from the Qutiva down to the harbor, half a league below.

Looking to the south as he stepped out on to the main avenue, he could see the flickering lights of the Red fleet riding at anchor. The great ships of the line were festooned with hundreds of lanterns in celebration of the victory. The entire city was thus decorated, though Hazin knew that the celebration was not so much one of joy but of relief for having been spared yet another battle, for when emperors fall there is always a battle and, at times, a massacre. The mob that had only weeks before been so supportive of Hagana were now relieved by the news that he was dead.

At Hazin's approach, the crowds clogging the Processional Way parted, drawing back with averted eyes and bows. A few made subtle gestures to ward off the darkness or clutched the amulets of rival cults.

The guards flanking the open portals of the Green Gate offered the usual salute at his approach, but then one of them stepped before his standard bearer, demanding identification. Hazin stood in silent rage as an assistant fumbled in his haversack for the necessary papers bearing the Imperial Seal.

"I see here only a request for the presence of Grand Master Hazin Vaka," the commander of the guard announced, "nothing concerning an honorary escort."

A scene now ensued, the argument dragging on for several minutes. The assistant indignantly argued that no master should walk without an escort. The commander of the guard replying that the imperial escort was sufficient. It was obvious what was being played out, and finally Hazin stepped forward.

"Ilvani, wait here," Hazin said softly. He fixed the captain with his gaze. "Your name."

"Ragna, captain of the Green Gate"—he hesitated the briefest of moments—"Your Holiness."

"You will be in my thoughts, Ragna," Hazin replied with a cool smile, and the captain, though trying to maintain a calm exterior, blinked, eyes lowering.

Hazin smiled. This one knew he was dead, orders or no orders from the emperor. The touch of a courtesan armed with a finger needle that would barely scratch the skin would be enough, or a powder slipped into a tavern drink. Wait awhile, though, let him contemplate, let him learn fear, then manifest the fear before killing him.

Imperial guards flanked him. There was no chair waiting, and he said nothing. The approach to the palace zigzagged up the steep hill, passing the villas of the lesser nobles, court officials, who now anxiously awaited their fate with a new emperor of the throne, and chosen consorts of the bed chamber, the place of each palace on that hill in direct relationship to their favor or disfavor of the moment. At each turn gun positions were cunningly laid out, often concealed behind finely wrought stonework, or small pleasure gardens, guards barely visible in recessed alcoves. The muzzle of a land cruiser was barely visible, hidden inside a stone arched stable. Several light fieldpieces, ready to be rolled out at an instant's notice, were parked in a courtyard.

The place had been a fortress only a month ago, manned by ten thousand of the elite imperial assault troops. They had sworn allegiance to the new emperor without a moment's pause, for what was the use of dying for someone who was dead? They were gone now, back to their barracks on the far side of the island. All that was left were the Imperial Guard—gilded fools in Hazin's eyes. A hundred of his Shiv could take them in an hour if he so desired.

Turning the final corner of the Processional Way, he was disgusted to see that the inner gate was closed. Nor was there a banner of the Order displayed to mark his arrival. This outrageous oversight caused him to again look at the captain, who stood impassive, except for a slight twitching of his jaw.

The gate finally swung open, and he passed beneath the archway and into the outer courtyard, where a chamberlain, a gelded one, awaited and silently pointed the way, a whiff of costly perfume trailing in his wake.

They passed through the outer audience chamber, where the ceremonial holding of judgments took place on the first day of the new moons, a ritual harkening back across thousands of years when the emperor was no more than a rude clan elder in a felt tent. It was nothing more than a farce play now, already scripted as to who would be sent to the circle and who would leave with hide still intact.

At last the meandering tour through the outer rings of the palace, past cautious observers and whispering nobility, gave way to the inner circle, the private domain of Emperor Yasim. The chamberlain opened the door, then stepped backward, eyes averted.

Hazin strode in.

Yasim was alone, standing on a veil-draped balcony, goblet in hand, back turned. Hazin knew that the room was double walled, cunningly designed and inspected daily by the chamberlain so that no eunuch of the court could get close enough to eavesdrop on what was being said.

Hazin did the proper bow, right hand touching the floor.

"A drink to refresh you, Hazin."

His voice was relaxed, betraying the slightest touch of the narcotic malva, a perceptive sniff of the air catching its pungent scent. Hazin looked over to a side table. A few light snacks were arranged, fresh slivers of meat, clean goblets of wine, and fermented milk.

As he took an empty goblet, he quickly looked for any abrasions, or slick spots that might indicate dried poison. It was a tiresome game and he doubted the emperor would ever be so direct, but a lifetime of training always prevailed.

Years of slowly increasing self-administered doses of most of the common and several of the preferred uncommon poisons had built a certain immunity. Combined with the oils he had drunk prior to coming here, he should be proof against a clumsy effort by anyone other than the emperor who might make the attempt and thus hope to pin blame on the imperial household.

He took several slivers of raw meat, poured a few ounces of blood, and stepped out onto the veranda.

A cooling breeze was coming down off the mountain, sweeping away the choking heat and stench of the summer's day.

"You are well?"

"Yes, sire."

Yasim turned, cool eyes appraising as Hazin sipped his drink.

"Frankly, it is a surprise to see you alive."

Hazin smiled.

"My last communication with your Grand Master, or

should I say your late, lamented Grand Master, was most interesting."

"Please enlighten me, sire."

"The cost of my victory at Ra was dear, very dear."

Hazin wanted to laugh. "My victory . . ." It was the Order that had given him victory. This fool had simply footed the bill. Fifteen assassinations, the turning of the Greens through the threat of a genocidal attack on their families and, above all else, the death of Hanaga, which had cost more than anyone had ever been willing to pay.

"Your order is expecting the second half of the payment by tomorrow."

Hazin smiled. Direct, far too direct. It almost took the amusement out of the game.

"And, my sire?"

Yasim turned away. "How did you survive, may I ask?"

"The battle or my return?"

"The battle. The death of my brother is of far more interest than the internal squabbling of your precious society."

Ah, so he is linking things together here, Hazin thought, his features revealing nothing.

"Easy enough. The captain of the frigate I arrived on, he was of my order."

"Tell me, how many captains of my ships are of your order?"

Hazin looked down in the goblet, swirling the drink. The blood was still warm from the body it had been drawn from in the next room, as was the meat. An emperor could afford such a luxury, meat bred for texture and taste, the blood slowly tapped out from an open vein as required.

"The cost of such information, Your Highness," and he shook his head.

"How about a trade, then?"

"Yes?"

"You leave here alive, I know who of my ship's captains are of your order."

Hazin smiled. "Too high. The bargain would be known, and then who would trust me or my order? I would be dead in a fortnight. There have been Grand Masters who have had reigns nearly as short, but I would prefer not to establish such a record."

"So you prefer not to leave here alive? Know that it is obvious that your Grand Master preferred that you die in that last battle. That is why he personally gave to you the task of killing my brother."

"That was obvious," Hazin said dryly. "And that is why he is dead."

Yasim turned away, going over to a sideboard where he picked up an ornately carved statue. It was a delicate creation in ivory, an abstract work of intricate swirls and curves. Hazin recognized it as one of the new school of Davin, an artist who had gained imperial favor of late. He wondered if Davin would still be in favor a moon from now.

"This took a year to create," Yasim said softly, hands gently cradling the work. He sighed, holding it close for a moment then turning it over, lightly stroking it, fingers tracing the intricate design, then placed it back on the table.

"May I inquire as to the reason for my summoning?" Hazin ventured.

Yasim smiled. "There are times when you are the personification of subtlety, and then other times when you are as direct as the thrust of a dagger. Patience."

Hazin returned to the table where the drinks were and poured another goblet full of the fresh blood. This time he sprinkled in a mixture of spices and a dark, heavy liqueur laced with a touch of malva.

The emperor smiled. "I did not know you indulged."

"When it suits me."

"And it does not dull you?"

"It does not dull, Your Highness. And besides, we of the Order are used to headier stuff."

"I know."

Hazin returned to the curtained veranda. The silky gauze was sheer enough that the view of the city was spread before them, the twinkling lights of the city below, the open harbor where the fleet lay at anchor.

From the temple of Ashva a dark pyre of smoke curled—their burnt offering for the day—while from the rival order of Vishta a brilliant fire blazed atop their pyramid temple. In the firelight he could see the writhing forms, their shrieking cries of agony carrying on the wind.

He wrinkled his nose with disgust at such primitive bar-

barity, made worse by the fact that the contemptible fools actually believed that there was a purpose to such sacrifices, that their idols desired the blood of human sacrifice. It served its purpose, though, for it kept his own in line. To be cast out of the Shiv was to be placed into the hands of one of half a dozen of the other cults.

It was such a delightful, intricate swirl of intrigue that gave purpose to life: the religious orders, the houses of the nobility, the eternal quest for dominance. He could not imagine a world without such interplay taken to the edge, for each maneuver held within it life or death. To dance upon the edge of the abyss, to cast one's foes into that abyss, to at times see them fall while blessing your name, never realizing that you were the one who destroyed them was the thrill of existence.

"You still have not reacted to what I have said," Yasim said softly, coming up to Hazin's side. "Your Grand Master wanted you to die. Why did you wait till after you had fulfilled the contract to kill him? Why not before?"

Ah, so here was an inner fear, Hazin realized. For twenty years I stood by Hanaga's side, yet killed him without hesitation. He wonders why I did not turn and take the Grand Master first. He knows that if I had, Hanaga would be alive today and it would be he who was dead.

"I could not refuse the order of my master to assassinate your brother. It was a contract, and it was binding. To strike such blood required the highest of our own order, not a lowly initiate or brother. Only a master should slay one of the royal line, and then only by the blade."

It was such a ridiculous lie, and yet he could see that Yasim almost believed him.

"Why my family tolerates you, Hazin, has been an open question of late. Many say that your order should be destroyed while there is still time."

"Would Your Highness desire such?"

Yasim looked over at him warily.

"There are fifty million of our race in your empire," Hazin announced dryly. "Another twenty million or more human slaves. Did you ever wonder how many of them might be of the Order?"

"It is a question of regular debate," Yasim replied.

Hazin smiled. "I can assure you that if you struck tonight, if all the other cults joined you, if you could keep it a secret and fall upon all our temples in one blinding flash, still thousands would survive, and you know what they would do."

"Are you threatening me?" Yasim asked quietly, looking over the rim of his goblet as he took another sip of his drink.

"Is it not the other way around, Your Highness?" Hazin replied coolly.

Yasim turned away. "What of this encounter that was reported to me?"

"Which encounter, Your Highness? There have been so many these last few days."

"This ship you destroyed while fleeing the battle."

Hazin laughed. "Majesty, I did not flee. When your brother met his gallant demise in the explosion that destroyed his flagship," and he smiled, "I was blown overboard and rescued by a frigate. The ship I was on flew the colors of the Blue Banner. To linger while your fleet closed would have been foolish bravado." To reply with the official story regarding Hanaga's death amused him and clearly frustrated Yasim.

"Foolish bravado, Hazin. Something you were never noted for."

"Those with bravado rarely live. Let my initiates show such traits. It is expected of them, not of me."

"You avoid the question, though. Tell me of the human ship. They were of these rebellious humans, the envoy to the Bantag reports."

"Who told you?"

Now it was Yasim's turn to laugh.

So someone within his ranks was in the pay of the emperor. Why would he tell me? Why would he betray one of his own? Was it an offering of some kind?

"Actually, the ship was inconsequential," Hazin stated, turning the goblet in his hand so that the gems caught the lamplight and flickered.

"Oh, really? I would not call a force that destroyed three of the northern Hordes to be inconsequential."

"The ship is what I was referring to, not what it represents."

"The ship, then."

"It was primitive, what little we could see of it in the dark. Heavily reliant on sail, though it was under steam when we met it."

"Its guns?"

"One hit only. The damage to our aft turret was minimal. It barely penetrated the turret's armor, and that was at less than a thousand paces. The size of it was about the same as our frigate."

"Do they have anything larger?"

Does he know we sent spies? Hazin wondered. The operation had been very secretive.

"I doubt it, Your Highness. This is the third vessel like this that has been taken, nothing bigger. I believe it is all they can produce."

Yasim walked over to his desk, an ornate affair in the style of Subuta, which had enjoyed a resurgence ever since the Emperor Hanaga had expressed interest in the school. Yasim produced a bound report bearing the imperial seal and held it up.

"These are the reports from the minister of ambassadors. I assume your spies already have obtained a copy."

Hazin smiled and said nothing. Half the ministers of court gave copies to his order before they even reached the hands of the emperor, at the start for payment, but after a while out of fear of what would happen if they ever stopped.

"According to what we have learned from the Bantag, this human rebellion in the north started with half a thousand who came through a Portal," Yasim said while casually leafing through the pages.

"Within two years they fielded an army, and not just an army, but with it the creation of steam-powered machinery to manufacture weapons and support their effort. The Tugars were defeated, followed by the Merki and finally the Bantag, each of them stronger and more advanced than the last.

"The Bantag developed steam machinery as well, the art of it learned from the captives taken by the Merki and traded. By the end of the war both sides had flyers, land cruisers, iron ships, rapid-fire guns, telegraphs, all of these things unknown to the northern world only twenty years before."

Hazin nodded as if this information actually was anything new.

"We have been too preoccupied, Hazin, with our own affairs."

"When the fire is in your kitchen, Your Highness, one does not think of what his neighbor is cooking."

"Do you think these humans have control of a Portal?"

The question caught Hazin off guard, but he quickly recovered. Did they in fact control such a thing and the emperor knew it?

"I doubt it."

"Why?"

"Because if they did, they would be far more advanced. No one can control a Portal. It is beyond us and will remain beyond us for generations to come."

The emperor looked at him with a crafty smile. "The dream of your order, isn't it? If they had a Portal, you would already be there and controlling it."

Hazin's features remained impassive. Again, he wondered who was the traitor in his ranks. A Portal was the holy of holies of his order; the path to power, the path to the stars. It was the legendary Kalinvala, who had come through a gate more than two hundred years ago, who had transformed the Kazan from ignorance to all that they now had, and who had founded his order. Finding a Portal was the ultimate goal that he had established for them, shrouded in religious mysticism in order to control the ignorant.

"You know that the leader of the Bantag, the one called their Qar Qarth, came through a Portal." As he spoke, the emperor nodded toward the report.

Again Hazin was silent. Of course he knew. Did this one take him for a fool? And the Qar Qarth was ignorant of how it worked or why he had come here. The information he had of his world was useful enough, it was the same world as Kalinvala's, though far more advanced across the hundreds of years, but unlike Kalinvala, the Qar Qarth had little technical knowledge, only general information, though the information was intriguing enough, especially when it came to a weapon that could annihilate entire cities. To obtain such a thing would be a dream.

"So what do you advise regarding this human rebellion, this nation they call the Republic?" the emperor asked.

Hazin shifted, looking back out over the city so that the emperor could not see him smile. "Crush it."

"Why? They are no threat. We've endured twenty years of war for control of this throne, and it is finished. Other issues here are far more pressing. In five years, ten, perhaps then."

Issues here, Hazin thought. Such as turning on my order. "In ten years they might be the ones coming to dictate terms to us," Hazin replied. "Realize as well that their existence has been kept a secret even from our own people. If word ever got back to our slaves of the success of the human rebellion in the north, it could be a threat."

"The Shiv perhaps. Might they rebel against you?"

Hazin laughed. "They are of my order and incorruptible."

It was the emperor who now laughed. "No one is incorruptible, Hazin. You most of all know that."

"The Shiv exist because of us, and they know it."

"Your experiment with them is something that the other orders and even those of the nobility increasingly fear. You are playing with fire."

"The breeding of a warrior race to do the dying for us? It is an interesting experiment, nothing more. They are chained to us by our selection and by the gods we created for them."

The emperor shook his head. "The Republic. Answer that."

"As I said, crush it."

"And what of the other houses still to contend with if I should divert my attention elsewhere?"

"Unify through this war, or should I say, this crusade. The Bantag are our brothers. What they are now enduring could happen to us. Tell the other houses that."

The emperor came to stand by Hazin.

"Crushing them is a small thing, Your Highness, a very small thing."

"And of course you will lease the troops. Yet more expenses on top of expenses I cannot now afford."

Hazin smiled. So here at last they were getting to the true purpose of this summons.

"Go on, I am fully attentive, Your Highness."

"The cost of the victory over my brother was rather excessive."

"Yet you agreed to the contract."

"Wouldn't you in my position?"

Hazin laughed softly. "Your brother set the bid mark, which you had to exceed."

"Don't you think I know that? It will bankrupt the throne."

"Your brother didn't seem to think so."

"He never considered such things. I have to."

"Are we brokering a deal here, Your Highness."

"I do not broker deals," came the sharp reply.

"Then let me see if I can surmise the offer. The Grand Master with whom you negotiated with is dead. You agree to my ascension as Grand Master, and in return I forgive the debt owed to my house."

The emperor said nothing, his gaze fixed on Hazin.

"I could say that I sent the Grand Master to his ancestors out of loyalty to you."

The emperor smiled sarcastically and Hazin laughed.

"Fine, then. The debt can be forgiven. You will declare a holy crusade to aid our beleaguered brothers to the north, revealing what happened to them, declaring your outrage that your brother knew of this but kept it a secret since he was too preoccupied with vying for the throne. Such a declaration will of course cast you in a positive light and at the same time divert attention to a new cause."

Yasim looked at him warily. "Sometimes you are too cunning, Hazin. In thinking of me, what is it that you seek for yourself?"

"I must have some payment to the Order. To totally forgive the debt, especially after the effort made to secure your throne, would be unforgivable, and I would fall within hours of announcing it. Here is what I propose. We help you to crush the human Republic, you can make payment in part from the loot taken, the money counters of my house will be satisfied, and you shall appear as a liberator.

"Your fractious cousins and countless nephews could be promised fiefdoms vaster than all that you now hold. Offer them new empires and they will fall in line."

The emperor became more animated, looking over at Hazin with eager eyes.

"Let your cousins weaken themselves. Then, when the time is right, confiscate their lands. Use that as payment and eliminate them at the same time."

Yasim could not help but smile. "You will make a deadly Grand Master," he whispered.

"All in service to you, my lord."

"I'm not so stupid as to believe that, Hazin."

"Nor am I so stupid as to challenge you. With the unfortunate and untimely death of my old master, I have all that I desire in this world. What need is there for more? Besides, my fate will be linked to yours, and you, sire, are an entity that I know."

Yasim slowly nodded in agreement.

"Might I therefore suggest that tomorrow you dispatch a fast frigate to the Bantag coast carrying ambassadors and some military advisers? Inform their Qar Qarth that war is about to begin."

"When?"

Hazim fell silent, as if carefully calculating.

"It's a long run for the frigate, and a collier will have to follow in its wake to refuel it for the return journey. Give a week for the frigate to reach the Bantag coast, then another week for your envoy and advisers to reach their Qar Qarth. Offer to them full military assistance if they will abandon the reservation they are trapped on and move south to the coast to link up with us."

"Assistance such as?"

"The Shiv."

"You would commit them to such a place?"

Hazin smiled inwardly. He knew Yasim would leap upon the offer, believing that the mailed fist behind the Order would thus be directed elsewhere. It showed a weakness of Yasim to react without fully contemplating the hidden meanings.

"They, fighting alongside the Bantag, will be a powerful force against the Republic."

Yasim nodded in agreement.

"The uprising would therefore stir first in the east, diverting the Republic's attention. Then time the arrival of the fleet to strike along the main coast of the Republic. We know where their main naval base is. Annihilate it in one blow, land your own troops there, and resistance will begin to fall apart."

"A dangerous time of year to campaign," Yasim replied, his enthusiasm suddenly cooling. "Storm season. Also, my fleet has been hard pressed. Much needs to be repaired and refitted."

"Strike hard now," Hazin said. "In three weeks' time most of the refitting can be accomplished. If anything, your sailors, your warriors, are at their best. In addition, the campaign will immediately divert attention, consolidating forces that were fighting against one another into a common crusade. It will meld them together. Wait until next year, and that chance might be lost."

Yasim hesitated, looking over the railing of his balcony to the city below.

Walking across the balcony where the emperor stood, Hazin leaned against the railing. It was shortly past midnight, the end of the most torturous and difficult day he had ever known, and all had fallen into place. Overhead he heard the distant hum of a flyer, faint, almost imperceptible as it drifted northward. He smiled.

A nod from the emperor indicated that agreement had been reached and the audience had ended.

"I'll pass the necessary orders to begin preparation in the morning."

"I will see you at the celebration of your ascension, my lord," Hazin said formally, bowing low. He left the room, gaze lingering for a moment on the chamberlain, the bloated eunuch. He wondered what this one thought. He must know that his days were numbered, that he had been far too loyal to Hanaga.

The eunuch drew closer. "Grand Master," he whispered. "May I come to your temple tomorrow to speak to you?"

Hazin smiled graciously. "Oh of course, Tugana, of course. Though there is nothing to fear, Yasim even mentioned you in our conversation. Rest assured that your position is safe. I pointed out that your loyalty was to the family and not to Hanaga himself."

He saw the wave of relief in the poor fool's eyes.

"But do come anyhow. There is much we can discuss."

Perhaps it might be worth the effort to ensure this one survived. Then he would be in debt and could be useful.

Hazin followed the eunuch out the side door so that the guests waiting in the outer chamber would not see whom the emperor had been talking to. The captain of the Green Gate waited to escort him out of the compound.

All was playing out as desired. Hazin felt in such a munificent mood that he decided that this captain would not suffer when he died for his insult. A blade no thicker than a wire inserted into the base of the skull by a courtesan of the Order would do the trick. Perhaps even allow him the pleasure of lying with her first as a small gift before death.

Yes, all was unfolding as he had planned. He looked to the North and smiled, wishing Cromwell a safe journey home.

NINE

Exhausted, Richard Cromwell sat before the president of the Republic. He struggled to keep his hands from shaking as he gratefully took a cup of tea, the third one Andrew had offered him since the interview started.

"Can you tell us anything else about the plane you flew?"

"I'm sorry, sir. I tried to stretch it to land. I should have set it down on the beach along the Minoan Shoals rather than try and make the last ninety miles to Constantine."

Andrew extended his hand in a calming gesture. "You might have been stuck out there for days before someone spotted you. I don't blame you for trying the final stretch. I'd have done the same thing."

"Still, I lost the plane damn near in sight of land."

"Just lucky one of our frigates spotted you going in. But is there anything else you can tell us about their weapons?"

"Ship designs, I can give you only general information. I worked on some of it on the train ride up here and can compile more information in a day or so. Perhaps if some of the design engineers from the technical college asked me questions I might be able to remember."

Andrew nodded approvingly and looked over at Pat O'Donald, the only other person he would trust to be at this meeting and whom Richard had requested attend as well.

"Is there anything else you can remember, lad?" Pat asked. "Did you hear of a date when they plan to start, details about machines? Can you tell us anything else about this Hazin, or those beastly men?"

"The Shiv?" He wearily shook his head. The interview had been going on for nearly three hours without stop, and it was obvious to Andrew that Cromwell was past the point of exhaustion. He had been fished out of the ocean less than two days ago, taken straight to Bullfinch, then put on an express train straight back to Suzdal.

"Frightful, sir. They don't seem quite human. I'm not sure if it's because they have been bred for so long that they are different from us, or if it is their cult or the drugs that Hazin gives to them."

Pat, who had shown remarkable restraint throughout the meeting, could finally contain himself no longer.

"Cromwell, a personal question."

Andrew could see Richard stiffen. "Yes, sir. About your son. That's why I asked that you attend when I met with the president."

"You knew him?"

"Of course, sir. We trained together at the academy flight school and were berthed together on the *Gettysburg*."

Pat showed a hint of embarrassment. The fact that he did not know such common details about his son's life was troubling.

"Did he say anything? I mean, did you talk at all about things before the *Gettysburg* was lost?"

Richard hesitated, looking not at Pat but at Andrew.

"Go on, son," Andrew said softly.

Richard shifted, coming almost to attention as he turned back to face Pat. "Your son is alive, sir."

"My God!" Pat cried. He bolted up from his seat and began to pace furiously. "I knew it. I just knew the lad was still alive!

"How? Did he escape, too?"

Richard shook his head.

Pat seemed torn with emotions. He was relieved of the horrible anxiety that had controlled his life since Andrew had told him that the *Gettysburg* was destroyed and a lone survivor had escaped. Now, to suddenly discover that his boy was still alive, but a prisoner, was all but overwhelming.

Pat looked at Andrew, desperation in his eyes.

"Could we arrange an exchange? Remember, the Tugars did it with Hawthorne. We did it with the Merki and Bantag. Damn it, Andrew, I'll go myself."

Andrew extended a calming hand, his gaze still locked on Richard. "I think Mr. Cromwell here has more to say."

Richard nodded his thanks and took a deep breath.

"Out with it, boy. Come on," Pat snapped anxiously.

"Sir, I offered your son the chance to escape with me. He refused."

"What?" Pat roared. He advanced menacingly on Richard, but Richard didn't flinch.

"Are you calling my son a traitor?"

"No, sir, I didn't say that. On the night I escaped, I asked Lieutenant O'Donald to come with me. He refused."

"The weight," Pat interjected, grasping for answers. "He must have realized how desperate your plan was. A hundred and fifty pounds more and you might not have made it."

"That's not what decided the issue, sir," Richard replied, and Andrew realized that Cromwell had brushed over a point. Taking Sean would have meant dumping nearly thirty gallons of precious fuel, but he'd been willing to do that anyhow.

"Out with it then, damn it!" Pat shouted.

"Sir, I hate to be the bearer of this news. Your son, something happened to him."

"They tortured him, didn't they, the filthy bastards."

"Pat, would you please let Mr. Cromwell explain," Andrew said quietly but his voice was hard, the tone expecting compliance.

Richard looked over at Andrew with the slightest flicker in his eyes. It was obvious that he hated what had to be done, but would go through with it regardless.

Pat sat down, pulled out his handkerchief, and wiped the sweat from his brow. "Go on then, Cromwell."

"Yes, we were tortured."

"That's rather evident," Andrew interjected, for the wounds on Richard's face were still evident, lips still puffed up.

Richard started to say more, but fell silent.

"They broke him, didn't they?" Pat asked.

"It wasn't just the torture, it was something they put in our water. It was a drug. I have heard about how morphine affects men who were wounded."

Andrew looked at Cromwell unflinchingly. His own addiction to morphine after being wounded at Capua was one secret of his life that only those closest to him knew. It was frightful as well that after twenty years he still thought of it at times and had to fight the craving. Emil had told him that it would be like that for the rest of his life.

"Was it morphine?" Pat asked.

"I don't know. It made you feel like you were floating, the pain was gone, but you could still see and think clearly. It also made what Hazin said terribly persuasive. It was a horrible thing to fight against."

"Yet you resisted."

Pat looked over at Andrew, ready to make an angry comment, but a gesture stilled him.

"Yes, sir. At least I think I did," Cromwell replied.

"And my son?" Pat asked.

"Hazin seemed to single him out for special attention," Richard replied.

Andrew could sense that Cromwell was skirting the truth, but knew it was best, at least with Pat in the room, to not press for any further details.

"What do you mean, 'attention'?" Pat asked warily.

"After the torture we were separated, and I didn't see Lieutenant O'Donald again until just before I left. I assume Hazin talked to him as he did to me."

That information set in motion a disturbing thought. Perhaps, Andrew wondered, Cromwell was unwittingly a pawn in some sort of power game. Perhaps everything he had learned about their plans was false.

"My son, damn it," Pat interrupted. "Get on with telling me."

Richard exhaled noisily and quickly finished his cup of tea and set it down.

"I'm sorry, sir. There was another factor, a woman. Sean became involved with her and didn't want to leave her."

Pat's temper edged back slightly.

"This woman, was she a slave of Hazin's?" Andrew asked.

"Yes, sir. She was a member of the cult."

"She was assigned to seduce Sean—" Andrew offered.

"That's what I assumed," Richard interjected hurriedly.

"So you are telling me that now my son is in the ranks of this Hazin."

Richard hesitated again.

"Go on."

"Sir, he accepted rank," Richard replied softly, as if the words were too distasteful to be spoken aloud. "He said that the only hope for the Republic was to have someone from our side in their ranks, so that when we were defeated he'd be in a position to help what was left. He said that Hazin was the future."

Andrew sat back, forcing himself to compose his features, to not show shock or anger.

"And this news comes from the son of a traitor," Pat cried, coming back to his feet.

"Pat!"

"It's a damnable lie."

"Pat, there's no purpose to him telling us this if it was a lie."

"It's to cover his own tracks, to cover leaving Sean behind."

"If he'd done that, it would have been best to say nothing at all."

Throughout the exchange Richard remained impassive, even though Pat was within striking distance, hand half raised.

"Mr. Cromwell," Andrew asked, his voice hard, "why did you not communicate to Admiral Bullfinch, or to anyone else, that there was another survivor? Why did you wait till now?"

Richard lowered his head slightly. "Sir, I felt I should first tell this to Senator O'Donald. That it was better to hear it straight from me first rather than read it in Gates's paper."

Richard looked back up at Pat.

"I'm sorry, sir. I thought about saying nothing at all, but in the end I figured it was best to let you know that at least your son is alive. I'd like to think that in his own way he is following an honorable path, that he hopes in the end to help somehow.

"And, sir, no one other than the three of us knows of this. I swear that to you, and frankly, I would prefer if it stayed here and was never spoken of again."

Pat looked stricken, features so pale that Andrew thought for a moment that his friend was about to collapse. Pat sat down heavily.

"I'm sorry, sir."

Pat held his hand up, motioning for him to say no more.

"Mr. Cromwell, I think you need a good rest."

"Yes, sir. Thank you, sir, I am rather tired. It was impossible to sleep on the train."

"You're staying here in the White House tonight. My wife is just down the hallway. Tell her that I want you to have a decent meal and a good night's sleep. She'll see that the staff takes good care of you."

"Thank you, sir."

"You are to share with no one what we've discussed here. I'll ask as well that after you have your dinner, you remain in your room. I don't want other folks, particularly some congressmen visiting tonight, to see you. Someone might recognize you and questions will start to fly."

"Sir, believe me, I plan to be asleep within the hour."

Andrew offered the slightest of smiles. If not for Pat's presence, he would come around the desk to shake Cromwell's hand.

"Go get some rest, Lieutenant."

"Thank you, sir."

Cromwell stood up, put on his cap, and formally saluted. He started to turn but then stopped, looking at Pat.

"Sir, about Sean. He was a good officer. I think in his own way he still is."

Pat lowered his head, saying nothing.

As the door closed behind Cromwell, Andrew looked over at Pat.

"Merciful God, Andrew. Do you believe him?"

" 'For I alone have lived to tell thee all,' " Andrew whispered.

"What?"

"Moby Dick."

"What the hell is that? It sounds awful."

"Never mind."

Andrew walked over and opened the window facing the main plaza of the city. A gust of hot air swept in, dry, not comforting at all. The Great Square of Suzdal lay below, teeming with activity, merchants from across all the states of the Republic hawking their goods from open-air booths. In the far corner, under the sign of the Cannon Tavern, brokers from the stock market were gathered in their traditional summer location, waving their arms in some unintelligible manner, each movement a signal as to whether they were buying or selling shares and at what price. A procession of Rus monks was making its way into the great cathedral for the mid-afternoon service, followed as always by a cluster of old women wearing black shawls. More than one of them were widows from the Great War, still mourning twenty years later.

All this activity seemed so ordinary, so peaceful, that he wondered if anyone would actually remember this particular day. For that was the nature of peace, he realized, to become commonplace, quiet, unassuming in its passage of days that slipped gently into years and lifetimes.

"I don't believe him," Pat announced sharply.

"I have to."

"Damn it, Andrew, my son, did you hear what he said about my boy?"

Andrew looked back at his oldest friend, feeling the anguish churning within Pat. "Yes, I heard what he said about Sean. I don't want to believe it, Pat. Perhaps he is wrong. Regardless of that, though, I have to believe everything else he said. To do otherwise is pure folly."

Pat drew closer, putting his hand on Andrew's shoulder, and Andrew was surprised to see tears in his comrade's eyes.

"I made a mess of things, I did, Andrew. I should have married the girl, helped to raise the boy. But the army, Andrew . . ." and he fell silent.

Andrew offered no response, the excuse so obvious.

"No. Damn my soul, I didn't want to be tied up. For that matter, I wasn't even sure at times if the boy was mine."

Andrew started to voice an angry response, but remained silent.

"The boy's my blood, it was as plain as day." He turned away, covering his face.

Andrew left him alone for the moment. So much about his friend he loved without reservation—his unflinching courage, his bravado, his ability to counter the melancholy that would often creep up in his own soul, ready to seize control. After the defeat by the Merki, and especially after he was wounded at Capua, it was Pat who had applied the steady hand and stirred the fires once again.

Because of that he felt, if not acceptance, at least a tolerance for Pat's mistakes. After the war, with no focus, no next battle calling, he had made a mess of his life, turning to drink as more than one veteran had, and to women. But Livia had been special, and now he would be forever haunted for his mistake in not realizing that, and not taking his son into his heart from the beginning.

Pat noisily blew his nose, wiping his tears away with a dirty handkerchief, and looked back at Andrew. "You must consider who that young man is, Andrew." He nodded to the door that had closed on Richard.

"What's that?"

"The son of Tobias Cromwell."

"So?" he said, a touch of warning in his voice. He had endlessly preached across the years the ideal that in a Republic the sins or the greatness of a father did not affect how the son should be treated. As in the Constitution of the first Republic he had lived in, Andrew had written in an article forbidding the denial of rights to a citizen regardless of what crimes his father had committed. The acceptance of Richard Cromwell into the academy had been a test of that resolve.

Pat was silent, and Andrew could see clearly that more than one would raise the question, especially when word spread of the accusation against Sean O'Donald. The son of a traitor coming back with a fanciful tale of an invasion, capped with an accusation against the son of a senator, was more than many would accept.

"Pat, we have to focus on our duty first."

Pat nodded, looking absently out the window. The cathedral bell tolled, announcing the start of mid-afternoon services. The mingling of half a dozen languages drifted up from the plaza. Andrew sat back down behind his desk.

Turning in his swivel chair, he looked at the display case behind him, which contained a presentation sword from the men of the 35th Maine, given after Gettysburg, his Medal of Honor and the commissioning papers signed personally by Lincoln.

In the wavy glass of the display case, he could dimly see his reflection, It was hard to believe that that image was actually himself. The graying beard, the furrows across the brow, the receding hair, the thin narrow face, he almost looked like Lincoln.

He absently rubbed his empty sleeve. For a moment the "ghost arm" was alive, itching uncomfortably.

Back home, Lincoln was most likely long gone now. I'd give most anything to be back there, if only for a moment, to know what happened, to know how the war there ended, to know if the nation had healed, to find out about old friends, who undoubtedly number me amongst the dead.

I thought I could serve out this second term in peace, retire once and for all in another five years, finally to teach, to write, to enjoy the summer cottage on the shore of the Inland Sea, not far from where Ogunquit had washed up close on to thirty years ago.

"Pat?"

His friend looked back, features pale, as if an infinite sadness had at last crept into a soul that had without care enjoyed life prior to this moment.

"Pat, we have to figure out what in hell we are going to do."

"Based on the word of one boy?"

"He's not a boy, Pat. He's five years older than most of the cadets who graduated. He grew up in the lower depths of hell and survived. I think he is turning into a leader we can count on. I trust him."

"Well, I for one don't."

"Damn you, Pat!" He slammed the table with his fist. "This is no time to think of yourself! This is no time to think about what the hell you should have done for your son when you had the chance." He hesitated for the briefest of moments and then pressed on. "Consider him dead," and his voice was cold, remorseless.

Pat opened his mouth, but was unable to speak.

"I'm sorry, Pat. We have to focus on the issue, not on what we cannot change."

"I thought you, of all people, would understand, Andrew."

"When I can, I will."

Pat looked at him sadly. "Andrew Lawrence Keane, I've counted you a friend since the day we shared our first drink. What has happened to us?"

"Pat, nothing, other than we are older, and when I walk out of this room I have to be president. That must come first. Your being a senator has to come first. Later we can mourn for all that we've lost."

"Fine then, Andrew. I see." He sat down woodenly in the chair across from Andrew.

Andrew lowered his gaze. Now that he had Pat's attention, what next? Since the end of the war the problems had been political, holding the Republic together, suppressing the Chin separatist movement, passing the language-unification laws, but this was different. And Pat was right, any plans they made would be based on the word of one lone officer who many would find suspect.

"Where's Vincent?" Pat asked, finally stirring.

"Still out on the frontier. This report from Cromwell explains the tension out there. The Bantag are in touch with the Kazan, and something is afoot. If war comes with the Kazan, it will explode with the Bantag as well."

Pat nodded. "You should get Hawthorne out of there. With a lone regiment he'll be overwhelmed."

"I'll send a recall message immediately."

Andrew didn't mention that he wanted his own son out of there as well. If a war was about to ignite, he didn't want Abraham to be two hundred miles inside Bantag territory.

"And the fleet?"

"Based on what happened to the *Gettysburg,* it doesn't sound good. Their smallest class of fighting ships are obviously a match for our armored cruisers. Against their ships of the line it will be suicide."

"Withdraw them up the Mississippi?"

Andrew turned and looked at the map above the display case. The river was a deep-channel all the way up to the Inland Sea; back home, more like the Hudson than the Mississippi. Would they pursue? Undoubtedly. From Cromwell's report, one of their main ships of the line could lay off the mouth of the Neiper and shell Suzdal to pieces.

No, there'd have to be a blockade set up. The narrows below Cartha would be the best place, but it would take time, weeks, more like months to build the proper fortifications, lay in the guns, and build up a garrison that could resist a ground-based attack.

"For the moment I'll let Bullfinch think about the response. That's what we're supposed to be paying him for anyhow. Hell, I was a line officer. Things with ships I could never quite understand."

"Fort Hancock," Pat muttered.

Andrew looked back, wondering if there was a mild rebuke there. In that debacle the Bantag had successfully launched a surprise amphibious attack and cut off Pat's army on the Shenandoah River.

No, he was just remembering.

"What about the Bantag?" Pat asked.

Andrew sighed, still gazing at the map.

"They'll join. If the Kazan land on the coast south of them, and they come with what Cromwell says they have, the Bantag will join. Hell, if the roles were reversed, wouldn't you?"

"Punitive strike now, Andrew."

"What?"

"We could mobilize a hundred thousand men within a week and move them to the frontier. We have over two hundred aerosteamers and five hundred land ironclads. Throw that force at them now, drive a wedge between them and the sea."

"Oh, damn," Andrew sighed, and he slowly shook his head.

"Why not?"

"What did you just tell me ten minutes ago about how people will react to what Cromwell said? Pat, I can't preemptively start a war with the Bantag based upon a sole report."

"And Hawthorne's report, what about that?"

"The same there, It's merely a surmise, a reading of intent. We have no proof other than a single revolver. I can't go to war over that."

"Then provoke them."

He thought about that. It could be done, but wouldn't Jurak figure out as well what Andrew was trying to do? He was no fool, and he had a million square miles to fall back into. A band of a few thousand Bantag, fighting in their own territory, could run rings around the fresh recruits the army now had.

Too many variables were beginning to close in, and now, after the first rush of excitement over what Cromwell had reported, a cooler voice was whispering to him.

I'm overreacting, he thought. Perhaps the boy is wrong after all. There could even be a plot within a plot, that he was deliberately let go to provoke us into a first move.

The first move, that was the problem here. If we are wrong, the Separatists' Movement will have a golden opportunity; they could even bring on another constitutional crisis. The Chin would use any pretext to attack the Bantag and, if let loose, it would be a debacle. The Greeks might very well ally with the Chin in order to leave the Republic, and then everything fractures.

Yet to wait, to do nothing, was repugnant to his nature. He had a window here, a month perhaps, six weeks at most before the onslaught hit, according to what Cromwell had said. And yet all that was based upon a lone report.

"Damn," he sighed, clenching his fist, looking back at Pat.

"We're stuck. I can't order an unprovoked attack on the Bantag without clear evidence that they actually are allying with the Kazan.

"As for the Kazan, we know nothing. Absolutely nothing. We have one report from a pilot to whom I'd give anything if he had changed his name, and on that, our fate might rest in the weeks to come."

Andrew stood up, returning to the window. The stock market was still at it. A scribe was furiously running back and forth on the catwalk above the Cannon Tavern, writing the latest prices on the huge chalkboard that ran the entire length of the building. A jade merchant with a particularly annoying whine, who had leased a crucial corner directly in front of the White House, was chanting about the beauty of his stones. Off in the distance, beyond the smoke billowing from the steel mill stacks, he caught a glimpse of an aerosteamer lazily circling, then turning, cutting figure eights in the sky, a student learning his art.

"Pat, nothing is to be said as of yet. Nothing."

"How long do you plan to keep the lid on?"

"No one knows that Cromwell has reported here other than the admiral and the crew of the ship that brought him in, and Bullfinch wisely had them quarantined. We have a couple of days before the rumors begin to circulate. I want you to line up senators you can rely on, Gracchus, Petronius, Valincovich, and Hamilcar."

"Alexandrovich," Pat added, "he's an old vet, we can count on him."

"To keep his mouth shut?"

Pat hesitated. "I'll threaten to break his arms if he breathes a word."

"All right then. The speaker and the vice president are not to know. They'd spill it out in a heartbeat."

"They'll be furious when they find out."

"Let them. I'll have Vincent call a mobilization drill. It was slated for next month anyhow. We can use the excuse that it was getting too routine."

"The stock market boys, the factory owners, will scream. Their schedules are planned around losing their men four weeks from now."

"Let them scream. I'll make some statement about it being a realistic drill this time. We shift the maneuver area to our grounds on the Chin territory."

Pat started to shake his head. "Gods, Andrew. The Chin will read into that. Hell, one of them breaks wind, and they spend days reading into it. They'll think our holding maneuvers on their territory is a veiled threat."

"Let them think what they want."

"I want a meeting with Webster, Varinnia Ferguson, and a few people she trusts first thing in the morning. We're going over everything Cromwell told us—in fact, I want him here, too. We have precious little time, but we have to start thinking about counters to everything he says they have."

Pat smiled.

"What is it?"

"A bit like the old days again."

"I'd prefer something different."

Pat solemnly nodded. "Yes, Andrew, I agree."

Andrew returned to his desk and looked at the calendar page set to one side. "Damn. There's a dinner tonight with some Chin congressmen. I can't cancel that. Then a play."

"Better go. Besides, I heard it's a good one. *The Yankee and the Boyar's Daughter*."

"Oh, God, not another one."

Pat smiled. "Complete with tableau of the historic victory at the First Battle of Suzdal. Performed in English, no less, with Dimitri Vasiliovich as the Yankee."

"It sounds like you actually enjoyed it."

"Oh, I did. Rare fine good acting it was."

Andrew groaned. He was bored to death with the utter silliness of patriotic plays, which had become the rage of late, all but taking Shakespeare off of Players Row. But if he did not attend, the more astute might read something into it, put it together with the change in the summer mobilization rehearsal. No, he would have to attend and listen to Dimitri's hysterical overacting.

"All right, then. Tomorrow I'll clear my schedule. You get word to Webster and Ferguson, make it first thing in the morning. I think our focus at the start should be the navy, what we can do there within the next couple of weeks. Let's plan to meet at the shipyard."

His tone indicated that the conversation was at an end, and that bothered him. This was Pat, after all, not someone who had to be eased out of the office so that the next appointment could be kept.

"Andrew?"

He nodded, already knowing what was to be asked. "Let's just keep the word about your boy between us for right now. Cromwell kept it till he could meet with you. I trust he'll continue to keep it. Perhaps he was wrong after all."

Pat smiled. "I don't believe it for a minute, Andrew. Do you?"

"No," Andrew lied, "of course not."

TEN

The sun was rising as Abraham Keane, riding alone, crested the ridgeline. Before him the encampment of the Golden Yurt was spread out across the open plains, the early morning light casting long shadows, the steppe to the west disappearing into a dark blue horizon.

A shaman's chants drifted on the hot wind. Smoke curled from campfires. Some cubs, engaged in a passionately fought game, rode in swirling knots, sweeping down to reach for the ball. Not so long ago he knew that the bag would have contained a human head. Now it was just stuffed with old felt rags—at least he hoped that was the case.

He saw the Qar Qarth riding out from behind his yurt, mounted on his favorite stallion, a magnificent white animal. The two of them were a striking sight. The horse pranced, legs raised high, and Jurak was obviously enjoying the ride, knowing that all eyes were upon him.

Abe leaned back in his saddle, taking in the view, enjoying the moment. The thought of going back to the cities of the west, to the crowds, the stench, the noise, after riding patrols, after watching sunrises and sunsets on the open plains where heaven and earth met on a horizon that seemed to disappear into eternity, was impossible to contemplate. This is the place where he wanted to stay.

Jurak drew closer, his mount kicking up plumes of dust. The cubs paused in their wild melee and bowed respectfully from the saddle, then returned to their pursuit once he had passed.

Abe stiffened and saluted as Jurak reined in by his side.

"The night passed well, Qar Qarth Jurak?"

"Yes, and yours?"

"Our circles are peaceful, as I see yours to be," Abe replied, offering the ritual words that indicated he had come without warlike intent.

Jurak leaned over and affectionately patted the neck of his horse.

"You ride well," Abe said.

"I have to in order to survive here. I wasn't born to it the way my people are. I'll admit that when I first came here, I hated riding. There's something about being atop a beast that could kill you, and who at the same time is actually rather dull of mind, that bothered me."

Abe laughed softly. "My father still misses his old war-horse, Mercury. He said Mercury was the only horse he ever knew that had brains."

"I remember that horse. The battle at what you call Rocky Hill. Your father was a magnificent sight riding along the front line, followed by his battle standard. He was the incarnation of war at that moment. I'll never forget the way his men cheered, and I knew that as long as he lived you would never be defeated. He has my respect."

"I shall tell him you remember him thus. He will be honored."

Jurak looked away, letting go of his reins so his horse could crop the short grass.

"There is a reason for your visit, son of Andrew Keane. The flyer that dropped the message over your camp last evening sent Hawthorne scurrying up here for one last talk, and now you have come at dawn. Hawthorne has already said his farewells. Why have you come back?"

Abe nodded, letting go of his reins as well. "I've been ordered to tell you something. It is not official. It came from my father to me, and no one else knows."

He could see that he had Jurak's interest.

"Go on, then."

"My father conveys to you his respects."

"Yes, the usual formula between rulers, but what is the message?"

"You are not to move south."

"I have argued this point with your General Hawthorne for over half a moon." Jurak pointed back to the regimental encampment where even now the tents were being struck, the column forming up. "Our talks ended with no resolution. Why do you come back here alone to repeat yet again that which we could not agree upon? Does your general know you are doing this?"

"Yes, sir. He gave his permission."

"Why?"

"Sir, he said that," and Abraham hesitated, "that you

respected me because of my blood and would believe me. I asked as well to come alone."

Jurak laughed. "You are brave like your father."

"I know I have nothing to fear from you."

"At this moment, yet."

"I would like to think it would stay that way."

In the weeks that he had come to know Jurak, Abe felt that he had learned some of the nuances of this leader of the Bantags. He had heard Cromwell talk about it back at the academy, how when you lived with them, you learned quickly to recognize each as an individual rather than as part of a faceless horde. You knew who was more cruel than normal, who might give a favored pet an extra scrap of food, when someone was angry, happy, sad, or vengeful. In short, you learned things about them the same way you did about humans.

He felt he had gained some knowledge of Jurak, at least a vague understanding of this alien ruler of what was to him an alien race. Jurak possessed a keen intellect, as fitted someone from the future who had been thrown into a primitive world. In a strange sort of way he thought Jurak and his father were alike. For he too bore knowledge this world had not yet come to grasp. He had led the Rus in a war undreamed of before his arrival.

But it had been Jurak's fate to come too late, when events were already unfolding beyond his control. Across the years afterward all he could do was brood, to maneuver for a way to survive, not just for himself but for the fallen Horde he ruled as well.

He looked at Jurak carefully, sensing the wariness, the sudden alertness and caution. The wind stirred the mane of his horse, the plume of his helmet. The light about them was soft, diffuse, mingled with the shadows of early morning.

"Is that all there is to the message?"

"Yes, Qar Qarth Jurak, that is all that he sent directly to you. No one else, either in our government or our military, knows except for General Hawthorne."

"There is more, though," Jurak pressed, leaning forward, gazing down at Abe.

"Yes, to you personally."

"I am waiting."

"My father asked me to tell you that he knows what is about to happen."

Jurak looked confused for a moment and then smiled, shaking his head and laughed softly.

"Are we playing some sort of game, Abraham Keane? You threaten me and watch how I react? If so, I thought better of your father and of you."

Abe, however, could tell that Jurak was troubled. Abe had yet to learn the finer points of their language, to recognize the tonal inflections for emotion, a crucial element to master since tone often influenced the exact meaning of the word. Still, he could sense the unease in Jurak's voice.

"Then tell me what your father speaks of when he says that he knows what is about to happen."

"War with the Kazan," Abe said, almost whispering the word. "You will receive an offer from the Kazan to ally with them shortly. War will ensue within the month, and my father asks that for the good of all you stay out of it. Either stay here or move north, but do not turn south."

Jurak's features remained impassive. "Why? Why now?"

"I have no idea," Abe replied. "I am only telling you what he sent to me, nothing more."

Jurak gazed at him thoughtfully. "I suspect you are telling the truth."

Abe bristled slightly. "I have never uttered a false word to you, Jurak."

Jurak nodded. "And is there anything else, then?"

"Flyers will be doubled patrolling the lands to the south of here. If you should leave treaty land and move south toward the coast, it will be viewed as a hostile act."

"And you will attack."

"Yes."

"And to you, though? What more was there to you?"

"My personal orders? I've requested a transfer to a troop assignment, and General Hawthorne has agreed. I'm to stay with the 3rd Cavalry, which will take up station on the border. Sir, if you would move, I will ride with that regiment against you."

Abe looked straight into Jurak's eyes.

"So why did you tell me?"

"I trust you."

Jurak leaned back in his saddle and laughed so loudly that the cubs who were playing but a hundred yards away slowed in their game to see what was so amusing.

"Something is happening back west, or," and Abraham paused, "or to the south. Is there an envoy in your camp, Qar Qarth Jurak? Are you expecting yet another envoy with news about the war?"

Jurak did not react. His mask was impenetrable.

"Don't play the subtle envoy with me, boy. Whether I know anything or not I will never share such information with you."

"I understand that. I understand what divides us as well."

"I don't think you fully do. In your eyes I am something strange, a remainder of an older day of glory. I fought your father, and it appeals to your sense of romance to now say that we could be friends."

"It is not a sense of romance," Abe replied heatedly. "What I've said to you is genuine."

There was a moment of softness in Jurak's eyes. "Yes, you are young enough that I believe you." He shook his head. "Too much will forever divide us even though a few such as you will try to breech that wall. Do you know, Abraham Keane, that I have eaten human flesh?"

Abraham stiffened. He could feel a cool shiver course down his back.

"Yes, I had assumed that," Abe finally replied.

"That fear is primitive, instinctual. Enemies can kill each other and yet drink a cup with the sons of those whom they have slain, if the slaying is viewed as honorable. Over their cups they praise each other and speak of the glory of the old days, as you and I have done. But the eating of flesh, that is a dread beyond death. That, and the humiliation of slavery."

He looked back at the cubs playing their game.

"They're of age to be warriors. They were raised on the tales of their fathers, who fought your father, and of their grandsires, who still remember the old days of the everlasting ride to the east, the glory of the wars with the Merki and the Tugars and, yes, the harvesting of cattle."

He looked at Abe, his gaze cool and penetrating.

"You don't like that word, *cattle*. None of your race does."

"It is a reminder of a time that is gone."

"Gone to you who were born after it, but alive in the memory of many of my people, and still dreamed of by those cubs. If I whistled to them now, ordered them to drop their game and slay you, they would do it."

"You are their Qar Qarth. Of course they would obey."

"No, Keane, they would do it because they wanted to. And beyond that, they would devour you upon this very spot and do so with glee, do it while you are still alive and screaming, as they have heard their fathers describe it done."

"Why are you telling me this?" Abe replied, voice edged with anger. "So that I can hate you? I was trained as a soldier of the Republic. I know of every battle, of all that happened before. I know that at Hispania and at Roum our men executed prisoners, tortured and mutilated some. Atrocities are committed in the heat and madness of battle."

"But you never felt them," Jurak said sharply. "You don't know war. I do. I guess that's always been the way of it. The generation that fought a war looks at its young, not imagining they too could do the barbarities required.

"Those cubs, look at them carefully, Keane. The next time you see them, they will be coming to kill you."

"Is this what you truly want?" Abe asked.

"No, damn you," Jurak snarled with a deep throaty growl. "I know where this will end, as do you."

"Then stop it."

"How?"

"Just stop it."

Jurak laughed. "Perhaps your father will be a victim of the very sense of justice he is famous for. If you had slain us all twenty years back, this would not now be happening."

"But we didn't. Shouldn't that sway your thinking now?"

"Blood. It is about blood and race. I wish it was different." His voice trailed off, but the look in his eyes told Abe that there was nothing more to be said.

"Then this is where we part, Qar Qarth Jurak."

He nodded. Reaching down to the side of his saddle, he pulled out a scimitar that was still in its scabbard and handed it over to Abe.

"A present in parting, Abraham Keane. It was forged for a cub and thus should fit your hand well."

Abe took the present and unsheathed it. The fine wavery lines from the forging of the blade shimmered in the morning sunlight. He held it aloft, feeling its balance, then slowly resheathed it, nodding his thanks, unable to speak.

"Strange as it sounds, I hope it protects you well."

"I have no such gift to offer in reply."

"Nor was one expected, young man. It's a present to your father as well in a way, to protect that which he cares for. Call it a small repayment of the debt I owe to a human who was your father's closest friend."

Abe smiled sadly and then, on impulse, extended his right hand.

Jurak hesitated, then finally extended his own hand, taking Abe's in his. "I hope we don't meet again, Abraham Keane, for you know what that would mean."

"Yes, I know."

"Ride with the wind. I will let no one pursue you. That should give you fifteen leagues or more. Avoid the Gilwana Pass. That's the grazing grounds of the Black Speckled Clan. They more than most have no love for you. Nearly all their warriors died in the Chin Rebellion."

"And what shall I tell my father?"

Jurak smiled and shook his head. "Nothing. His message was clear enough."

"Farewell, Qar Qarth Jurak."

"Then farewell, Keane."

The Qar Qarth picked up his reins and spurred his mount, which leapt forward with a start.

Abe held his own reins in tight, his mount shying as Jurak's stallion surged forward. So it's war, Abe thought coldly. Strange, I half want to see it, to understand it as my father did. And yet he found it difficult to hold back tears as he watched Jurak ride back to the Bantag encampment.

The train, pulling a single car, glided to a stop at the station, out of which descended a woman, followed by several of her assistants.

"Varinnia, how are you today?" Andrew asked, coming forward to take her hand.

Richard immediately recognized her. Varinnia Ferguson

had often lectured at the academy to senior year cadets on applied engineering. She was, of course, yet another legend of the war, and that legend stilled any comments when she had first come into a classroom. Her face had been horribly burned, she was barely able to write with one wilted hand, but the flames, if they had touched her mind, had done so in a different way, making her seem as if she would burst into fire from sheer energy and passion for her subject. By the end of her first lecture all had forgotten how she looked, and there wasn't a cadet who wouldn't thrash anyone who dared to make a crude joke about her appearance.

She had another side as well, for as the wife of Chuck Ferguson, she had worked not only as an engineer and inventor but also as a political revolutionary, bringing about the amendment for women to vote and, at the same time, creating a tradition in the young Republic for women to go into medicine and engineering.

At her approach, Richard instinctively came to attention. She nodded to William Webster, secretary of the treasury, then turned to look appraisingly at Cromwell.

"Young Lieutenant Cromwell, I understand you are the reason for all this excitement."

"Commander Cromwell as of this morning," Andrew interjected with a smile.

Stunned, Richard turned to the President.

"Sir. I hardly think—"

"No self-deprecating comments, Commander. Admiral Bullfinch was an admiral at the age of twenty-two. Age doesn't matter in this country. It's wisdom, guts, and more than a little luck that counts."

Cromwell was silent.

"Besides, you need the rank to do some of the things expected of you. Plus, it's a statement on my part as well."

"A statement, sir?"

"That he believes you," Varinnia said. "When word of this becomes public, your promotion will make a statement." She looked back at Andrew. "I assume Gates will be pulled in to do the proper articles on him, and on everything else."

"I've already talked to him. That's why you don't see any newspaper scribblers following us down here this morning. He agreed to hold off on the story."

"Oh, really?"

"Either that or I shut down his papers for a few days and he loses thousands. There's a fine line between censorship and a nation's security. I convinced Gates it was the latter rather than the former."

She nodded approvingly. "Let's get to work."

She led the way from the station, which was empty on this Sunday morning, down to the naval dockyard on the Neiper, fifteen miles south of the city.

As the procession headed out, Cromwell noticed that Adam Rosovich was one of her assistants, and he fell in beside his old acquaintance from the academy. After offering a smiling salute, Adam extended his hand.

"On the train ride down here Ferguson told us a bit about what happened to you," Adam whispered. "Are you all right?"

"I'm fine."

"Is it true that the *Gettysburg* was lost with all hands?" Richard nodded.

"Damn, I had a couple of friends on her. Poor O'Donald, he was a good man."

"Yes," Richard sighed, "a good man."

"You look like hell, Richard, like you took the worst end of a brawl at the Roaring Mouse."

Richard smiled. "If only it had been that easy. So how is it with your plush and comfortable job at the ordnance design office?"

Adam sighed. "Boring. I wanted to fly, but I've been up exactly once, to test." He fell silent and gave him a conspiratorial smile. "But that's supposed to be a secret. Anyhow, even then I just rode in the backseat. There's a lot of good ideas floating around. I've been trying to push that pet project we talked about at the academy."

"The aerosteamer carrier?"

"Exactly, but you should hear the old admirals howl. I thought Admiral Petronius was going to have my head when I presented a paper on it a couple of weeks back. 'It goes against all doctrine,' he roared. 'We need more guns, not buzzing gnats,' were his exact words."

Richard nodded. He'd seen the exact same type of ship Adam was dreaming about riding at anchor in the harbor of Kazan.

"I keep trying to tell them that with the new weapon we're developing, aerosteamer carriers will become crucial. We'll no longer just use them for scouting. But they'll have none of it. I think Dr. Ferguson agrees, but the rest of the board moves like a snail in a snowstorm."

The group slowed as they approached the main gate of the shipyard, and the two fell silent.

Nothing stirred in the early morning except for a few surprised sentries guarding the entry gate, through which hundreds of workers flowed during the regular work week. One of two guards accompanying Andrew went over to the sentries and quietly but forcefully began to impress upon them that the president had never been here. A nervous lieutenant, coming out of the guardhouse inside the gate was turned back and taken inside.

Andrew walked through the gate, Varinnia on one side, Webster on the other. Richard and Adam followed. Just inside the gate Richard recognized the stooped-shouldered form of Theodor Theodovich, head engineer of the Republic Aerosteamer Company, chief contractor for all airships built for the Republic. Beside him stood a tall gray-haired naval officer, still slender in spite of his obvious sixty years or more of age.

"Admiral Petronius," Adam whispered.

The two offered their salutes, which Petronius answered without comment.

When Richard looked over at Theodor, he smiled.

"Old Jack Petracci told me you were a damn good pilot," he said, extending his hand.

Richard, who normally fought at all times to contain any display of emotion, could not help but be impressed and gladly took the hand.

"Later today I want to sit down with you and go over every detail you can remember of their flying machines. I read the notes you jotted down. They show good technical judgment, Cromwell."

"I just wish I could have brought the plane all the way in."

"You're lucky you made it as far as you did and spotted that ship. That was damn near good enough."

"You once flew with General Petracci, didn't you?"

Theodor grinned. "Scared the hell out of me. After the war I swore I'd never go up with him again, and I've kept that promise."

Richard looked at him admiringly. He and Petracci were the only two flyers from the Great War who were still alive.

Clearing the gate, the small entourage maneuvered through the railyard, weaving around flatcars loaded with steel plates, keels, beams, masts, and all the thousand other ship parts cast in the foundries north of the city. All was silent, and a cool fog was drifting in from the river, heavy with the less than pleasant smells that drifted down from the teeming city to the north.

The naval yard had been constructed after the war, a massive project that had taken five years and required the movement of millions of tons of earth and rock to construct a dry dock, slips and ways, piers and workyards.

Tied off at the main piers were the almost complete cruisers *Shiloh, Perryville,* and *Wilderness.* The decks were still flush, since turrets, superstructures and masts had yet to be added. All three of the ships had been launched only within the last month and then tied off for final completion.

Along the next dock were five frigates in various stages of completion. Nothing new was in development, because the eight ships represented all of the budget allocations Andrew had run through at the start of his second term. Some of the southern members of Congress were arguing that all further ship building should take place at Constantine. It seemed a natural choice, being directly on the sea. Continuing the work at Suzdal was seen as a maneuver to keep money inside Rus and away from the shipbuilders of the southern states, who had far more experience. The only argument against it was the threat from cyclones.

"What's the deepest draft we can get in here?" Varinnia asked, looking back at one of her assistants.

"Thirty-three feet in the main channel and from slip number one. The others are all at twenty-five feet."

She led the group over to where *Shiloh* was tied off. She was one of the *Gettysburg* class, three hundred and fifty feet in length and drawing nearly five thousand tons.

"Compare that to what you saw, Cromwell," she said, pointing at the ship.

"It wouldn't last ten minutes in a fight with their ships of the line."

Andrew and several others of the group shifted uncomfortably.

"Why?"

"Their largest ship had breechloading guns that I estimated were ten inches, perhaps even twelve. I spotted six turrets on several of them, two forward, two aft, and two amidships."

"The amidships guns, how do they bear?" she asked.

"They're positioned so that they can fire directly forward or aft. Therefore, it would have four guns for a bow or stern chase, and five guns for a broadside. I think I spotted a number of secondary guns of lighter caliber as well.

"In the night fight, I think I saw a couple of ships that had three guns forward and one or two aft. It looked like several different designs, but all of them were heavy, twelve thousand tons, maybe as high as eighteen or twenty."

"Did you see these guns fire?" Petronius asked.

"Only in a night action. The one we spotted."

"We?" Petronius asked. "Who was your spotter?"

Richard hesitated for the briefest instant, noticing that the president was watching him carefully.

"It was Lieutenant Sean O'Donald, sir."

"And what happened to him in this action of yours?"

"He didn't come back," Richard said slowly, hoping that Petronius would interpret his words in the way he wanted. The admiral simply nodded.

"Range on these guns?"

"That's the interesting thing," Richard replied. "Like our fourteen incher, I believe their guns must have a range of ten thousand yards or more. The question is hitting at that range. It looked as if most of the action was taking place at a mile or less."

"Could that be because it was a night battle?" Theodor asked.

Richard shook his head.

"No, sir. I heard later that the battle had started in late afternoon. The ship that . . ." He hesitated, looking at Andrew, who shook his head. "The ship carrying the rival to the throne was hit early in the action, at a range of nearly a league, which all considered to be remarkable luck."

"That information could be valuable to us," Varinnia interrupted. "Very valuable, but it will take time."

"Fire control?" Theodor asked.

"We've talked for years about it," Varinnia replied. "My husband's notes include talk about a man on the old world, the one named Babbage. When firing at long range, gunnery is a question of numerous variables too complex to solve in the necessary time. We have the theory of using optical triangulation instruments to figure out the range. Calculating from there, though, is the problem. We could have a hundred of our finest engineers and mathematicians on board a ship, give them the estimated range, and by the time they got done calculating gun elevation and powder load, both ships would be back in port and their crews on leave."

She shook her head, but Richard could sense her excitement as she contemplated the problem.

"If we could find a way to calculate, in advance, the elevation, angle, and load of the gun, fire it, then have a new calculation within thirty seconds for the next firing, factoring in the observed hit of the previous shell, we could defeat anything afloat."

Varinnia and Theodor launched into a heated discussion for several minutes, which Richard tried to follow. The two argued about shell flight time, relative change of distance and angle, and something called differential engines, until Andrew final interrupted with a polite clearing of his throat.

She looked over at him and smiled. Richard could sense a genuine affection between the two.

"Mister, or I should say, Commander Cromwell, tell us the number of ships in the emperor's fleet," Petronius asked, having stood to one side during the technical debate.

"I can't say for sure. That shifts as alliances between families change. When I flew over the harbor, I counted eight great ships of the line, each of them easily three times the size of our *Gettysburg* class. Twenty or more ships of the second line, about half the size of the capital ships but still bigger than our largest vessels. I would estimate they had eight-inch guns. Finally forty, perhaps fifty smaller ships, like the one that defeated the *Gettysburg,* somewhat smaller than our cruisers, around the size of our frigates."

"Speed?"

"The great ships I can't say for certain. I saw several of their frigates maneuvering out of the harbor while I was being taken off the ship, and I would say they could reach eighteen knots, perhaps twenty."

The group around Varinnia broke into feverish whispers. She turned to join them, occasionally looking back at him as if they were doctors conferring just outside the hearing distance of a patient who was desperately ill. Again he caught only snatches of phrases—steam turbines, cruise range, fuel storage to gross weight ratios.

He waited patiently, sensing a certain desperation on their part.

Andrew came over to join him, taking off his stovepipe hat, which one of his guards quietly took from his hand.

"An honest appraisal, Commander Cromwell," Andrew asked softly, drawing Richard aside.

"Yes, sir."

"Can we match them?"

Richard reluctantly shook his head. "Maybe in three years, or five. If we could capture one of their ships and tear it apart, then start making them."

"In that time they'll overrun us."

"Yes, sir."

"Then, we have to come at it from another angle," Andrew said, raising his voice enough so that the others could hear.

The arguing group fell silent.

"Another angle. Figure out their weakness as of this moment and attack it, at the very least to buy time so that we can then apply a long-term plan."

"Their weakness is political," Webster interjected. "I can figure that much from the report of this young commander."

Richard sensed a distrust on Webster's part. Was it because of O'Donald? he wondered. Surely that would leak out sooner or later. Had Andrew already shared that bit of information with the only member of his cabinet who was an old survivor of the 35th Maine?

"Our flyers versus theirs perhaps?" Theodor asked.

Richard gave a nod of approval. "I think we have the speed on them. The machine I flew had the range—it was made for that—but it was slow. It was built to span the long distances between their islands."

"How you flew it for a day and a half is beyond me," Webster said, and again Richard wondered if there was a question about the truthfulness of his report.

"I was desperate, sir," Richard replied evenly. "That can drive a man to do most anything."

"Basing decisions related to flyers and tactical application on a vague report regarding just one of their machines is more than a bit reckless," Petronius interjected. "I would think that if this whole thing is even true to start with, they'd have given this young lieutenant here a worthless machine."

Andrew let the flicker of a smile light his features and held out his hand before Richard could respond.

"Two things we must do," Andrew said, fixing everyone with his gaze. "Long-term first. If we can buy a year, two years, what can you do?" he asked. "I need to know that now, today. You can give me the details later. I know you people have been cooking up a lot of wild ideas. That's what you are paid to do."

He looked over at Ferguson, who smiled conspiratorially.

"I want a concise proposal on long-term development plans by this afternoon. I think I can get the support you've been screaming about, and which I have honestly wanted to get for you all along.

"This afternoon I will meet with several senators to let them in on this. We have to put together, at once, a proposal for a naval buildup unlike anything we've ever done before, then ram it through Congress before they have time to think about it, while they are still afraid. Give them time to think, and then the arguing will start and months will drag out, which we obviously can't afford."

"And suppose the whole thing is for naught," Webster asked. "Six months from now, when we've spent millions, then what?"

"Bill, do you honestly believe that?"

Webster hesitated. "It's a lot to gamble based on the report of one man."

"I'd rather bet on it now than wake up one morning to

hear that the Kazan fleet is steaming into Constantine, or worse, coming up the Mississippi to blow us apart. Until proven otherwise I have to assume it is correct."

Richard stood silent, stomach knotted, wishing he was, at this moment, anywhere else.

Webster finally grumbled in agreement and fell silent.

Richard looked over at Petronius, who stood with arms folded, saying nothing.

"To match their ships of the line?" Varinnia announced. "Three years at least. There isn't a slip here big enough to support such a project. We'd need to increase the size of this facility four fold at least. We could shift frigate production over to the smaller yards at Roum and Cartha."

"That will help get votes," Webster replied, and Andrew nodded in agreement.

"The number of ships?" Andrew asked.

"We should do it the same way we make guns, artillery," Varinnia replied. "I've always said the way we put ships together is all wrong. It is not an assembly-line process like we have for other things. Make standard design for several classes of ships, then get the factories rolling."

She pointed at the half-completed cruisers lining the piers.

"We put these together like craftsmen, turning out only enough pieces to fit each ship. It all goes too slowly. We must have total standardization, train more workers, then start churning them out one after another."

"But it won't be that easy," Petronius replied. "Consider the question of scale. Armor plating is difficult to cast, and for what you are thinking about, by the gods, we don't know much of anything. How thick is the armor, how deep do their armor-piercing shells penetrate, how do they delay the fuses so they burst inside the target rather than on top of it? We've talked about steam turbines, even built small-scale models, but one big enough to move a frigate?" He threw up his hands in frustration.

"You have a few months to work that out," Andrew announced. "Just to gear up will take time. The sheer labor needed to expand this shipyard will take months before the first keel is even laid down. Put everyone you have on the problems and come up with the designs."

"They're amphibious," Richard said as the conversation

paused for a moment. "I doubt if they are simply going to hit Constantine and be done. They'll land an army. They could put thirty thousand or more ashore anywhere along the two thousand miles of our coast and in six months make it half a million. I was told, during that battle they had already placed tens of thousands of troops ashore and built landing strips for aerosteamers, all within a couple of days."

All fell silent as they digested the enormous implications of what he'd said.

"The first question is, when and where will they strike, if they are indeed coming," Petronius interjected, breaking the silence. "Deal with that first."

"Constantine," several of the group said at the same time, followed by nods of agreement.

"How do they even know where Constantine is?" Webster asked.

"As I said in my report," Richard replied, "they sent spies here years ago. They must have charts drawn up, showing our bases."

"They know where Constantine is, and that is the first place they will head for," Andrew stated.

"Do we order Bullfinch to pull out?" Webster asked.

"No," came the sharp reply from Andrew. "Do that and the Greeks might very well leave the Republic, and then we have a civil war on our hands. We have to fight to hold it."

Andrew looked over at Richard. "Go on, I want to hear what you are thinking. Should we try to hold Constantine? Or should I say, can we hold Constantine?"

Richard took a deep breath. "We fight there with what we have right now, and we lose, sir. Their main ships could shell the fortifications and the naval depot to rubble. They land, encircle the town, and it is over."

"We can't concede to them, in the opening move, a base on our coast," Petronius replied sharply.

"I fear, sir, that they will take it regardless."

Richard could sense Andrew's tension, and he wondered if he was sounding too defeatist.

"The other place they will land is on the Bantag coast," Varinnia announced. "It's obvious."

Andrew nodded sadly in agreement.

"So we have two battles, on two fronts."

"Consider the prospect that they might strike on three fronts," Webster interjected. "They could very well venture up the Mississippi, knowing that it will blockade us, in a way, actually cut us off from our states along the coast. There's only one rail line down there, so far, to Constantine. They know we are reliant on the river as well."

"There is one other factor," Richard said slowly. "For the moment, we are the desperate ones. For them this, as much as anything, is a political maneuver."

Andrew looked over at him. "What do you mean?"

"Just that, sir. There is a game within a game and we are but pawns. It is the struggle between Hazin and the emperor for power. If we could drive a wedge there, it might buy time. Second, there is contempt for us. The Hordes quickly learned desperation. You threatened their ride, their source of food, of survival. Whether we live or die at this moment matters to the Kazan not at all."

He fell silent, wondering if he had said too much, but the group around him were gazing at him intently.

"Go on," Andrew said.

"The farsighted might perceive that twenty, fifty years from now there could be a conflict to the death over which race will survive on this world."

"I always held some hope that it would be different," Andrew replied, an infinite sadness in his voice.

"Those bastards?" Webster snapped. "The world is too small for both of us. You can dream about it, Mr. President, but those here who lived under the yoke of the Hordes know different."

As he spoke, Varinnia's assistant nodded in agreement.

"Later, Mr. Webster, later," Andrew sighed. "Continue, Commander."

"In the long term, this will be a political war as well. I know that doesn't bear on the issue at hand, but I had to mention it. I suspect that Hazin is urging the emperor to attack in order to divert him. You see, if they didn't fight us, they'd fight among themselves. Perhaps their nobility would turn on this cult of Hazin's and destroy it."

"If only we could trigger that."

"I don't know how," Richard replied. "I wish I did."

"There's one final question for this morning," Andrew

said. "Assuming we face their fleet within the next four to six weeks before the storm season strikes. What do we do?"

"Based on what he said," Webster replied, "surrender the ships or pull out."

Andrew looked over at Webster with a flash of anger in his eyes. "We can't withdraw, nor will we ever surrender."

"We fight, and they get blown apart and thousands of good men die for a hollow gesture based on political considerations."

Richard stepped back from the two as an argument ensued. Long ago, while still a slave, he had learned that when rulers fight, the lowly should be nowhere in sight.

As he moved to the edge of the group, his attention focused on the half-completed ship.

"I always feared these were not enough."

Varinnia was by his side, Adam behind her. He nodded, sensing it was best to say nothing.

"Beautiful ships, but the problem with the sea is, so much rides on so little. A dozen ships can decide the fate of a nation. On land, with massed armies, you can fight a battle, lose it, perhaps even lose near on to an entire army as we did several times, but with the right backing industrially, by the time your opponent advances you can have a new army in place and quickly adapt your tactics to what you've learned from the last fight.

"At sea it comes down to a few thousand men, a few ships. Lose that fleet, and before you have time to build a new one they are standing off your harbors, destroying the crucial yards needed to rebuild. One battle at sea, maybe two, and the issue is basically decided. Maybe in a way that is better. I've always dreaded the mass slaughter created by the weaponry I helped to build."

"Admiral Bullfinch calls it the power of a fleet in existence," Richard replied. "Says that he used to talk about it with his roommate when he was at the old Naval Academy back on earth."

"So these ships will die if they go to face the Kazan."

"They'll be sunk the moment they come into range of their guns."

She looked at Keane and Webster, who were still arguing, then turned back to Richard. "Tell me, is there a way that they can fight without having to come within range?"

As she spoke, Richard could see Adam standing behind her, ready to burst with excitement. "I think Lieutenant Rosovich has the answer to that," he replied.

ELEVEN

"What is it, Sean?"

Ashamed that she had caught him thus, he slipped out of the bed and retreated to the small veranda attached to their bedroom in the palace of Hazin.

Slipping on a light robe, Karinia came out to join him. "What's wrong?" she whispered, "I woke up, and it sounded like you were crying."

He lowered his head, covering his eyes with his hands. "Nothing," he whispered. "A bad dream, that's all."

"Tell me about it." She sat down beside him, hands lightly touching his shoulders, rubbing them.

"My mother. I dreamed she was still alive, back in Roum. She asked me why I had done what I have."

"Done what?"

"Stayed here," and he uncovered his face.

Ever so gently she touched the tears on his cheeks as if they were some strange curiosity she had never experienced before. She touched a teardrop on her fingertip to her lips.

"And my father, yelling drunkenly. Funny, that's one of the few memories I have of him from when I was a boy. Him drunk."

"Did he hit your mother?"

"No. He was never like that. A good-natured mick, they called him. He'd laugh too loudly, always with some of his friends from the army when he came to Roum. He'd give me some present, then have the servants shoo me off to bed. In the morning he'd be gone and my mother would cry for days afterward. He was with her in the dream, asking me the same thing."

"You regret staying?"

He looked over at her and forced a smile. "For you? No, of course not."

He let his fingers lightly trace the line of her jaw. His hand cupped her cheek for a second, then fell away. He stood up, leaning over the railing. Below was the main courtyard of the temple. In this, the hour before dawn, initiates of the first order, Kazan and human, were dimly visible, lying on the flagstone pavement with arms spread wide. At dusk they had drunk of the holy waters, and even now they drifted in their visions. Occasionally one would moan softly.

Guards paced back and forth between the rows. Several of the bodies were completely still, blood splattered around them, their heads neatly laid to one side. Even as he watched, one of them, caught in a horrible vision, began to stand up, crying out. He was dead within seconds, body collapsing, spraying blood. He had failed, falling victim to the inner terror. He had not learned stillness in the face of fear.

"Ghastly in its power," Sean whispered.

"The first thing you learn," Karinia replied. "Weakness is the destroyer."

He stepped back from the spectacle below, looking over at her. "My tears were weakness."

She smiled. "No. Just love." She moved into his arms. "I vaguely remember my mother," she whispered. "My father, any of our fathers, none of us know. He is simply selected, then is gone."

"Were you selected for me?" Sean asked.

She slipped from his embrace, returning to the bed, beckoning for him to follow, which he did.

As he lay down beside her, she lightly traced a fingertip across his chest. "Yes, I was selected."

He pulled back slightly and sat up.

"Don't be angry. Consider it an honor, my love. It was Hazin who told me to go to you. I obeyed, but after I met you the obedience became pleasure."

He shook his head. "It makes it seem false."

"Why? Because that is not how it is done in your old world?"

He nodded.

"Hazin wanted you for the Order. There is nothing wrong in that. If not for that, you would be dead now."

"That's not what I mean."

"What, then?"

"Arranged like that."

"Don't they do that where you come from? The Chin still arrange marriages, don't they?"

"How do you know that?"

She smiled. "I just know. Consider it an honor conferred by Hazin. You are not of us, yet he wishes your blood to be joined with us. I should have been destined for someone pure, of ten generations or more, but he chose you. That indicates his regard."

Sean looked over at her, not sure how to react. She seemed a dream of perfection, yet beneath the softness of her light olive skin, she had a strength that at times, in moments of passion, seemed capable of overwhelming him.

She was not the first woman he had been with. There had been Svetlana, one of the girls at the Roaring Mouse, and even Lavinia back in Roum, who, at age eighteen, he had at times thought of in terms far more than passion. He had made her vague promises about finishing the academy and his first tour of duty, at which point the military freed him and would allow him to marry. He wondered where Lavinia was now, if she mourned him, if she still cared or had already forgotten him with someone else.

The way I've forgotten her, he thought. He looked over at Karinia. She was different, and he wondered if in some way she was not even quite human.

Yet that was indeed what had convinced him to stay. It was not the visions given to him by Hazin, the cunning and oh so persuasive arguments of the inevitability of history on this world, or even the quest to find a Portal and thereby reach the power of the stars. No, it was the raw, primal power of this race the Kazan were breeding. They were the inevitable culmination of man, and once unleashed, nothing, and especially the Republic, with all its turmoil and teeming, foolish voices, could stand against them.

"My mother, in the dream, she said something."

"What?"

"That I was a traitor."

Karinia laughed softly. "To whom? Yourself, your country?"

He nodded.

"Rather, it is your Republic that would betray you. We understand a thousand centuries of history, Sean. This world is the old world of the Kazan, of their barbarian cousins who once rode the northern continent. From here they leapt to the stars, subjugated a hundred worlds, and then came the Great Falling, the casting down and twenty thousand years of darkness.

"The Portals are the key to everything. All were dead here, annihilated, and then the Portals somehow opened, the gate between worlds. A few came from one world, and then another. Their descendants multiplied, but understood nothing of before.

"Our race. Our race somehow was on more than one world as well."

He looked at her in surprise.

"Didn't he tell you that?"

He shook his head.

"The world your father came from, the world that those who lived under the northern hordes came from, it is the same place. Perhaps the ancients of the Kazan made a gate there, perhaps several, and took ancestors of yours from long ago. There was another Portal here, in the realm of the Kazan, that is where my blood comes from. It was this order, then, who decided to make the blood pure, to recreate us."

"I understand how," Sean said softly, almost fearfully, as if someone was listening. "I do not understand why."

"You will, when Hazin decides it. Sufficient to know that what he offers is the only alternative. Both races united, both races pure. Your Republic could never achieve that, and you know it. We are the future of this world, not the Republic."

He nodded. That he knew was true. Man against man there was no question. The Kazan, all the Hordes, were bigger and far more powerful physically, but in battle that size had its drawbacks. They moved slower, and the northern hordes lacked the technical skills. The Kazan had those skills, but when it came to lightning speed and sustained physical endurance, humans had the edge. The Shiv combined a physical presence and power that was terrifying. A power that could unite the two races to one purpose was indeed unstoppable.

"And if you could control it," she replied, again her fingertips tracing his arm and then his shoulders, "would you turn it against Hazin?"

He looked at her, wide-eyed.

"The truth."

"I am nothing to the Shiv. In battle," he paused, still shocked by what she had told him only the evening before, "in the arena that you told me about, any one of them could crush me."

"That's not what Hazin wants of you. He has a hundred thousand who can crush. They, almost all of us, are trained to nothing else. To think like your opponent, to understand them, that is what he wants from you. You can be the face that those of the Republic will see, will rally to.

"There is nothing but power. All else is meaningless. And when life ends, it ends. Thus morality is a charade to dupe the foolish."

"The god of the Shiv?" he asked.

She laughed. "A legend for the initiates, for those who need such things. Those of the inner circles know that nothing exists beyond this life. Therefore it is power, my lover, power and nothing else that matters and that drives the game of our lives." She smiled. "And that power then gives us the pleasures we desire."

He wanted to pull back from her, but even as she spoke, the look in her eyes drew him in, her touch feeling like fire.

"Do you know why your father was as he was?"

"No, I wondered that often as a child. My mother was beautiful, educated, and she loved him. He threw all that away."

"It's because he was drunk not with liquor, but with the memory of power. He commanded armies. He crushed his enemies and saw them driven before him. He knew triumph like few have ever known. And then it ended and he had nothing but memories.

"Could such a man ever settle down, sit in the corner of a room and watch the days drift into a blur, to lie with but one woman until they grew old and died? Believe me, Sean, once the elixir of power has been drunk, it will haunt you.

Forever after your life is divided between all that happened when you held it, and then all that came afterward, when each day is spent remembering rather than gazing toward what still lies ahead.

"That is what Hazin offers you. What I offer you."

"And if I turned away, would you turn away from me?" She smiled softly. "Why do you ask?"

"Because I love you," he whispered. "And fear you. Fear that you would leave me."

"Ah, so I would haunt you forever afterward. Sean O'Donald, you know how to compliment."

"And my power, what of it? Would it haunt you?"

"What you could be if you but allowed it. Hazin saw that in you and in your foolish friend."

"You are not answering the question I asked."

"Nor will I, lover. I must keep at least one secret from you." She smiled. "It is, after all, part of the game that all lovers play with each other."

He slowly nodded.

"Today you will see the Shiv in a new way. When you watch them, consider what it would mean to lead them in battle. Your father's successes will pale to insignificance when compared to what you could do."

She gently pulled him back down by her side and drew him close.

"Do you love me?" Sean asked, and he was ashamed that his voice betrayed his fears.

She kissed him gently.

"Here, at this moment when it is just the two of us alone. Yes, I do," she whispered.

The blaring of the trumpets was an annoyance Hazin was forced to accept. He just wished that they didn't have to stand directly behind the imperial box.

The fanfare echoed around the great amphitheater, the brazen call of the nargas, the war trumpets joining in. A hundred thousand came to their feet, clenched fists raised to the emperor as he came out of the shadows of the entry corridor and stepped into the light.

A thunderous cheer erupted and redoubled as he raised his hand in salute.

Hazin stood at the back of the imperial box, just behind

those of the inner blood, the eunuch chamberlains, the royal attendants of the chamber, and the chosen concubines of the moment. He preferred this spot. It allowed him to watch without being watched.

While the emperor stood, accepting the adulation of the mob, his guards stood warily to either side. One of them examined the royal chair, expert hands running across the cushions to check one last time for a hidden needle or pressure detonator. He stepped back, gave a subtle nod of approval, and the emperor sat down.

It was the day of celebration of the ascension to the throne, and since dawn the city had been a madhouse. Free food, from ten thousand human sacrifices butchered since midnight, had been distributed to the mob, and the feasting had gone on for hours. A thousand barrels of drink laced with mild doses of gava had been set up at nearly every street corner, thus inflaming the passions of all.

The crowd in the arena, the lucky hundred thousand who could cram their way in, were wild in anticipation for what was to come. The all-night revelry and now the promise of the show had stilled the few voices that had questioned the surprise announcement of a new war to be fought in the North.

Those who were to entertain stepped out from the archway beneath the emperor's box, and the cheering redoubled as they paraded around the perimeter of the arena. All of them were of the Shiv, armed with swords and a variety of exotic weapons: throwing daggers, curved scimitars, poisoned spokes, bows, even modern rifles.

The parade circled and reentered the archway. There was a moment of silent expectation, followed by a renewed roar as the first fighters came out. Stripped naked except for a loincloth, they bore the traditional short swords, which harkened back to the days long before the Shiv, when human slaves were selected to fight over the body of their master. The fallen then served as their servants in paradise.

A dozen fighters formed a circle, evenly spaced like spokes on a wheel, their blades ceremonially pointed to the center. All turned to look at the emperor, who gave a nod.

The action exploded. Several banded together, others stood alone, others turned to rush upon an opponent to the left or right. Within seconds the first man was down, clutching at his bowels as they spilled out. His victor didn't bother to deliver the coup de grace but instead raced off. Cheers went up as the wounded man, one hand holding his guts, threw his sword, catching his opponent in the back and sending him sprawling.

The knot of three who had joined together systematically maneuvered as one, taking down three men in quick succession, until they encountered two others who had banded together.

The disemboweled fighter retrieved his sword and waded into the melee, taking the leg off an opponent before falling to a decapitating blow, his death triggering scattered cries of sympathy.

The three were down to two, but in so doing had defeated the others. In an instant the last two turned on each other. The one swung a split second faster than his former companion, neatly taking his head off with a single blow. The fight had lasted barely longer than a minute.

Applause broke out. Some of the patrons rushed to the galleries below to collect their winnings from the money dealers, for each of the fighters had been numbered and bets had been placed on the order of their death or who would survive.

As ritual demanded, the lone warrior approached the box, saluted and then fell upon his own blade, choosing the slow method of cutting into his stomach rather than through the chest or throat. It took several minutes for him to die. He didn't utter a sound. His eyes gazed straight ahead, facial muscles barely twitching as he cut across his stomach, and then finally drove the blade up through his own diaphragm and into his heart.

As he collapsed, an ovation erupted. The emperor looked back over his shoulder at Hazin and nodded, a gesture all of course would see.

At the far side of the arena two more Shiv had been led out and tied to stakes. Their ordeal would, if properly conducted, last until midday. Neither cried out or even flinched as the inflictors of the Test laid out their tools, knives, pliers, pincers, and hot braziers filled with glowing coals.

One of the two set directly to work, gouging out the eye of his subject with a stilettolike blade, holding the orb up before his victim, then crushing it between his fingers. The other was more subtle, a blade heated to a glowing white, lightly flicking against bound fingertips, lips, then drawn slowly across the stomach so that the smoke curled up.

Gasps of approval echoed as the two who were bound did not move.

Hazin stood up and withdrew from the imperial box, going to the section of the arena where those of his order sat. He spotted who he wanted and sat down by his side.

O'Donald's features were pale, his eyes wide with horror.

"Do not show revulsion," Hazin whispered in English. "Do that and you will forever lose face and any hope of survival."

"Merciful God, what in hell are you people doing?" Sean gasped.

"First, there is no god, and if there was, what is happening here proves he is without mercy. It is entertainment, but also a lesson."

"Entertainment? Torturing people?"

"There are two things neither your species nor mine can resist watching. The first is the act of love, the second the act of annihilation. Curious, don't you think?"

A gasp went up from the audience. The second torturer, after long minutes of subtle play, had gone for the cruelest of cuts and now stepped back so that all could see the results. His victim lowered his head and then let out a shuddering sob of agony.

His cry triggered an eruption of loud cries of derision and jeering taunts. Even those of the Order rose to their feet, though they remained silent. Most of them turned their backs to the arena floor in a show of contempt for the victim.

The first torturer, whose victim had yet to cry out, finished his subject within seconds, driving a blade up under the jaw and straight into his brain until he slumped over. Freed from his task, he now joined his companion. The two threw themselves into a frenzy of mutilation. Their victim's shrieks were tauntingly echoed by the mob.

Sean lowered his head and gagged.

"Watch it," Hazin hissed.

Sean looked up at him, features drawn.

"Watch it."

"Why? What in hell is this?"

"It is the ritual. Those of the Shiv down there are selected to die as a demonstration of their strength, of their devotion to the emperor. Every man you saw in the parade will die this day. The question is how they will die. What you are seeing is power, O'Donald. That they face pain unflinchingly, that they go to their deaths without a murmur of complaint, is what they have been trained for. Most of them see it as an honor to die thus. They have been allowed to breed. They know their sons and daughters will be told of their glory, and thus the next generation is strengthened yet more."

The shrieking of the dying man was all but drowned out by the cries of derision from the crowd.

"That one's children, however, will have their throats cut within the hour, and his consort will be the one who does it. His seed will be extinguished, his immortality denied. Listen to his cries of pain, O'Donald. That is the real agony, not what they are doing to his flesh, but rather what they are doing to his soul. He let weakness show just for an instant, and his soul is now condemned forever."

Sean looked at him wide-eyed, and Hazin smiled.

"And yet you just said there is no God," O'Donald whispered.

"I know that, I have allowed you to know that, but the lower orders? I give them something to believe in, to die for. I cannot lead a holy war and promise nothing to those who die. Instead, I want them to rush to their deaths gladly, believing, as the others who just died down there believed, that it is but a flicker of pain that will be followed by the fulfillment of every desire imagined, forever. The garden, O'Donald, that is the pleasure they aspire to.

"Imagine such power. What could a hundred thousand of these men, believing that, do against anything the Republic could put in the field?

"It is too bad your friend Cromwell fled. I must admit that I actually liked him. He did not quite have your frightfully cold intellect. Instead, it was his spirit, to lead, to fight, which appealed to me. If I could have but convinced him, what a commander he might have made."

Even as the torture continued, another act came forward, a demonstration of poisons. Subjects were tied to stakes, and a priest of the third order cut each man with a dagger.

Leather-voiced announcers explained to the audience the type of poison on each blade, its effects, the pain produced. Some were poisons that acted quickly, the victims barely convulsing before gone. Others were poisons of vengeance, designed to produce unspeakable agony and dread. The crowd watched fascinated, as one of the victims writhed convulsively, white foam dripping from his mouth.

Hazin could see that O'Donald was slowly being drawn in, repulsed and yet fascinated, unable to look away no matter how he wished to. He knew as well that though the crowd was fascinated, they were also terrified, for such poisons were known to be reserved for special enemies of the Order. The captain of Yasim's guard of the Green Gate had tasted one just last night, for Hazin's original decision to be merciful had been replaced with one that inflicted several hours of agony before death.

"The writer Vasiva described these games five hundred years ago," Hazin whispered, drawing closer to O'Donald, putting a reassuring hand on his shoulder. "He wrote of a man of supposed virtue by the name of Sutona, of the school of self-deniers, who believed that pleasure must be controlled and moderated, and who denounced these spectacles. Vasiva challenged him, declaring that this supposed man of virtue was a hypocrite, for he denounced that which he had never seen. Sutona went to the spectacle with Vasiva, and do you know what happened?"

O'Donald looked away from the dying man and slowly nodded.

Hazin smiled. "Yes. He became addicted. Within the hour he was racing to the money changers to make his bets, and he lost all his fortune by the end of the day."

Hazin laughed and shook his head. "Understand it without passion, without judging, with the realism to see into the hearts of your race and mine, O'Donald, and to thus see them for what they truly are. But do not let it control you. That is the secret."

He could see that the gava that Karinia had dosed O'Donald's morning meal with was taking effect. His eyes were becoming glazed, breath coming more rapidly. The drug was seductive, subtle. The receiver was never really aware of its onset.

Even as he spoke, O'Donald's gaze was drifting away

from Hazin, looking back at the show. The man being tortured with knives and hot irons had dissolved into incoherent babbling. The crowd, growing bored with the mewing cries, were taunting the torturers now.

From under the emperor's arch more combatants emerged. These were matched pairs, fighting with identical weapons in tests of skill and cunning. Though all the fighters moved with lightning-like speed, the crowd fixated on one pair in particular. Both of them were armed with two razor-sharp double-edged blades, which were indistinct blurs, flashing in the sunlight as they danced, weaved, parried, and thrusted.

Two others fought barehanded, coming together for an instant, slashing blows exchanging, then leaping apart, warily circling before closing again. Karinia, who sat on the other side of O'Donald, was lightly toying with him, brushing his hair, kissing him on the cheek, whispering something, and he smiled, nodding, his attention still fixed on the fights, drawing in his breath when one of the knife fighters made a cunning backhanded sweep, cutting his opponent's throat. The dying man, however, leapt forward, even as blood fountained like a geyser, driving his blade into his opponent's chest. The mob erupted with a roar of approval for the double kill. Both of the men drew apart and amazingly stood erect, struggling to bow to the emperor before they collapsed. Their gesture brought the crowd to its feet in an ovation.

The last of the matched pair died. This bare-handed fighter had broken the back of his opponent, leaving him to thrash about. Picking up a blade from the knife fighters, he then disemboweled himself.

O'Donald rose to his feet, mouth open.

"Watch what comes next," Hazin whispered. "It is a more practical demonstration.

A line of men, dressed in the black battle fatigues of the Shiv, rushed out from under the arch, carrying no weapon other than bayonets. From another archway at the east end of the arena a team of two men came out carrying between them a gatling gun mounted on a tripod. They were not wearing the black uniform of the Order, but instead were dressed in the blue jacket and khaki of the Republic. They set their weapon in place as the twenty fighters went to the west end

of the arena and spread out into a line. Those in the stands
behind them scattered in every direction, jumping into en-
tryways, fleeing like a receding wave. Roars of laughter
erupted from the rest of the crowd. In front of the emper-
or's box, guards set up what appeared to be heavy sheets
of glass, slipping them into place around the imperial chair.

The twenty saluted, holding bayonets high. Out in the
middle of the arena, the torturers and the poisoners took
off, running for cover.

The gatling opened up. The twenty rushed forward with
a wild cry: "Shiv! Shiv! Shiv!"

They had gone barely a dozen feet before the first was
bowled over, the gunners swinging their piece, to try and
stitch up the line. The men around the first to fall went
down, hugging the packed sand. Others farther out continued their rush.

The gunners quickly shifted, catching several on the left
flank. A few high rounds plowed into the stands above them,
triggering pandemonium. Those in the middle were already
back on their feet, one of them picking up the body of the
first fallen, holding it in front like a shield even as he ran.

The gunners desperately played their fire back and forth.
But as they focused on one flank, the other flank, or the
middle, sprang up, crouching low, sprinting forward. Three
made a desperate rush, racing along the edge of the wall
under the emperor's box and then straight in while the
gunners tried to finish off the other flank.

O'Donald, still standing, began to shout, cheering the attackers on. At the very last instant the gunner swung his
barrel around, dropping all but the last man, who had been
running behind the other two. He leapt over the fallen even
as he was hit, and flung himself onto the gun, knocking it
over. The assistant gunner, with drawn revolver, shot the
man in the head. But the gun was momentarily down.

The surviving attackers charged forward with wild cries.
The gunner and his assistant struggled to right the piece.
The distance closed, only feet separating the lead attacker
from the gun.

The gatling stuttered to life, slicing across the closest
man. He staggered, came to a stop, and then stood there
for several long seconds, legs braced to the ground like oak

trees, shuddering, flinching as each round hit, but continuing to absorb the blows.

The assistant gunner stepped around to one side, leveling his revolver, putting a round straight into the man's head. The bullet finally caused him to collapse, but it was too late. The half dozen survivors surged at them, the next man in carrying the body of a comrade as a shield.

The assistant gunner emptied his weapon, dropping two more while the gunner continued to fire, rounds exploding into the shield of flesh. The attacker closed, flinging the body onto the gun, knocking it over again. The final rounds arced up into the audience as the gun fell, and then he was in with bayonet held high.

The arena roared in a mad frenzy, and O'Donald was part of the insanity, the lust for blood and for killing, screaming as bayonets flashed, rose and fell, rose and fell.

A lone attacker staggered to his feet, holding a bloody knife aloft, and even those of the Order erupted into applause.

"Who were you cheering for?" Karinia asked, still hanging on O'Donald's arm.

Sean, eyes glazed, look over at her. "For those who would win," he said, voice choked.

Hazin left him, drifting back down to the imperial box. The emperor was on his feet, hand held up in salute as the lone survivor, gasping for breath, stepped to the middle of the arena. The man held his blade aloft in salute and in a gesture so rare as to be remembered years afterward, the emperor extended his hand, palm up, a sign that the man was not to take his life.

"You will need such leaders when this is for real," the emperor said, looking over at Hazin.

Hazin said nothing, sensing yet again the game within the game. It was he, after all, as the Grand Master, who selected those who were to be sacrificed on the sand. The survivor had been one loyal to the last Grand Master. Now he held a potential that was unknown, a supporter of an opponent whose name would be spoken of throughout the city this night, who would be greeted by his brothers as one returned from the dead in glory. He was *fetahid,* one who has returned, and to try and take him another way would be folly.

There would be time enough later, Hazin thought, wondering which of his rivals within the Order would see this human as a possible tool to be turned to advantage.

The battle was the climax of the morning's show. Next would come the tedious routine of executions of criminals of Kazan blood, something the baser elements of the crowd enjoyed, especially when a notorious case was at last brought to justice, but nowhere near as exciting as watching humans slaughter one another.

The counters of the dead were busy at work, dragging the bodies off, down through the northern gate, the gate of the dead. Below, the bidders waited. The more dramatic the death, the higher the price would go, the winners dragging off their prizes as a trophy of prestige for the evening's feast.

The emperor, yawning, a display to indicate his boredom with the tedious bloodletting to come, stood up and left his box. He motioned for Hazin to follow.

Withdrawing under the shadow of the entry arch, the emperor followed his guards down the corridor and turned into a private chamber, a comfortable hideaway where the imperial presence could relax or amuse himself. The guards closed the door behind them.

"Quite a show. Who was the human that survived?"

"Just one of my Shiv. A commander of a thousand."

"Hmm, seems a waste to throw such training and skill into the arena. Any particular reason?"

"A hundred are chosen to die each month, and all volunteer for the honor."

"Still, I do wonder how it is they are chosen."

Hazin smiled, but was silent.

"A good way to cleanse. No matter what you claim of your breeding and training, surely they must desire to live."

"Those that desire it too much find themselves on the sand," Hazin replied. "It is a lesson for all to ponder. Even you and I shall face that someday."

The emperor, who had pouring himself a drink, turned, obviously wondering what was the veiled meaning of Hazin's words.

"Nothing intended, Your Highness. Just an observation."

"I've been meaning to ask you about the escape."

"Escape of whom?"

"The captured human. How did it happen?"

Sooner or later he knew that an imperial spy would find out. Cromwell had flown low over the harbor. The plane had to have been spotted and questions raised.

"As all escapes do. He found an opportunity and fled. Those who were at fault paid. You watched several of them die today, those tied to the posts for poisonings."

"So all of them have been punished."

"But of course."

"Hmm." He sipped his drink, eyes half closed, warily gazing at Hazin. "I take it all is in readiness for departure."

Hazin nodded. "You should know that from your fleet commanders. All ships of the Red Banner designated for the attack are to sail within seven days. The assault transports for the Shiv will follow a day later. Fifty thousand men. As long as your ships fulfill their tasks, in three weeks the Shiv will land on the Bantag coast. One umen will support the assault on their main port, called Constantine. Eight supply ships will carry additional arms for the Bantag.

"I am not comfortable with committing my land cruisers to that attack. It leaves my reserves here dangerously thin."

"From what threat, sire? Any potential rival sees what can be gained there. The fiefdoms carved out will be vaster than all of Kazan. Why run the risk of engaging in a fight against you when such power and wealth can be had simply for going along with this attack?"

The emperor put down his drink and drew closer to Hazin. "What is your game, Grand Master?"

"Sire?"

The emperor smiled. "There is a game within this game. Your arguments for attacking the Republic are simple enough on the surface. They are a growing threat, and it is better to slay the cub in its cradle than wait for it to be full-grown. The wealth in resources to be taken, the diversion of my fractious cousins, all of it seems simple enough, but with you there has to be more."

"I have all I desire already, sire. You ensured that when you supported me against the last Grand Master, who threatened both of us. There is nothing else."

"I find that hard to believe."

Hazin stiffened, stepping back a pace. He stared straight into the emperor's eyes, and the imperial gaze dropped.

"Do not interpret what I said the wrong way, Grand Master."

"Of course not, Your Highness. I never interpret anything the wrong way."

There was a moment of awkward silence.

"I assume you are going with this expedition."

"Sire?"

"Just that. It is, after all, the greatest effort in the field your order has attempted. I assumed you were going."

Hazin was silent.

"In fact, as your emperor, I order it. Admiral Biza has already been informed to that effect."

"I see."

The emperor smiled.

"An honor I did not expect, to be requested to journey with you for this campaign."

"Of course not, but you shall find it amusing."

Hazin started to turn away, not bothering to wait for a formal dismissal, and then he looked back over his shoulder.

"The poisoning show was most interesting today, wasn't it? The third man on the right, the one whose face turned black as he swallowed his own tongue in convulsions, I designed that myself. It is remarkable stuff—tasteless, odorless. A dozen drops kill almost at once, but only three or four drops are far more interesting."

He said the words coldly, impressing upon this rival the knowledge that if anything should befall him, one of his order would find a way to get through all the guards, all the precautions, and gain revenge.

Without waiting for a reply he slammed the door shut, leaving the emperor alone with his fears.

TWELVE

Exhausted, legs so numb from yet another day of riding that he could barely stand, Abraham Keane came to attention and saluted.

"Lieutenant Keane reporting, sir."

Vincent Hawthorne, smiling, returned the salute, and

nodded for Abe to take a camp chair by the fire. Vincent absently poked the coals, then leaned back, drawing a puff on his cigar, and exhaled.

"Son, I'm heading on back to headquarters tomorrow. Though I would prefer if you stayed with my command, I can't deny your request for a field assignment, so you'll stay with the 3rd, A Troop."

Abe nodded his thanks. It was a choice assignment, the scout company.

"We're not escorting you back to Fort Malady?"

Vincent shook his head. "I'm taking that flyer that circled in. I'm expected all the way back in Suzdal. The 3rd, however, has been ordered to turn back around and shadow the Bantag. Ten regiments of cavalry are being deployed from their forts. You're going straight back to where we were a week ago, then continue to push southeast."

Abe said nothing. Ten regiments meant ten thousand men, but if it turned into a fight they'd be outnumbered twenty to one.

"Gatling companies are going out with each, so that should beef your strength up a bit, and two squadrons of aerosteamers will be flying patrols. Land ironclad units are being sent up as well."

"Two squadrons? That's only twenty-four planes, sir."

"I know. Your father has something else in mind for the rest of the Aerosteamer Corps."

Abe knew better than to ask, but his curiosity was aroused.

"We finally got a flyer report yesterday afternoon that Bantag encampments all along the western frontier were packing up. This morning the flyer returned to report that the main encampment was empty, having already moved a dozen miles to the southeast."

"Could they just be following the herd of mammoths or bison? They're still inside their own territory," Abe said hopefully.

Vincent shook his head.

"No, I don't think so. Jurak knows well enough what the warning implied. Either he is doing it now to see what will happen, or something was already planned long ago and is now taking place."

"I could sense that," Abe replied sadly. "The message, it

was no real surprise, almost as if we are all moving toward something inevitable."

"Get some rest, you'll move out at first light tomorrow. Kind of absurd, I know. It's a demonstration, Abe. A couple of days after we cross back into their territory, Jurak will have word that we are in pursuit. I just hope it convinces him of our resolve, but I doubt it. Once inside their territory again, expect a fight."

Vincent meditatively puffed on his cigar for a moment and spat.

"Perhaps this isn't the time or place to say it. The 3rd is a damn good regiment. It was formed during the Great War and still has a few of the old vets in it. A couple of the officers on top, though, can be a bit headstrong, and they are contemptuous of the Bantag."

Vincent felt uncomfortable with the commander of the army sharing such information.

"You're just a green lieutenant still fresh out of the academy, but I've watched you over the last month, and you're a good officer. That's why I put you with the A Troop of the 3rd. You'll command it. Both the captain and first lieutenant are down with dysentery."

Abe nodded. It had swept through the regiment on the way back from their assignment and dozens of men were down with it, two having died. It was a common enough complaint in the cavalry.

"Shouldn't someone of higher rank command A Troop?" Abe asked.

"It's not a favor to your old man. It's simply because I think it's the right assignment for you now. Give you some experience. The troop's got a good NCO. Trust that Sergeant Togo, he's a good man. He'll play along with letting you be the officer, but if he nods to the right, turn right and the hell with protocol. Sergeant Major Mutaka is one of General Ketswana's old Zulu comrades from the war. He's one of the best in the army, and he'll keep an eye on you as well."

Abe started to ask if his father knew that he was being transferred, but then realized that he most likely did not.

"I know your itch, I had it, too. I hope it doesn't get scratched too hard, though, the way mine did."

He looked over, silent for a moment.

"This advance by the cavalry, call it bait, son. Jurak might just stop, turn around, and act like nothing happened at all. Then we'll withdraw. If Jurak turns and fights, we have a clear cause of war the public will accept. I think he'll leave a rear guard to slow us down, but will keep on moving southeast to the coast."

"It's the Kazan, then. Isn't it?"

Hawthorne nodded. "Keep safe, Lieutenant. I gave you what you wanted. Just don't make us both come to regret it."

"You have your orders, Mr. Cromwell. Are there any questions?"

"No, sir."

Richard, clutching the heavy, locked briefcase, sealed with a presidential stamp, waited to be dismissed. Andrew hesitated, looking down at the map spread out on the conference table in his office.

"It's so damn vague," Andrew said as his finger traced a line out from Constantine and into the Southern Sea. "Here be dragons and unknown lands."

"Sir?"

"Old maps on Earth. When they didn't know what was out there, that's what they used to write in the blank spaces. It's a vast blank space once past the Cretan Isles. We never should have made that agreement to venture no farther. We wasted fifteen precious years."

He let his finger run along the line that Cromwell had flown, a full thousand miles farther toward Kazan.

"If what Hazin told you is true, they could be off our coast inside of three weeks."

"I'd make it at least a month, sir. They have to conserve fuel. An armada that size will go only as fast as the slowest ships."

"I understand your reasoning, but I have to assume the worst."

"Yes, sir."

"Mr. Cromwell, concerning your mission . . ."

"I volunteered the moment it was discussed," Richard replied evenly.

"I know. I know the whole routine about honor, duty." He paused, his hand absently rubbing the empty sleeve.

"Frankly, I'd prefer if you stayed with Bullfinch. There's a place with his staff if you want it."

Richard smiled. "I'm the one most qualified to scout."

"Just because you saw their ships once, at night, and flew one of their airships. I don't see those as deciding factors for who flies scouting missions. To be blunt, I don't want to lose you. I'll need men like you. Second, well, there is the political issue."

"You mean getting rid of me might be read by some as a message?"

Andrew shook his head. "Damn, I never wanted to get into politics. Being a colonel was straightforward. Even commanding an army in a losing war was easier."

He turned away and started to pace.

Rumors of what was happening had finally broke. Yet again a senator with a mouth too big and a few too many drinks had spilled the news to some friends in a tavern. From there it had exploded across the city that the mobilization for maneuvers was actually a front for war with the Bantags and that Hawthorne was already leading a punitive expedition into their territory.

Once that news broke, another senator, figuring everything was out in the open, had told the rest to some of his in-laws who had major interests in the market, and thus would profit immensely if a new naval appropriations bill was run through. The insiders made their buys the following morning, then quietly let the other shoe fall. By noon the issue was finally raised by a Chin congresswoman on the House floor, and by dusk it was a firestorm, fluctuating between war hysteria, terrified panic, and renewed rumors of secession.

"We couldn't have kept it quiet much longer anyhow. What we were doing to the three armored cruisers and five frigates was already drawing notice. I had hoped to keep a lid on it, though, until we had something absolutely positive. Some will whine that I provoked this war as a means of reunifying the country. A lot of questions will be asked tonight at the joint session about why the *Gettysburg* was beyond the treaty limits."

Standing by the windowsill, he lightly tapped his clenched fist against the frame while looking down on the crowds milling about in the square. A few protesters had shown up earlier, claiming that the entire crisis was a hoax, one sign proclaiming CROMWELL, TRAITOR BEFORE, TRAITOR AGAIN! An angry crowd of sailors on leave had set upon them, and it had taken half the constabulary force of the city to quell the disturbance.

Several people on the plaza, recognizing Andrew in the window, began to shout, and he drew back, shaking his head and pulling the curtains shut.

"I wonder how many days Lincoln had like this," he sighed. He fixed his attention back on Richard, as if the commander had just suddenly materialized in the room.

"Yes, Mr. Cromwell. Please consider what I just said."

"I think it would be best all the way around, sir, if I followed through on what I volunteered for."

"A statement, is it?"

"Yes, sir."

"All right. I know what it means to you."

"Thank you, sir."

Andrew took his head. "Son, I think in a month's time this Republic will be in the most desperate struggle it has yet faced. This foe, unlike the old Hordes, is far more insidious, far more seductive, and thus far more treacherous. The Hordes, no matter how hateful their practices, were warriors of honor in their own right. Jurak added a new element, though still honorable in his attempt to split us politically. The message of this Hazin, however, will appeal to far too many. But beneath it, there is a cruelty unimagined."

"Yes, sir. I knew that from the beginning. I only wish O'Donald had seen it as well before he was trapped."

Andrew nodded sadly. "Stay alive, Cromwell. This might drag out for years, and I'll need you." Andrew let go of his hand.

Saluting, Richard left the room, briefcase clutched tightly in his hand.

Andrew, watching him leave, could only shake his head in weariness and then returned to the preparation of his speech before Congress, asking for a full mobilization to war.

"Did you see the copy of the president's speech last night?" Flight Lieutenant Adam Rosovich asked, looking over at the chief engineer from Republic Aerosteamer Company.

Theodor nodded. "Hard to see how anyone could argue against it. Hell, he laid it out clearly enough. These Kazan are insane, and they are coming this way. We have to fight."

A sharp, steady breeze whipped the two as they walked across the plank deck as the armored cruiser *Shiloh* came up to full speed. This was its first test run. Men scrambled around the two. An engineer came up to Theodor and pointed to the single smokestack, which had been shifted from center line to the starboard side.

"That thing is leaking like a sieve. The fittings below deck are a mess, sir," he shouted.

Theodor smiled and simply nodded. "We can fix it later. The purpose now is to see if this damned idea really works. Then we turn around and head back to Suzdal."

The engineer shook his head wearily and walked away, shouting oaths at several crew members who had stopped to gawk at the spectacle that was about to take place.

Adam approached his airship, a brand-new single engine Falcon. The engine was already ticking over, propeller a slow-moving blur. The crew chief, in the cockpit, scrambled out as Adam approached, and saluted.

"Everything ready, sir. Engine temperature at two hundred and forty, I've revved her up to twelve hundred, all controls checked. Just remember, sir, she's got no ammunition on board and only ten gallons of fuel, so she'll settle in real light."

Adam smiled, nodding his thanks. His chief, an old Roum aristocrat who had joined the air corps because he was fascinated with aviation, was obviously delighted that his young pilot had been selected for this first experimental flight.

"Just bring her in nice and steady now, sir," Quintus continued, a bit nervous. "Remember that you're trailing that ugly-looking hook. Just let it catch."

"Quintus, leave the boy alone. He's already practiced this on land half a dozen times," Theodor shouted, his own tension ready to explode.

The two fell into an argument, Quintus though a sergeant, still maintained a certain bearing of nobility and refused to be disciplined by anyone, even the chief designer for the Republic's entire air fleet.

Adam ignored the two, gave his machine a quick walk around, and then climbed up into the cab positioned just forward of the propeller.

The Falcon, the latest model to come out of the Republic's design shop, had a curious twin boom fuselage that swept to either side of the prop, with rudder and elevators aft. Its bi-wings were sleek, canted back at a ten degree angle, missing the tangle of support wires, which had been replaced by single vertical support booms out near each wing tip.

Adam pulled down his goggles, slipped his feet up against the rudder pedals, and looked down at Quintus, who broke off from the argument in mid-sentence and gave a thumbs-up. Adam swung the rudder back and forth, then checked the elevator control by pulling the stick back and then forward, and finally the ailerons.

He revved up the throttle, watching the temperature gauge, which dropped slightly then held steady. The new revolutions per minute gauge ticked up over a thousand. It felt like the machine was about to surge forward with a jolt. The only thing holding it in place were the wheel clocks and tie-downs.

He edged the engine back down and gave a thumbs-up in reply.

The launch crew, urged on by Quintus, scrambled around the plane, freed the wheels, and released the tie-down straps. With two men holding each wingtip, Adam gingerly edged the throttle back up, slowly letting the plane roll forward.

He caught a glimpse of Theodor holding both hands over his head, clenching them together in a victory salute, and then he focused his attention forward.

Shiloh was up to full speed at fifteen knots. Over the last week a crew of half a thousand men had hurriedly covered over the entire topdeck with wooden planking, while shifting the exhaust stack to one side, then built a small wooden bridge forward of the stack. It was, without a doubt, the strangest ship Adam had ever seen, designed for one purpose only, to carry and launch aerosteamers, not just two as were now carried on the armored cruisers for scouting purposes, but twenty Falcons and two-engined Goliaths.

The President had cut through all the years of debate with a direct order: convert the three armored cruisers to aerosteamer carriers and have them ready to fight within a fortnight. His argument was straightforward and simple. If the report about the Kazan battle cruisers was true, the armored cruisers of the Republic were obsolete and to continue building them was a waste. Besides, the change over to a plank decking on the hulls was far simpler than the two months of fitting out that would be required to install the guns and other equipment for the three cruisers.

Admiral Petronius, who was slated to command the new flotilla of cruisers, had resigned in protest, but his resignation was refused by the president, who ordered him to take command regardless of his personal feelings. Adam looked up at the bridge and saw Petronius's baleful gaze, and he wondered if the admiral was praying to his pagan gods for him to crash on takeoff.

Just forward of the small wooden control tower the launch crew stopped and at Quintus's command stepped back. Adam looked down at Quintus, who was gazing at the ship commander's bridge. He wasn't really sure what to do next and decided it was best to salute. The admiral returned the salute.

Adam settled back in his seat and slammed the throttle forward. The engine seemed to hesitate for a second, RPMs suddenly began to climb and the Falcon ever so slowly began to roll forward. With only a hundred and fifty feet of deck, the takeoff distance seemed impossibly short.

There had been talk of putting steam catapults forward, but there simply wasn't enough time to rig them up. The engineering crew would have to work on the conversion after the ship had sailed. Adam wondered if all the mad haste was going to cost him his life in the next ten seconds.

The Falcon continued to build speed. The edge of the launch deck was only feet ahead as he pulled back on the elevator . . . and nothing happened.

Once over the edge, the rumbling of the wheels on the rough wooden deck stopped. In the strange silence, the aerosteamer began to fall. Instantly he reversed controls, pushing the stick forward. He had forty feet to drop, the cruiser had been moving at fifteen knots, the wind had been light but steady at just under five knots. All he needed was another fifteen knots to hit minimum flight speed.

He waited to the very last second as the Falcon drove toward the water. He pulled back and it leveled out, wings holding him aloft; so close that the wheels actually skimmed the water. Heart pounding, he lifted up half a dozen feet and let her build up speed.

He flew on straight for half a mile, letting his speed build up to sixty knots, then eased back on the stick. Putting in a touch of airelon, he brought the Falcon slowly upward in a banking turn. Looking over his left shoulder, he could see the cruiser and the antlike figures scrambling on the deck.

He laughed with childlike delight. If ever he'd felt totally alive, this was the moment. Being the first to try this mad scheme, to be soaring alone into the heavens, the world drifting away beneath his wings.

Climbing through a one hundred eighty degree turn, he leveled out, setting altitude at three hundred feet. In less than a minute the *Shiloh* was off his port wing a half mile away.

Ungainly and strange as it looked, to him the carrier was a beautiful sight. Such a vessel had been discussed in advanced design school, but never had anyone attempted to make one. Admiral Bullfinch and so many others on the Design Board had firmly blocked it, claiming it was a total waste of effort. Aerosteamers were scout planes, and all that was needed was one or two float planes on a cruiser.

Well, all that debate was gone forever, and he was ecstatic to be the one to prove it. If he'd crashed, the scheme would have been canceled, and Petronius would have gotten his old tub back.

Adam grinned, not today, dear sir, not today.

A mile aft of the *Shiloh* he began his slow banking turn. Nothing fancy, though he knew he could put the Falcon up on its wing and still maintain control. The Falcon was the first aerosteamer ever to be rolled and looped, at least deliberately, and still hold together, but for today, it was slow, gentle, and steady flying.

He came out of his turn at two hundred feet and lined up straight on the landing deck. He felt a momentary ripple of fear. The damned thing looked so impossibly small, just three hundred fifty feet long and thirty-five wide. He was glad he was trying this first with a Falcon rather than a Goliath. With its fifty-foot wing span, a pilot would have to land off center to the port side in order to avoid clipping the bridge.

Concentrate! . . he screamed at himself. This wasn't quite as easy as he had boasted it would be. Lining up on the fantail of the ship, he closed in. Then he watched his target slip ahead. He'd forgotten for a second that the place where he wanted to land was steadily moving forward at over twenty feet a second.

He raised his nose slightly, edged in another hundred RPMs, saw that he was coming in a bit high, and dropped the RPMs back down again. Right hand on the throttle, he gripped the control stick tightly. One of the things he liked about the new Falcon was that just before stalling there'd be a slight shudder on the stick from the airflow breaking up over the wings.

He edged the nose higher, the plane dropping as it lost flying speed. Watching from the corner of his eye, he saw the creamy wake rolling away from the ship, then the edge of the landing deck. He cut the throttle back, felt the shudder on the stick. The metal wheels hit the deck with a clattering shriek. Panic flashed through him as the nose dropped. It seemed that he was racing straight at the bridge. Then, with a snap, he was jerked to a stop. The tail hook had snagged the cables laid across the deck, which were weighted down with sandbags.

He chopped the throttle back completely. As he pulled off his helmet and goggles, he was suddenly aware that he was sweating profusely.

He unstrapped the safety harness, stood up, climbed out of the cockpit, and dropped to the deck. Instantly he was surrounded by a shouting, joyous mob—engineers from the design team, Theodor leading the way, Quintus and the launch crew swarming in around him. He caught a glimpse of the admiral up on the bridge, who, though looking a bit glum, formally saluted.

"What do the Yankees say?" Adam laughed. "A piece of cake. Now let's try the Goliath."

He tried to walk, but suddenly his knees felt like jelly,

and he had to sit down. The crowd around him broke into appreciative laughs.

Theodor shooed them back and took a seat beside him. "How does it feel to be the first man to take off and land on an aerosteamer carrier?"

"A what?"

"That's what we're calling them. Aerosteamer carriers."

Adam smiled, afraid to speak, the sudden surge of fear still holding him. So much could have gone wrong. He should have simply fallen over the edge of the deck and then drowned. He could have come in too high and slammed into the bridge, or too low and crashed against the fantail. What sounded so easy in late-night arguments, or when first tested only a week ago on a regular landing strip, now seemed little short of insane.

"Scared?" Theodor asked.

Adam smiled, shook his head, then, looking into Theodor's eyes, he slowly nodded in agreement.

"I was petrified every time I went up," Theodor said. "Flew eighty-two missions during the war and afterward and near peed myself on every one. In fact, if I remember correctly, I did pee myself when we started to burn and crashed at Hispania. Nothing to be ashamed of."

"It's not as easy as we boasted it would be," Adam whispered.

"I know, I could see that. If we don't have fifteen or more knots of wind, it'll damn near be suicide unless we get those catapults in place."

Theodor sighed.

"The president wants these three ships ready to sail within the week. We've got to train sixty pilots to do this, and then"—he hesitated—"and then fly straight into their fleet and attack."

He looked back at Adam.

"We'll bring the Goliath up from below. Do you feel up to trying it, or should we call it a day?"

Adam smiled. "No problem. Let's get it done."

Theodor clapped him on the shoulder. "Take a break, son. It'll be a half an hour or more before we have it topside and ready to fly."

Adam refused Theodor's help as he stood up and walked toward the bridge. He smiled again as dozens of men surrounded him, shouting congratulations and slapping him on the back. He waved good-naturedly, a bit of a swagger in his walk, reached the edge of the wooden top deck, found a ladder, and scrambled down to the main deck below.

What had once been intended as the main deck upon which the superstructure, turrets, and mounts for the three masts were to be placed had been covered over with yet more planking. The flight deck, twenty feet above, ran the entire length of the ship, vertical support beams to hold the deck hastily bolted into place. What was now the lower deck acted as the storage and maintenance deck, which would be filled with aerosteamers, their munitions, and supplies. It was presently occupied by a lone, Goliath twin-engine plane, wings folded in, rudder detached.

A steam whistle sounded, the alert signal that the ramp was about to be lowered. The deck overhead just forward of the fantail suddenly opened, powered by half a hundred men on pulleys. The hinged deck ponderously dropped down to form a ramp to the lower main deck.

A crew scrambled around the Goliath, hooking a hoist cable to the nose. Topside, fifty men began to pull, and ever so slowly the ungainly-looking aerosteamer rolled up the thirty-degree incline, crew chiefs shouting orders.

As Adam watched, the entire show seemed somehow unreal—and also far too slow. It might work here, on the calm Inland Sea, with no enemy in sight, but a better way would have to be found. A ship would have to be designed from the keel up for this job. But for now this was all they had, and in thirty minutes he was going to have to fly that thing, bring it back, and land it.

Turning, he rushed to the railing, leaned over, and vomited.

It all seemed like a dream.

Sean O'Donald stood on the foredeck of *Ulgana,* the Kazan ship of the line named after the third keeper of the underworld. Looking aft, he was awed by the sight, the sense of power the ship conveyed. Its three forward turrets, each carrying a massive ten-inch gun, barrels raised to maximum elevation, were pointing broadside to starboard in salute as they passed the emperor. The entire starboard railing, from

bow to stern, was lined with the crew, clenched fists raised
in salute.

His view of the emperor's flagship was blocked by the
massive bulk of the Kazan sailors, and he turned away,
attention turning to the harbor. Over a hundred transport
ships filled the great bay. Since the day before yesterday,
five umens of the Shiv, three legions of imperial troops, a
full division of land cruisers, and another of heavy artillery
had been loading up, and the ships were starting to weigh
anchor, ready to fall in astern of the main battle line, com-
prised of eight main battleships like *Ulgana,* a dozen heavy
cruisers, and more than twenty frigates.

Even the lightest frigate would be a match for anything
the Republic could put to sea, and that realization chilled
what little doubt still lingered in his heart.

Am I really a traitor as Cromwell said? he wondered.

He could see Hazin up on the bridge, rendering the
proper ceremonial salute as they passed the emperor.

So unlike anything I ever imagined of their race, he
thought. Always my father called them beasties; barbarians
fit only for extinction. Yet in the brief time he had spent
among them, he had seen things never imagined.

Suzdal, even Roum, when compared to the glittering capital city, were but stink holes. Smoke-belching factories surrounded Suzdal, sometimes blackening the sky even at
midday, and Roum was but a shadow of her former glory,
a fair part of it still in ruins from the Great War.

Even the poorest of Kazan lived better than many in
Suzdal. None were left to starve. Food and shelter were
given by the emperor, and entertainment provided. While
in Suzdal many still worked twelve-hour days in stygian
darkness in the mines or choking in the great foundries.

Even the entertainment now intrigued him, a demonstration of remorseless courage unlike anything he had ever
imagined. If that was how the Shiv performed in battle,
nothing, not even all the veterans of the legendary 35th
Maine, could stand up to them.

They were the future, he realized, not the grasping of
the Republic, which seemed so divided against itself, which
pitted rich against poor, state against state, all a mad babble
of voices, led by men like his father who bellowed and
drank. There was no elegance, no culture, no unity of pur-

pose, and that was what truly intrigued him, the single mind that could control all and offer a dream of the future.

In a month's time the fleet of the Republic would be gone, swept away in its first encounter, and for that he felt true regret. Though he no longer loved what he had once served, nevertheless he had taken an oath and more than one friend would be on those ships.

But, as Hazin said, the price of power, the price of glory, must be paid in blood.

Once defeated, once the Shiv and the imperial umens had landed on the Bantag coast and Constantine pounded into surrender, the Republic would disintegrate. The internal bickering, the pulling to different goals, the resentment of south to north and frontier to the settled west, would ensure that.

What Hazin offered, though, and what had been the factor that had captivated him, was a final ending to the divisions.

Hazin held out a dream, of human and nonhuman united in one empire, which the Republic could never achieve. That was his reason for being here now, he realized. It was not Karinia, though she had opened the door. It was the dream of a final ending without total annihilation of one or the other.

Once achieved, the secrets of the Portals could at last be explored, revealed, and opened. Then everyone would see the truth behind the Order and all that it promised. An escape from this mad world, a quest to places undreamed and, if need be, to conquer them.

He knew that even now his thoughts were still laced with drugs that coursed through his soul, altering his dreams, shaping his every wakeful moment, but he did not care. He felt liberated by the joy of the moment, the unity of purpose, the chanting of the emperor's name, the great power of the ship he rode that, alone, could crush any who resisted.

Facing back to the bridge, he saw Hazin and raised his clenched fist in salute. To his amazement, Hazin turned, smiled, and returned the salute, a gesture that brought tears to his eyes.

THIRTEEN

"Well, Commander Cromwell, all this fuss and excitement simply because we fished you out of the water."

Still standing at attention, Richard figured it was best not to reply. He stepped forward and laid the briefcase on Admiral Bullfinch's desk.

"Do you know what's in here?" Bullfinch asked.

"Sir, the presidential seal is intact."

"Damn it, man, I can see that. But you must have a sense of what the hell it is they are doing up there in Suzdal."

"I attended several meetings, sir, if that's what you mean."

"Relax, Cromwell. I told you to be my eyes up there, I want to know."

Richard took the word *relax* to mean that he could stand at ease, and he did so.

Bullfinch leaned back in his chair, looked appraisingly at Richard. "Hard to believe you are old Tobias's son."

Richard stiffened slightly, and Bullfinch put out his hand and waved it in a conciliatory gesture.

"No, no, don't take offense. It's just, remember, I served under your father for over a year. They pushed my class out of Annapolis early because the navy was desperate for officers. I'd hoped for one of the new steam frigates; instead I got a transport ship. Damn, how your father hated that. I mean the ship, not me. He wanted action the same as I did." Bullfinch smiled wistfully. "We both got more than we'd bargained for."

As he spoke he popped the seal on the case and opened it, pulling out several thick folders that, in turn, had been sealed as well.

"Looks all very official and businesslike. Now tell me, Cromwell, what did you see, and what do you think about all this?"

"The president's speech, I read it in the papers on the way down. I think he laid it out quite clearly. The Kazan are coming, so now is the time to mobilize and present a unified front."

"I read that as well," Bullfinch snapped. "Andrew at his best, but that's not what I asked for. What is it that you really saw?"

Richard hesitated. He was being asked to comment on things political, a realm he wished to avoid whenever possible.

"Out with it, Cromwell."

"Indecision and confusion, sir."

"Ah, now we are getting down to facts."

"No, sir, just my opinion as you asked for it."

"They trained you well at the academy, Cromwell."

"Sir?"

"The military and politics to be forever kept apart. Facts versus opinion. Cromwell, politics has precious little to do with facts and everything to do with opinion, so go ahead."

"President Keane clearly understands the issue."

"In other words, he completely believed you."

"I wouldn't venture an opinion on that, sir. He said that we have to believe my report, for to do otherwise is folly."

Bullfinch grunted, his one eye baleful, gaze locked on Cromwell.

"You realize, Cromwell, that if you are wrong, if it should turn out that these bastards are not attacking, then the entire navy will look like fools. Half the senate will scream we cooked the whole thing up to ram through another appropriation. I do not take kindly to being made to look like a fool. Do you get my drift, Lieutenant?"

"Yes, sir," he said, thinking it best not to correct the admiral concerning his new rank.

"The father of Sean O'Donald is one of my closest friends, Cromwell. On the other hand, your father was one of my most bitter foes. The fact that I now have to accept the word of one son over another, an accusation that Sean O'Donald cannot even defend himself against, is an outrage to me."

"You know about Sean, sir?" Cromwell gasped.

"The whole damn Republic knows about him." He reached over to the table behind his desk and picked up a copy of Gates's *Daily*.

"Some damn congressional assistant spilled it last night,

and Gates printed it, damn his hide. Sherman was right: every damn newspaperman should be given a choice, either hang them or hand them a gun and put them on the front line. This will break old Pat's heart. It will kill him, Lieutenant, kill him."

Richard did not reply.

"You were in this office less than two weeks ago, still dripping wet from your alleged adventure. Why the hell didn't you tell me about this? As you commanding officer you should have reported to me any allegations you might have against a brother officer first rather than have it spill out like this."

As he spoke, he coiled the paper up and slammed it several times on his desk and then in disgust threw it so that it landed at Cromwell's feet.

"Sir." He struggled to control his voice, to not let a hint of anger show. "I kept it in confidence because I believed it proper to first inform Senator O'Donald personally."

"You mean, you told him this to his face?" As he spoke, Bullfinch rose half out of his chair, pointing at the paper, shouting so loudly that Cromwell knew that every officer and sailor in the outer office was most likely standing stock still, soaking in every word.

"Yes, sir. He was the first to know. Him and the president. I have discussed it with no one else since, other than now with you. If some"—he paused for a second and then let it spill out, raising his voice so that the unseen audience could hear his reply—"damn loose-mouthed pencil pusher in Congress ran and told the press about it, I can assure you, sir, it did not come from me. I resolved that no one other than Lieutenant O'Donald's father would ever know of what happened out there, and I kept that promise to myself and to him."

Bullfinch settled back slightly. His features were still red, though, so that it looked like he was barely containing his temper.

"You better pray for war, Lieutenant," he said, his voice low, "and pray damn hard, because if it doesn't come, I'll have you shoveling shit in the most godforsaken outpost I can find, and remember, sir, you owe the Republic eight years service for your education, so you can't resign and get away from me."

"Sir, I will pray for exactly that to happen. I'd rather shovel shit for the next eight years than see my comrades blown out of the water."

Bullfinch, taken aback by the reply, looked at him with obvious surprise, and Richard decided to press in.

"And they will be blown out of the water, Admiral, if we go at them in a ship-of-the-line fight, trading broadsides at three thousand yards. As I told you before, the *Gettysburg* lasted barely ten minutes against one of their lightest ships. You asked for an opinion, sir, and that is it, and it is the opinion of the president and the Naval Design Board as well."

There was the slightest flicker of a smile on Bullfinch's face, but his gaze was still hard, features red.

"Damn you, Cromwell," he said. "At least I'll say this, unlike your father, you have some guts."

Richard sensed his control slipping. He lowered his eyes, and that triggered even more anger within, knowing that Bullfinch would see the action as a backing down.

"Sir." He took a deep breath, struggling to maintain his composure. "The issue here is my report and the response from Suzdal. I'd prefer if any allegations you might have about my father remain outside this conversation."

Bullfinch blinked and, if possible, his features reddened to the point that it seemed as if he would explode. He exhaled noisily and then sat back.

"I'll be damned if a lieutenant tells me what I can and cannot discuss in my own office."

"As a commander in the service of the Republic," he replied, unable to contain being called lieutenant one more time, "I believe I have every right to object to a personal insult, sir, as long as that objection is done in a professional manner."

Bullfinch reached up, rubbing the ugly scars that creased his right cheek and forehead. "I'll be damned, sir. Now you are quoting the rules of the service to me, no less."

Richard was tempted to add that Bullfinch had helped to write them, but he was back in control of himself again. Getting into a shouting match with an admiral at a time like this served no useful purpose, either to the navy or to himself, or to the memory of his father, a man whom he had never even known.

Bullfinch cleared his throat, opened the topmost envelope on his desk, and slowly read through the first few pages.

He finally looked back up, acting as if Cromwell had not been standing there waiting patiently for him to continue.

"Insane," Bullfinch sighed, and he almost seemed to collapse as if all wind had been taken out of his sails. "This whole thing is insane."

Richard remained silent.

"Do you know what they are ordering us to do?"

"No, sir, not officially, but I had a sense of it. I attended three meetings with the president and two with the Design Board before being detailed back here."

"And you actually saw these ships, these Kazan battleships, as they are called here?"

"Yes, sir. Eight of them were anchored in the harbor at Kazan, as was most of the rest of the emperor's fleet."

"I hope to God you weren't behind the mad scheme to tear *Shiloh* and her sister ships apart, because if so, orders or no orders"—he tapped the papers on his desk—"you will most definitely be handed that shit shovel before you get out of this office."

"No, sir. I was at the meeting at the dockyard when Professor Ferguson raised the subject."

"Did you influence that woman at all?"

Richard hesitated. "Sir, she asked my opinion, sir."

"And that was?"

"*Shiloh* would go to the bottom inside of ten minutes once their battleships got within range. If we had thirty, forty ships like *Shiloh*, maybe enough would survive to close in and make a kill, but twenty thousand men under your command would die doing it."

Bullfinch looked back at the papers, picked them up, and riffled through them again.

"I'll say this at least," he announced slowly, "she has saved our asses more than once." He looked up again at Cromwell. "You didn't know her husband. I did. He was a damn good friend, even if he was strange. His mind always seemed to be off somewhere else even when you talked with him. But good God, when you got into things technical, he just exploded with ideas and plans that, damn me, always seemed to work. If he hadn't disobeyed Andrew with that rocket scheme, we'd have lost the war at Hispania, and that's a fact." He smiled wistfully, the tension gone for a moment as he remembered things past.

"Varinnia was a real beauty, she was, tragic what happened in that fire. But maybe it was a blessing for us all. Ferguson had the strength and moral character few men have to look beyond the flesh, to see and discover a mind as brilliant as his own beneath. No, perhaps even more brilliant because she was a perfect match, a mind that could organize and bring to completion all his mad schemes.

"And when he died, Lord, how we were terrified. He'd always been our ace up the sleeve. But he had unleashed something within her. In those last months when he knew he was dying, he crammed in years of training, and after he was gone she took off like a blazing comet. She was able to find others like herself, train them, point them in the right direction, and let them loose."

He sighed again and then seemed to be embarrassed with his mental wandering. "Still, even if it came straight from her, I'd tell her right to her face that this time she is out of control. She's trying to do in days what should take months. Hell, that inane decking on Shiloh will raise the center of gravity a good three feet. The ship will be so top-heavy she'll roll in the first good gale."

"She knows that, sir, and the response is, don't sail into a gale."

Bullfinch laughed. "In another month the cyclones start."

"In a cyclone even our best armored cruisers have gone under."

The admiral slammed an open palm on the papers. "The president orders and I obey, but by heavens, Andrew Lawrence Keane was an infantry officer before he became president. He and that Design Board, and even the damned secretary of the navy, who couldn't figure out which railing to piss over when the wind is up, don't know what it is to fight a battle at sea, and I do."

"Sir, that was conveyed to me quite clearly by the president just before I left. What you have in those files"—Cromwell pointed at the papers on the desk—"are undoubtedly recommendations and proposals for ship changes, transfers of command such as the air corps, and overall strategic suggestions. The president told me to inform you that you have his full confidence, and how the battle is to be fought is under your control, not his."

"Well, thank you very much, Cromwell," Bullfinch responded, his voice edged with sarcasm. "I was beginning to think that all I was supposed to do is push these papers around and sit behind this desk."

Richard did not reply, but even a blind man could have seen that there was more that he wanted to say.

"Go on, out with it," Bullfinch growled.

"Sir, when I first came in here, you asked for my opinion."

"And now you're going to give it."

"With your permission."

"Then do it, damn you."

He stepped closer, trying to assume a more relaxed position, eyes not fixed on Bullfinch, but instead on one of the papers scattered about the desk: a sketch of a Kazan battleship. He pointed at the drawing.

"Sir, what is coming at us is unlike anything we ever imagined in our worst nightmares. For the last fifteen years the Kazan have deceived us. The ships they assigned to patrol their outer waters were derelict wrecks from fifty years past. All the time they were watching, observing, gathering information while they fought amongst themselves to settle their own differences."

"Wish the hell they'd slaughtered one another."

"The paradox is that the fighting amongst themselves created the threat that exists now. Their fleet has a generation of battle experience behind it.

"I regret having to say this, but we must assume that Lieutenant O'Donald has told them everything he knows about us, technical and political. The Kazan will come armed with that knowledge."

"And these Shiv?" Bullfinch asked.

Cromwell visibly shuddered. "Terrifying, sir. They view us the same way a tiger would look at a kitten. They've been bred for two hundred years by the Order. Why the emperor tolerates the Order's existence is beyond me, other than the fact that he must fear them and their power.

"That, sir, is part of the reason for this war. I suspect it is an excuse to divert the emperor."

"But you told me that their leader, Hazard . . ."

"Hazin, sir."

"This Hazin is cunning."

Richard nodded. "The most cunning mind I have ever met."

Bullfinch looked at him closely. "I sense an admiration in you, Cromwell."

Richard reluctantly nodded. "I must confess I was intrigued. I thought he would be like a leader of the Hordes. I was a slave, sir, for the first six years of my life. I remember their cruelty, their rage. Hazin was educated, with knowledge that is beyond us. He could cite ancient poets and philosophers, then ever so subtly shift, pulling out your most hidden thoughts. He is a match for the emperor. In fact, I believe that before this is done, the emperor will be dead and Hazin will control all."

"You liked him, didn't you?"

Richard lowered his eyes. "He is our enemy."

"But personally?"

Richard looked Bullfinch straight in the eye. "No sir, he is our enemy."

Long ago he had learned to read lies, to catch the ever so subtle shift in voice, the momentary flicker in the eyes and tensing of features. It came from searching the faces of his cruel childhood masters. He wondered if Bullfinch could read that now.

Yes, he did like Hazin, and in a different world he might consider him a friend, no matter how loathsome his dreams, morality, and obsession with power. He had never met a mind like his, or a personality that could be so frightfully engaging and controlling.

He knew Hazin had seduced him, had seen him as but one more pawn in a game of power. And yet it was Hazin who had granted him his life.

Bullfinch nodded. "That is all, Lieuten—Commander Cromwell."

"Yes, sir." He stiffened to attention.

"Your own personal orders I assume the president told you."

"Yes, sir, he did. He said I was the most qualified to lead the section, though he preferred that I accept a staff assignment with you instead."

"My staff?" Bullfinch laughed. "Hardly likely."

"I assumed you would prefer it this way, sir."

"You at least guessed right on that one, Cromwell. We have a million square miles of ocean to watch. As the air corps moves down here, you will serve as liaison to them and for training. You'll do more flying in the next month than you did in the last four years. Try not to get yourself killed doing it, Cromwell."

"I plan to be here for the fight, sir."

Bullfinch shook his head. "What we have here," he sighed, pointing at the papers and then looking back up, "scares the living hell out of me, Cromwell. I hope my threat to send you on that shit-shoveling detail comes to pass, for all our sakes."

"I hope so, too, Admiral, but I can tell you, unless we pull off a miracle, we'll all be in hell before you can hand that shovel to me."

"Lieutenant Keane, over here!"

Abe urged his exhausted mount to a loping gallop, leaning forward in the saddle as they zigzagged up the face of a low butte, following an ancient mammoth trail. Sergeant Togo, the troop's lead scout, was crouched low on the crest, horse concealed just below the lip of the rise, and Abe swung out of his saddle, slipped to the ground, and took the precaution of unslinging his carbine and bringing it along. As he scrambled up the last few feet of rocky ground, the scout extended his hand, motioning for him to keep low.

He crawled up over the edge of the rise.

"Careful, sir, don't kick up any dust."

The sergeant pointed over at the next butte a couple of miles to the east.

Abe raised his field glasses and within seconds spotted more than a dozen Bantags, dismounted at the base of the butte, watering their mounts along the far banks of a muddy stream. They were out in the open, clearly visible, one of them carrying a red pennant, signifying a commander of a thousand.

The low summer grass covering the open ground between the butte and the stream was burnt brown with the heat, and crisscrossed with hundreds of tracks, crushed flat in some spaces across the width of a hundred yards or more.

"We're on a main column here," the sergeant announced. "Hard to tell at this distance, but the mounts look dun-colored, Betalga's clan. Damn, he is one mean bastard."

"Wish we had a flyer," Abe sighed. "I haven't seen or heard one all day."

"A million square miles and twenty-four flyers." The sergeant shook his head.

"Look at the water and the far bank, sir."

Abe carefully looked at the ground, which shimmered in the summer heat, not sure for a moment what he was looking for. Then he realized that the river above the crossing was still fairly clear, while for several miles below it, the water was churned a dark, muddy brown. The far bank looked wet, rutted with deep tracks.

"They've crossed here."

"Thousands of them. I bet the tail end of their column of yurts isn't a mile or more around that next butte. Remember, we crossed that same ford coming back."

Abe wasn't sure if he remembered and said nothing.

"This group was camped north of where we were. They're swinging in behind Jurak's main column, covering his withdrawal."

Abe looked back down over the side of the butte he had just climbed. Five companies of the 3rd Cavalry were strung out in columns, weaving their way up a dried ravine. In the lead troop, his unit, the men had dismounted, a few relieving themselves, others sprawling on the ground, munching on hardtack, drinking cold coffee from canteens while Togo scouted forward.

He caught a glimpse of Major Agrippa's guidon. He was the commander of this half of the regiment and was moving up past the head of the column. The yellow banner stood straight out in the hot, southeasterly breeze that was as dry as a bone, carrying not a hint of moisture from the sea four hundred miles to the south beyond the Shintang Mountains.

If that was indeed where the Bantag were heading, once they got up into those mountains they'd be all but impossible to control. But then again, he wondered, how could a couple regiments of cavalry change their mind?

"Keep an eye on them, Sergeant, see if you spot anything else." Abe pointed at the ravines and low, bare hills that flanked the valley ahead.

"It's crawling with them. I can smell their stink," the sergeant grumbled. "Tell the major it doesn't look good up ahead. It's a natural spot for an ambush. I suggest we stop here and then probe forward real careful like."

Togo pointed at the buttes that flanked the approach to the ford. "They could have a full umen hidden behind those buttes, and we'd be none the wiser. I think we should send scouts out to circle them first. For good measure, send a courier back to the rest of the regiment to come up before we go venturing any farther."

"The other half of the regiment is fifteen miles or more off," Abe replied.

"Just the opinion of a lowly enlisted man, Lieutenant," Togo replied, looking up balefully at him.

"I'll tell him," Abe replied.

He slipped off the top of the rise, remounted, and endured a nervous, gut-churning slide back down the face of the butte. Major Agrippa arrived at its base to meet him.

Abe reported the sighting along with Togo's recommendations.

Agrippa grinned. "Good work, Lieutenant." He turned and ordered a sergeant to ride back down the line and to urge the men up, forming into companies by line.

Agrippa turned and looked back at Abe.

"So you think they're just ahead, Lieutenant?"

"Sir. I'm new at this, but I trust Sergeant Togo's judgment. He grew up in the northern plains. It looks like we're crossing into the track of Betalga's clan. They can field well over an umen."

"Their males will be spread out across a hundred square miles of ground, Lieutenant. They've got to hunt to survive, and this is damn poor ground."

The lead company came up out of the ravine behind them, and Agrippa pointed for them to deploy to his left, calling for them to form a skirmish line.

"Sir, maybe you should go up and take a look with Sergeant Togo. The ground around the other side of this butte is flat and open like a bowl, two miles across, the stream at the far end. In the flanks, though, there's a lot of ravines, washouts. It's impossible to see what's in them."

"They crossed through here. We've been picking up signs all day, Lieutenant. I'm not looking for a fight. We'll just advance, get into the rear of their column, and make it real clear they are to stop in place."

"You could have ten thousand of their riders on us inside an hour."

"Lieutenant, they wouldn't dare attack if we gain their column of yurts. We could slaughter their mates and cubs. They know that. They'll back off, and then we turn them around."

Abe swallowed hard, realizing that the men of his troop were watching the exchange. "You men mount up and fall in," he snapped angrily, then looked back at Agrippa. "Sir, should I get one of my men to head north, find Colonel Yarsolav, and have him come up?"

"Yes, you do that, Keane. Let him know we are into the rear of their column and bringing them back."

Abe hesitated.

"Keane, this isn't the old days back when I was a lieutenant in the last war. The Bantag barely have one gun for every ten men. We've got two gatlings with this column. So just relax and follow your orders the way you were trained to do. You might think a lot of the Bantag, but they're little more than beggars now, so just follow your orders."

Abe stiffened. "Yes, sir."

"I'll make sure you get mentioned in the dispatch when I report how we turned these bastards around and forced them to come back."

Abe saluted, turned, and called for his other scout, Togo's brother.

"Listen to me carefully," he whispered. "Your brother's got a bad feeling about what's ahead. Ride north like hell. You should find Colonel Yarsolav and the other half of the regiment about fifteen miles from here. Tell them to get down here at once. Suggest as well they send a dispatch back to Fort Malady before advancing. I think we're going to have a fight here."

"You mean, old Agrippa is riding in after them." Abe nodded and the trooper groaned. "Damn, I never should have volunteered for this unit."

He spurred his mount and galloped off. The rest of the column was coming up out of the ravine. The compact line

kicked up plumes of dust as they deployed to left and right
on either side of the butte.

Agrippa rode down the line, shouting orders, telling the
men to draw their carbines, deploy around the butte, and
spread into open skirmish order. He caught a glimpse of
Keane and rode over, his horse already lathered with sweat.

"Your troop to the front, get a couple hundred yards
ahead of the main line, beat that grass, make sure none of
them devils is hiding. And remember, don't shoot unless
fired upon. If they want a war, let them be the ones to
start it."

Abe was tempted to tell him the grass was barely knee-
high, dry as tinder, and a Bantag cub couldn't hide in it,
but orders from majors were orders. Calling his fifty men
to form, he rode the several hundred yards to the north
flanking the butte and swung out into the open plain
beyond.

"Open order skirmishers, advance at the walk!" Abe
shouted, and pointing straight toward the ford, he started
the advance, his men spreading out in a line two hundred
yards across. Togo rode up to join him, looked over balefully, and drew his carbine.

"Did you talk to him?" Togo asked.

Abe bristled slightly at the accusatory tone in Togo's
voice, but, remembering Hawthorne's advice, he did not
react.

"Yes, I told him exactly what you said and threw in my
own opinion as well. I sent your younger brother off as a
courier to the main column."

Togo grunted and said nothing more.

He heard a bugle call from behind, and looking back,
Abe felt a cold shiver at the magnificent sight.

Two companies came galloping out to the north of the
butte, and a hundred yards to the south two more companies emerged, followed seconds later by the limber-drawn
gatlings.

Each flank formed into a line eighty mounted men across
and two ranks deep, company guidons in the middle. Carbines were drawn, barrels flashing in the sunlight. Bugles
sounded, announcing the advance at a trot.

Abe picked up the pace of his own line, anxiously looking to either flank. They covered the first mile, the tension

mounting. The ground ever so gradually undulated, slowly rising up, dropping down, then rising again.

They were following the tracks of the clan column, dried grass mashed flat, ruts from the heavy wheels cut into the dry soil, horse droppings everywhere, the droppings still damp. He tried to act composed, remembering his father's story about going into action for the first time in Antietam. But this wasn't Antietam. He didn't know if this was the start of a fight, a war, or just an exercise to please Major Agrippa's vanity.

"Ahead, sir."

One of his troopers was pointing. The ford was less than a mile away. A lone Bantag rider had come up out of the streambed, red standard held aloft. Several more joined him, one turning to gallop away.

"The left, sir!"

He looked where another trooper was pointing. A flash of light up on one of the flanking buttes, gone, then flashing again. Sunlight on a sword blade, a signal, he couldn't tell, but it gave him a queasy feeling, as if he were sticking his neck into a noose.

The range was down to less than half a mile, Heat shimmers made the Bantags look like ghostly figures, elongating, flattening out, shifting, changing shape. They continued to close.

He looked back again. The sight was still inspiring, battle line now joined across a continuous front nearly a quarter mile wide, guidons standing straight out in the hot wind, gatlings following several hundred yards farther back. Looking forward, the range was down to less than six hundred yards.

"Smoke!"

Several men cried out at the same time, pointing to the left oblique, just forward of the streambed. For a second he wondered if it was a rifle shot, waiting for the zing of the bullet. He had never actually heard a bullet fired at him, but the veterans had always talked about the beelike hum, the flicker of air as a round brushed past.

More smoke, now in front, then to the right, puffs igniting, small white plumes. Several of the men cocked their carbines, reined in, took aim even though the range was absurdly long. He shouted for them to hold fire.

More smoke, white plumes curling up, then laying flat out in the wind. All across the front curls of smoke were igniting, flaring. He saw a flicker of fire, and within seconds it was a wall of flame rising up, spreading out, leaping before the wind.

"Halt!"

The first whiff of smoke was already upon them, the sweet scent of dried grass burning, strangely triggering a memory of autumn days at the country home, burning leaves.

The crackling roar of the spreading inferno could be clearly heard. His mount shied, snickering with fright, ears lying back.

For several long seconds he sat there, dumbfounded, not sure what the hell to do next. He looked back over his shoulder. The line was still advancing, the men lower down in the hollow, but surely they had seen. He caught a glimpse of dust to his left, sliding down the butte—a wave of riders several hundred strong.

He looked forward again. Beyond the rising wall of flames he saw the standard bearer, up in his stirrups, red pennant held high, waving back and forth.

"Back!" Abe swung around, pointing to the rear. "Back to the hill at a gallop!"

As he spurred his mount, it reared up, nearly throwing him. It turned around, and for a mad second he thought it would race off straight at the wall of fire, which was now leaping before the wind, flames dancing high, a front of fire half a mile wide raging across the plains as fast as the wind.

He viciously sawed his mount around, leaned forward, and dug in his spurs. The horse shied again, then fell in with the rest of Abe's troopers, who were off at a gallop, racing straight back toward the rest of the line.

The other four companies were coming up out of the hollow, but the line was slowing. Some of the men were standing in their stirrups to see what was ahead. Those on the left flank were pointing toward the butte to the north, where the expanding line of riders were storming down.

He headed straight for Agrippa.

"Lieutenant, what the hell?" Agrippa screamed, and then he looked past Abe, eyes wide. "Bugler, sound retreat!"

Men were already turning, not even waiting for the call. Abe screamed for his troop to stay with him, but everyone was jumbling together, forward companies falling back into the second line, men turning about, several losing their saddles. A trooper in front of Abe, riding flat out, suddenly tumbled as his mount stepped into a hole, snapping its leg. The man crashed down, his screaming horse rolling over on top of him, crushing him.

He looked back. The fire was leaping with the wind, actually gaining. Hot embers were swirling around them, smoke blanketing the ground like a fog, blinding him.

Coughing, eyes stinging, he focused all his attention forward. He weaved around another pileup where two horses had collided, throwing their riders. One of the men was obviously dead.

In all the confusion, he suddenly felt a bizarre sense of detachment, wondering what he was doing, why this was happening, what he was supposed to do next.

The unfurling wall of smoke made everything look dreamlike, surreal, with shadows moving to either side. Then he heard a strange fluttering sound, the air hissing. Directly ahead he saw a man jerk, half rising out of his saddle, then slump over, ever so slowly falling, left foot catching in the stirrup, his face a bloody pulp.

They're shooting at us?

Is this what it is like? he wondered. Strange, he felt no fear, just a curious surprise that someone was shooting, trying to kill him. Did Jurak order this? Ten days ago I was in their camp, I sat with them, talked, and now this.

He saw another man go down, horse screaming, rearing up in mid stride, twisting in agony, rolling. The rider tried to kick free of his stirrups, then disappeared beneath the writhing mass. The sickening crunch of their hitting the ground snapped him out of his dreamlike state.

All command was broken down. Everything was mad panic and chaos.

He caught a glimpse of a larger shadow to his left. A team of four horses raced past, one of the precious gatlings. The limber wagon and piece were bouncing and careening, gun crew atop the limber desperately hanging on.

He edged over toward them. "To the butte!" he screamed. "Follow me!"

He weaved in front of them, looking up, catching a glimpse of the pale, red sun visible through the smoke, nearly directly overhead and slightly to his left.

Keep the wind directly on your back, he realized. We were riding straight into it before.

As he rode straight on, time seemed to stretch out. He could feel his mount beginning to slow after a hard morning's ride and now this mad gallop.

"Come on, damn it, come on!" He raked his spurs in again.

A shadow emerged from his right, hard to distinguish for a second. It was bigger, far bigger than a trooper.

A Bantag rider burst out of the smoke, scimitar raised, grinning, roaring a wild battle cry, coming straight at him. Wide-eyed, Abe saw him coming, his fingers still tightly clutching the reins, carbine dangling from his shoulder sling, slamming uselessly against his hip.

The Bantag closed.

Abe ducked, heard the hissing whistle of the blade slashing the air . . . and then the Bantag was gone, disappearing into the smoke, riding on.

The ground started to rise. Grass gave way to rocky slope, and as he gained a few precious feet of altitude, the smoke seemed to miraculously part. He was above it, at the base of the butte. He reined in hard, turning, nearly losing his seat again as his mare's back legs nearly collapsed.

All around him was chaos. Troopers were coming up out of the boiling white ocean of smoke. Several were dismounting. Down in the confusion below he saw hundreds of men riding, most coming straight toward him, others veering off to the left and right. On both flanks a disciplined wall of riders were hemming them in, closing the ring. Rifle shots echoed, flashes of light in the swirling smoke.

Another bullet zipped past, kicking up dust on the rocky slope behind him. He could see half a dozen Bantags less than a hundred yards off. One of them armed with a rifle had just fired, aimed straight at him.

The others had bows and were firing flaming bundles into the confusion.

A bugler came up out of the smoke, hat gone, eyes wide with panic.

Again the sense of detachment. Am I frightened? What the hell do I do?

He stood up in his stirrups. "Major Agrippa!"

Even as he shouted for his commanding officer, he realized the absurdity of the gesture. Wherever the damned fool was, screaming for him wasn't going to help.

"Bugler!"

The man was kicking his mount, trying to urge him up the steep slope of the butte.

"Damn you, bugler! Over here!"

The bugler slowed, looking at him.

"Over here, damn you!"

He swung around, came up, and in a gesture that struck Abe as ridiculous he came to attention and saluted.

"Blow recall! Blow it and keep blowing it!"

The man looked at him as if he were speaking in an alien tongue. He wondered if he even understood English. He appeared to be Rus, but he wasn't sure.

"Recall!"

There was a nod of recognition. The man spat, wiped his lips, and raised his instrument.

At nearly the same instant Abe's horse reared up again, this time shrieking in pain. It turned, trying to run in panic. He regained control, felt the limping walk and saw the fathers of an arrow, the shaft plunged deep into his mare's chest, just inches from his right leg.

The high clarion call of the bugle echoed, and Abe moved close to the man's side. Standing in his stirrups, he pulled out the scimitar, which had been a gift of Jurak's, and waved it back and forth over his head.

More men were coming out of the smoke, looking around in confusion. Hearing the bugle call, they spotted an officer and started toward him.

"Up the slope, men! Up the slope as far as you can ride, then dismount and set up a covering fire!"

A sergeant major, obviously an old trooper, picked up the cry, riding back and forth along the rocky slope, repeating Abe's command, urging individual men and small clumps of riders forward, driving them up the slope.

The gatling crew came out of the smoke. The lead horse

had its foreleg nearly shot off, blood spraying with every agonized step. The driver reined in, and the gun slewed around, nearly upending. It was obvious that there was no way in hell that it could go any farther. Abe rode down to them. "Unlimber that piece! Push it as far up the slope as possible."

He spotted a half a dozen troopers, following a lieutenant and moving in some semblance of order.

"Lieutenant, have your men dismount. Get this gatling and ammunition boxes up the slope!"

Without waiting for a reply he turned away. Riderless horses came out of the smoke. A flurry of shots erupted to his right, and he saw a score of mounted Bantags were coming up around the flank of the Butte, having circled round.

God, if they are on the crest above, we're dead.

The sergeant major, who had been detailing off men looked up and saw the threat. Abe rode toward him.

"You better get some men on top, sir!" he shouted. "I'll feed them up to you as they come in!"

Abe nodded, and the sergeant screamed for the knot of troopers gathering around him to follow the lieutenant.

Abe started up the rocky slope, feeling a moment of anguish over the labored gasps of his dying mount, which seemed to somehow sense what still needed to be done before giving up.

He zigzagged up the rocky incline, passing several dozen men deploying on a narrow plateau. Several of them were firing and reloading, shiny brass cartridge casings scattered around them.

He looked back. A score or more troopers were following him up the slope.

He was momentarily aware, yet again, that bullets were smacking into the rocky ground, kicking up plumes of dust, exploding shards of rock. An arrow whistled past, striking sparks as it hit a boulder.

He caught a glimpse of an adder, coiled up, hideous looking, head raised, mouth opened and ready to strike. An hour ago, the sight would have filled him with terror. He ignored it, riding within half a dozen feet of it, then pushed on.

The slope seemed nearly vertical, and a narrow trail, a

beaten path left by mountain goats, was the only way up. He felt naked, exposed as he looked down to his left.

The entire panorama of the madness was laid out below. The fire was sweeping past either side of the butte. The ground back across nearly two miles was blackened, hot spots still smoking. Dozens of fire-charred bodies littered the plain, a ghastly sight. Dying horses, flesh smoking, staggered about, shrieking in agony. Curled-up bodies of dead troopers lay in the smoking ashes. A rippling explosion, sounding like a string of Victory Day firecrackers, detonated, followed by a dull whooshing explosion. One of the gatling limbers was burning. An ammunition wagon was upended nearby, its four horses still trapped in their traces, down on the ground, kicking and thrashing.

The Bantags to either flank had drawn back to let the fire pass, but were now circling back in. Down at the very base of the butte a wild melee was being fought, the most daring of the attacking host having pressed right into the middle of the smoky confusion. Abe could see the flashes of scimitars rising and falling.

The trail ahead switched back yet again, and directly above he saw the crest. His poor mount, gasping for breath, blood frothing, struggled the last few feet.

He heard the click of a rifle being cocked, and looked straight up into the muzzle of a gun.

"By all my ancestors," Togo gasped, "get up here, damn it!" He lowered his weapon and disappeared. Seconds later Abe heard the gun go off.

He pushed the last few feet, came over the crest, and saw Togo leaning over the other side of the butte, which at its crest was less than thirty yards across.

"They're coming up from behind!" Togo shouted, even as he levered in a fresh round, leaned over, and fired again.

Abe swung off his mount. Uncasing his carbine, he grabbed a bandolier of ammunition secured behind the saddle.

The next trooper in line came up behind him, and before he was even dismounted he had his revolver out, leveled it, and fired, dropping a Bantag who was trying to ride up onto the crest.

Abe looked back down the trail. More than a dozen men were still following.

"Come on!" he screamed.

He loaded his weapon, turned, and started toward Togo. The sergeant screamed something incoherent in Japanese. Abe wanted to ask Togo how the hell he had gotten up to the top of the butte ahead of everyone else, but kept silent.

He gained the edge on the other side and looked down. Several hundred Bantag had circled in behind the butte, which acted like a wall, blocking the fire that was sweeping along with the wind to either flank. Some of the Bantag were trying to ride up, but their horses were simply too big and cumbersome to mount the slope; that was the only thing that had saved the troopers on top from already being overrun.

Most of them were dismounting, starting up through the rocky ground, climbing hand over hand.

Togo fired again, and Abe clearly saw the bullet smash into the upraised forehead of his target, blood exploding, Togo grunting with delight.

Abe lowered his weapon, took aim, and then, amazingly, he found he simply could not squeeze the trigger. He had his target clearly in sight, a young one, frame not yet filled out, bow slung over his shoulder, face down as he climbed, not even aware that death was closing in.

"Lieutenant?"

He gladly turned away, looking back. A corporal had gained the crest. "Where the hell do you want us?"

"Over here. Drive those riders back." He turned away from the crest. "Sergeant Togo, deploy the men out on this line as I feed them in!"

He ran back to the other side. For a second he felt a wave of horror.

Two hundred feet below was pure chaos, no sense of command. The smoke from the fire around the base of the hill was beginning to clear, replaced by yellow-gray puffs from carbine fire.

Intermingled, swarming in around them, were scores, a hundred or more Bantags, most using scimitars, some armed with bows, a few carrying old bolt-action rifles from the war.

A war, he thought. Damn it, this is war.

Several dozen troopers broke from the flank of the butte, trying to ride around it to the west, instinctively heading back the way they had come. From around that side a score of Bantag charged. In seconds it was over, blades flashing, bodies tumbling, all the troopers dead.

Amazingly, the bugler he had ordered to blow the recall was still at it. But no one else was left out on the burnt plain except for the dead and dying.

As more troopers rode up the slope, the sergeant below grabbed men, pushing them up.

"Who's in command here?"

It was Agrippa, gaining the crest on foot, face puffy and scorched, breathing hard, eyes dilated.

For a second Abe looked around, caught off guard, waiting for someone else to answer. Then he looked back. "I am."

"I'll take over, then. Get these men mounted and ready to follow me. I've lost my mount, so find one for me as well."

The bugle below fell silent. He looked back over. The man was falling out of his saddle, a Bantag rider withdrawing his scimitar from the trooper's back.

"Lieutenant, do you hear me, mount up."

"Where did you say we're going, sir?"

"We'll go down the other side and break through. Now follow orders!

The sergeant major down below was heading up the slope, pushing the last of the survivors before him.

"Did you hear me, Lieutenant?"

"Yes, sir, I heard you."

"Then do it."

Abe stared at him. "Why?"

"What did you say, Lieutenant?"

"Why, sir? What the hell are you going to do once we get down there?" He pointed down at the prairie. Clusters of Bantags were riding over the smoldering ground they had just retreated across, casually dispatching the last of the wounded, while to the flanks and rear a circle of skirmishers were closing the net in tight. A knot of troopers had gained a small ravine, but were quickly being annihilated as scores of Bantags swarmed in on them, heedless of loss.

"We're going to get the hell out of here, Lieutenant. We'll go down that slope." He pointed to the west.

"Sir, there's hundreds of Bantags down there, and we don't have more than sixty up here." As he spoke he indicated the skirmish line deploying along the rim of the butte. One of the men was already dead, head blow off by a well-aimed shot, but the rest were pouring out a steady rate of fire.

A corporal, every inch the professional, was pacing the line, crouched low, offering encouragement, pointing out targets, cautioning the men to make every shot count. He paused in his work, looking straight at Abe. His gaze spoke volumes. The corporal had heard every word. He simply shook his head, nodded down to the plain below, then drew a finger across his throat.

Abe took a deep breath, turned, and faced the major.

"May I suggest, sir, that we stay here. Most of the battalion is dead, sir. We go down there, and we won't get half a mile before they finish us off."

"What? What the hell did you just say, Lieutenant?"

"With all due respect, sir. We are on the high ground. Up here we can secure the flanks for the men still down below. Ride back down and we're all dead, and the gatling position down on the east slope will be wiped out as well."

"We're dead if we stay here," Agrippa cried and pointed back to the east.

The distant riverbank that they had been riding toward was swarming with hundreds of Bantags.

"They're coming!" Agrippa cried, shifting his gaze to the troopers, who had slowed in their firing and were watching the confrontation. "Mount up and let's get moving before it's too late."

"They'll slaughter us if we go off this hill."

"Mount, damn you, get mounted!"

Abe looked back down at the base of the slope. Not a single guidon was in sight. Out on the plain he saw a Bantag galloping off, triumphantly holding the yellow flag with the crossed sabers of the battalion, flame-scorched, waving it over his head as he raced toward the ford.

"Mount, Lieutenant, and that is a direct order. I don't give a good damn who your father is. Now get these men moving!"

Abe turned back. "No, sir."

"What?"

"No, sir, and I don't have time for this. We're staying here. This is the only defensible ground we have. The Bantag didn't want this fight. They aren't going to stay. We just have to hang on!"

"You are relieved, Lieutenant, and by God, I'll have you court-martialed for direct disobedience of my commands."

"Go ahead," Abe shouted, "do whatever you damn well please, but these men stay here! Your mad charge got them into this mess. I'll not see the rest of them slaughtered because you panicked."

Several of the men on the firing line, including the corporal, were looking at them.

Abe stepped closer, trying to regain control of his emotions. "Listen, Major. We can hold this position. Now pull yourself together and help me to lead these men."

"Be damned. Now mount up."

Before he fully realized what he was doing, Abe swung his carbine around and pointed it at the major.

"Sir, if I hear one more word from you, I will blow your damn head off. You got us into this mess with that damn stupid ride straight into an ambush that my scout warned you about. Now stay exactly where you are and shut the hell up."

In spite of the roar of battle Abe felt as if he were trapped in a world of silence. He could see the corporal standing upright, staring at them. Togo, with a half dozen men gathered around him, was directing fire down the north slope, securing the flank, not aware of what was going on behind.

Agrippa started to reach for his revolver.

"Don't, sir. I am not playing a game. Touch that weapon, and you are dead."

Agrippa looked at him, mouth gaping open like a fish that had been speared and dropped into the bottom of a boat. His eyes darted back and forth, settling at last on the corporal.

"Over here," he gasped, and the corporal reluctantly approached.

"Remove that weapon from this man and place him under arrest," Agrippa hissed.

The corporal looked back and forth between the two, and then his gaze shifted beyond them.

"Goddamn, what the hell are you people doing?"

It was the sergeant major Abe had grabbed at the bottom of the hill, pushing a dozen men on foot in front of him. Crouching low until clear of the edge of the butte, he stood up, slowly moving toward the two officers.

"Sergeant major, arrest this man," Agrippa hissed.

The sergeant hesitated.

"Sergeant, we are staying on this hill," Abe announced. "Major Agrippa wants us to charge back down and make a break to the west. It will mean abandoning our comrades still down below. I have tried to reason with him, and he refused. So either he backs down now, or I shoot him."

The sergeant major cautiously approached the two, the entire group breaking their tableaulike poses when a high arcing arrow hissed down, striking the ground between them, and then went skidding off.

The staccato roar of the gatling ignited, and Abe shifted his gaze for a second to the sergeant.

"Deployed on the plateau just below us," he announced. "We managed to get a couple of thousand rounds up with it. The men are digging in."

"Sergeant! Get the men mounted."

The sergeant, moving with steady purpose, stepped between Agrippa and Abe and faced the major. Taking the officer's revolver out of its holster, he stuck it into his own belt.

"Sir, you're injured, sir. I think you need to lie down."

"Sergeant?"

"I can see you're badly burned, sir. Corporal, get something to drink for the major here."

"I'll have all of you court-martialed," Agrippa cried.

"Sir, will you look over there," the sergeant replied, speaking softly, as if sharing a few kind words with a friend.

The major turned, looking to where the sergeant pointed.

The revolver in the sergeant's hand flashed upward. Agrippa fell, sprawling in the dust. The sergeant stood above him, holding the pistol by the barrel.

"Damn," he whispered, "I think a ball just grazed the major."

He looked back at Abe and wearily shook his head.

"You were right, sir, but damn it, your ass and mine are in the fire once he wakes up."

Abe could not help but smile. "Thank you, Sergeant."

"Look, sir. I think most all the other officers are dead. The damn bastards tore into anyone with a guidon following. I think we got about a hundred men all mixed up down there and up here, but by God if we keep our nerve, we can hold. They're already pulling back."

Abe had been so preoccupied with Agrippa that he had forgotten about the battle raging around them. He looked back to the east. The Bantag along the riverbank were holding their position. He could see them moving about, clustering around a rider coming in bearing a guidon.

Looking to either flank, he could see they were pulling back. Some of them had dismounted, hiding behind dead horses, scattered boulders, keeping up a slow but steady fire. To the west, down in the ravine where they had been less than an hour before, he caught glimpses of riders dismounting. The half dozen supply wagons that had been left to the rear were being looted, drivers all dead. The back door was closed. Another bullet zipped passed, sounding like an angry bee.

I'm under fire, he realized. That one down there behind the pyramid-shaped boulder is aiming straight at me.

"We're stuck here, sir," the sergeant announced, "but we can put up a hell of a fight at least until we die of thirst or run out of ammunition."

"Damn, I wish we could have gotten one of those wagons up here."

"How old are you, Lieutenant?"

"Twenty-one, Sergeant." He hesitated. "And you?"

"Old enough to be your father. I was in the last war."

"I could tell that, Sergeant."

The old man grinned. "Hell, I could have thought you were, too, the way you were down there."

Another bullet sang past.

"Like the old days all over again," the sergeant grumbled. He looked down at the still unconscious major.

"Remember, Lieutenant, he got nicked by a spent round. I'm heading back down to the gatling now. You just keep them back from our flanks, sir."

The sergeant disappeared back over the rim. Abe looked around and saw a few of the men still staring at him.

"What the hell are you looking at? Get back on the firing line, and make every shot count."

As the men turned away, he caught the eye of the corporal. "Make sure the major is all right," Abe said, and walked off.

He was startled by the sight of his mount, still standing, eyes wide with pain, bloody froth dripping from her open mouth.

"Oh, God," he sighed.

He leveled his carbine, which was still cocked, and aimed it at the poor beast's forehead. Abe closed his eyes and squeezed the trigger.

FOURTEEN

Andrew opened the door, then extended his hand, greeting Varinnia and the other members of the Design Board as they came into his office and sat down around the table.

Fortunately, the secretary of the navy had been diverted and was down at the naval yard for an inspection. The old Greek autocrat, a political compromise announced before the election to ensure holding that state, was far more interested in drink and the pursuit of young Rus beauties than business, so there would be no inane questions and delays. The 1st Aerosteamer Group was sailing at nightfall and final plans had to be checked.

Varinnia opened without delay, clicking off the details of the conversion of the three armored cruisers.

"The last of the aerosteamers are being loaded even now," she concluded. "The major problem is one of space and moving them around. The ramp to the lower deck is simply too slow and cumbersome. One of the workers suggested installing a steam-powered lifter, or elevator as he called it. If we had another week, we could do it."

"If the wind goes up to twenty knots," Theodor interjected, "we should be able to put all the planes up on the main deck before going into action. With wings folded and packed in, they'll occupy two hundred and twenty feet of deck space. That will give us a hundred and thirty feet for takeoffs. Falcons go first, then the Goliath, thus giving the heavier aircraft just over three hundred feet."

"How about landings, though, with all those planes?" Andrew asked.

"Well, they'll all take off. With luck, they'll all come back."

She fell silent, the implication clear. Part of the plan was based on the fact that not all the planes would be returning.

"As each plane lands," she finally continues, "it gets pushed to the front, clearing the aft deck for the next one."

"Sounds doubtful. You'll have damaged aircraft, wounded pilots."

"Actually, it's rather insane, but that's the only way we can get them up in some semblance of a group, which will be the key to making the attacks work."

"Their weapons?"

Varinnia sighed. "They were designed for launching from our frigates at a range of five hundred yards. Rosovich tried dropping one yesterday, and it damn near killed him when it exploded on impact with the water. He brought the plane in, but it was junked.

"We figure the fuse was too sensitive. My people are modifying them now. Impact with the water snaps the safety on the detonator. The next impact, against the target, sets it off."

"How many do we have?"

"Forty-three."

"Damn," Andrew gasped. "Can't you get more? I think you're telling me there isn't enough for those boys to do some practice runs first, even to test the damn things out."

"I suggested that Mr. Rosovich do a demonstration run as the ships cruise down to Constantine, but for the rest of the pilots, we'll just have to rig up drums filled with sand to simulate the weight."

"Just great."

"It's all we have, sir," Theodor replied. "Remember, we had moments like this back in the last war as well."

"Damn it," Andrew snapped, "that was the last war. We've had fifteen years knowing the Kazan were out there, and now we are sending boys up with sand-filled barrels so they can practice getting killed? Damn all of it."

He lowered his head for a moment. If I had complete

control, he thought, we'd have pushed the edge back with the Kazan, found out what was beyond the treaty barrier, and the hell with the stay-in-our-own-boundaries majority.

He closed his eyes, thinking about the telegrams piled up on his desk, each of them screaming for attention; messages from senators and congressmen telling him that their constituents were blaming him for provoking a war, that we should go out and meet the Kazan and make a deal, that the entire thing was a contemptible hoax to get money for the navy, which would be spent in Suzdal.

"Is there anything more that we can do between now and when we might expect their fleet?"

The members of the board looked at one another.

"Precious little," Varinnia replied. "We're trying to upgrade the frigates with rapid-fire one-inch gatlings. If they can dodge in close, it might be effective. Some of the new steel-tipped shells will be distributed to the armored cruisers, and Theodor here promises he can push us up to the production of two aerosteamers a day. That could give us upward of two hundred and forty airships by the end of the month."

"Not counting the ones on the three aerosteamer carriers?"

"That includes them."

He nodded sadly.

She shuffled some papers, which an assistant had pulled out of a briefcase. "Here you'll find our proposals for next year's appropriations."

"Next year?"

"Sir, we have to assume that somehow we will fend off the first attack. That's the only possible way we should be thinking, both privately and in public."

He noticed the slight edge of rebuke in her voice, and he accepted the briefing that she passed over, printed on the new typing machines.

He scanned through the last page and whistled softly.

"You are asking for one hundred and fifty million dollars?"

"For the navy alone," she quickly interjected. "Air corps is another hundred million and the army another hundred and fifty million."

"Good Lord, Varinnia, that's nearly ten times this year's

budget for ordnance development and procurement. Where the hell are we supposed to get that kind of money?"

"The same way you did last time," she ventured.

"Last time? We had no money. It was, for all practical purposes, a military dictatorship in spite of what trappings we made about the Republic. People worked and somehow we got them food and shelter. The country has changed now."

"Do we want to survive?"

"Of course we do."

"Then this is what I think we need."

Andrew felt his stomach knot, and a fearful voice whispered that suppose Pat was right, suppose this entire thing was a mad cooked-up story by Cromwell. There was even the underlying fear that Cromwell might very well believe he was telling the truth, but Hazin had fooled him. No invasion, just the threat of it to trigger a political crisis. My God, if they did wait, we might very well collapse on our own accord. It seemed as if the crisis had already triggered a frontier war with the Bantag. Reports had been coming in since late yesterday of skirmishing all up and down the frontier, and the Chin were howling bloody murder.

He closed his eyes, feeling a monumental headache coming on. "Explain this to me," he sighed, rubbing his closed eyes.

"First, we have to settle within the navy the question of emphasis. Do we go for the larger ships to match the battleships of the Kazan, or do we build aerosteamer carriers? The first path will take at least eighteen months to launch the first vessel. We had rough designs and calculations worked out. The Suzdal yard could be converted to handle two of them within six months, and two more within a year. I'm proposing as well the expansion of the yards at Roum and Cartha. That should lower the political heat a bit."

He nodded.

"If the aerosteamer scheme actually works, and the war nevertheless continues, remember the old formula, that for every offensive maneuver a defense will be found. If they have both the heavy ships and aerosteamer carriers a year from now, we are trumped. I'd suggest both."

"What I figured you'd say."

"Then to the second point. The controlling of fire."

"What do you mean?"

"Cromwell said something that stuck with me. I asked Petronius and even he agrees. Our guns can fire to over fifteen thousand yards. On rock-solid land they could expect to hit a stationary target the size of a Kazan battleship at that range. But put those guns on a ship, even one sailing in a dead calm, and all bets are off. Right now we're lucky to hit at a mile, and Cromwell estimated they were hitting at three thousand yards. If we could figure out a way to control the firing out to maximum range, we would have them."

He could sense the edge of excitement in her voice. "Go on."

"Working with several of my naval gunnery team, I've come up with several basic problems that have to be solved.

"First there is range finding. That is simple enough and might explain those pagodalike towers Cromwell said are on their battleships. If you knew precisely, to the inch, the distance between those two towers you would have a base line." As she spoke she traced out a triangle on a sheet of paper.

"Once you have the baseline, you measure the relative angle to the target from the top of the two towers. You know the width of the baseline, you know the angles. Combine that knowledge and you can figure the range."

"So then you shoot. That sounds easy enough."

Several of the men and women sitting around Varinnia chuckled softly. "That's the easy part. We need to coordinate all the guns together, then rig them to a single trigger. I'm thinking of some sort of liquid mercury switch. You have to fire when the ship is level in its pitch and roll, because the mercury inside the tube completes the electrical circuit only when it is precisely level, and then the guns fire."

"I suspect there's more," Andrew announced.

She smiled crookedly. "We've just started. The farther away we are from the target, the longer the shell takes to get there. At ten thousand yards it's over twenty seconds. In that time, the target could move a couple of hundred yards. Add into that the relative angle of travel of the target in relationship to you. What we need to be able to then do is calculate where the target will be, not where it is at, when the shells land. There are some other factors as well, wind speed, for example, and then finally our own motion and angle of direction in relationship to the target. If two ships are running parallel to each other, it isn't all that bad, but both will be maneuvering, turning, and thus relative angles and distances will change second by second. We're calling it the rate of change, and that component makes it very difficult to predict. All of that has to be calculated within seconds, then recalculated again, and yet again, while at the same time observers are calling down the splashes and correcting the range.

"You want to build a machine to do this, don't you?"

"Sir, it is the only way. I doubt if I could explain this to most of the senators on the appropriations committee— they'll have to trust me, or you, on it—but I can tell you it might take years and it will cost money, lots of money. But if we can figure this thing out, if we can shoot at ten thousand yards and they can't, we have them. Also, there's an advantage to hitting at greater ranges."

"And that is?"

"Plunging fire," Theodor interjected. "Ships have always had their heaviest armor on their sides. But when you start hitting them out at ten thousand yards the guns are at maximum elevation. That means the shell travels a couple of miles high, pitches over, then comes screaming straight down, through the more vulnerable top part of the deck."

"What about just making old-fashioned monitors? They're low to the water, and difficult to hit." But even as he asked the question, he could see the heads shaking.

"That might work here on the Inland Sea, but this is the Great Southern Ocean. Even on a good day you've got six-foot seas. Any kind of blow, and it's suddenly twenty-five-foot seas. No monitor can survive that."

"All right then," he sighed, "what else?"

"Improved shells, harder tipped for penetration. We've been talking about researching this new type of explosive refined from boiled cotton. It'd make our guns a lot more powerful, and the bursting charge in shells would be devastating.

"There's a lot more. Our experiments in making laminated armor, both for ships and the newer class of land ironclads, recoil absorbers for artillery, new rations that are packed in cans, it's all there."

"You've dredged up everything you could think of over the last five years, haven't you?"

"And a few new ones besides."

"Varinnia, I almost think you are enjoying this."

Though her burned features were a mask, he could see a flash of anger and instantly regretted his foolish statement.

"I want this country to survive. Last time around it was men my husband's age who were doing the fighting. Now we have boys. It's far harder now watching them go out."

"I know," Andrew sighed.

"We've got to get to work, Mr. President. Theodor is sailing with the *Shiloh.* I want to check some last-minute details. Will I see you down at the naval yard later?"

"I'll try to make it. I've got meetings with congress all afternoon, but I'll try."

As the group stood, the door to the office opened. Andrew looked up, annoyed, wondering who would be barging in. Kathleen stood in the doorway, features pale, a piece of paper in her hand.

She saw who was there, but couldn't contain herself.

"One of the telegraphers from the War Office brought this over," she announced, her voice tight, struggling for control.

Andrew took the sheet of flimsy paper, slowly read it, read it again, then stuffed it into his pocket.

"What is it?" Varinnia asked.

"Our son's regiment," Andrew whispered. "Half of the regiment was surrounded yesterday. Last report indicates they were wiped out. Abe was with them."

"A lovely sight, my emperor."

Emperor Yasim nodded in agreement. He looked over at Hazin, who had come up to the railing, and like him, was leaning over, hands clasped. The two of them were alone on the imperial bridge, the rest of the watch respectfully having withdrawn to the starboard side. Hazin had transferred over to the emperor's flagship the day before, and the emperor was obviously nervous about him being aboard his own ship.

The fleet of the Red Banner seemed to fill the ocean.

Looking astern, Yasim could see the other seven battleships following in the wake of their flagship, each one perfectly positioned a quarter league astern of the next. Flanking outward, encircling the battleships, were the dozens of cruisers and frigates.

They were still well inside the waters of the empire, but years of continual warfare had trained them well. The transports carrying the imperial legions and the Shiv were far astern, for it was not proper that such vessels sail with the elite.

Yasim looked over at Hazin and smiled. "The sickness of the sea, how do you fare?"

Hazin nodded, and Yasim chuckled.

"I for one am rarely bothered by it. Strange how that is."

"Perhaps because you were born to this, my lord, and I was not."

"That's why I thought the cruise would be good for you."

Hazin looked over warily.

"You know, I could but snap my finger"—Yasim motioned to one of his guards, who was standing at attention, gaze fixed at them—"and that warrior would come over here, break your back, and toss you over the railing."

Yasim laughed softly.

"No one would ever speak of it. We could simply report you lost by accident. Then we could turn these ships about, sail back through the transports, and sink every one of those laden with your Shiv. That would finish the Order."

"Would it?"

"Is it the sickness of the sea, or a sudden nervousness I detect in your voice."

"The sickness, damn it," Hazin snapped.

"I'm not so sure. That was a plan suggested by more than one before we sailed."

"How interesting. I'll have to run inquiries when I return."

"I figure you already have."

"Yes, it was discussed with me. Shall we discuss your amusing plan?"

"By all means, Hazin."

"Which of these guards is truly yours?"

"I actually might be innocent enough to believe that all of them are."

"That would be unworthy of you. That, my lord, has always been the base of the power of the Order. No one ever really knows who we are."

"At times I wonder if it is all a hoax. You have your disgusting Shiv that you've bred, a few foolish priests in their white robes, and actually little if anything else."

"If that was the case, why did you venture fifty million in gold to us against your brother? Why did you ensure my elevation in order to have that debt canceled. If you did not fear us, you would have slain the last Grand Master, slain me, and burned our temples, but you did not. Why?"

Yasim looked back over the railing. Yes indeed, why? he wondered. *Why not kill him now? I know he plans eventually to kill me and seize the throne.*

"You're thinking about killing me because you fear that I am plotting to kill you."

Yasim looked at Hazin and then slowly extended his hand. "For once, just for once, a moment of peace between us."

"You were the one who started this line of conversation, my lord."

"Enough, Hazin."

"Yes, my lord."

"I know what would happen if I slew you. The needle would find me."

Hazin said nothing.

"Damn, how we slaughter each other," Yasim sighed. "My brother. I remember our youth, my first teacher, the eunuch Galvina. How I loved him."

Hazin laughed softly. "Sire, he was one of us."

Startled, Yasim looked over at him.

"There was some serious bidding for a while between those who wanted him to kill you and those who did not. Obviously those who did not won."

"Damn you," Yasim whispered.

"Go on, though, sire, your story."

The emperor nodded. "Galvina tried to teach me never to love those of my blood. That all my brothers, my cousins—we would turn upon one another in the end. It had always been that way, for our race will tolerate nothing less than the strongest, the most ruthless upon the golden throne. The weaker barbarian clans to the north might allow an eldest son to rule and force the others to bow, but we of the Kazan needed ruthlessness.

"In my heart I rebelled, for I loved my brother Hanaga, and I knew there was a time when he loved me. Remember the incident when we were but cubs out sailing in the harbor and the boat overturned?"

Hazin nodded.

"I got tangled in the sails and went under. It was Hanaga who saved me. He could have left me to drown and thus have one less rival, but he saved me."

"He was honorable in his way."

"What was it like to kill him?" Yasim asked.

"It was the task assigned by the Grand Master. It was not for me to have feelings about it. I did as the Order required of me, an act that you were to pay for. So do not look at me that way, sire. It was you who, in the end, held the knife. I but gave him his release."

His words cut deeply, and Yasim lowered his head. "Galvina the eunuch was right: love no one."

"It has always been that way, it must always be that way."

"Tell me, what have my surviving cousins offered you?"

"To kill you?"

"Yes?"

"Not as much as you have to keep you alive."

"Damn all this. It is waste, contemptible waste."

"Sire, it is our way. Show weakness, and you will die."

Yasim looked at him in surprise, wondering if here, for an instant, was genuine counsel, advice freely given, without calculation.

"Go on, I sense you wish to say more, Hazin."

"Sire, we have been trapped on our islands for thousands of years. Until two hundred years ago, we did not have the knowledge, the ships capable of spanning the vastness of this sea, until the coming of the Prophet and his companions. They gave us the knowledge to begin the revolution that has taken us, in a hundred years, from ships of wood to ships of steel, from ships of sail to the power of the great engines below these decks.

"Now we can expand, and we must. I believe something has happened with the Portals. There were the Prophets, and now we find that the leader of the Bantag, their Qar

Qarth came from another world—I suspect the same as the Prophets. This place is the meeting point between worlds.

"Sire, that I will tell you is part of the plan of the Order, to gain the Portals, to unlock them, to control them. For whoever does that first will survive. Whoever fails will perish."

"And whoever controls them will have the power to rule," Yasim interjected.

"The Order answers to you, sire. They would be yours."

Yasim smiled. "And the Shiv?"

"It started as an experiment, nothing more. We bred pets for our amusement, even our affections. We bred beasts to give us milk. The barbarians to the north bred horses that came from the human world to fit their size. Why not breed humans as well?"

"There is something I have never felt comfortable with concerning that."

"Why?"

"They are intelligent. You've read the writings of Ovilla."

Hazin laughed. "That they just might have souls? Nonsense."

"They are self-aware, Hazin."

"Perhaps horses are, too, but horses do not make guns, ships, machines that fly. The humans to the north breed wild, like beasts. I seek perfecting them and then the harnessing of them to our needs.

"With the Shiv we present two things to the humans who defeated our cousins. The first is the threat of them. They are unstoppable in battle and will fight with superior cunning. Second, they offer a hope that will weaken the will to resist.

"It will appear that we offer a way to end conflict. A way for humans and our race to live together."

"Under your order."

"Which answers to you," Hazin replied quickly.

Yasim smiled. "Go on."

"As the Republic is defeated and the Hordes to the north are placed under your banner, your cousins will be diverted, and in that time your throne will be secured. The internal wars will be forgotten in an external war of conquest. That has been the bedevilment of the Kazan for a thousand years.

"Prior to the coming of the Prophet, the wars were at least contained, the destruction limited, but even you will admit that within the last two generations, the carnage has become unsustainable. The weapons have become too destructive, too powerful."

"Yes, I know that. I believe my brother Hanaga did, too."

"What happened at Bukara, for example."

Yasim wondered if there was an accusatory tone in Hazin's voice. He had leveled Bukara, which had gone over to his cousin Tagamish. Over two hundred thousand had died.

"They had given a sacred pledge of support and then betrayed it. That was always our custom."

"Before, you would have slain but the leaders of the city and their retainers. The entire city, though?"

"War changes. The city was a base. Its factories in the hands of a rebellious cousin unacceptable, and we could not hold it. Destruction was the only answer."

"That is my point," Hazin replied. "You did what was necessary, but that necessity is destroying us, while eventually the Republic of humans will expand until it is too late."

"Visha started the change. We have reached the limits within our empire. So we expand.

"Your Shiv, though, I wonder what they will lead to."

"Perhaps we should try the same experiment with our own race," Hazin said, his voice barely a whisper.

Yasim felt a wave of revulsion, and he wondered if his reaction showed.

"Seriously, my lord. Why not? Allow our strongest, our most fit, our most brilliant to breed."

"The rest?"

"There are ways to discourage them, or if need be prevent them."

"Impossible."

"Is it?"

"You've contemplated this?"

"I contemplate all things possible," Hazin said with a smile.

Yasim slowly shook his head.

"You might see differently someday. But as for the Shiv, we have several alternatives. They were simply an experiment that has proven fruitful. Now we shall unleash them upon the North. If the Republic breaks apart, which I suspect it will after the first onslaught, they can rule. Then, if we actually achieve a gate, we can push them through and see what the results are."

"Or slaughter them all," Yasim said quietly.

Hazin smiled. "Yes. Once they've served their purpose, that might be necessary. You see, there is always the prospect that the experiment will work too well, that they just might be superior. That is why I suggest what I do as to our own race."

"My original thought, Hazin, was to kill you now, to sink the transports. Your words push me closer to doing it."

"Majesty, never whisper your inner thoughts too loudly."

"Damn you."

"We are locked in an embrace, sire. You fear me and that is wise. I need you, for never would the families of the blood accept a base-born bastard such as me as emperor. If we understand that, together we can have our arrangement.

"Believe me, sire, kill me, slaughter all the Shiv, and there will still be another such as I, and yet another behind him, or her. Always remember the old adage that it is better to have an enemy that you know beside you than an enemy that you do not know behind you."

Yasim turned away, hands clasped behind his back, and walked to the far end of the bridge. The staff who had been gathered there respectfully withdrew through a hatchway into the cramped quarters of the weather bridge.

The scum is right, he thought. War is the eternal nature of the race, but if it continued internally, we would eventually annihilate ourselves while the humans to the north inherit the planet. If I ever breed a son, I want to hand him an empire, not a smoking ruin.

Yet will he ever rule? Will there be a Hazin standing behind his shoulder with a hidden needle of poison? If I have more than one son, will they slay one another as I've slain my brothers?

He looked back at Hazin, who was leaning over the railing, back turned.

This war against the Republic, I must win it swiftly, he realized. Let my cousins be in the forefront, kill off as many of them as possible, and let the others think it was for glory, promising the survivors more and yet more to drive them forward.

And then annihilate the Order once the war is won.

As Emperor Yasim of the Kazan contemplated these ideas, little did he realize that his rival, standing but forty feet away, was contemplating the exact same path.

"You did what?"

Qar Qarth Jurak flung down his cup and stood up to face the courier.

"My Qarth wishes to report that a regiment of the Yankee horse riders has been destroyed."

"By all the Ancestors, that is not what I ordered. I said, hold them at a distance."

"My Qar Qarth, they were within an hour's ride of our column of yurts. It was either that or submit to slaughter. I was there. They deployed into battle order, weapons drawn, and were preparing to attack."

"Which regiment?"

The courier, bowing, went back to his lathered mount and pulled out a flame-scorched yellow flag and handed it to Jurak.

"Third Regiment, Army of the Republic," Jurak read. He balled the flag up and tossed it to the ground.

That was Keane's regiment. He remembered the brass number on the boy's collar. If the boy was dead, then the full fury of the father might very well be unleashed.

"Did you kill all of them?"

"Not yet all. Some of them gained a hilltop, but surely they are all dead by now. We could see that the only ammunition they had was what they carried on their horses. The wagons were taken. The other half of the regiment came up to support them and fell into the second trap. All of them died."

Jurak looked around at those gathered about him. More than one was grinning with delight, a few venturing to approach the courier to slap his shoulders. One of them ceremonially offered him the gift of his knife, the traditional present for a bringer of glad tidings.

"This means we are at war," Jurak announced.

"We were never at peace to start with," one of the Qarths growled. "We merely waited until a new generation could be bred to avenge their fathers."

Word of what the courier had reported was spreading

like wildfire through the encampment. A shaman began a chant to the heroic dead, calling on the Ancestors to greet them with drink and the flesh of cattle, a chant not heard in the camp for over twenty years. The chant was picked up, other voices joining in. A nargas sounded, its deep brazen tone chilling, awe inspiring.

Jurak stared at the fire, kicking the glowing embers with the toe of his boot.

So it has begun, he realized. In the morning they might think differently, though. We must push hard, outrun their pursuit and gain the mountains, then pray that the ambassador of the Kazan spoke the truth, that an army will land bringing with it the weapons we need to survive.

He lowered his head. He had liked the boy. A pity he was dead. A pity for this entire damned world. He wondered what the elder Keane was actually thinking. Would he be motivated now by hate? Would he seek out his old foes, but this time slay them all? Or would it now be the other way around, that the Bantag shall join with the Kazan and slay the Republic and all who lived there?

Either way, he felt, I shall lose, and my people, the Bantag, shall lose.

FIFTEEN

"Now remember, you clear the deck and keep your nose down, let her drop. You've got over thirty feet to play with before leveling out. If anything goes wrong and you have time, push her to starboard. That way when you go in the drink you'll be off to one side and not get plowed under by your ship."

Adam Rosovich, with Theodor by his side, paced in front of the pilots and gunners gathered around him on the deck. A brisk wind was up, whipping his hair, and he turned into the breeze.

"We've got a good thirty-knot blow running between the ship and the wind. You shouldn't have any problems."

He looked around at the pilots. More than half of them were graduates of this year's class from the academy. Most of the rest had come out a year or two ahead of him. One of them had been his senior cadet commander when he had been a first-year plebe. It felt strange to be giving advice and orders to them. The new captain's bars pinned to his collar seemed ponderously heavy, and in a way he felt like a fraud. He had gained the rank simply because he had been available and done all this first. Granted, he would admit to himself that he was a damn good pilot. But the technical side of it had actually captivated him during his work with the Design Board, and besides, it was a hell of a lot less suicidal than the assignment he now had.

"Finally, we're trying something different here than what you trained for on land. When you clear the aft deck for landing, if you don't touch down and snag, we want you to give it full power and get the hell up again, then go around."

"Full power?" one of the Goliath pilots asked incredulously. "What the hell are you talking about? You should cut throttle completely and if need be nose it in."

"Sir," Adam replied quietly, staring at the pilot who was five years his senior and commander of the squadron on *Perryville*.

There was a momentary pause as the pilot looked around at his comrades for support. Finally he showed a trace of a definite grin. "Yes, I'm waiting for a logical answer, Rosovich."

"Look, O'Reilly. Let's say you're tenth in line coming back from the strike. We're pushing the planes forward after they land. You miss your approach, go drifting down the deck, throttle off, nose down, but you keep missing the snag wires. Where the hell do you wind up? You plow into the next plane in line, maybe two or three of them. You chop open a fuel tank, that new benzene fuel goes spraying around, and suddenly the whole ship is on fire.

"Mr. O'Reilly, therefore, if you miss the approach, the landing officer is going to wave you off. You obey him, by God. You hit the throttle, bank to port, and get the hell out of the way."

"All right, Adam. But another thing, that damn benzene. One bullet and it explodes. At least kerosene just burns. What the hell is the Design Board trying to do to us?"

Theodor stepped in front of Adam, ready to confront the

anger that had been simmering ever since the new burners for the engines and the new fuel had been revealed.

"It's a question of energy and weight," Theodor said. "With benzene you get a lot more heat per pound of fuel. Weight is crucial, gentlemen. You might have to push this out to maximum range, and the benzene fuel will give you an extra fifty miles, which might make all the difference in this flight. I don't like the risk any more than you do."

"You're not flying it," someone whispered from the back of the group.

Theodor bristled, but it was Adam who stepped forward. "Any man here who dares to question Theodor's bravery better step forward right now."

No one moved.

"You know what he did in the last war. Does anyone want to challenge that?"

There was no response.

"All right then. Everyone get ready for a go around."

A groan went up. Theodor looked over at Adam, but said nothing.

"And remember, for the first time we're all doing it with full loads." He pointed at the lined-up aerosteamers. Each of them had a barrel strapped underneath filled with sand.

Actually, all the planes would be lighter than when they did it for real. The guns on the Falcons were empty, and the fuel load was just enough to take them around on the exercise. There simply wasn't enough wind to get them off otherwise.

The group broke apart, the ten pilots who were flying headed for their aerosteamers, which were packed onto the deck. The pilots of the second group drifted off to stand along the side railing.

Adam looked up at the bridge, caught the attention of Admiral Petronius, saluted, then pointed a clenched fist forward. Petronius wearily shook his head, finally saluted back, and turned away.

Theodor laughed softly. "You know, there's a lot of debate up on that bridge about who is actually in command on this ship."

"I take orders from Petronius like everyone else, but when it comes to actual flight operations, I guess I'm in charge."

"Heady job for someone barely out of the academy."

"Wasn't it the same in the last war? You were what, twenty?"

"Something like that."

The lead aerosteamer, a Falcon, was rolled into position by its crew. The routine had been practiced for several days as the *Shiloh* cruised down from Suzdal to its first refueling stop at Cartha. That ancient city was fifty miles astern. The vast river, now named the Mississippi, was several miles wide. Straight ahead, Adam could make out the high ground that rose up like a bastion on the east bank—the Merki Narrows.

With the Falcon in place, the launch chief, a new position created by Theodor, and given to Quintus who had suggested the position, stood ready, holding the flapping red flag, a visual indicator of wind speed and any last-second variants.

Behind the lead Falcon the second and third machines were already revving up, running through the final check.

The launch chief waved the flag in a tight circle over his head, pointed it forward and ducked down.

As the lead pilot threw in full throttle, his support crew let go of the wingtips and ducked to either side. The Falcon lumbered down the deck and lifted off a good thirty feet before reaching the bow.

"Note it down," Adam said, looking over at yet another new creation, the launch and landing observation mate. "Plane number one should keep his wheels down as long as possible. He pulled up too soon. He'll argue he had the speed, but if the wind had suddenly dropped, he would have stalled and gone in."

The second plane took off without mishap, followed by the other four Falcons of the first squadron. Now came the heart-stopping moment, the big two-engine Goliaths.

The four airships were lined up at the aft end, all of them set off center so that their port side wings extended half a dozen feet over the side of the ship, just barely giving them enough clearance to get their starboard wing past the bridge.

The first of them started up, slowly rolled down the deck, bounced, lifted a few feet, touched back down, then lifted again, and gained altitude. The other three followed without mishap, and Adam, who felt like he had been holding his breath through the entire operation, exhaled noisily.

"Time?" he asked, looking over at Theodor.

"Thirteen and a half minutes."

Adam shook his head.

He looked aft. Once the launching had started, and the first four planes were cleared, there was enough room aft for the rear ramp to be lowered so that the planes of the second squadron could be brought up from below and prepared for launch.

As each plane cleared the ramp, launch crews struggled to swing the folded wings into place and lock them, then started up the engines, which would take nearly ten minutes to fully heat up.

Adam paced back and forth nervously, every few minutes looking over at Theodor, who was still holding his watch.

"Too long," Adam snapped. "Damn, the lead squadron will burn an hour's worth of fuel waiting for us."

"I know."

The six Falcons of the second squadron lifted off. The wind had picked up slightly, and all six were cleanly airborne by the time they reached the end of the launch deck.

Finally, the last four Goliaths came up.

"Don't screw this up," Theodor shouted. "You want them to follow you, you better do it right the first time."

Adam nodded, heading to the aft ramp as his aerosteamer emerged. He squatted down, carefully examining the weapon strapped underneath. The other Goliaths were carrying sand, but he was carrying the real thing, the first live test of the new weapon.

He climbed up into the cockpit and revved the engines even as the launch crew walked the plane forward, rapidly ran through a final check of controls, looked over at Quintus, who waved his flag in a tight circle and then pointed forward.

He slammed the throttles up. The massive caloric engines hissed, fumes from the burning benzene washing over him. With the extra five hundred pounds on board the ship felt heavy, the launch deck impossibly short as he rolled forward, thankful for the extra fifteen knots of wind blowing up from the south, sweeping along the deck. The wings bit, controls felt lighter, and he lifted. The fact that the airship had only enough fuel on board for the demonstration flight was worrisome, and he wondered how it would handle when fully loaded.

The morning was slightly hazy, thin wisps of mist drifting across the Mississippi. He flew steadily forward for the first mile, watching his gauges, letting airspeed build up to sixty knots, then turned out of the wind. The other planes, which had been circling in their holding pattern to the starboard of the *Shiloh* at an altitude of a thousand feet, were waiting for him.

He wondered what they were thinking, how many were cursing him, how many thought him mad, how many might actually believe in what they were trying to do.

He wagged his wings, signaling for the group to follow, and all but one fell into line, flying in formation abreast, heading back up the river.

Several miles astern of *Shiloh* was *Wilderness,* and a mile behind her the third aerosteamer carrier *Perryville. Wilderness* had recovered all the planes from her practice, the deck was packed with them and Adam had a cold thought, wondering what would happen if a Kazan aerosteamer should ever catch them thus, planes loaded with benzene lining the deck. The last of the *Perryville*'s planes were coming in, and to his dismay he saw a burning slick on the water behind her, bits of wreckage floating. Someone had gone in. The light frigate tailing the group had come to a stop, sending a rescue boat over the side, but it was hard to tell if they had managed to pull anyone out.

The practice target for the day was clearly marked along the east shore of the river. It was the hulk of an old ironclad monitor from the last war, anchored in place. The once proud ship had been stripped of her two guns. Observers from the Design Board, who had been dropped off from the escorting frigate to observe the strike, lined the bank. Someone, not trusting the eyesight of the pilots, had splashed red paint on the side of the ship and hung a red flag from atop the rusted turret. Muddy splashes ringed the ship, and to his delight he could see where a barrel of sand had exploded directly atop the turret. Whoever had scored that one deserved a bottle of vodka once they reached Constantine.

The Falcons were practicing bombing today, but the

board was still debating if the several hundred pounds might not be better spent on additional ammunition for their gunner in order to provide covering fire for the far more lethal load carried by the Goliaths.

Adam, leading the way, circled in over the monitor, holding at a thousand feet. He looked over at Captain Sugami, leader of the 1st Squadron, who was flying a Falcon just off his wingtip, pointed down, and saluted.

Sugami, grinning, saluted back, and led the way, nosing over, cutting into a broad circling turn to bring his unit around to the north for a run down on their target straight into the wind.

Adam realized that in a way the entire exercise was ridiculous. The target, anchored fore and aft, was stationary, no one was shooting back, there was no smoke, and most of all there was no fear, other than the usual knot in the stomach one had when flying a crate loaded with explosives.

The first squadron turned into their attack position, as discussed, three miles out from the target, flying line astern, Falcons first, followed by the Goliaths.

Sugami, in the lead plane, landed his barrel of sand almost square on the monitor's turret. The next three planes did nearly as well, but the last two were abysmal, one missing by a good hundred yards, the other crabbing at the last second. His barrel hit fifty yards off the ship's bow.

The four Goliaths followed with mixed results. One slammed his barrel directly across the bow of the ship. The other two hit within a couple of yards. The last was either a fool or his release mechanism was jammed, for the barrel didn't fall until he was a good quarter mile beyond the target.

Adam motioned for the second squadron to go down while he continued to circle. The results were roughly the same, perhaps a little bit better, with two Goliaths making hits this time.

No maneuvering, no shooting, no smoke, he kept thinking throughout. His heart was beginning to pound. What would the real moment actually feel like?

Finally he was alone, the rest of his planes heading back to the *Shiloh*. He swung out over the target, skimming along the shore, looking down at the several dozen men and women from the design team.

As he nosed over, picking up speed rapidly, he could feel the five-hundred-pound weight of the weapon slung beneath his cockpit pulling the Goliath down. He leveled out a bit too early, eased down another fifty feet, and went into his banking turn. Coming out of the turn, he lined up on the ironclad.

From three miles out it looked absurdly small, almost difficult to spot except for the red paint and flag. He closed in, wondering what the range was for the Kazan guns, how much fire would be coming at him, what was their tactical deployment, whether they had armed escort ships ringing the targets.

Range was less than a mile. He dropped lower, down to fifty feet, eased back on the throttle, bringing airspeed down to fifty knots. A hint of turbulence buffeted a wing up, and he steadied it out. There seemed to be a slight surge with the engine, but he ignored it. Range was a half mile, and now the ironclad was looking bigger, but the real thing would be far bigger, a dozen times bigger, and shooting at him.

He leaned into the sight, nothing more than a piece of pipe with a crosshair set inside. He aimed straight amidships today, since the target wasn't moving. When its real aim half a ship's length ahead of the bow, a few seconds more . . . he pulled the release.

The Goliath surged up like a bird of prey that had just dropped a burden that had proven too heavy. He gave the plane full throttle, then banked over sharply, circling around, remembering to stay well clear of the monitor. Turning out and away, he caught sight of a foaming wake.

The damn thing was working! It was under its own power, cutting through the water, exhaust from the compressed air spinning the propeller!

He thought he actually caught a glimpse of the underwater, self-propelled mine moving through the water at fifteen knots. This time it was tracking straight in, closing on the side of the monitor.

And nothing happened.

A second later he caught a glimpse of it again . . . on the other side of the ship! It had gone right under the target.

Cursing, he winged over, following it. The underwater shell continued on its way, going another two hundred yards until finally its compressed air tank lost pressure. The weapon slowed, came to a stop . . . and finally there was a violent explosion. Water cascaded a hundred feet into the air as it struck the bottom of the river.

"Damn it all to hell."

It had tracked too deep. Maybe the monitor didn't draw enough water, but still, he knew how this would affect his men. They figured the whole thing was a suicidal gesture anyhow. The fact that this, the fourth test, had been a failure as well wasn't going to help.

Dejected, he turned south, heading back toward the *Shiloh*. Suddenly there was a flash of fire. Even from six miles away he knew what had happened as he caught a glimpse of flame spreading out astern of the carrier. Someone had crashed and most likely died on landing.

And this is how we are supposed to stop the Kazan? he thought grimly.

Andrew hesitated before knocking on the door, and the mere fact that he did shocked him. The city was quiet this time of night, just after midnight, when he often enjoyed going for a walk. Ditching the guards was an old routine, and they went through the show of expressing their dismay when he returned. He suspected that as usual a couple of them were following at a discreet distance under orders from Kathleen.

He could see that lights were still on where Pat lived, which had been Andrew's home until the presidency forced him to move back into the White House. Reaching the porch of his home, he felt a wave of nostalgia. It was where they had raised their children, and it was in that front parlor that they had held the wakes for the ones who had died. How many evenings, he thought with a smile, did we sit on this porch, the children playing in the New England–like town square? The few men left of the 35th Maine and 44th New York would often gather here in the evening, drinking lemonade spiked with a touch of vodka, laughing about the old days, remembering comrades lost. The tales kept growing, enlarging in memory through the years until it seemed that they had once lived and fought in a golden age.

The children would frolic in the front yard, sometimes stopping to listen, other times wandering off to play tag around the statue dedicated to the memory of the fallen, or dance around the bandstand where, on summer evenings, light waltzes and traditional Rus tunes would be played.

He turned back to the task at hand, lifted the heavy eagle brass knocker, and let it drop.

No answer. He rapped again, several times. Finally he heard a mumble from the parlor. Knowing what it meant, he opened the door and walked in.

Pat was sprawled out on a sofa. Andrew was glad Kathleen was not along. She'd had the sofa specially made, patterned after the designs popular back on Earth just before they had embarked on "their journey." It was a beautiful piece made with dark walnut and upholstered with a light green silk. Pat, dusty boots still on, had his feet up over the side, an empty bottle of vodka on the floor next to an overturned spittoon and another bottle, which was lying on its side, half empty. The place stank.

Bleary-eyed, Pat looked up and frowned. "Get the hell out and leave me alone," he growled.

Andrew, without saying a word, headed for the kitchen. A low fire still glowed in the wood stove. Picking up a handful of kindling, he tossed it in, found some tea in the pantry, and set a kettle to boiling.

"What the hell are you doing?"

He looked up. Pat stood in the kitchen doorway, leaning heavily against the frame.

"Getting you sobered up, damn it," Andrew snapped.

"What for? Now leave me alone."

"How long have you been on this drunk? Two days, three?"

Pat grinned foolishly. "I don't know."

"We've got things to go over."

"Let it wait till morning. I'm tired."

"A wire came up from Bullfinch an hour ago. There's a report of smoke from ships being sighted inside our boundary. It might mean they're coming a hell of a lot quicker than we expected. Bullfinch is sending up an aerosteamer now. It will be out there by dawn."

"So?"

"Pat, if they're inside our boundary, as defined by the treaty, that means Cromwell was right and we're at war."

"Cromwell. God damn his soul." Pat turned, staggering back to the parlor. Andrew could hear a bottle clattering and followed.

Pat was standing by the parlor window, bottle up, ready to take another drink.

"Drop it, Pat."

Pat looked over and smiled, but there was a light in his eyes that Andrew knew well.

"Drop it, Pat," he said slowly.

"Are you going to make me, Andrew darlin'?"

"If I have to."

Pat laughed, tilted his head back and started to drink.

Andrew strode across the room and struck the bottle away. It slammed against the window, shattering a pane.

Pat turned with a roar. Grabbing Andrew by his shirt, he slammed him up against the wall. "No one, not even you, stops me from a drink," he cried.

Andrew remained motionless. "Let go of me, Pat," he said softly, "I'll fight you, by God, if you want, but let me take my jacket off first."

Pat looked at him, wide-eyed. The front door out in the hallway was flung open, and two of Andrew's bodyguards rushed in, one of them with pistol drawn.

"Get out!" Andrew shouted. "Get the hell out of here!"

"Sir?"

The two stared at them, obviously terrified, with their charge pinned to a wall by a drunk senator.

"I told you to get the hell out of this house!" Andrew yelled, his voice nearly breaking. "Wait out in the street until this is over."

The two looked at each other, a few words were whispered, and they backed out the door, not bothering to close it, and waited on the porch.

"Are we going to fight, Pat?" Andrew asked.

Pat let go of him, and Andrew, without waiting for a reply, fumbled with the buttons of his Lincolnesque long-tailed jacket. He let it fall to the floor and raised his one hand and balled it into a fist.

Pat stood stock still and then turned away, shoulders beginning to shake. Within seconds he had dissolved into sobs.

Andrew came up to his side, put an arm around his shoulders, and led him back into the kitchen, settling him down in a straight-back chair next to the stove. He found two mugs and poured out the boiling tea. Clumsily holding the mugs in his one hand, he kicked another chair over to Pat, sat down, and offered him one.

Pat, face covered with his hands, continued to sob.

"Come on, old friend, drink some of this."

Pat looked up, face red from crying and far too many years of drinking. "And you with one arm wanting to fight me, no less."

"Because I'm your friend, Pat."

That started the tears again.

"I'm ashamed of meself, Andrew darlin', ashamed I am." He slipped into such a heavy brogue, Andrew was not sure of what he said next.

Finally he looked up at Andrew and, surprisingly, made the sign of the cross. "May the saints damn me forever if I ever touch you again in anger."

"Just drink the damned tea," Andrew said wearily. He almost preferred Pat belligerent rather than sunk into a maudlin display of Irish drunkenness.

Pat did as ordered, half draining the scalding brew, then finishing the rest while Andrew sipped his own. He sat back and waited for the effect. A long minute passed. Pat stood up, staggered out onto the front porch, and got sick. After a long while he came back, features pale, and Andrew tossed him a towel. Wiping his face, he dropped the towel onto the floor and sat back down while Andrew found another cup and refilled it. This time Pat drank more slowly.

"It's my son, you know," Pat finally said. "The fact that he did what Cromwell said. I still can't believe one of me blood would do such a thing."

"Our children, Pat, sometimes one never knows."

"Your own boy? I'm sorry. Any word?"

Andrew shook his head. "Hawthorne said he's sending up a couple of extra aerosteamers to patrol out toward their last known location. I told him not to do anything special . . ." and his voice trailed off.

"The whole frontier's exploded. Fifth cavalry was completely wiped out, their fort overrun. Fourth and Seventh are in a running fight, retreating. The only thing that saved them was two aerosteamers. The Bantag got one of them, but the gatling fire kept them back long enough so the regiments could ford a river and get the hell out.

"There's going to be an uproar in Congress when it opens in another eight hours. The Chin are talking about forming up their own militia, going out, and massacring any Bantag they find. One of the Qarths, old Kubazin, is staying put, says he's keeping his land. I want him left alone; he's staying within the treaty agreement, but the Chin want to go and kill him and everyone else.

"Pat, it's chaos out there and it starts up here come morning. A fair number of senators are claiming the whole thing is a mad mistake and are looking for someone to blame."

"You," Pat croaked, looking down glumly at his tea.

"I can stand that. If the Kazan are indeed coming, in another day or two that song will change. But then it will be a different tune—how we weren't prepared, how we somehow provoked the attack, how the Republic is finished and will never work." His voice trailed off as he looked at Pat, realizing that while he had been pouring out his woes, his friend was still dead drunk and consumed with his own anguish.

"Our boys, Andrew," Pat sighed.

Andrew felt a sudden welling up of tears, and he struggled not to break, not now. All he could do was nod. "I thought our war would have finished it. That it would never touch our own."

Pat looked up and smiled weakly. "I just wish I'd set mine on a different path, when I still had the chance." He took another sip of tea and lowered his head again.

"You're a dreamer, Andrew me friend, if you thought our war was the last of it. Our parents dreamed it. Mine did when they sent me away from Ireland, saying America would be safe, and look at the right fine slaughter you and I found ourselves in there."

He hesitated.

"If your boy survives, and I pray to the saints he does, his boys after him will fight as well."

Andrew said nothing, realizing with a profound sadness

that his friend had not included his son in that prayer as
well.

Lieutenant Abraham Keane froze. Something was ahead,
something had moved.

He could sense Sergeant Togo beside him, crouched low,
knife out. As the seconds passed, the high wispy clouds that
had obscured Baka, the greater of the two moons, parted.

Togo relaxed. A rabbit, nearly under their feet, leapt up
and bounded away.

Andrew exhaled noisily. Togo held his hand out, motioning for him to remain still. Off to his right, he could
see the glow of a fire flickering in a ravine, a gruff voice,
silence for a moment, then barking laughter. The next wave
of high-drifting clouds covered the moon.

Togo crept forward, Abraham and the rest of his men
following. Every step kicked up tiny plumes of dust, ash,
and the smell of charred grass. Another smell drifted on
the breeze as well, and he suppressed a gag.

Again the moonlight appeared, and all of them froze,
crouching low. Abe looked back to the east. The butte
stood out clearly in the moonlight. A flash, seconds later
the report of a rifle.

Darkness again, they pushed forward. Togo slowed again,
touched Abe on the shoulder, pointed. The ground ahead
dropped away to reveal a broken wheel sticking up out of
the shallow ravine. Togo got down on his hands and knees,
crawling the last dozen paces, Abe at his side.

Three days in the sun had made the stench all but un-
bearable. He caught a glimpse of what was left of the
horses. The Bantag had butchered them for the meat, but
not the offal. Abe was startled when a buzzard, which had
been resting next to the remains, tried to fly off, squawking,
belly so distended that it could barely get into the air.

Abe pressed his face to the ground, gasping, trying to
deaden the sound of his vomiting.

Togo, ignoring his misery, pulled him over the lip of the
ravine and down into the awful mess, then hissed for the
others to follow.

"You men with the canteens," Togo whispered, "get up
the ravine, fifty yards at least from this filth, scoop up an

embankment to block the water and start filling the canteens."

"Lieutenant, some cartridges might have spilled out of this wagon. Feel the ground."

The clouds parted again, and in the moonlight he caught a glimpse of one of the drivers—what little was left of him after the butchering.

"Still think Jurak's your friend?" Togo whispered fiercely.

Abe started to retch yet again.

"Damn you, Lieutenant, there is no time for that now," Togo hissed.

Startled, Abe looked over at him.

"Look, damn it. Look."

Abe crawled across the muddy bottom of the ravine. A wagon had upended, its torn canvas top rippling in the breeze. Inside the wreckage he caught a glimpse of the second driver and turned away.

"In here," Togo whispered.

Abe, startled, saw that the sergeant had come into the wagon from the other side and was kneeling alongside the stinking smear of what had once been a man.

Abe hesitated, took a deep breath, and then slipped up to the sergeant.

"The bastards looted it clean, but here's a broken ammunition box. Help me."

Abe heard the rattle of shells as Togo swept them up from the floor of the wagon and started to dump them into his haversack.

"Come on, Lieutenant. If they saw that buzzard fly off and not come back, they might get suspicious."

The stench was all around him. He felt as if it was seeping into his clothes, his hair, penetrating his skin. He tried not to breathe as he swept his hands across the bottom of the wagon. Then he felt something rolling underneath. He scooped up several carbine shells.

The discovery made him forget his anguish. Half the men back up on the butte were completely out of ammunition, and the rest had only two or three rounds apiece. He rejoiced as if he had stumbled into a cave filled with jewels.

"Why didn't they take these?" Abe whispered.

"You might not believe it, but those hairy bastards have sensitive noses," Togo whispered. "Our old comrade here scared them off if they came back looking for more later. Now shut up and get these shells."

Abe slowly crawled about in the dark, feeling the wooden boards, recoiling for a second when he touched something soft and yielding. Then, realizing that more shells were underneath the noisome mass, he closed his eyes, pushed it aside, and grabbed more of the precious cartridges.

The haversack draped from his shoulder grew heavy as the minutes passed, and then he became aware that Togo had stopped working. He was crouched half up, tensed, hand out, motioning to Abe.

All his instincts seemed to flare at once. He felt the hair at the nape of his neck stiffen, his heart thump. Ever so slowly he backed out of the wagon, Togo by his side, neither saying a word.

A cascade of crumbling dirt trickled down from the top of the ravine. He started to draw his revolver before he saw the glint of Togo's knife in the moonlight.

He slipped his revolver back into its holster, reached around to his other hip, and slipped out a bayonet. He followed Togo to the side of the ravine, pressed up against the wall, and waited.

In the silence, Abe heard something breathing. Again the shadows parted, moonlight flooding the ravine, and on the far wall of the gully he saw a shadow moving.

Togo pointed at the shadow, then held his knife up.

Abe took a deep breath and nodded.

The two went up the side at the same instant.

A dark silhouette towered above him. It was turning, swinging something. He ducked under the blow. After a grunt of pain, the silhouette doubled over, dropping a rifle, which fell with a clatter that sounded like a tree crashing in the stillness.

The shadow lashed out with a clubbed fist, and Togo spun backwards. The mass of darkness leapt on top of the sergeant.

Abe stood there, transfixed as the two struggled, rolling on the ground.

"Kill him!" Togo hissed, "kill him!"

Time stretched out. He wondered who this was. Could it

be one of the cubs that Jurak had pointed out to him only days ago? He didn't seem full-grown for a Bantag.

"Keane!"

Abe saw an arm go up, heavy blade shiny in the moonlight.

He leapt upon the back of the Bantag. Grabbing the arm, he pulled it back, jerking the arm with such force that he heard the bone snap.

There was a howl of pain.

Terror drove him. He let go of the broken arm and grabbed the Bantag's head with his left hand, and then slashed down with his right, driving the blade into his victim's throat.

He felt something hot splashing out. The howl disintegrated into a gasping, bubbly groan.

He cut again, feeling the blade hit bone.

Togo kicked his way out from under the Bantag.

"Damn, Lieutenant, don't hesitate next time!"

Abe, barely hearing him, continued to slash, feeling the life slipping out of the Bantag. He begged for him to die quickly, to end it.

Togo pulled him back. "Enough, Lieutenant, he's finished! Now by all the gods let's get out of here!"

Togo rolled back down into the ravine, but Abe stood up, still holding the blade.

A gutteral challenge echoed from the next ravine, where they had spotted the fire.

"Lieutenant!"

He saw a shadow standing up, then another.

"Lieutenant!"

Abe looked back down at the body, which was still kicking spasmodically.

"I'm sorry," he gasped, and leapt back down into the gully.

"What the hell is going on?"

It was one of the men from the watering party.

"We're on the move," Togo hissed.

Togo led the way, running up the ravine, Abe and the returning soldier following. They met the men still filling canteens.

"We've only got half of them full," one of them cried.

"No time," Togo snapped, and he sprinted on.

Abe waited as one of the men plunged another canteen into the muddy pool. Drawing his revolver, he turned, looking for Bantag. The seconds dragged out.

"Finished!"

The soldier began to stand up. There was a blinding flash, the roar of a rifle shot shattering the stillness. The man with the canteen seemed to lift into the air and was flung backward.

A Bantag stood atop the ravine. Flash-blinded, Abe turned, crouched and fired, then fired again. He caught a glimpse of the Bantag crumbling, clutching his stomach.

The man whom he had been guarding was dead, arms spread wide, half a dozen canteens flung out on the ground beside him.

The water, the precious water.

He snatched up the straps of the canteens and started to run.

As soon as he had turned his back on the dead man, a mad panic took hold, and he ran blindly, weaving his way up the ravine. He heard another rifle shot, this one directly above. He blindly raised his revolver, fired again, and kept on running, slipping on the muddy ground.

He came around the next turn in the gully and almost screamed with fright. In the moonlight he saw the glint from a gun barrel.

It was Sergeant Togo, weapon leveled straight at him.

Togo lowered the gun, then a split second later raised it and fired.

Abe turned and saw a Bantag directly behind him. He hadn't even heard his pursuer closing in. The Bantag spun around, clutching his shoulder.

"Come on, sir!"

Togo sprinted off and this time Abe followed, keeping close. Ahead he could hear his men running. They were reaching the top. Above the lip he could see the butte, the Great Wheel overhead.

Strange, the night was so crystal clear. The fact that he had time to recognize that struck him as curious.

The gully where they had been began to curve away from their mountain fortress. The quarter mile of open prairie that they had crept across before now separated them from safety.

The men ahead had slowed, not sure what to do.

Togo didn't hesitate. He turned to look back, crouching low. "Full out now, boys. Don't stop for anything. If a man goes down, grab his water, but he's on his own. Now run for it!"

The group started off.

Abe looked back, saw flashes of torchlight in the ravine, deep voices calling. He started to run. Togo was in the lead, but something compelled Abe to keep to the rear, following his men. He heard the clatter of hooves, and from his left saw several Bantag coming up out of a deep gully, urging their mounts forward.

At the sight of them everyone redoubled their efforts, the men gasping, canteens slung over their shoulders, banging on their hips. For a second Abe was tempted to let his own canteens drop, to cut them loose, but he hung on to the precious load and to the haversack brimming with cartridges.

At first it seemed that the riders had not seen their prey. Then they turned and started straight for them.

From atop the butte he saw a flash. A second later the sharp crack of a rifle shot echoed. A waste of a precious round.

The riders closed in, one of them standing in his stirrups, and though he could not see, Abe knew the man had a bow and was drawing it.

One of his men went down, clutching his leg, canteens clattering.

There was a flash of a pistol. Togo was firing, and though he missed the rider the horse reared and turned away. The other two continued to follow them. An arrow slashed past Abe, the rider pressing in, both hands off the reins, tossing aside his bow and drawing a scimitar.

Abe crouched, both hands on his revolver. He cocked it and waited. As the Bantag closed in, he emptied his cylinder. Horse and rider crashed to the ground in front of him. He turned, but the third rider was gone, where he could not tell.

Holstering his empty revolver, Abe ran up to the downed trooper, who was clutching his thigh and gasping.

"Can you run?"

The man looked up at him wide-eyed.

"Take the water!"

His English was broken, thick with the brogue of the Gaelic.

Ignoring Togo's orders, Abe put an arm under the man's shoulder and helped him up.

"Run!" Abe hissed.

The two set off, staggering and weaving. He was tempted to throw off their canteens, but the butte looked so close, so damnably close, and he pushed on.

He could no longer see Togo and the others.

He heard hoofbeats, looked over his shoulder, and saw four more riders coming in at the gallop.

"Run, damn it, run!" Abe cried. The wounded trooper gasped, cursing in Gaelic, staggered alongside him, hopping on his one good leg.

The pursuit came closer, thundering. He could hear their wild shouts and sensed they were filled with a mad joy, the joy of the hunt and the kill.

The wounded trooper started to push him away, shouting for Abe to run. Abe turned, pulled his revolver back out, raised it at the lead rider and then remembered that it was empty.

He stood there, stunned. The rider filled his world, a darker shadow in the darkness of night.

The rider tumbled backward, falling, illuminated by a brilliant flash.

A volley crackled around him. Half a dozen troopers came up at a run, crouching low, carbines raised. One of the men grabbed Abe, pushing him forward. Another scooped up the Irish soldier, the two of them shouting at each other in their native tongue.

Abe felt his legs turn to liquid, and for a second he was frightened that he had wet himself in terror, but then realized he was soaked with sweat.

Barely able to walk, he accepted the helping hand of a trooper for the last fifty yards to the butte, the ring of skirmishers closing in around him.

Scrambling onto the base of the mountain, he collapsed behind a barrier of rocks piled up over the last three days as a rough stockade covering the west side trail of the mountain.

In the shadows he looked around at his companions. Men

were gasping, bent over. The wounded man was sprawled out, cursing while his companion pulled out a knife and slashed the trouser leg open to examine the wound.

"I told you to leave the wounded behind, sir."

Abe, knees raised and head between his legs, looked up. Togo was holding a precious canteen, and he offered it. More than a day had passed since his last sip of water, and he eagerly took the canteen, the canvas cover slippery with mud. It was uncorked and Abe tilted his head back. The muddy drink seemed like the finest he had ever tasted. He took a long gulp, then remembering how precious the liquid was, he stopped and offered the canteen back.

Togo squatted at his side. "Go ahead, Lieutenant, take another drink, you need it."

Abe struggled to refuse but gave in, but this time allowing himself only a sip before recorking it.

"Damn it, sir, that was rather stupid if you don't mind my saying so."

Abe took a deep breath and exhaled slowly. "Sergeant Togo, if I remember the way things work in this army, I'm supposed to be in command, not you. I wasn't going to leave a man out there to be butchered."

Togo leaned back and a soft chuckle greeted Abe's words. A gentle hand clapped him on the shoulder.

"For a Westerner, you did good out there, sir, real good."

Abe shook his head, suddenly embarrassed. "Sorry I froze on you."

"What?"

"With the Bantag, back at the wagon."

"Your first kill with a knife, wasn't it?"

Abe slowly nodded.

"You'll get used to it."

"I hope not," he whispered, remembering the bubbling gasp, what the Bantag was saying. He had heard it before in Jurak's camp, the ritual prayer to the Ancestors, calling upon them to witness.

The companion of the wounded soldier came over, knelt down, and started to speak in Gaelic.

Abe shook his head.

"English. Speak English, trooper."

"Oh. Me baby brother, sir. Thank you, sir." The man fell silent, embarrassed, then withdrew.

Togo leaned closer to Abe. "You did the right thing, Keane. The men here will follow you to hell after this."

Abe laughed softly. "Sergeant, we've been trapped here now for nearly four days. I thought we were in hell."

"It's only started."

"Lieutenant Keane, is the lieutenant all right?"

Keane looked up. It was Sergeant Major Mutaka.

He slipped down behind the rock wall just as a rifle shot zipped in, kicking up a shower of splinters. One of the men cursed and peeked up over the side.

"Damn, there's a whole parcel of them out there."

The sergeant major sat down with Abe. "You hurt, sir?"

"No, I'm fine, just winded."

Before he could say more, Togo quickly related what had happened.

"I figure we got around half a quart of water per man, not much, but it will keep us going another day. The lieutenant and I got lucky. We found four or five hundred rounds of carbine ammunition as well."

Abe, remembering the haversack slung around his neck, reached down and opened it up. A sickening stench wafted up, and he quickly closed it.

"If we do this again tomorrow night," the sergeant major announced, "sir, you stay behind. I know why you volunteered to lead the first one, but you've proven your point with the men. So do us all a favor and let one of the other lieutenants go."

Abe would not admit it, but he was more than glad to nod in agreement.

"And, sir. The major started coming around while you were gone. Started saying he was in command again."

"Oh, damn. What did you do, Sergeant? For God's sake I hope you didn't hit him again."

Mutaka chuckled softly. "No, sir. It's twice now I've whacked him. Any more, and I think it'd kill him."

He paused, and Abe wondered if the sergeant was quietly waiting for some sign to simply go and finish the job.

"Sergeant, don't even think about it."

"What, sir?"

"We both know, so let's drop it."

"Anyhow, one of the boys finally admitted he had a quart of vodka still stashed away in his saddlebag. How he'd hung on to it without drinking it is beyond me. The captain drank it all and passed out, so we don't have to deal with it for a while yet."

"Thank God."

Two men had rigged up a stretcher from a blanket and two Bantag rifles. They started back up the steep slope carrying the wounded soldier, his brother walking beside him.

"There, I see another one," a watching soldier whispered, pointing over the rock wall. He started to raise his carbine.

Abe crawled up beside him and peered over. He could see several of them, crouching low, weaving their way across the flat open plain. On impulse he touched the trooper beside him on the shoulder and shook his head.

He looked back at the stretcher team heading up the slope, keeping low, quickly moving from the cover of one boulder to another. He was suddenly aware that it was getting lighter. On the other side of the butte the first dim glow of dawn must already be visible.

He knelt and cupped his hands.

"No shooting!" he cried, struggling to remember the Bantag words. "Your wounded and dead we honor. Take them back to their yurts."

The men around him shifted uncomfortably. Togo cursed softly under his breath.

One of the Bantags slowly stood up, then held his rifle over his head with both hands, the sign that he would not shoot. Others stood up, and Abe was surprised to see not two or three but a dozen or more, one of them less than fifty yards away. He wondered if the closest had seen the stretcher party going up the slope and had been waiting for a kill.

Wounded and dead out on the ground in front of the butte were picked up and carried off.

The lone warrior, rifle over his head, remained still until the last of the bodies had been retrieved. Finally he lowered his gun and turned away, walking upright.

"Not even a thank-you, damn them," Mutaka hissed.

"I didn't expect one," Abe replied softly.

He started up the slope, Togo falling in by his side.

"This isn't no gentleman's war, sir," Togo whispered.

"I know that, Sergeant."

"But, sir, maybe you were right," Togo finally conceded.

Abe thought of the warrior he had cut apart with the knife and then what was left of the two troopers in the wrecked wagon. What the hell is right out here? he wondered. Was this what my father saw? Is this what he felt?

They gained the crest of the butte, the horizon before him shifting from deep indigo to a pale glowing red. The troopers who had gone on the expedition spread out, passing out canteens. Desperate men eagerly took the precious loads, gulping down a drink, but Abe could see that in almost every case a man would drink but briefly, then pause and pass it on to a comrade waiting beside him.

He could see the men who had been with him returning to their friends, squatting down, whispering, and gradually heads would lift, turn and gaze in his direction. Under a roughly made shelter, rigged from blankets and ground clothes, was the hospital. The surgeon was a lone surviving medical orderly who had worked without rest for three days on the forty odd men who had been wounded and dragged to the top of the butte. The orderly was already at work, the men who had gathered around to watch were turning as well, looking at Abe.

The look, he realized, they are giving me "the look." He had seen it wherever his father went, the gaze, the flicker of a smile, the slight straightening of the shoulders. Always he had associated it with his father, and for a second he wondered if somehow his father had come into their midst and was standing behind him.

But then he knew that it was him they were looking at. These were now his men.

Embarrassed, he lowered his head, slumped down behind a boulder, and within minutes was asleep, untroubled by the nightmare he had just survived.

And when he awoke an hour later with dawn, he found that someone had put a blanket over his shoulders and left a cup of water by his side.

Dawn was obscured by banks of clouds marching along the eastern horizon, their interiors glowing with flashes of lightning.

It had been a hard night of flying. The summer heat was at its height, the ocean below heavy with warmth that, during the night, would continue to evaporate, the warm air rising, changing it to clouds and then towering thunderheads. To drift into one was almost certain death. The wind shears were capable of ripping the wings off a steamer in a single, cruel slash. It was the perfect brew for the beginning of the cyclone season.

Richard had weaved and darted around the storms, going down so low at times that salt spray coated his windscreen, then rising up again through canyons of open air. The stars twinkling overhead guided him as they had guided all navigators who sailed or flew at night.

In the dawning light he looked out across the massive wings of his four-engine aerosteamer, one of the new Ilya Murometz models, capable of ranging outward a thousand miles. He had run with all four engines through most of the night, wanting to get as far out to sea as possible, pushing the range. His fuel was nearly half gone. For the journey back he'd cut two of the engines off, add buoyancy by releasing additional hydrogen into the aft gasbag, which was tucked into the huge, hundred foot tail boom, then lift to the thin air of fourteen thousand feet.

His forward and aft observers had been violently sick through most of the night flight as they bobbed up and down in the warm thermals, and it was hard to keep them at their tasks. Both of the men kept groaning, their agony echoing through the speaking tubes.

Richard tried to block out the sounds. He was just as susceptible as they were and had leaned out the port side window more than once.

His copilot and navigator, a hearty Rus flight sergeant, had taken the entire ride as an immense joke, laughing at the agony of his three companions. Propped above and behind Richard in the top gunner position, he kept shouting ribald songs to the wind . . . and then fell silent.

"Cromwell, off to starboard!"

Richard looked to the right, but saw nothing.

"Igor, what the hell is it? You are supposed to tell me what you see," he cried, turning to look up past the feet of the man behind him.

"Smoke. I see smoke."

Richard called to his forward observer, who came back with a negative. Banking the huge aerosteamer slightly to port so that the windscreen to his right rose, he tried to see what Igor was shouting about, but saw nothing.

"Igor, get down here, damn it!"

Igor slipped back down into the cabin and sat in the chair beside Richard. He could see that Igor's face was beet red from the wind as he pulled up his goggles and grinned.

"I saw it. Smoke, lots of smoke." As Igor spoke, he pointed off to starboard, roughly twenty degrees from their heading. Igor then reached around behind the seat and pulled out the plot board, their map tacked to it. Igor's estimates of their speed and heading had been checked off every fifteen minutes. According to the chart, they were fifty miles northwest of the previous day's sighting of smoke.

Richard knew it was all guess work. Without the sun it was impossible to shoot a sighting, and even when it was out, most of the time the navigator would calculate that they were two hundred miles north of Suzdal and in the Great Northern Forest. Shooting an angle might work on a boat, but in a plane, surging and falling with the wind, it was a waste of time.

So everything had to be based on airspeed, and estimated winds, and in ten hours they could be a hundred, even two hundred miles off from where they were supposed to be this morning. For that matter, the pilot of this aircraft from the previous day could be two hundred miles off from where he claimed he was.

They had not sighted any known landmark so far, not the Tortuga Shoals, the Caldonian Isles, or the Archipelago of the Malacca Pirates. Their only fix had been on the Minoan Shoals, ninety miles due south of Constantine, and that had been less than two hours into their flight. It was all guesswork, and he wondered if Igor, given his reputation on land, had been secretly sipping vodka during the night.

"You take the controls, Igor, and aim us toward where you think you're seeing things. I'm going topside for a better look."

"You'll see, Commander," Igor said with a grin, "and we'll get the credit."

"Great, just what I wanted," he replied glumly. Unbuckling from his seat, he scrambled up through the circular opening just aft of the pilot's seat and popped out, bracing himself against the breech of the topside gatling. He remembered to clip the harness around his waist to the safety ring and then stood up into the wind, pulling down his goggles, then clipped on the speaking tube and earplugs.

Bracing his hands on the top wings, he felt a momentary thrill. The great wings of the Ilya Murometz, more than a hundred feet across, spread out to either side. Clouds whisked by overhead, stretching to the hazy glow of the all-encompassing horizon. The plane banked, Igor, demonstrating a good touch on the controls, gently bringing them around and then leveling out.

"I think I'm flying straight toward it!" Igor shouted, and Richard winced. In the earplugs the man's voice was far too loud.

Leaning against the wind, Richard looked straight ahead, but saw absolutely nothing but the milky haze of the horizon. "I don't see a damn thing."

"Look careful. It's coal smoke. Darker. I know, I've seen it from our ships many times."

Richard squinted, tried to use his field glasses, and gave up after a few seconds. The plane was bouncing too much.

He squatted back down a bit and leaned forward, as if the extra few inches might somehow clear the view. He carefully scanned ahead, not even quite sure where the horizon ended and the ocean began . . . and then he saw it, a dark smudge.

It gave him a chill, and he had a sudden flash of memory, of the indistinct smudge on the horizon at sunset the night the *Gettysburg* went to her doom. It was a barely distinguishable difference in light, a darker shadow against a light gray sky and sea.

"About five degrees to port!" Richard shouted. "Ask Xing up forward if he sees it yet."

The plane slipped ever so slightly, then leveled out again.

"Xing is blind," Igor cried, "he sees nothing. You see it, though."

He still wasn't sure. Had he thought he'd seen something simply because he was looking so hard for it? But then it reappeared, a dark greasy smudge.

"Yes! Hold us steady on this bearing. You're almost straight on it."

Igor laughed.

Long minutes passed, and gradually the darkness began to spread out.

"I can see it from in here," Igor announced. "That Xing is blind. Throw him off now. It will lighten the load so we get home."

Richard said nothing, trying again with the field glasses, momentarily catching it, then losing it as the plane surged yet again.

Finally he saw something more, a dark spot, looking like the blade of a knife turned almost edgewise, two small dark pins rising from it. The pagodas of a battleship?

"Give us a little more speed, Igor."

"Cromwell, our fuel. A little reserve would be comforting."

"Just edge us up another five knots. We've got plenty."

"Not if we have to start running."

"Just do it."

He heard the slight change in tone of the engines.

He extended one hand, holding his fingers open before his face at arm's length. The smoke extended far beyond either side of his fingertips. If they're still twenty, thirty miles off, it was definitely not one ship. That much smoke had to be dozens of ships.

"A little lower, we're brushing into the cloud base."

The nose of the aerosteamer dropped slightly, and he could feel airspeed picking up. After several hundred feet they leveled out again, where the air was slightly clearer.

He saw not one ship, but dozens of ships. In the van was definitely one of the battleships that he had seen in the harbor, the distinctive twin pagodas almost lined up on each other. Forward, surrounding the huge vessel, were half a dozen smaller ships, tiny slivers of darkness against the gray sea. Plumes of smoke trailed out behind them, drifting into a cloud astern, obscuring what he was convinced were more ships yet farther back.

"Got it!" Richard cried, and finally he heard Xing up forward shouting as well.

The moment of exuberance gave way to a knot in his gut, a strange mixed emotion that was part that they'd made a sighting, but with it a realization that the nightmare was indeed true.

Now what?

He was tempted to order them to turn around and get the hell out of there. The Kazan had some catapult-launched scout planes and a small ship for carrying additional planes and launching them. If they catch us and we don't get back, the fleet will never know. They were nearly six hundred miles out, two days sailing, more likely three. Go back now and we can get a better read as they come closer in.

Yet, on the other hand, in another ten minutes we'll find out what they really have.

"Commander?"

It was the first time Igor had called him that, and he could not help but grin. Igor was nervous, and it showed in that one word.

"Straight in, Igor. Xing, I don't care how blind you are, start keeping a watch for scout planes. Octavian, same with you in the tail. If they spot us, you know they'll send something up, and I want to be long gone."

The dark shadow began to rapidly spread out, an indication that they were closing in.

He now had two battleships in view, then three, and in another moment five, all of them riding in line astern, each a mile or so back from the other.

He firmly braced his elbows on the wing, leaned down, and raised his field glasses. This time he caught and held the target. The lead battleship had a smaller vessel to its windward side, connected to it by what appeared to be cables. Why? Transferring coal perhaps? That could be the explanation for how they could travel so far and hope to return.

He looked farther back, until the fourth battleship caught his eye. It was flying the red banner of the emperor, just below it the gray of the Order. It was the flagship, and both of them were on board.

Sweeping over him was the memory of Hazin, the curious strange mix of emotions, of loathing and yet of attraction, of outrage and, also, most disturbing, of admiration and even of awe. He wondered if poor Sean was with him.

He felt a prickling sensation that felt almost like a warning; that somehow Hazin had sensed him and was turning his attention on him.

"Ship off the portside wing."

It was Octavian, his voice pitched high with excitement.

Richard turned, craning back to look, and then he saw the ship, half a dozen miles upwind almost directly abeam. How they had missed it was beyond him. It was a cruiser, obviously riding forward point, and he wondered if they had gone past any other ships.

"I see it," Igor announced, "and if he hasn't seen us he's blind."

The chill triggered by thoughts of Hazin deepened. Anxiously he scanned around, and then he spotted two Kazan scout planes, nearly forty-five degrees astern of the starboard beam of his own airships, noses high, climbing steadily. They were maneuvering to come around him from behind.

He unclipped, turned, and descended into the cab. Dropping into his seat, he immediately pitched the huge aerosteamer over into a sharp banking turn to port, feeding in full throttle and edging the nose back to head to the clouds.

"We've been spotted! Octavian, keep a watch as we come around. Xing, wake up. Igor, I want you to sketch the ships as you saw them, then get yourself topside!"

"Oh, I see them!" Octavian cried.

"Then watch them, damn it, and tell me if they're closing."

Igor sat hunched over the chart board, pencil flying as he wrote down numbers and quickly drew tiny figures across the bottom of the paper. After several minutes he pushed the board down into its rack, unclipped and scrambled up into the topside gunner's position.

"They're closing on us," Octavian shouted. "I think they're faster, can climb better."

Cromwell eased the nose even higher, watching as the altimeter gauge slowly rose through eight thousand feet. Then they were into the clouds, the world going white. He added an extra two hundred feet, sweating out the two minutes it took to climb.

Now he was flying blind, watching the compass, the bank indicator, and airspeed. The plane bumped and surged, rising up, then dropping so that for a moment they popped out of the clouds, then back again.

Had they been spotted? Did the bastards now have a bead on them?

As the surging continued, he felt a cold lump in his gut.

If the enemy scout planes don't get us, he realized, this weather will. Looking at the fuel gauges, he wondered if they could stretch it to get home. Going higher, climbing into the heart of the turbulence, was out of the question now.

He said nothing, flying straight on as best he could.

Igor slipped down beside him, picked up his chart, looked at the gauges, then over at Richard, and he was silent as well.

"So they've spotted us."

Startled, Sean O'Donald looked over at Hazin, who had quietly come up behind him. All he could do was nod.

The entire fleet had sprung into action. All ships had gone to battle positions, smoke belching from stacks so that a thick haze swirled about them in the following wind. Scout planes from the lead battleship had been launched to join the pursuit, and two more had gone aloft from the second ship of the line to maintain a watch above the fleet.

The precision of the operation, the practiced ease of the crew, which went about its duties as if they were routine, only reinforced to Sean what seemed inevitable: in the forthcoming battle the empire would sweep the seas.

"Interesting that they had a patrol plane this far out," Hazin said. "Tell me, is that normal?"

"Not really. I don't know where we are, though, so I cannot judge."

"One hundred and ninety leagues from the Constantine coast, according to our navigator. He's the emperor's best, but he has been known to be wrong."

"Then we are inside the treaty line."

Hazin nodded.

"So they know. They must have been looking for us."

Sean turned to look back to the northwest. The plane had disappeared into the clouds. It had been barely more than a speck in the sky. He wondered who the pilot was.

"I would think it was Cromwell," Hazin said.

Though he had tried to get used to these insights, nevertheless they continued to startle him. Never could he be sure if it was simply an uncanny ability to read subtle indicators, or was it truly the ability to step into another mind.

"The emperor, I can imagine, will be all astir. He had hoped to gain their coast and launch the first attack without their notice." He laughed softly, turned, and walked away.

SIXTEEN

Shaking the fatigue, Richard lined up on the landing field as Igor called off the airspeed. Buffeted, the plane rolled onto its portside wing. Both of them strained on the rudder pedals and crossed the controls to keep the wing down and crab in.

He felt the wheels touch, they bounced lightly, came back down, and held the ground. Turning, Igor pulled the quick release to drop the little remaining hydrogen left in the aft bag. In the stormy twilight, ground crews came running in from either side to grab the wings. They rolled to a stop, and Richard collapsed back in his chair. The side hatch popped open, and a ladder was extended up. He tried to get out, but his legs refused to cooperate. Finally a crew chief had to climb in and help him down. Reaching the wet grass, he sat on it heavily, gladly accepting the flask of vodka. Igor plopped down beside him.

The ground crew took over the massive plane, rolling it toward its hangar. Richard saw a horse-drawn carriage bumping across the field. Carefully he came to his feet, glad for the help of a ground crewman with unbuttoning his flight coveralls.

The carriage rolled up and stopped, portly Admiral Bull-finch stepping down.

"Your buzzing over my headquarters leads me to believe you spotted them."

"Yes, sir."

"Tell me."

Richard gave his report standing in the middle of the landing field, with Igor laying the chart against the side of the admiral's carriage. The driver shielded it with a poncho from the splattering rain that came down in heavy drops.

Several of Bullfinch's staff rode up, dismounted, and joined him, taking in every word that Richard said, looking at the chart, and then back to Bullfinch.

As Richard spoke, Bullfinch looked over several times at Igor, who nodded in support, and Richard wondered if he truly believed him and needed someone else's approval for confirmation.

"How was the weather coming back?"

"Like this, sir, getting worse all the time. Lines of storms building all the way out."

"Not a cyclone yet," one of the staff announced.

"Could be to our advantage, though," Bullfinch stated.

He looked at the chart again.

"How much do you think they know of our coast?" the admiral finally asked, looking back at Cromwell.

Richard realized that the true question was, how much would Sean know and tell them along with any information that might have been gleaned from other lost ships and from Malacca pirates.

"They might know of the Minoan Shoals," Richard volunteered. "It's a fair marker." He pointed out the shoal waters and chain of islands on the map, which stretched east to west off the main coast just ninety miles away. "They hit that, then it's a straight run in, no blundering around off our coast, thus giving us additional warning."

Bullfinch nodded. "That's where we form," he announced.

Richard looked at him with surprise. Bullfinch slowly turned and smiled.

"A comment from the commander?"

"Sir, I spotted at least five of their battleships and thirty or more support ships."

"And?"

"We have eight armored cruisers and twenty frigates. When I left last night, I heard the aerosteamer carriers are still coming down the Mississippi."

"And won't be here for another day and a half. I know that."

"The Minoans will put our air corps at extreme range for full bombing loads."

"Look at this weather, Cromwell. Do you think your planes will be flying in it?"

"I did."

"Well, you might be a more gifted pilot, sir. I think it's a fair bet, though, that we are in for a bit of a blow. Not a cyclone, as they call them here, but a fair blow nevertheless. I doubt if your airships will be doing anything for the next couple of days."

He turned and looked back at his staff.

"Ten knots they're making, according to Mr. Cromwell. That means they've closed over a hundred miles since he saw them this morning. Another hundred by dawn, which could put them near the Minoans at dusk tomorrow. We'll meet them there.

"It should be blowing, visibility will be down, and as you heard in Mr. Cromwell's report, their guns are big but useless beyond three thousand yards. In a good storm with high seas it will be even less. We race in, slash, try to get this red flagship. Sink that and their precious emperor goes to the bottom, and we break them. I just wish to hell we had some of those self-propelled mines that the Design Board decided to waste on their aerosteamer scheme instead."

He turned and looked back at Richard. "Any problems with that, Commander?"

Richard looked at the chart, then at the admiral. He could see in the man's eyes that the plan was formed and nothing would change it.

"Better than waiting for a nice warm sunny day and a good flat sea for your aerosteamer carriers and air corps. Meanwhile, they blast my ships apart, then come and blow this town apart and take it."

Richard had to concede the point. There was a certain audacity to the venture, an audacity which the veterans of the last war were noted for, the betting everything on a single shake of the dice.

"Good luck to you then, sir. Any orders for the air groups and carriers?"

One of Bullfinch's staff chuckled. "Come out and bomb the wreckage when we're done with them. The *Gettysburg* might have been caught by surprise, but by damn we won't be."

Bullfinch turned, and his withering gaze silenced the officer. He motioned for Cromwell to follow, and the two walked off a few dozen paces.

"Look, Cromwell, I must admit I do not like you."

Richard stiffened, but Bullfinch's tone was different, almost apologetic.

"I understand, sir," Richard finally replied.

"No, I'm not sure you do. Yes, in part it was your father, but even I will admit that in his own way, before we came here and everything got unhinged, he was a good sailor and taught me a lot that I never learned at Annapolis.

"It's just that you suddenly come landing in my lap with this wild tale about the *Gettysburg* being lost, the Kazan, an emperor that sounds like a fool, and a religious fanatic with a race of god-like men and Horde warriors."

Richard could not help but smile. He nodded in agreement. "I can see that now, sir."

"And then there was Pat O'Donald's boy. No one likes to hear that a beloved friend's son is a traitor."

"I never said he was a traitor, sir."

"Well, it sure as hell sounded like it to me," Bullfinch snapped. Then he sighed. "Look, son. Your coming back with this tale, it caught me—it caught all of us—off guard. In a way it made some of us look like fools for going along with this treaty as long as we did. Also, your tale that they could blow us out of the water, well, that is basically saying that old Admiral Bullfinch can be blown out of the water."

"I never said anything like that, sir."

"You're obviously not someone who hangs around Congress," Bullfinch replied sadly, "but believe me, that's what will be said."

"Sir, I was with the president and he has nothing but admiration for you. I think that's what counts."

"Be that as it may, you are, to many of us, a snotty lieutenant bearing a wild tale, who gets jumped in promotion, then comes back here as a special messenger from the president to tell me what to do. Do you get my drift, young man?"

Cromwell reddened. He was suddenly aware as well of just how exhausted he was. What little food he'd eaten before the twenty-hour flight had long since gone out the window. His stomach was in aching knots, the few sips of vodka had gone to his head, and all he wanted was some sleep. Everything else at the moment seemed to be drifting away. But he focused his attention, seeing the look in Bullfinch's eye.

"Yes, sir," he sighed, "I can well understand."

Bullfinch hesitated and noisily cleared his throat. "And for that I apologize."

Startled, Richard shook his head. "You're an admiral, sir. I don't think you need to apologize to me."

Bullfinch laughed softly. "Well said, and from anyone else I would think that you were trying to kiss an admiral's royal rump."

Richard found that whatever hard feelings he'd felt had just burned out. He lowered his head. "I'm sorry as well, sir."

"Fine, then. I want you to stay here ashore for a couple of reasons. I want you to get some rest and in the morning make a report, with drawings of the ships. Then have a courier take an express up to Suzdal. I'll be gone by then, and dispatches also will be waiting to go, detailing my plan of operations.

"I've got a pretty good weather nose, Cromwell, and that young lackey of mine in the fancy uniform over there is right. There'll be a bit of a blow tomorrow, maybe the day after as well. With luck we'll get a punch in, maybe a couple of solid punches, and get back out under darkness and foul weather.

"Cromwell, I can't simply stay here and do nothing, and for the next couple of days I don't think any of you boys will be flying."

Richard nodded, finding that he was in agreement.

"If the weather clears, you know where we'll be. Bring in everything you have."

"Yes, sir, but what about the aerosteamer carriers?"

"With luck, they can follow up on what is left."

He stopped and looked off for a moment, then turned back.

"Actually, I think they might be the future, Cromwell, if we can ever figure out how to make the engines more powerful and get the speed up so your attacking a ship isn't all but a guaranteed suicide. So for the moment I think they're ahead of themselves, but what the hell, on this world, we've always been ahead of ourselves."

Bullfinch extended his hand and Cromwell took it.

"I've included a personal note to the president in my dispatch. Hang on to it, and if something should happen— you know what I mean—see that he gets it."

"I don't plan on sending it, sir."

Bullfinch withdrew his hand and smiled. "Son, we both know my chances. I'm sailing with my fleet. Just see that he gets it."

Bullfinch did not even bother to wait for a reply. He walked away, shouting obscenities at his staff as he urged them to mount up and get to work.

Richard saluted him anyhow as he disappeared into the dusk.

Dawn broke wet and soggy across the broad expanse of the lower Mississippi. Theodor, with Captain Rosovich by his side, watched as the dispatch boat, which had come out from the small riverboat town, cast off from the *Shiloh*. Its lone occupant hoisted a small sail, which bellied out, and the boat heeled over as it started to tack back in toward shore.

Smoke belched from the leaky stack, whiffs of coal gas coming up from below deck where the joints where leaking, and the *Shiloh* started up again. A sailor came up the ladder that had been lowered over the side. Running past the two, he ducked through a hatchway into the bridge, pausing to pass a bundle of Gates's *Daily* to a first mate. Men were already queuing up, handing over ten cents for the five cent paper. Theodor tossed him a coin and opened the sheet up.

The headline splashed across the top was the largest Adam had ever seen, taking up nearly a third of the paper. The banner was but a single word:

WAR?

"What the hell is Gates doing?" Theodor growled. "Of course it's war. Look at this."

He pointed at the left column below the headline:

FIGHTING ON BANTAG FRONTIER

Adam leaned over and grabbed the paper. "President's son reported missing," he read aloud.

He closed his eyes and lowered his head.

"It happens a lot," Theodor said hurriedly. "A couple of days later they turn up. Believe me, I know. I was reported dead several times."

"Still, it doesn't look good. The Bantag moving to the south, that's clear enough indication that something is up."

"Mr. Rosovich?"

Adam saw an ensign standing in the hatchway to the bridge.

"The admiral wants you, sir."

Adam looked over at Theodor, who quickly folded up the paper, stuffed it in his back pocket, and followed Adam through the hatch and up the ladder to the bridge.

It was a roughly made affair of wood, nothing more than an enclosed wooden platform made of three layers of railroad ties to at least give the illusion of protection. There was a chair for the captain, a wheel, compass, barometer, and speaker tubes lined up against the starboard side. All of it was a far cry from the original plans for the *Shiloh,* with a proper steel cupola and a proper captain's quarters.

Rear Admiral Petronius was gazing balefully at a telegram, as the two came onto the bridge. "I did not ask for you, Theodor Theodorovich."

"I invited myself anyhow," he replied with a smile.

Adam remained silent, know that Petronius held Theodor personally responsible for what had been done to the *Shiloh* and the other two ships of what was supposed to be his flotilla.

"This dispatch went up to Suzdal this morning. Fortunately, the station master back there heard it on the wires"— he pointed at the town that was drifting astern—"and seeing us approach saw fit to at least make sure we heard about it as well."

Petronius held the telegram at arm's length in order to read.

"Kazan fleet sighted dawn yesterday, five hundred fifty miles southeast Constantine, steaming northwest ten knots. Shall sortie with entire fleet to engage. God Save the Republic. Bullfinch."

"They went without us?" Theodor asked.

"Obviously, or am I making this dispatch up?" As he spoke he waved the sheet of paper.

"Petronius, I didn't mean that. It's just that if he had waited another day and a half we'd be there to support him."

"In this weather?" Petronius snapped, indicating the line of rain squalls sweeping across the river. "If it's this way here, it must really be cutting loose on the coast."

"Still, it'll pass. He should have waited."

"Are you a sailor?" Petronius replied. "Well, if not, then don't dare to pass a judgment on the weather."

"I'm a flyer," Theodor announced, his voice edged with anger. "It'll pass. He should have waited for everything, throw everything at them at once."

"Well, he won't, and I wouldn't either. Any comment, Mr. Rosovich?"

Adam swallowed and shook his head. "If Admiral Bullfinch sailed, he must have had good reason to do so, sir."

Theodor looked over at Rosovich as if he had just sold out.

"I'm tempted to tell the chief engineer down below to bring us down to half speed. The engines are barely broken in, and we're banging them to pieces steaming at this rate. We'll miss the fight and that's that."

Theodor shifted uncomfortably and looked over at Adam.

"Sir," Adam said quietly, "our orders were to make best possible speed to Constantine to report."

"Report to who? The local madam? The fleet's sailed, sonny, and we missed it."

"Still, sir, the orders said the best possible speed."

Petronius crumbled up the telegram and tossed it on the deck.

"Wrong place at the wrong time, damn it," he growled.

Neither of the pair spoke.

"Best possible speed then, Mr. Rosovich. And that thing you were going to build up forward, what about that?"

"The steam catapults," Theodor replied. "I've decided not to."

"Pray why?"

"It would mean tearing up fifty feet of deck. We have the parts, and they would have been installed for the two scout planes, but I don't want to risk having a deck torn apart and going into action with the job half done. It will have to wait."

"This speed that Mr. Rosovich keeps hollering about and the wind. Suppose there isn't enough wind."

"You just said there'd be a blow, Petronius."

The admiral glared at him. The rest of the bridge crew went rigid, staring straight ahead.

"Then see to that damn leaking smokestack. You came along for some purpose or other, make yourself useful."

Both of them, taking his comment as a dismissal, backed out of the bridge and went down the ladder.

"If I wasn't interested in seeing what the hell happened to you, Rosovich, I'd get off this boat at the next town," Theodor announced, shaking his head.

"He's just shaken up, that's all."

"Shaken up?"

"He just found out all his old friends are going down to death or glory, and he isn't with them."

"Death or glory? You think that's what war is?" With a sigh Theodor walked away.

The attack came the hour before sunset, catching Abe by surprise. The first wave swarmed up out of the ravine where they had snatched the water a day and a half ago, a position that the Bantag had occupied heavily the following night. Six men had ventured down there last night, but their heads had been found at dawn, carefully placed in front of the redoubt on the west slope.

In spite of the outrage the sight had triggered, Togo was impressed by the gesture. Usually the Bantag ate the brains of fallen cattle in order to kill their spirits. The return of the heads was meant as a sign of respect to a courageous foe.

The mounted charge came forward at a gallop. Abe had posted himself by the unit's best marksman along the north edge of the butte, trying to spot a shot for him. Earlier in the day they had seen the standard of a leader of a thousand in a ravine to the north. Twice the sniper had taken a shot at him and missed. He was just lining it for the third time, a long gamble at six hundred yards, when the cry went up that an attack was under way.

Abe, crouching low, ran to the west side of the butte and looked down. The charge was already halfway across the six hundred yards of open ground. In a remarkable display of horsemanship, the riders were hanging over the sides of their saddles, keeping the body of their mount between them and any incoming rounds.

He had less than twenty men watching the west side. Turning, he screamed for half the men on the east side to come over.

As the charge thundered in, the troopers waited for the range to close. Abe could see that the redoubt at the base of the butte would be overwhelmed. He stood up and leaned over, cupping his hands. "Sergeant Volnov! Get out!"

The sergeant didn't need to be told. He already had his detachment of ten men up. The men let loose a single volley, which dropped several riders, turned, and started up the steep slope, while above them their comrades opened with covering fire.

The charge pressed in, riders swinging up into their saddles for the last fifty yards. More than half of them were armed with bows, and a deadly volley slashed out, catching two of Volnov's men. Both of them collapsed, rolling back down the side of the butte.

The rest of the men dodged from rock to rock, firing as they went, several running out of ammunition. Another man was hit, and when a comrade turned to pull him back up, he too was hit, in the chest. Both of them fell, sliding down to the Bantags, who were dismounting and swarming into the redoubt. Screaming, the men disappeared under a swarm of Bantags with drawn scimitars.

Troopers on the rim of the butte, cursing madly, fired straight down into the seething mass until the attackers finally withdrew, scrambling over the far wall of the redoubt and dropping down behind it.

"More on the north side!"

"Keep these bastards pinned down," Abe cried, and he sprinted back over to the other side.

A second wave of riders was surging up out of another ravine, riding in the same hidden manner as the first group. The northern slope of the butte was far too steep for a mounted assault, and he instantly knew where they were heading. Running to the east side, he scrambled over the edge and looked down to where the gatling was positioned on a rocky outcrop twenty feet above the plains. The gun had run out of ammunition the morning of the third day. The outcrop, however, was their only other way off the butte, and a rock wall had been built up around it with twenty men holding the tiny fort.

He looked back to the north. The first of the riders was still a quarter mile off but coming on fast. He knew the lieutenant down there would use what ammunition he had left trying to hold it, and he sensed that the Bantag knew it as well.

"Lieutenant Hamilcar! Get out!"

"Lieutenant Keane, we can hold it!"

"Get out, Lieutenant, get out!"

Hamilcar hesitated for a few precious seconds, then turned, shouting to his men to move. Picking up a rock lying atop the empty ammunition limber, Hamilcar smashed it down on the breech of the gatling and then hammered the barrels several times for good measure. Throwing the rock over the wall of the redoubt, he followed the last of his men up the slope. Covering fire snapped from the northern rim, then rippled around to the east as the charge swept around the base of the butte. One of Hamilcar's men caught an arrow in the leg before reaching the summit, but he did not stop. Gasping, the men piled over the edge. The sergeant major, by Keane's side, helped to pull them over. Everyone cursed and ducked as bullets nicked the air, and arrows, aimed nearly straight up by the mounted archers, came clattering down around them.

Hamilcar, his skin pale and dry, was the last one in. "We could have held it, Keane."

"And used the last of our ammunition doing it. Then they overrun us."

"Damn it, Keane," Hamilcar wheezed. "So now what? We can't get off this Baal-cursed rock with them holding both ways out. Now what?"

Even as he spoke the last words Hamilcar's eyes seemed to go unfocused and then rolled up. He silently collapsed.

"Get him under some shade," Keane said, looking at two of Hamilcar's men. They nodded and wearily carried him over to the hospital shelter.

He'd lost five men to heat stroke, and from the look of Hamilcar he feared he'd lose him as well. From down below he could hear taunting shouts, occasional arrows soaring up and then clattering onto the hard ground.

He looked around at his men.

"Holding the redoubts was no longer worth it," he shouted, slowly turning, looking at each man as he spoke. "They knew our routine, and you saw what happened to Magnus and his men last night."

"So now what, sir?" someone cried, and he could hear the resignation in the man's voice.

Keane turned to look at him, a ragged-looking trooper with a bandage around his knee. The rag was caked with dirt, and from the look of it, it was covering a leg that was starting to rot.

"We hold."

"I'm down to three rounds, Ishi has only got one left, and I told him to save it for himself." As the wounded man talked, he pointed at the body of the man lying next to him. Fresh blood was seeping out of a head wound. The trooper was feverish and so near to hysteria that he didn't even realize that his comrade had been killed in the last firefight.

From down below the taunting continued. Togo crept up to the edge and shouted something. It was met with a flurry of rifle shots and cries of outrage.

"What did you say?" Keane asked, trying to divert the men.

"I discussed his relationship with his mother," Togo replied with a caustic grin.

The joke fell flat, and there was no response.

Abe was tempted to simply sit down, curl up, and go to sleep. His last sip of water had been doled out at noon, and he felt as if the heat was about to finish him as well. The two canteens of water still left were in the hands of the medical orderly, to be doled out a small cupful at a time to those men he felt he could still save.

Shading his eyes, Abe looked off to the west, Distant clouds had drifted across the horizon during the day. A lone thunderhead had swollen in the southwestern sky during the afternoon and had passed agonizingly close. For a few minutes there had even been a cooling breeze, but then it had marched on, touching the ground with lightning as it continued on its stately way.

A mad raving came from the hospital shelter. It was the major again. Either the repeated blows to the head, the heat, or simple fear had driven him over the edge, and he had fallen to alternating bouts of desperate pleading for water followed by wild oaths about court-martials and firing squads.

Abe felt he was finally losing control of the situation, that he had overstepped his bounds in the first minutes of the battle and now was paying the full price. Perhaps the major had been right all along. They should have gotten the hell out. Now they could be riding under a thunderstorm, soaking up the rain, laughing about their narrow escape.

"Damn it, Keane, let's just load, charge, and be done with it," the wounded trooper cried. As he spoke he tried to get to his feet. As Abe looked around, several of the men stood up in response, and gradually more began to do likewise.

He looked over at the sergeant major, desperate for some advice, but he could see that he had none. The old Zulu almost seemed detached, as if standing on a parade ground, waiting to see what the young cadet would do next. Togo was sitting on the ground, rifle across his knees, watching and saying nothing.

What now? What the hell do I do now? He suddenly wished more than anything that his father were there. The Colonel would know what to do. Everyone was always telling him how old Keane always knew what to do.

And then he started to laugh. The laughter came because of the utter absurdity of the whole situation. He slowly turned, looking at the men who were standing, and continued to laugh. They gazed at him, some startled, some terrified that he had gone mad as well. The rest were just silent, dejected and beyond caring whether the lieutenant was mad or not.

"Don't you get it?" Abe shouted. "We're not going to die out here. I'm the son of the bloody president of the Republic. I'm the only surviving son of Andrew Lawrence Keane!"

No one spoke and he shouted it again.

"I'm the son of Andrew Lawrence Keane."

"So who the hell cares," a corporal growled. "It's over."

"Like hell it is," Abe cried, and to his amazement, tears of moisture were in his eyes, streaking down his face. "The whole goddamn army will be out looking for me. How the hell is General Hawthorne supposed to go back to my old man and say, 'Mr. President, sir, I'm sorry we lost him. I guess he's dead. Better luck next time, sir'."

As he spoke Hawthorne's words, he did a fairly good imitation of Vincent's high tenor voice, and the sergeant major began to grin.

He stopped laughing almost as suddenly as it had come upon him.

"I tell you"—his voice dropped and self-consciously he wiped the tears from his cheeks—"my father will not leave me out here to die. I know him. He'll say that he won't do anything special because I'm his son, but that won't matter. The word will go out to do everything possible."

He paused and then shook his head.

"No, that's a lie. He won't do anything special, he'll do what he would do for any of you men, blood relative or not, Yankee or Chin, and he'll try to pass that as an order. But those around my father, the men who love him, they'll take special steps to find us because they do love him."

He fell silent for a long moment and the tears fell again.

"That's why we'll live, that's why they'll find us. It's because this army will never abandon its own. That was the army my father created. That is why I promise you we'll survive this day, and the day after until they finally come and get us."

SEVENTEEN

"To go in harm's way."

"Did you say something, Admiral?"

Bullfinch looked over at his young staff officer and smiled. "No, nothing."

He stepped out of the armored cupola and, leaning forward, grabbed the railing of the open bridge. Two observers, glasses raised, struggled vainly to maintain their positions, sweeping the horizon.

A squall line of rain slashed in, driven on the thirty-knot wind, stinging as it hit. A gust swept off Bullfinch's oilskin nor'easter hat. It spun across the bridge and went over the railing, disappearing into the foaming sea.

The bow of his flagship surged onto the crest of a fifteen-foot wave, foam spraying up, tons of water cascading over the deck as the ship corkscrewed down into a trough and then started the climb onto the next wave.

The sailor to his right lowered his glasses, leaned over the railing, unceremoniously vomited, then raised his glasses again. Bullfinch actually felt pity for the boy. In spite of the warm tropical air, he was actually trembling from sickness and most likely from fear.

"Anything, sailor?" Bullfinch shouted.

The boy lowered his glasses and looked over, features a pale shade of green. "Not since we saw that frigate, sir."

"Well keep a sharp watch. They are out there, I can feel it, you can smell it."

The boy nodded weakly and resumed his watch.

In fact, they actually had smelled them. A heavy line of squalls had battered the ships throughout the afternoon as they approached the Minoan Shoals. The fleet had moved in line astern of the flagship as they struggled through the Three Sisters, a mile-wide passage that cut through the middle of a chain of islands and sandbars that stretched for more than forty miles.

With his flagship *Antietam* leading the way, several of the lookouts had reported that they had smelled coal smoke on the wind, and several minutes later two of them claimed to have seen a frigate-size ship, with an unusual silhouette, sailing two or three miles off, and then disappeared as the next line of rain closed in.

That was a half an hour ago.

Turning his back to the wind, Bullfinch reached under his sealskin coat and pulled out his pocket watch. An hour till sunset, but already he could feel the light beginning to fade.

Five miles past the shoals to leeward, not a good position to ride out a storm at night.

He leaned over the railing and looked aft. The fleet was still running astern. The last of them had to be through the Three Sisters.

Come about? Put the Shoals between us and them during the night?

He felt a terrible loneliness. Suppose they aren't here? Andrew said they might make a run for the Bantag coast. But nothing was there other than a bunch of savages. No, all doctrine ran toward hitting your opponent's main base first by surprise, bottling him up, smashing him. Then they'd have the sea and could do as they pleased. If they were coming to Constantine, they would make for these shoals first, and get their bearing, rather than go blundering along an unknown coastline and then give the Republic warning.

For that matter, had they even arrived yet? Cromwell had said ten knots. Suppose, though, it was eight knots, Bullfinch thought. That would put them a good hundred miles still out. Or twelve knots, then they might very well have rounded the shoals this morning, we sailed straight past each other and even now they are closing to bombard Constantine.

He had sent scout frigates out at full steam to cover the flanks of each end of the shoals, but no reports. But then again, that could mean that they were already at the bottom of the sea, destroyed before they could return.

He knew he was tearing himself apart with all the variables and chance errors and decisions that made up a battle at sea. Make the plan as best you can, he realized, then stick to it until you get a solid fact that changes things. You figured they'd run first to the Shoals, perhaps slow there for at least a few hours to bring their fleet together, perhaps even weather the night here, then move along its length to gain a bearing, finally rounding it either to the east or west. We come in through the middle and hopefully hit them by surprise, then get the hell out.

So it's here. But where the hell are they? In this storm they could be five miles off to port or starboard. Perhaps they'd already gained the shoals and had turned, running east or west to round them, moving cautiously to avoid running aground.

He looked back again at his own fleet, less than half of it visible. All of them were running now on engines, all sails furled as they plowed into the teeth of the storm.

What next, damn it, what next?

With the light beginning to fade, he had but two choices. Either come about, get to leeward of the shoals, and sit out the night; moving to pounce before dawn. If I do that, it will be a fifty-fifty chance—we either run east or west. Or we move straight on here into the night, gain about ten miles out, then turn either east or west and try to come in from behind.

Best possible choice, I've got to run with that.

He could sense that everyone inside the cupola was peeking out through the narrow view slit, watching him, knowing he was trying to sort out all the different elements, to come to a conclusion. They most likely knew his every idiosyncrasy, the way he hunched his shoulders and rubbed his scarred face and eyepatch when he was lost in thought. He realized he was doing that, and turned the gesture into wiping the rain from his face.

Another wave cascaded over the bow, sending up spray bits of spindrift flying back, sweeping the bridge.

He turned his back to it, saw the men peering at him through the viewing slit.

"Signal the fleet. Line abreast, storm formation."

As he stepped back into the cupola, the signal flags went up. He doubted if the ships astern could see them since the wind was running almost due fore and aft so that the flags would appear edgewise to those astern.

The command, however, also went up to the signals officer in the enclosed maintop. The shutter telegraph would relay the order as well.

He felt the pounding vibration of the engines ease off slightly. Captain Nagama, who was in direct command of the ship, had passed the word to ease back to half speed. Behind them the other cruisers would surge forward, breaking in an alternating pattern to port and starboard of the flagship. Each cruiser would assume a position six hundred yards to either flank, while the frigates, running at flank speed, would cut through the line to assume a forward position half a mile farther out.

"Gentlemen," Bullfinch shouted, trying to be heard above the whistling of the wind, which cried with a demented moan as it cut through the cupola, "we'll head in line abreast till dark. That will sweep us ten miles out beyond the Shoals. We'll rig for night running, hooded lanterns fore and aft. Then we turn, still maintaining line abreast, and cut speed to four knots. Once night falls, half the crew can stand down from battle stations to get some food and rest. We then alternate battle stations watch till an hour before dawn."

"The heading, east or west?" Nagama asked.

"Which way is the wind bearing?"

"South, southwest. It's beginning to back around to westerly."

Running slowly with a following sea would be deadly, water crashing over the sterns, driving the ships, pushing them in toward the shoals. If the Kazan were out here, he reasoned, they would be running into the storm as well.

"West."

Nagama nodded in agreement.

He looked past Nagama and could see the *Spotsylvania* coming up at flank speed, maneuvering to take position.

Then several things seemed to happen at once. One of the lookouts on the bridge, the boy along the starboard railing, turned, glasses dangling around his neck. With his hands cupped, he screamed something unintelligible. A speaking tube shrieked, the one from the foretop lookout. The communications officer uncapped it, leaning over to listen, eyes suddenly going wide . . . and a geyser of spray erupted a hundred yards off the *Spotsylvania*'s port bow. It almost seemed like an illusion, a column of water shooting up nearly a hundred feet, then gone an instant later, whipped away by the wind.

Everyone seemed frozen in a tableau as the words of the forward lookout drifted over them.

"Ship off starboard bow. Range one mile!"

Bullfinch pushed his way past Nagama, ducking through the hatchway and out onto the open bridge. The lookout was pointing directly forward. "See 'em, see 'em" he was screaming.

With one eye gone, his vision was not the best. Bullfinch squinted until he saw them. Three ships, starting to turn to the west, bow wakes planing up. They seemed to have simply materialized out of the mist. He could see smoke boiling away from the first ship to fire. There was another flash, a brilliant hot light, then another.

Bullfinch turned back to the cupola. "Signal hold course! Close for action!"

He felt the engines going up to flank speed. The forward turret with its massive fourteen-inch gun fired with a thunderous report, and smoke completely blanketed his view for several seconds.

A high whistling shriek cut overhead, went astern, and detonated two hundred yards aft in the foaming wake of the *Spotsylvania*. The two forward below-deck guns, one of them a five-inch breechloader, went off, creating more smoke.

He could see other ships emerging from the mist. Frightfully, the ones appearing now were bigger, vaster than anything he had ever seen afloat, with a huge tower perched forward rather than a mast. The forward guns of the monster fired. Scant seconds later he heard their thunderous roar and actually caught a brief glimpse of a streak of darkness, one of the shells, clipping a wave crest off his port side, tumbled end over end, howling like a banshee.

Looking past the shell, he saw where another of his cruisers was maneuvering in alongside, the *Atlanta,* its forward gun firing.

His charge pressed in. The enemy's forward cruisers were making ninety-degree turns, and for the next few minutes he was at a disadvantage. The enemy was crossing his T, able to bring all guns to bear, fore and aft, while only his forward guns could fire.

He turned back, facing the cupola, and cupped his hands. "Signal all ships. Fire on largest target!"

As he turned back, he instinctively flinched at another howl. A huge plume of water surged up less than fifty yards off the port side amidships.

Another shell passed, this one high, disappearing. His own ship was frustratingly silent. The crews were still reloading. Even in the best conditions it would take the massive muzzle loader another five minutes. Finally, the breechloader fired again. He looked forward and roared with delight when the shot slammed into the side of one of their cruisers, at a range of less than fifteen hundred yards. Seconds later great gouts of smoke cascaded out of the cruiser's aft smoke stack.

The great ships, screened by the cruisers, were turning

as well. He counted four of them now, two thousand yards farther back than the cruisers. If not for their bulk they would be all but invisible in the rain and deepening twilight.

One of his own frigates, running at flank speed, sailed between him and the *Spotsylvania,* inching forward, its rapid-fire three-inch gun pumping out a round every twenty seconds.

As more shells came in, the battle spread out. His own cruisers were maneuvering, trying to form a line, but looked instead like an inverted V, with the flagship in the fore, while to the south two great lines were forming. Between the lines frigates were coming forward as if charging.

Shot was flying in both directions. Already he could tell that they were at a severe disadvantage. Not only were they completely outgunned, but the rate of fire of the Kazan's heavier weapons was superior as well. The only thing that seemed to be saving them so far was the violence of the sea. The fifteen-foot swells made it all but impossible to fire at an even keel.

So instead everyone just seemed to be madly firing, trying to let off their individual guns as best they could, and the air was alive with fire.

At eight hundred yards he saw another shot hit an enemy cruiser. Cursing, he looked back again at the command cupola, shouting for them to repeat the order to concentrate on the largest ships.

There was a brilliant flash to his right. It was the *Spotsylvania.* A heavy shell had detonated just forward of its bridge, directly into the topside turret. The shell had penetrated the armor and blown inside the narrow confines of the five-inch armor surrounding the heavy gun. It burst asunder, the massive bulk of the fourteen-inch barrel half lifting out of its mount, fragments of armor hurdling a hundred feet into the air. He ducked as another shell came in, clipping through the masts overhead, severing the mainmast just above the maintop. The impact caused the shell to explode with a thunderclap, and fragments slashed outward in every direction, causing sparks to fly off the cupola directly behind him.

A different sound erupted. Looking back forward, he saw that the two forward gatlings had opened up. Their tracers arced out across the stormy sea. The stream of fire rose and fell as the gunners tried to compensate for the roll of the ship, walking the stream of fire across the water and straight into the nearest enemy cruiser, which was now less than a quarter mile away.

The range was insanely close, what he had hoped for, but now that it was here he struggled to control his terror. As admiral there was little more that he could do. He had brought the fleet, and he had given the final orders to close. Now it was up to the individual captains to fight their ships.

The battle had not played out as he hoped. If luck had held, they might have culled one or two of the enemy's capital ships in the darkness and smashed them at close range. It was obvious now that they had been anticipated and spotted first as well. As they steamed southward at flank speed, more and yet more enemy ships were coming into view. Flashes of light rippled across the sea from the dozens of guns firing. The roar commingled into a maelstrom of sound that nearly rivaled that of the storm's.

The *Atlanta* died first. He was looking over at her when a shell slammed directly into the bridge, crushing the command cupola. Fire blazed out in every direction. Several seconds later another round splashed into the water but a few feet off her bow. The blow was close enough, however, to lift the ship half out of the water, shaking it the way a terrier would shake a rat.

The water around the *Atlanta* was lashed to a foam as half a dozen more rounds of various calibers impacted. An enemy frigate, having rushed through the line of cruisers, came straight in, passing between the *Atlanta* and his own ship, all guns firing. Gatling gunners on the Republic's cruisers stitched the frigate, and sparks detonated where the explosive rounds slammed into their target.

Suddenly the *Atlanta* was lifted out of the water by a massive explosion erupting just aft of the bridge. The back of the cruiser was broken, bow and stern ends instantly settling.

He looked forward again. The line of enemy cruisers was less than two hundred yards off, Nagama steering straight between two of them. For a few brief seconds he had the advantage. The heavy ships beyond dared not fire for fear of hitting their own, while only half of the cruisers' guns could be brought to bear.

He felt the ship surging beneath him, wondering for a second if the engine had been hit, then realized that Nagama, in a mad, audacious move, had ordered all engines backed, to slow down and give the gunners maximum opportunity to hit their targets.

The topside forward turret containing the fourteen-inch gun began to turn, lining up on a target to starboard that was presenting its stern, normally the most vulnerable part of a ship. The range was ridiculously close, less than one hundred yards. He could almost sense the gun commander in the turret shouting, standing to one side, hand on lanyard, judging the roll, waiting for the precise moment on an upward sweep when the target appeared to be just above the sight.

A brilliant flash of light snapped out from the turret, and the concussion flattened the water. The round slammed into the stern just at the waterline and blew. The entire aft end of the enemy cruiser seemed to disappear in boiling smoke and flames.

A wild cheer echoed through the ship. The other two heavy guns below deck fired seconds later. Another round struck the superstructure. The three guns aft fired as well, scoring yet another hit, which tore into where the first round had hit.

He could feel the engines starting up again. The flagship was heeling back, digging in. Then the entire vessel seemed to jerk sideways, as if struck by a giant hand.

Bullfinch was knocked off his feet. He cracked his forehead against the railing and it split open. He lay there stunned for a moment, then pulled himself back up. Black smoke and flame poured up through the aft vents and ventilation hoods. Something must have struck them through the hull, exploding inside and astern.

He looked back at the cupola. Nagama was on his feet, leaning over, shouting into a speaking tube. A tracer slashed past, and then another. He looked to his right and saw an enemy frigate barely two hundred yards off, heeling hard over to swing in alongside them. As he saw a forward gatling firing, the thought struck him that the gunners were aiming at him personally.

Another tracer, ricocheting off the cupola, passed within inches of his face

He ducked down and then saw that the lookout by his side was dead, a fist size hole in his back, face looking up, still a shade of green from the seasickness.

Another explosion overhead sheared off the foremast. Heavy debris rained down, forcing him to run to the shelter of the cupola. He ducked inside as steel and wood slammed into the deck.

Nagama barely spared him a glance. "Still forward?" he asked.

Bullfinch took a deep breath. They were in the middle of a fight now. To even get signals out in all the confusion with the fore gone and the main signal station in the maintop most likely gone as well was impossible. If he tried to turn out, the other ships might see, might think that the flagship was out of control, or worse yet, running.

"Forward!" Bullfinch cried. "Close with that big bastard directly ahead."

The big bastard, as he called it, was less than a thousand yards off.

Even as he looked at it, the ship's forward gun fired, followed several seconds later by one of its aft guns.

Some instinct told him they were aimed straight at him, and a couple of seconds later, even inside the cupola, he heard the shriek as the round came in. The first one passed within feet of the deck, plowed into a wave cresting off the port side, and blew; close enough that fragments tore across the deck, taking out a gatling crew. The second one hit a wave just forward, failed to detonate, tumbled, and slammed into the bow, penetrating the armor, and went crashing through the main gun deck.

Through one of the speaking tubes he could hear the tearing of metal, followed almost instantly by screams of agony. Up on the deck steam vented out from a severed line.

Another blow hit and then another, slamming him to the deck. He pulled himself back up, saw Nagama kneeling, mouth a smear of blood. The captain was coughing, spitting out broken teeth, wiping his face, then standing back up. Bullfinch looked out through the viewing slit. The bow was a mass of crumpled wreckage. The steam catapult for the scout plane, which had been left behind, was standing nearly straight up and then twisted back like a bent piece of wire.

The ship was shearing off. Nagama, coughing and gagging, tried to shout orders through a speaking tube. The wheelman was down, hands over his face. The signal officer took over the helm, struggling to bring the ship back to a bearing straight at the battleship ahead, less than seven hundred yards away.

He looked to starboard and felt a swelling of pride that brought tears to his eyes. Two of his armored cruisers were still with him, the *Spotsylvania* and the *Sumter*. Both were trailing fire and smoke, *Spotsylvania* with all three masts shattered, forward turret a smoking ruin, *Sumter* its entire aft end wrapped in flames.

Behind them he could see several of the enemy cruisers were turning, but at least two others were aflame. One of them was listing heavily to starboard. Its railing was already below the water, and antlike figures were falling into the raging sea. Frigates, both his and the enemy's, crisscrossed back and forth across the foaming sea, trading shots, gatlings firing, light guns flashing. The wreckage of a frigate, one of his, drifted past to port. Its fantail rose out of the water, propeller still turning; from the bow all the way up to the superstructure it was submerged. Just beyond it an enemy frigate was burning furiously and then disappeared as its magazine detonated.

"Forward gun, can it still fire?" Bullfinch shouted.

Nagama looked over at him, eyes wide. Bullfinch shouted the question again, and still Nagama didn't respond. Bullfinch realized the man was deaf, eardrums shattered by the last explosion.

He gently moved him aside, found the speaking tube to the forward turret, and uncapped it.

"Bullfinch here," he shouted, "can you hear me?"

Curses and the sound of steam vents echoed with a tinny shriek through the brass tube that snaked down from the bridge and then up into the turret.

"Here, sir."

"Can you still fire?"

"Reloading now, but steam for the rammer is dropping."

"Get it done and aim for the battleship straight ahead. Hold fire till I tell you to shoot."

"We're trying, sir."

"Just do it!"

He left the tube uncapped, looked over at the signal officer at the helm and simply pointed ahead.

He could do nothing now but ride out the storm and pray they'd survive the next few minutes.

A drumroll of exploding shells marched across the wind-tossed seas, visibility dropping from the smoke. With the sun setting, a surreal gray-green twilight engulfed Bullfinch's world, punctuated by brilliant thunderclaps of fire.

"Sumter!"

He didn't know who had shouted, but turning, he saw the valiant cruiser breaking apart. A shell had torn into the burning stern and exploded, tearing off the aft end. The ship skidded around, fantail breaking off, bow beginning to rise as tons of water poured into the bowels of the ship.

He looked forward. His target's two aft turrets fired almost in unison, and he braced for their impacts. One of the shells passed so close to the cupola that the turbulence staggered him. An instant later it felt as if the entire aft end of the ship was rising. The concussion slammed him against the side of the cupola. Stunned, he lay there for a second, trying to sense what had happened to his ship. One of the speaking tubes whistled, and he pulled himself up and uncapped it.

"Who is this?"

"Engine room. Something hit us. The plates are buckled, and we're flooding . . ." The words were cut off by an explosion that he felt in the soles of his feet even as it blasted through the speaking tube. He could hear screaming and what sounded like steam venting. Even as he tried to shout a question, smoke came boiling up out of the tube.

They were losing speed and he looked over at the signal officer. He was turning the wheel, but it was no longer attached to anything. It was spinning freely.

"Can you go below and steer with the main cables?" Bullfinch shouted.

"I'll try, sir."

He sensed it was useless, but sent him anyhow. The ship was beginning to die, and the target was so tantalizingly close, four hundred yards off.

Another of its forward guns fired. Another geyser shot up just forward of the bow an instant later. Damn, was their gunnery that bad? But even as he wondered about it, he saw the *Spotsylvania* take a devastating hit amidships. The smokestack tumbled overboard, and the mid deck superstructure peeled back. The blow had detonated deep inside the ship, fire soaring upward.

"Forward gun."

"Still here, sir."

"Ready?"

"In another minute."

"Shoot when you can bring it to bear. Try to hit the bastard toward the stern, get its engines and steering. Can you do that?"

"We'll try, sir."

"Good luck."

There was no reply.

An enemy frigate cut directly in front of them, all guns firing. Tracers walked up the deck, and a round shrieked through the view slit, pinging around inside the cupola like an angry bee. Everyone ducked and cursed until it fell spent on the deck floor.

Something exploded against the side of the cupola. A heavy fragment broke off on the inside, slicing across the narrow space, smashing the wheel to splinters.

Several seconds later the forward gun fired, startling him. He looked forward, and then howled with delight as a blossom of fire ignited just above the waterline of the enemy ship, astern of its rear turret. The force of the fourteen-inch shell visibly shook the behemoth, and a secondary explosion followed several seconds later, peeling back part of the deck.

The triumph, however, was short-lived, for his wounded foe now returned fire. Its four heavy guns fired in sequence. The first two shells missed but the third one landed a devastating blow.

For a moment he wondered if he were dead. The sensation reminded him of when he was hit at the Battle of St. Gregory's, when an explosion destroyed one eye and left him temporarily blinded in the other. The world was black. He felt a building panic.

Then he saw fire, a wall of it billowing up just outside the cupola. He started to crawl toward the hatch and caught a glimpse of Nagama, lying on the deck, clutching his shoulder, arm gone, blown clean off.

He went back, grabbed him, and pulled him toward the hatch.

The deck started to tilt, slowly but noticeably to port, helping them along.

They slid out through the hatch and he looked forward. The bow was gone, as was the forward turret. Men were scrambling up from below, many of them wounded. A number of them had reddened faces and hands. The outer skin had been boiled off from the flesh underneath by a blast of pressurized steam.

There was no need for him to order abandon ship. Everyone knew it. Everyone was scrambling for their lives.

Someone grabbed Nagama from him, dragging him down the steps to the main deck, pushing the captain over the side.

Bullfinch looked around. It was hard to make sense of what was happening. Burning ships dotted the sea. It was impossible to figure which were his, and which had been kills. His men had been magnificent, and he felt a swelling of pride. Green boys really, precious few of the veterans of the old days, but they had fought like demons to the end.

And yet he knew that their effort had been in vain. Only one of the great enemy ships was burning. The armada would roll over them and keep on going. He had played the gambit and lost.

He saw the turrets of one of the battleships turning, barrels laying flat across its deck, aiming straight at his flagship.

He barely felt the explosion that swept him and what was left of the *Antietam* into the embrace of the sea.

The funeral pyres of dying ships dotted the night.

Emperor Yasim sat alone in his stateroom, stunned by the violence. He had survived half a dozen major engagements, but never had death whispered so close. At one point a shell fragment had punched through a viewing slit, decapitating the bodyguard standing next to him.

The thought of the blood spraying on his face caused him to go over to the silver basin and wash yet again.

Through an open porthole above the basin he saw a flare going up and detonating. Seconds later tracers lashed the water. One of his frigates was hunting down survivors in the water.

The eastern horizon was growing light, and the storm was beginning to break, though the wind still held and the seas continued to run. Occasional glimpses of the misty horizon revealed a dim red glow.

He returned to his bed and lay down, placing a cooling cloth over his forehead. He prayed that his stomach would settle, that the seas would settle, that he could somehow sleep. A spasm of nausea hit, and he sat up in anticipation, but then it passed.

Why am I here? he suddenly wondered. This could have waited. The humans were no real threat as of yet. Why did Hazin want this?

The ferocity of the human attack had been startling. They had charged straight in regardless of loss. Thanks to the vigilance of a lead frigate, which had hurried back with the report of their approach, they had been prepared. Plus, with his uncanny sixth sense, Hazin had made the suggestion to change formation before the frigate had even reported in. If not for them, the enemy ships would have struck straight into the van of his fleet when it was spread out across half a dozen leagues.

Instead, the lead of the van had slowed, the rearmost ships had come up, and together they had cautiously advanced through the storm, striking hard. But even then, two cruisers were sunk along with three frigates. Most amazingly of all one of the battleships was out of action. Come dawn, two cruisers would begin the arduous task of towing it across the vast distances back to Kazan.

A knock at the door stirred him. He was tempted to ignore it, but he knew who it was.

He stood up, looking down at his uniform. His guards had immediately washed and changed him after the incident on the bridge, but after the long night of sickness, he wasn't sure if he had stained himself.

Satisfied that he looked presentable, he acknowledged the knock and the door opened. It was, of course, Hazin, excited about the battle. "Sire, let me congratulate you on this victory."

"Victory? I never expected this fight."

"Nevertheless, it served its purpose well. Rather than have to dig them out, or worse, having them slip away and our spending months searching, they came straight to us to be slaughtered."

"We lost two cruisers, and the *Kavana* is out of action. If we had been fighting a fleet of the banner, I would expect that. But against these humans? And it is so far from home. If a cyclone strikes, the *Kavana* will go under."

"Sire, we know that they had eight ships that they designated as cruisers. Seven of the eight are confirmed as sunk along with eight or more of their smaller ships. That, sire, is nearly their entire fleet. They are defenseless now. Admiral Ullani informs me as well that the storm is abating."

Yasim said nothing, but silently thanked the gods. At least, around Kazan, if a storm threatened a leeward bay or shelter could be found. The vastness of this ocean was too troubling and too fraught with peril.

"Be evening we will be off their coast. In two days' time a harbor will be secured for the fleet while the transports can proceed to the Bantag coast."

"Something tells me this will not go according to the plan."

"War never does. There will be some flyers attacking today, that must be expected. We might take some small damage."

"As much as last evening?"

"I do not know, Your Highness, but I doubt it. If the flyers were effective, they would have waited, held their fleet back and sent them all in at once. The fact that they did not indicates to me that the power of the flyers is negligible, and their admiral decided to risk all on an evening attack in the storm. Actually, an admirable move."

"Yes, admirable and costly."

"More so to them. It is all but finished now."

"You truly believe so, don't you."

Hazin looked straight at him and smiled. "With certainty."

Another swell rocked the ship, and Yasim turned, retreating to his bed, and lay down. The ship rocked again, and Yasim fumbled for the gold basin by the side of his bed and vomited weakly. Letting the basin drop, he laid back gasping.

Hazin went over to a side table, poured a cup of weak tea into a mug to use as a decanter, damped a towel with water, and went to the emperor's bedside, helping him to wipe his face. The emperor sipped down the tea, then laid back.

Hazin started to withdraw, then stopped. "Sire, a suggestion."

"And that is?"

"Let me transfer to another ship."

"Which ship? One that is infiltrated by your people?"

"Then one of the smaller ships if you suspect such. You pick it, a cruiser."

"Your reason?"

"The main battle has been fought and won. The transports bearing the assault troops are still a day behind us even with our delay here. I suspect your decision will be to send the main force into Constantine as planned, and let the secondary force and supplies continue on to the Bantag coast. A ship should be left here to convey that information upon their arrival."

"Any courier can do that. Why the Grand Master?"

"You suspect duplicity, don't you, sire?"

"With you, Hazin, it is the very air you breathe."

"Sire, that shell that struck the bridge. It killed the man standing between you and me. Suppose it had killed both of us."

"Then we would no longer be together, Hazin," Yasim said dryly.

"You have an unborn child. How long would its mother live if word should return of your death?"

Yasim looked at him in surprise. "How did you know that? It was supposed to be a secret."

"Secrets? From me?"

"Perhaps it is I who should then wait for the transports to arrive, thus sparing you such worries."

"Sire, we both know that is impossible. The emperors of the Kazan have always led their armies into battle."

Yasim did not respond, for another swell had rocked the ship and, grabbing up a gold basin, he shuddered, swallowed hard, then put the basin down, looking up weakly.

"Let me speak practically to you, to reveal the duplicity if I must," said Hazin.

"Go on."

"If you die, how long would I last? As you have had

dozens of rivals, so have I within the Order. Even as we are here, they are undoubtedly plotting back home with the families of your cousins who still survive, who are out here with you even now, but who will turn on one another if you are dead. I will be one of the first to fall when you are gone."

"So stay with me. Then if you have some premonition, you can end it swiftly."

"Sire, I can ensure the survival of your child, your own blood. That is my guarantee if something should happen, and that is the duplicity behind the practical suggestion."

"So noble of you, Hazin."

"Nobility has nothing to do with it. But there is another layer within the game, sire. Let the victory be yours tomorrow. If I am aboard, there will be more than one who will whisper that it was I, Hazin, who made the decisions and but handed them to you to carry out."

Yasim bristled.

"It is what some will say, sire, and we both know that. By transferring me, it could be even seen as your breaking away from me, leaving me behind to ensure your own place and glory and that I have fallen somewhat from favor."

"Why so concerned for me and my glory?"

Hazin smiled. "Practicality, survival, advancement. The warriors of the Shiv will win glory enough later."

Yasim laid back and closed his eyes. "Take the *Zhiva*. I can spare one more cruiser."

"A wise decision, sire. My staff and I will transfer at dawn."

Hazin withdrew so quietly that Yasim wasn't even sure if he had left until he opened his eyes to check.

There had to be a scheme within a scheme here, he realized. Though all the things Hazin had cited were true, there had to be another factor. But he was too weary to think about it now, and in spite of his sickness, he soon drifted off to sleep, not aware of the fact that the warm tea Hazin had handed him was laced with a mild drug to make him compliant.

EIGHTEEN

Dawn came slowly, with low scudding clouds racing in from the sea, bringing moments of driving rain that passed quickly to show brief glimpses of clear pale blue sky overhead.

Standing by the number three dock of the naval yard, Cromwell waited anxiously with the knot of officers. Beyond the gate blocking access to the pier, he could see hundreds gathered; enlisted personnel, naval yard workers, and wives, hundreds of frightened wives, their murmuring voices carrying with the wind.

It was obvious the frigate had been in a fight. Its foremast was gone, the aft turret was nothing but scorched ruins, and the ship was listing heavily at the stern, black coiling smoke curled up from several breaks in the deck.

A harbor tug eased it into the dock, lines snaking out from the shore. Sailors on board, more than one of them striped to the waist, their bodies blackened from smoke, grabbed the lines, securing them. The gangplank was barely down when a dozen officers raced aboard, the rest of the crowd held back by a line of sailors with rifles.

In less than a minute, one of the officers was coming back down the gangplank. Ignoring shouted pleas for information, he mounted up and rode to the gate, a detail of sailors falling in around him so that he could get through the mob waiting outside the navy yard.

If he wouldn't talk, the sailors lining the deck of the shattered frigate most certainly would. Within moments Cromwell heard the comments racing through the crowd on the dock . . . "fleet sunk . . . Bullfinch dead . . . everything gone . . . the Kazan are coming!"

The word seemed to leap like a lightning bolt to the mob beyond the gate. A wild hysterical cry erupted, a commingling of screams, prayers, curses, and weeping.

Hundreds tried to surge in as the gate slipped open to let the mounted officer pass, others turned and started running back to the city.

A flurry of shots startled Cromwell. The officer, pistol raised over his head, emptied his revolver, and the crowd quieted.

"All military personnel report to your stations," he shouted in Greek. "All dockyard personnel report to work. The rest of you civilians go to your homes and prepare to evacuate the city."

Cromwell shook his head at the last statement. The city would be in utter chaos within the hour.

He looked over at General Petracci who stood silent, leaning heavily on his cane. Jack had come in the evening before, transferring his headquarters to where most of his airfleet was now stationed.

Jack was ignoring the madness erupting around them, looking up at the sky.

"Lousy day for flying. Wind will be up. We better start getting ready."

"Ship in sight!"

Adam, who had been handing a wrench up to his crew chief, heard the cry as it raced along the main deck. All work stopped, and he felt a momentary panic. If it was an enemy ship they were dead; every aerosteamer had been secured below during the storm, the first of the Falcons was just starting to go up the ramp to the flight deck.

He left his chief and went through the wooden door to the base of the bridge at a run, then scrambled up the ladder to the tower. It was a violation of etiquette to enter the admiral's realm without being ordered, but if the fight was erupting he had to know.

The admiral ignored his presence, looking forward, glasses raised. Adam respectfully stood behind him, finally spotting the smudge of smoke and then the glint of reflected sunlight.

"One of ours," Petronius announced, "and she looks like she's been in a fight."

The early morning light struck the cresting waves, and if they were not in such danger, Adam realized, it would have been a beautiful sight. With the passing of the storm front the air was freshening, shifting around to the west northwest, bringing with it a drop in humidity as the wind came

sweeping down out of the mountains with a touch of cool-
ness to it.

The storm-green sea, which had been driven inward by
the southerly winds of the day before, was now a mad confusion of whitecaps and short, sharp waves, which hissed
and rolled.

The minutes dragged out, Adam finally borrowing a pair
of glasses from the first officer. Adjusting the focus, he
finally caught sight of the ship. It was a cruiser, and Petronius was right, it had obviously been in a fight. Smoke from
its stacks was swirling out, but there was smoke from several fires as well, white plumes of steam, and part of a mast
leaning over drunkenly.

He caught a flicker of light winking on and off.

"She's signaling," Petronius announced.

The ship's signals officer was out the door to the open
bridge, glasses up, with Petronius following. Adam cautiously stepped into line behind the admiral.

The signals officer turned to the enlisted man working
the shutter lamp.

"Send reply. '*Shiloh. Wilderness* and *Perryville* following
astern. *Malvern Hill,* please report situation."

Adam listened to the clatter of the lantern shutter, trying
to follow the Morse code, the sailor signaling so fast it was
hard to keep up.

The signaling done, Adam started to raise his glasses to
watch the reply, but the first officer reclaimed his property.
Stepping back, he listened as the signals officer started to
read the response from the cruiser *Malvern Hill.*

"Believe all cruisers of fleet destroyed," and a gasp swept
through the bridge. "Action last night five miles south of
Three Sisters, Minoan Shoals. Four enemy battleships and
numerous other ships engaged. One battleship believed
sunk. Three of our frigates following astern. End message."

Petronius, face pale, turned and looked around at his
staff, shaking his head.

"Ask him about Bullfinch."

Again the clattering and a quick reply.

"Believe dead. *Antietam* sunk."

"Position of enemy fleet," Petronius asked, making no
comment on the reported death of his old friend.

"Last sighted steaming west, five miles south of Minoan

Shoals. Believe they will attack Constantine by late afternoon. Am ordering remains of fleet to withdraw up Mississippi. Your orders?"

Petronius walked back into the shelter of the enclosed bridge and sat down in his chair. A gesture to a midshipman resulted in a steaming mug of tea, which Petronius slipped in silence for several minutes.

He finally looked up at the officers gathered round.

"Fight or withdraw."

There was silence, finally the first officer spoke up.

"*Malvern Hill* is shot to pieces, we can see that. Admiral Bullfinch is gone. If we put our backs against Constantine we'll be pinned and shot to pieces as well, sir. Captain Ustasha over in *Malvern Hill* is right, let's come about. The Mississippi is only two hours behind us. Pull back up the river."

There were nods of agreement, finally Petronius's gaze settled on Adam.

"The air corps has transferred nearly everything they have down to Constantine. They won't pull out without a fight, sir. They will launch a strike," Adam said. "We need to support it."

"In this wind?" the first officer replied. "It must be gusting to thirty knots."

"It will flatten by the end of the day."

"If that battle was fought last evening they will be off the coast of Constantine by three this afternoon at the latest," and as he spoke, he pointed forward, for the city was now less than five hours sailing time away at full speed.

Petronius looked from the first officer back to Adam and all fell silent.

"I'm with young Mr. Rosovich here," Petronius replied softly. "I've never turned my back on a fight, and I'll be damned if we do it now."

Adam looked over at him, obviously surprised by the response.

"But, sir," the first officer replied heatedly, "if Admiral Bullfinch and our entire fleet couldn't stop them and got annihilated trying, then what the hell can we do. We don't have a gun on this ship, just a bunch of crates that can barely fly."

"We can die trying," Petronius said, then paused, looking

around at the group. "But we'll do it with some intelligence, gentlemen, some intelligence."

For a wonderful, blessed moment, the high scattered clouds cast a shadow over the butte. Abe crawled out from under his shelter half, Togo calling to him.

He tried to walk erect, but his head was swimming. Feet like lead, he shuffled slowly, kicking up dust, a broken arrow, spent cartridges. He squatted down by the sergeant's side.

Togo was pointing toward the ravine to the north and offered his glasses. Several Bantag were out of the ravine, one of them holding a bucket, pouring water over the others. They paused, as if knowing they were being watched, and waved.

"Should I try a shot, Lieutenant? Arrogant bastards."

Abe shook his head.

"Save what we got," he croaked.

It had been a ghastly night, followed by an even worse dawn. Three times the Bantag had tried to scale the butte, the last fight hand-to-hand along the eastern rim. The dead from both sides lay where they fell; it was beyond asking the men to scratch holes in the hard ground, or to expend what energy they had left dragging the Bantag bodies off to push over the side. The one benefit of the charge was that nine of the Bantag dead had water sacks on them, enough so that a small cupful could be doled out to each man with enough left over for two cups for the surviving wounded.

Just before dawn the suicides started. Three men shot themselves in quick succession, while two simply stood up and charged over the rim. Abe had managed to stop two more, one by sitting and talking with the trooper until the boy broke down into sobs until he fell asleep, the second one with a fistfight that had sapped what little energy he had left.

Abe looked around at his perimeter. Maybe fifty men left who could fight, another forty or so wounded, dying, or beyond caring, lying comatose.

"Lieutenant," Togo whispered. "Your speech was all mighty fine, but if we don't get water and food, well, it'll be over with by the end of the day."

Abe wearily nodded.

"We wait till dark. You and the sergeant major," and he nodded to the old man who was dozing in the shade of a blanket propped up with several Bantag spears, "break out down the west slope. Maybe some of you can get into those ravines and find a way out."

"What about you?"

"I'll stay here with the wounded."

"A lot of good that will do, Lieutenant. This isn't the time to get sentimental or play some heroic game. You stay here, you die, and it won't be pleasant. Those buggers take you alive and figure out who you are, it'll be a slow death."

Abe shook his head.

"I don't think so, and they won't take me alive."

"Then I stay, too."

"No. If anyone can lead these men out, it's you."

Togo sighed and finally nodded in agreement.

"You know none of us will make it. They'll expect this."

"I know."

Togo laughed.

"Rice wine. A gallon of it, that's what I'll have when I get to where I'm going."

"Lieutenant!"

He got up and half crawled to where a trooper on the west side was calling, pointing.

Abe could see it, mounted Bantag in the ravine.

"Sergeant major! Round up ten men, get them over here."

A hundred riders swept up out of the ravine and came forward at the charge.

"Wait for it," Abe said. "Sergeant major, pass out the reserve ammunition one round at a time!"

The riders crossed the first four hundred yards without a shot being fired.

The last two hundred yards they swept in as before, low in the saddles. The Bantag dug in at the fallen redoubt resumed their harassing fire of launching arrows nearly straight up, shafts clattering down, striking ground. A trooper cursed as one caught him in the calf.

Measured shots snapped off, dropping several of the riders. Most of them dismounted, scurrying up to the wall and dodging in amongst the boulders and rocks. A few raced forward, coming up the slope, but were dropped by carefully placed shots.

The fight slacked off.

Several of the men looked at Abe, not sure of what was to come next.

"Just to see if we still had some fight in us," he announced. He didn't add that the reinforcements meant that any hope of breaking out had been sealed shut. The Bantag wanted to make sure that no one escaped.

"Sir?"

It was Togo, kneeling up and pointing.

He saw it too, and within seconds so did the others. There was a feeble shout, then men stood up, waving.

High up, half a dozen miles off, a dot was moving across the sky, slowly floating along . . . a flyer.

Men started shouting, taking off hats, waving, ignoring the flurry of sniper shots fired from the ravines. But the flyer continued on its way, never swerving from its course, tracking off to the northwest, growing smaller and yet smaller until it disappeared.

Abe knew that whatever faint hope still lingered with his men had finally broken at that moment. If a flyer had patrolled out this way and not seen them, it would not search there again. There were ten thousand square miles or more of ground where they might be lost, and that was assuming that the courier he had sent off had even made it back to the regiment.

Wearily he stood up and headed to the hospital tent, to take the medical orderly aside and ask him what was the most humane thing to do for those men who were unconscious when night came. He knew what the answer would be, and dreaded the thought. As he walked past the major, the madman simply sat there and glared, then broke into a taunting laugh.

Commander Cromwell walked down the flight line, thrilling to the sound of a hundred engines turning over, warming up; air crews and ground crews running past. He recognized several of them, classmates from the academy who had gone on to the air corps while he had joined the naval wing.

Every plane possible had been pressed into service, fifty

at this field, nearly seventy more at the other two fields hastily laid out in the narrow plains behind Constantine.

There had been over a hundred and fifty, but without hangars for the larger ships or sheltered tie downs, nearly a quarter of the entire air corps had been destroyed by the storm before a single shot was fired.

Cromwell reached his aerosteamer, the Ilya Murometz he had flown two days before. Igor was already up in the cockpit, running the final checks, and Octavian was in his gatling position astern. Xing, however, had been replaced after complaining of a sudden stomach ache. It was just as well, Richard thought, since the forward gunner was also the bombardier. Approaching the massive airship, he spotted the new aimer. Surprisingly, a Cartha like himself named Drasulbul. They shook hands, then he crouched down to look under the plane.

The four bombs were in their racks. At five hundred pounds each, it was the heaviest load any of the attackers would carry this day. He would have given anything to have the weapons on the aerosteamer carriers.

He walked around his plane, pausing for a second to watch as a Falcon took off. It barely rolled a hundred feet before it was up, nearly losing control in the gusty wind then leveling out. Another Falcon was airborne, and then a third.

He went up the ladder into the cockpit, slipping into the seat opposite Igor. His copilot and top gunner said nothing, just pointed to the gauge for the outboard starboard engine.

"Running a hundred revolutions a minute off, we're not getting the heat on the engine. It'll cut our speed a good five miles an hour. If it acts up, we'll lose it."

Cromwell stared straight at Igor.

"You suggesting we stand down?"

Igor gave him a tight lipped smile and shook his head.

"Just thought you should know."

"What the hell," Richard replied, "we'll make it there, that's the main thing."

"How far out are they?"

"Thirty miles, last report."

Two enemy scout planes had crossed over Constantine just before noon, flying high at well over five thousand feet. Neither of them had been caught by the four Falcons sent up in pursuit. Two of the Falcons had made it back with the latest fix. The watch tower on Diocletian Hill above the town had telegraphed a report just before he'd left the briefing, declaring that smoke was visible on the horizon.

Two more Falcons took off. A gust of wind upended one of them, wing clipping the ground and tearing off, the ship cartwheeling, then bursting into flames.

"Well there's one that didn't need his parachute," Igor growled.

Richard said nothing. Petracci had announced that except for the Falcon pilots flying cover, no parachutes would be issued. It saved nearly a hundred pounds per man, a crucial factor where every pound saved was eight additional rounds for the gatlings. As for the attack aerosteamers, they would be flying too low to ever use them. Besides, there simply were not enough to go around.

A crew chief came running down the flight line, stopping in front of Cromwell's plane and signaling for him to rev up.

Two more Falcons lifted, then two more. The ten Goliaths were next, lumbering off one at a time, straining to lift the ton of weight strapped under their fuselages.

The crew chief pointed to the right, signaling for Richard to begin taxiing out, a dozen men on the wings pushed, helping him to turn.

A Goliath floated past, propellers a blur. Three more Goliaths were ahead of him, the lead one turning, lining up to lift off . . . and then it burst into flames.

For several long seconds Richard sat, transfixed, not sure exactly what had gone wrong. He saw the aft gunner of the burning Goliath staggering out of the fire, wreathed in flames. No one was helping, men running in every direction. Richard's crew chief pointed up, then turned and started to run as well.

Richard slid open his side window and stuck his head out to look at an aerosteamer diving straight at him, a light sparkling from above its upper wing. A shot cracked through the starboard wings of his plane, striking the ground.

Then the realization hit.

"Igor, we're under attack. Get topside, do something. I'm taking this crate off!"

"You need both of us for that."

"Do it!"

Richard started to rev up his starboard engines. The Goliath pilot who was next in line looked over at him, and he pointed to the takeoff strip, then up.

The pilot nodded, and seconds later the two-engine ship swung out onto the runway, starboard wing swinging within a few feet of the burning wreckage. He started to take off, top gunner up in position, gatling firing, tracers snaking up.

The burning tail dragged past Richard, who brought his starboard throttles up to full. The machine simply hung in place. Cursing, he leaned over, grabbed the port throttles, and brought them up to half speed. The Ilya Murometz finally lurched as if breaking free from the ground, rolled a few yards, and then started to pivot. Richard scrambled to slam back the port throttles. Lining up on the field, he saw the Goliath preceding him flying low, flame trailing from its starboard wing.

"One coming in directly astern!" Igor shouted, and a second later his gatling opened up.

Richard pushed all four throttles to the wall, braced his feet on the rudder pedals, and started the takeoff, praying that the Goliath ahead would clear the field.

Speed slowly picked up, he caught a glimpse of a Falcon swooping low, cutting across the field at a right angle, gatling firing. Another Falcon was coming down, wing sheared off, spinning out of control. And a strange looking airship, propeller mounted forward, with a large, single wing, bulky fuselage trailing blue flame; it and the damaged Falcon impacted near the control tower.

He felt the controls biting and looked quickly at the airspeed gauge. The wind was the only luck factor at the moment, strong enough that after less than a thousand feet he leaned back on the stick. Igor continued to fire, cursing wildly in Rus.

"Damn—to our left!" he cried.

Richard looked off to port but saw nothing, then realized that Igor, in his excitement and facing backwards, had his directions crossed. He looked off to starboard and was startled to see one of the single wing planes flying directly alongside, pilot clearly visible. To his amazement the pilot actually raised a clenched fist, then the plane disappeared, nosing up, and winging over.

The Goliath ahead was still lumbering forward, unable to gain height, fire all along its wing. Richard realized that the pilot knew he was doomed and was trying to get clear of the aerodrome.

The Goliath nosed over and went in, its bomb load exploding a split second later. The blast soared up in front of Cromwell, rocking the Ilya Murometz, putting it up on one wing so that Richard felt as if he was about to lose control and add his explosives to the conflagration.

He fought the controls, wishing that Igor was beside him instead of in the gunner's slot. The great plane finally started to level out, and, looking over his shoulder, he could see the mad confusion of the fight. Half a dozen aerosteamers were on the ground, burning, and the hydrogen gas generator was on fire. Tracers snaked across the sky; two Falcons were diving, following a Kazan plane, which appeared to be slower. Seconds later the plane began to burn, nosed over, and went straight in.

He saw smoke rising from the second airfield, but the third still looked clear. The sky around him was aswarm with aerosteamers, weaving and banking, a fight unlike anything he had ever imagined. He realized that the last thing he needed was to be in the middle of the mad swirl and banked over to starboard, heading inland to get out of the fight and let the Falcons settle it.

He could see that the surviving Goliaths had the same idea and were turning out as well, a half dozen of the Falcons weaving in behind and above them.

After several miles he was forced to turn, not yet having enough altitude to clear the crest of the Diocletian Hills. Along the crest he could see thousands of soldiers standing in the open, watching the fight. The ground all along the crest was torn up with hastily dug entrenchments snaking out from either flank of the main fort that dominated the hill. The fact that they were watching, like spectators, told him that they were in the clear. Turning, he looked back. The battle was all but over. Airships were heading out to sea, flying low, several of them trailing smoke. Fires dotted the landscape between the hills and the city down on the plain, marking where two dozen or more aerosteamers had died.

We should have thought of it, I should have thought of it, and he cursed himself. It wasn't just the losses, although he feared that they were significant—maybe a third or more of the precious Goliaths. What was worse was the mass confusion. Falcons had flown off in every direction, their top cover was off chasing the surviving attackers. What was supposed to be a coordinated attack, everyone going in at once, was spread out across twenty miles of airspace. As for the aerosteamer carriers, which were to have arrived by now, they were nowhere to be seen.

"How many did they get?" Igor shouted, squatting down out of his gunnery position to look over Richard's shoulder.

"Too many."

"Now what?"

"We go in," and he pointed out to sea where a cloud of dark smoke blotted the horizon.

Adam Rosovich stormed back and forth across the flight deck, shouting orders, watching as each of the Falcons was slowly lifted up from below, turned around, wings unfolded and engines started.

"Adam."

It was Theodor, with a board tucked under his arm, a final check sheet for each of the planes.

"A word, son."

"I don't have time."

"Yes, you do. Now come over here."

Theodor led him over to the side railing. The sea below was still running high, waves rolling at ten to twelve feet, the crosswind breaking their tops, salty foam billowing off.

Adam looked up at the bridge beside him. The flag of the Republic was snapping, bent out; the ship's fifteen knot speed added to the crosswind coming in abeam from the northwest.

"Could you make it short," Adam asked testily, and Theodor put a hand on his shoulder.

"Relax, son."

"What?"

"Just that. You're making everyone nervous."

"What the hell do you mean?"

"Look, son. You're a good pilot, and you've got one hell of a sharp engineering mind. Varinnia saw that in you back at the academy, she had you picked out a year before you graduated, but, son, you are not the best of leaders at the moment."

Adam bristled.

"Friendly criticism, and please take it that way. I know what it's like to fly into a battle. In fact I'm the only man in this entire fleet who's done it before, and I will tell you, I used to puke from fear before I went in. You, on the other hand, are running around waving your arms and shouting orders."

"But . . ."

"Hear me out. These men are trying the best they can. I won't say they're doing a good job yet—hell, we're making this up as we go along—but they are trying. Your job is to lead the Goliath wing in the attack, not boss the deck crews. The best thing you can do right now is button up, take a chew of tobacco and just lean against the bridge there and say nothing. Act like you don't have a care in the world.

"You did your briefing for your pilots. Once everything is up on deck the waiting begins until the scout plane returns. When it does, if we have them fixed, I want you to just walk over to your plane like you're going out for a little spin around the field to impress some girl. No fancy speeches, the boys know what it is about now and the odds . . ."

His voice trailed off and he looked away for a moment.

"By Kesus just don't get yourself killed. You remind me a bit of old Ferguson, you've got a great mind and for my penny's worth I'd have Keane ground you the moment this is over. So just fly careful, will you?"

Adam nodded, realizing that every word Theodor had said was right.

"Thanks."

"Hell, I needed to say something. I'm about ready to bust, myself, with the damn waiting."

Adam looked up at the sky; the afternoon sun was tracking westward. Somewhere, off to their starboard, about eighty miles away, all hell must be breaking loose.

*   *   *

In spite of the fear, Yasim felt compelled to watch. It was a remarkable sight, the swarm of dots on the northern horizon growing larger, coming in. The outer ring of ships were positioned correctly, forming a screen between the main battle line and the coast, which was less than ten miles away.

His own aerosteamers were directly above. He tried to count them; twenty at least still survived. A few of the human aerosteamers, slightly smaller and faster it seemed, were mixed in, tracers streaming back and forth. Even as he watched, one of his flipped over, bursting into flames, and started to spiral downward.

The fight was trivial, unimportant. What was important was the attack coming in, the last desperate gasp according to Admiral Ullani.

Milky white puffs of smoke were igniting in the sky, the outer ring of ships sending up shells from their light guns, tracers streaking into the sky. An airship burst in a silent flash, another exploded seconds later.

They pressed on.

Yasim could not help but feel a touch of pity, of admiration. The attacks, which had been coming in for the last half hour, were completely uncoordinated, three or four planes at a time. The strike by the scout planes had been brilliant, catching them just as they were taking off, breaking up any hope of formation. It was going perfectly, just one more attack to weather and then they would press in to start the bombardment.

The dots were resolving themselves into thin lines, four of them bi-winged aircraft with two engines, and also several smaller, single-engine machines zigzagging back and forth above. And one larger, a four-engine plane almost as big as their own Zhu patrol aircraft.

Now past the outer ring of frigates, they dodged through the inner ring of cruisers, crisscrossing fire dropping one. They were less than a mile off now, leveling out; two sections of two. The four engine machine was joined with a two-engine companion trailing a quarter mile behind the first.

Every gunner forward was ready. He looked down at them, bright shell casings littered the deck from the repulse of the previous attacks.

A command echoed and everyone opened up at nearly the same instant, a staccato thunder, smoke rolling up as twenty gatlings and all the mid-range guns fired; gatlings with tracer rounds, the mid-range guns with explosive shells.

The fire swept out, water spraying up in front of the attacking airships, which continued to press in. Shell bursts blossomed. One of the twin-engine machines disintegrated in a violent explosion. The one behind it flew straight into the expanding ball of fire and debris, then emerged out of the other side, half a wing gone. It rolled up on its side then spun down, cartwheeling into the sea.

It was almost obscenely easy, and he could hear some of his warriors down on the foredeck break into laughter.

The other two banked slightly, swinging out and around the explosion, one of their escorts flying with them. The other two starting to pull up, moving to engage several of his own airships.

The action unfolded before him in a remarkable display of fire and explosions. The range closed rapidly. The two-engine plane started to trail smoke, then simply nosed over and went straight in. The four-engine plane continued to press in. Excited shouts erupted around him, several of his guard moving in closer. He could see flames licking out astern of this last plane. Part of its rudder snapped off, and the plane began to yaw, barely in control, now less than a hundred yards off.

It was a remarkable moment; the huge plane just seemed to hang in the sky, and then it nosed up, four black cylinders detaching. With the release of the weight the plane surged up as it winged over, one engine trailing smoke, tracers stitching through it.

The guards closed in around him, pushing him down on the deck.

He felt two violent jolts in quick succession, and, cursing, stood back up, annoyed by their overzealous efforts.

Two massive columns of water were already cascading down, drenching the deck. One of the single-engine planes appeared to fly right through the spreading mushroom of water, and he watched in disbelief as it flew straight for the bridge. This time he ducked on his own as the plane slammed into the second turret and exploded, hot smoke washing up over him.

He slowly stood up a second time. Bits of burning wreckage were strewn across the top of the turret, burning fuel splashed out into some several of the gatling mounts, when warriors, on fire, writhed in agony. He caught a glimpse of the four-engine machine, trailing smoke, clumsily dodging and weaving to escape, none of his gunners firing for the moment, either stunned by the blasts or the suicidal crash of the fast plane.

Yasim looked around at the officers on the bridge, who were silent.

"They have the spirit of warriors. I hope we have not misjudged this thing."

The moment the scout plane was in sight, Adam could contain himself no longer. Petronius, bent over a chart showing their position near the eastern end of the Minoan Shoals, gave him a curt nod and said nothing.

Adam stepped out onto the open bridge, joining the signals officer as the single-engine Falcon came spiraling in. A Morse lantern began to flash, the signals officer slowly reading off the message.

"Enemy fleet, seven battleships, fifteen miles south Constantine. While returning observed fires outside city, apparent air battle."

Petronius, who had stood up from his chart, walked out to join the group and nodded his head.

"We go?" Adam asked excitedly.

"With intelligence, Mr. Rosovich, intelligence, I said."

"The air corps, sir, the report."

"That battle is most likely over by now, Rosovich. A battle they were not trained for, I might add."

Petronius looked over at the sun, nodded his head, and went back to his chart.

Richard, one hand on the controls, reached over to Igor.

"Press it against your chest, damn you!" he cried, "Keep it pressed tight!"

Igor looked at him and actually smiled, frothy bubbles of blood on his lips. He weakly held the bundled up rag Richard was pressing to the hole in the side of his chest.

Igor, his flight overall, the deck, and the gunner's position behind Richard, were all covered in blood. He had seen thousands die in his youth, but still it never ceased to amaze him just how much blood could pour out of a person before they died.

"Another five minutes, we'll be down. Ten minutes, they'll stop the bleeding."

Igor still smiled. He tried to say something, but couldn't.

"I need my other hand to fly this," Richard cried. Letting go of the rag, he slapped his right hand back on the throttles, feeding in more fuel to the inboard engines. The pedals beneath his feet were useless, the cables snapped and the rudder half shot off in the last seconds of his approach.

"I should have just flown this damned crate straight in," he said. Repeating yet again a litany he had been torturing himself with ever since the bombs had missed.

A few seconds more, just ten seconds, even five and he could have brought them straight into the bridge. He knew it was the emperor's ship, knew he had seen him. The blast would have taken him, but it would have taken Yasim as well. And where there was Yasim, there was also Hazin.

Then a shot hit the rudder, another shattered the propeller of the already faltering starboard outboard engine, and he could feel the plane mushing into a yaw that would spin out of control. The only thing left was to yank back the stick and try to lob the bombs into the bow, and he had missed.

How he had got them out was still a mystery. There was little return fire on the way back out and he half wondered if the Kazan had fired off far too much ammunition and were ordered not to waste it on cripples that were obviously dying.

Well, this cripple he planned to bring in. Swinging out wide to avoid most of the frigates, he had finally turned in toward shore. Only then had Igor slipped back down from the gunner's position, looked at him, and without a word collapsed into the copilot's chair. Richard instantly realized that the man had remained silent about his wound, not wanting to distract Richard from flying them out.

As for the rest of the crew, he knew Octavian was dead and there was not a word from the Cartha up forward ever

since takeoff. Chances were the blast from the exploding
Goliath had killed him.

The shore was directly ahead, less than half a mile; the
city off to his right, the second airfield, the closer of the
two, just a mile back from the beach.

The port outboard engine finally seized and quit, jerking
to a stop with such violence that he could feel the shudder
run through the entire ship.

That was it. The hydrogen bags had been shot apart,
there was no lift left.

The plane began to slip, heading down the last few feet.
Cursing, he pulled the stick back, trying to beg just a couple
more seconds of flight to put them in on the beach.

The wheels hit the water, snagged, and the massive aerosteamer went in nose first, what was left of the forward
windscreen shattering as the ocean swept in.

Unbuckling, he reached over to Igor, unsnapping his
harness.

"Come on. You've got to help me!" Richard cried.

Holding on to Igor, he kicked his way up through the
topside gunner's hatch and out into the open, somehow
managing to hang on to Igor. The airship wasn't sinking
and, for a moment, he was confused. He pulled Igor up
and lowered him over the side, then dropped into the
water, feet hitting the bottom. He lost Igor for a second
then came back up, a wave knocking him over, the aerosteamer surging up and then ever so slowly flipping over
onto its back, steam hissing as the water hit the hot engines.

Afraid of getting tangled in the rigging, he let the surf
take him, going under, then coming back up again. He
caught a glimpse of Igor, floating facedown and swam over
to him, pulling his head up out of the water.

"It's only a few feet more. Hang on!"

He stood up, dragging his companion, another wave
knocked him down, but he held on to Igor, letting the surf
rush them in to shore.

He felt hands around his waist and saw that half a dozen
men were around them.

Their strength was a welcome relief, and he let them
carry him the last few yards to safety.

They laid him down on the rocky beach, one of the men

holding a bottle, which he gladly took, the rich Greek wine
warm and soothing.

They were all talking at once, pointing to the ocean. Not
a word they said understandable.

"Igor?" he asked.

They stepped back and saw his companion lying several
feet away, arms wide. A Greek woman was kneeling beside
the body, already closing the eyes, then making the sign of
the cross.

Richard turned his gaze away, looking back out to the
sea. The row of battleships were coming straight in. Already some of the frigates were but a mile off shore, opening fire on the city.

We've lost, he realized. Everyone dead, and they are
here. Hazin is here. I tried to stop him, and it was all
useless, bloody useless.

He closed his eyes and, tilting the wine sack up, he
drained it.

The wind slashed the length of the deck, the flag of the
Republic and the red launch flag standing straight out.

Adam tensed, watching as the last of the Falcons started
its roll. The deck beneath them was surging up and down,
one second pointing down at the ocean, seconds later pointing up at the late afternoon sky; the red sun almost directly ahead.

The Falcon lifted as the carrier rode up on the crest of
a wave, then dropped out from under the aerosteamer.

The launch chief turned, faced Adam, and held his red
flag overhead, then twirled it in a circle. Adam revved up
his engines. The chief pointed forward. Adam pushed the
throttles the rest of the way. His Goliath, the first in line,
started forward.

He carefully watched as the right wing passed within a
couple of feet of the bridge. He saw Petronius standing on
the open bridge. To his amazement the admiral offered a
salute, Theodor by his side, waving.

Adam snapped a salute back, then focused all attention
forward, watching the deck surge up and down, speed of
his roll out slowing as it pitched up, accelerating as it
went down.

His grip on the stick tightened. Even with the wind it

was going to be tight. There was no copilot beside him, no top gunner, every pound of weight stripped out except for fuel and what was slung underneath.

Another roll up, then starting down. He tentatively tried backing the stick, hoping to lift as the deck dropped, but he didn't have enough speed.

The deck continued to pitch down, his own speed picking up, and he rolled right off the end of the ship, heading down toward the foaming sea. Easing back on the stick he leveled out, ever so slowly climbing up to a hundred feet and then leveling off again, heading due west. Overhead the Falcons had formed up, circling around to come in above him. He looked back over his shoulder and caught a glimpse of the next Goliath, throttles full out, coming up to fall in on his left wing.

A half mile off was the second formation from *Wilderness,* and beyond them the flight from *Perryville.* Looking to starboard, he could see *Malvern Hill,* valiantly struggling to come up and join the three aerosteamer carriers, which had leapt ahead to gain position. Two more frigates had fallen in with the group during its dash southward to the edge of the Minoan Shoals, and they were now screening ahead of the main ships, yards bare, running on engines alone into the westerly wind.

Thirty miles to the Three Sisters, then a slow arcing turn out to the northwest, and then finally back in low, and out of the west toward Constantine. Two and a half hours of flying time, then an hour back to the carriers, which would run straight in toward Constantine for the pickup.

Fortunately, the lead pilot of the Falcons was a wizard at navigation. All Adam had to do was fly, and then go straight in on the emperor's ship if he could find it.

"Hazin!"

A Shiv lookout, up on the forward deck, was pointing off to the North. They were far off, on the other side of the shoals, hardly visible in the mist kicked up by the waves driving into the rocks a mile away.

The dots bobbed and weaved, rising and falling in his vision, and he turned away, shaking.

Was it truly a foretelling? Or fantasy, a dream vision of the future that had taken him to this time and place long

years ago? Or was it merely his imagination telling him it
was so?

He saw O'Donald down on the deck, attention still focused on the other horizon. The first of the transports was
just coming into view, the fifty ships holding the umens of
the Shiv.

Hazin could see, too, see him as in the dream, and it
fascinated him. Am I the master of my fate, he wondered.
Or has fate cast me into this moment, this role that would
change everything.

The gun in the number one turret began to lift up, steam
hissing from the exhaust line. The massive thirty-foot-long
barrel stopped, and Yasim half turned, covering his ears.
There was a blinding flash of light, barrel recoiling, water
going flat from the shock wave.

He raised his glasses, training them on the burning city.
Explosions were lifting up, fires spreading. Another explosion blew. It was impossible to tell if it was from his ship;
at the range of nearly two leagues it was impossible to track
where a shell might land. Closer in to shore the cruisers
and frigates were attempting to slam aimed shots into the
fortifications on the heights beyond the city. Aft, the number four gun now fired, again the shock wave.

For a human city it was actually rather impressive. On
one of the hills in the center of the city was a great golden
domed building. Yasim had overheard one of the gunnery
officers discussing the rivalry between the gunners in the
three turrets as to who would hit it first. The fourth turret,
damaged by the suicidal pilot, was still out of action. Water
was still leaking in from dozens of buckled plates below
the waterline, and all pumps were working hard to keep
ahead while the chief engineer directed repairs. He had
requested that the flagship cease firing, as the vibration of
the great guns firing was making the situation difficult to
control, but Yasim would not hear of it. Honor demanded
that his ship participate in the initial bombardment. At least
the fact that the bombardment required slow cruising had
helped, the ship barely moved at a league and a half in
an hour as it hovered off its target and pounded the city
to rubble.

The sun was low on the horizon, illuminating the clouds

of smoke from the gunfire and from the burning city, a beautiful sight, worthy of a hada, a seven-line poem of alternating five and seven words.

He tried to compose one even as he watched the billowing explosions, the first spreading across the city, a secondary explosion in what one of the gunnery officers described as most likely the Republic's main shipyard.

It was a glorious, beautiful sight—and yet he felt that something was not correct, not in place.

Was it Hazin?

There had to be a reason why, always the game within the game, like the toy he had had as a child; a golden ball that when opened revealed another within, and then another within that, and then yet another.

He had ordered his chamberlain to go through the ship's roster yet again, to have his chief protector question yet again any who might be suspect, who might be of the Order and concealed in the ranks. Yet they had found nothing.

Something was wrong, marring this moment, and then another explosion caught his attention, a cheer rippling along the deck. The golden dome had been hit, disappearing in a shower of flame and smoke, which glowed in the late afternoon light.

Then the alarm sounded.

Adam leveled out, pulled up his goggles to wipe the sweat from his eyes, wiped his hand on his pants leg, then gripped the stick again.

It was stunning. The city had been their beacon for fifty miles, smoke and flames as they flew a circular approach far behind the fleet, swinging around to the west before coming down to wave-top level and then flying straight in for twenty miles.

"Low, sun at your backs and in their eyes," Petronius had said. "The bastards will all be looking the other way, focused on the burning city, enjoying themselves, figuring the battle is won."

Petronius was right. The seven battleships were lying four miles off the coast, the frigates and cruisers lined farther in, with only two frigates several miles out on picket to the west of the battleships.

In the lead, Adam led his flight of eight Goliaths wide

of the frigates, and not a shot was fired until he was abeam the second ship. A few shells detonated, and then they were past, the battleships four miles ahead.

It was another mile in before he sensed that the Kazan were finally reacting. The battleships were moving slowly, guns firing, and then finally the last ship in line began to turn off the firing line to starboard, heading south, trying to run straight out into the open sea. Perfect, for it set them abeam, the widest target possible.

The second ship in line began to turn as well, still lumbering along. Adam grinned. Petronius had predicted that as well. Ships of that size would take ten, fifteen minutes to build up to battle speed, and by then it would be over.

He raised his glasses, scanned the first ship, then the second and the third, which was continuing straight on course. The fourth ship in line. That was it, the red banner.

He looked to left and right. The other Goliaths were roughly in position to either side.

He finally caught the eye of the pilot off to starboard. He pointed at the battleships, held up four fingers, and then pointed forward. The pilot nodded. He tried to get the attention of the man to port, but he was completely focused on the spectacle ahead.

He started to bank out, moving to swing beyond the range of the guns of the last battleship in line. It would add several dangerous minutes to the flight, but the emperor's ship was the one he wanted.

The first battleship was directly abeam, a mile and a half to port and still turning. One of the Goliaths on his port side banked up and started to turn in on the ship.

"No damn it, no!"

There was no way he could reach him. If he tried to turn to catch him, the others would follow and assume they were going in.

He flew on, cursing even more when a second Goliath rolled out to attack. Several of the Falcons flying above them broke to follow the two planes.

Adam looked back to his right and saw the groups from *Wilderness* and *Perryville* off to his left, a mile or two farther back, spreading out slightly, focusing on the first two battleships.

Far off to his left, close in to the burning city, the cruisers were breaking out of the firing formation, beginning to speed up.

Finally the shooting started, breaking the tension. Every gun on the aft battleship seemed to go into action, medium-caliber weapons letting loose. Seconds later an explosion ripped the sky directly ahead, several hundred yards off, fragments slashing the water.

The agonizing seconds dragged out; the third ship was abeam, beginning to fire as well, and then a half mile farther on and a mile off his port side was the target. A minute and a half he realized, a minute and a half and either its sinking or I'm dead, or perhaps both.

He lightly touched the release lever. He was tempted to pull the safety pin out, but decided against it, fearful that something might go wrong. He forced himself to continue on, watching the ship, gauging its speed, trying to calculate where it would be in another minute.

It was beginning to turn, swinging like the other ships, southward.

He looked back at the pilots to starboard; they were still with him. He raised a clenched fist, held it aloft, then jerked it down even as he kicked in the rudder and pushed the stick over.

The move was a little too aggressive with the half ton weight slung underneath, inertia wanting to push the plane along the path it had been following. Wings straining, he began losing altitude, dropping down to less than twenty feet. Leveling out, he felt he was off, aiming too far astern, and pulled the stick back slightly, gaining a few precious feet. He slipped in a touch of rudder, correcting the approach, and then everything broke loose.

Gatlings opened up from the deck of the battleship. The rounds fell short by several hundred yards as they arced up high and plunged down, but they appeared before him like a visible wall that he would have to fly through.

Amazingly the Falcons, which had been there to provide top cover if any Kazan aerosteamers were about, went in as well, going up to full throttle to move ahead of him. He wondered if they should have been ordered to carry a light load of bombs as well, but it was too late now for that. The first one went through the curtain of fire and seconds later was in the sea, wings snapped off, a second Falcon going down a hundred yards farther on.

Their actions brought him precious seconds of time, diverting fire from the slower attack planes. He spared a quick glance to starboard again; his remaining three Goliaths were still with him.

Looking to his left, he saw chaos. The aerosteamers from *Wilderness* and *Perryville* were boring in on the two battleships astern. Smoke was coiling up from a dozen or more wrecks dotting the sea, while tracers slashed back and forth. The lead Falcon was already over the battleship, soaring past it, his gun still firing.

A jolt snapped his attention forward. Another jolt came as a tracer slashed past his windscreen. A stream of tracers from a gun aft was snaking around, following him. Yet another jolt, and the sound of glass shattering. He was glad he didn't have a copilot, because the man would have been dead.

Range was half a mile.

An explosion. To his right, the Goliath on his wing was gone.

He focused forward.

Water sprayed up, slashing through the broken window. His ship dropped, as if the spray from the explosions would push him down into the sea. He surged back up, over correcting, losing speed. Pushing throttles to the wall, he nosed over and leveled out, then another jolt shredded the wing just inside from the port engine.

Six hundred yards.

Another round hit the forward windscreen, more glass shattering. Something tore at his right arm.

He reached down, wrapping his hand around the release lever.

More spray, tracers crisscrossing. A Falcon flew directly across his path, nearly colliding.

Four hundred yards.

He touched the rudder in, leaning into the sight, judging the angle. He pulled the lever.

Nothing happened.

He pulled again. And still nothing. The damn safety pin!

Fumbling, he reached around to the side of the lever, found the pin, and yanked it out.

Another jolt. He looked up and realized that he was off alignment, turning out and away. He jammed the rudder back in, realizing he was crabbing, that the torpedo would strike the water at an angle, and not nose straight in. If it didn't break up, the fuse might not arm.

Stick over, coordinate with rudder, straighten back out.

Three hundred yards.

He grabbed the lever and pulled.

His airship surged up. Now what?

Bank to port, starboard. He had never thought to discuss it, to plan it, he might pull across right in front of someone else. He pointed straight at the enemy ship and pressed in. The seconds passed, fire crisscrossing. He pulled up, skimming over the deck, too terrified to look to either side. Cleared of the ship, he nosed down slightly and raced out for several hundred yards without a shot being fired, then finally several of the guns on the enemy's port side opened up, tracers splashing the water around him.

He started to jink, still running low across the water. A half mile out he finally began to turn, for the enemy cruisers in close to shore had all come about and were speeding toward the beleaguered battleships.

As he turned, he finally looked back toward his target. The torpedo should have crossed the three hundred yards. A lone Goliath was zooming over the stern, a Falcon directly above it.

And then the bow of the ship seemed to lift, a massive column of water, several hundred feet high, a blinding flash sweeping over the deck, seconds later another explosion farther aft. As he continued to climb, he saw both battleships, sterns blazing, the farthest aft with its bow blown clear off, the ship already settling.

It had worked! By all the saints, it had worked. Now the only question left was how to get his crate home.

Yasim stood in stunned silence. Damage control parties raced past him without ceremony, dragging hoses. Flames swirled up from the foredeck, the ship all but dead in the water.

A thunderclap of fire burst across the western horizon, the battleship *Yutana* going up. Behind it, *Motaka* had rolled over, keel pointed heavenward.

"Sire."

He stirred from his thoughts and dark contemplations. It was Admiral Ullani.

"Sire, I suggest that you transfer your flag."

Yasim nodded, saying nothing.

"Sire, we can save this ship, but come dawn they might strike again. It would be best if you were on a vessel that can maneuver."

"Yes, yes, of course."

He looked back to the burning city. All this to achieve what? He wondered. This contemptible place, for what?

It was time to turn about, to find Hazin, to find out the real reasons for all of this, and then to kill him.

Minutes later a cruiser slowed, lines snaking out to the stricken flagship, swinging in close so that a chair could be run across to bring the emperor over.

Word had flashed through the ship that the emperor was leaving, from his third bodyguard, to a message runner, straight to an ammunition handler in the main magazine.

Twenty years prior he had taken the Oath of the Novitiate of the Third Order, had taken his assigned task and lived it across all the years, in a dozen battles, two hundred feet aft of Yasim and forty feet below him. He had even received, from Yasim's own hand, a commendation for heroism at Tushiva. And all that time he had waited, never knowing when the order would come or how it would come. It had arrived only the night before and only if the ship had already been hit seriously, otherwise he was to do nothing.

The ship had been hit, the emperor was fleeing, and the word had come.

He silently said the blessing of parting as he walked into the main ammunition locker. Powder bags for the great guns lined the walls, each in its own rack, sealed inside a wooden container. He had done the routine a thousand times, in drill and in battle. Lift the wooden container out of the rack and walk with it out of the powder locker room, the door guard opening and closing the barrier. An assistant loader would take the container and run it into the ammunition hoist; then he would turn, go back, and do it again.

This time he tore the lid off one of the containers, drew a concealed folding knife out from under his shirt and flicked the blade open. The hilt of the knife was cunningly made; a simple twist and a small container popped open, a simple wooden match falling into his open hand.

With the knife he slashed open the powder bag, a cascade of black powder spilling out. He pulled another lid open, did the same, and then a third. The door opened, one of the assistants putting his head in.

"Pava, what . . . ?"

The Novitiate of the Third Order held the match up, and with his thumb flicked it to life. Smiling, he touched it to the stream of black powder pouring out of the torn bag.

Richard Cromwell sat on the beach, drunk from the wine, watching as the fireball soared a thousand feet into the air. The civilians around him had been cheering the spectacle of the air battle and its aftermath as if it had been a chariot race. The explosion sent them into a new frenzy of celebration.

He was disgusted with the whole affair and felt no qualms about relieving them of another sack of wine, which they were more than happy to provide to the hero.

The emperor was dead, and somehow he knew it was Hazin who had done it.

They came just after sunset, five aerosteamers, soaring in from the northwest.

Togo, as always, heard them first. The men around Keane began to stand up, incredulous, several of them laughing, saying it was only a hallucination.

But it was not.

The first aerosteamer, a Falcon, winged over, swooping down on the ravine to the west, stitching it with gatling fire. Men who were so parched that they had not spoken for over a day, cheered hoarsely, pointing, laughing as the tables were turned. The next two were Goliaths, flying straight toward the butte. They came in low, throttling back, and for a second Abe thought that they were going to try some mad landing.

The lead ship skimming barely a dozen feet above them started releasing bundles, the first one almost hitting Abe, the second and third dropped near the hospital area. The fourth one sailed over the edge and disappeared.

The same performance was tried by the second Goliath. The first package fell short, but the second and third and fourth landed safely.

They made three passes, the men scattering with each pass, cursing when one hit too close, but then cheering and waving.

The last two aerosteamers were Falcons as well. They swept around the butte, tracer fire pouring down. One of the Falcons broke away and started back west, engine misfiring, but holding to its course. The two Goliaths buzzed back over one last time, wagging their wings. The men cheered. The bundles were already being broken open, discipline breaking down for a moment as the men leapt upon the full canteens bundled up inside, tearing them open, then gulping down the water. Abe saw cartridge boxes, rations, and a package stamped with the green insignia of the medical corps.

The last Falcon circled back in, a small package with a red streamer tumbled down, landing in the middle of the butte. One of the troopers hobbled over, picked it up and brought it to Abe. The Falcon continued to circle.

Abe tore the red streamer off and opened the package. Inside were half a dozen cigars, weighed down with a package of forty cartridges for a revolver, and a note.

> To the commander of the beleaguered force near Carvana Pass,
> My sincere apologies, sir, and please consider the cigars enclosed a small token of respect. We have been searching for you for five days. The airship that passed near you this morning reported your presence, the pilot wisely refraining from coming too close out of concern that it might trigger an assault to finish you before help could arrive. I hope its flying by without notice did not adversely affect the morale of your command.

Abe chuckled and shook his head.

> A relief column has been dispatched, supported by a company of land ironclads, and should arrive late tomor-

row. Airship support will return at dawn and maintain watch over you and also bring in additional supplies.

I must request, sir, a reply, which I believe you will understand given the nature of the situation. If Lieutenant Abraham Schuder Keane is with your command and still alive, would you please respond by waving the red streamer attached to this package. I apologize, sir, for singling out one particular trooper for concern when so many lives are at stake, but I hope you understand my reasons.

I look forward to meeting you, sir, and to personally congratulating you for what has obviously been an heroic stand.

I remain, sir, your ob'd and humble serv't,

General of the Armies Vincent Nathaniel Hawthorne.

Abe handed the letter to Togo and waited for him to read it.

"I'm tempted not to wave it," he sighed.

Togo looked at him, grinned, and shook his head. He picked the streamer up from the ground and started to wave it over his head. The Falcon banked over, wagged its wings, then circled back out, turning to the west.

Abe handed the cigars to Togo.

"I don't smoke," he announced.

Togo pocketed four of them, fumbled for a match in his haversack, and struck a light, puffing two of the cigars to life. He handed one to Abe.

"You do now."

Abe sat on the ground, canteen in one hand and a cigar in the other and watched the sun set.

NINETEEN

"My God, Abe, you look like hell," Richard exclaimed as the door into the waiting room swung open and the newly decorated major slowly hobbled in.

Both Adam and Richard came to attention and saluted,

the proper ceremony, regardless of rank, for a holder of the Medal of Honor.

Abe, still embarrassed with the whole routine of it all, returned the salute, and then came forward extending his hand.

"Both of you deserved it far more than me."

"Well, we aren't president's sons," Adam replied.

A hard look came to Abe's eyes.

"Abe, just joking, that's all."

Abe relaxed slightly.

"I told my father I would refuse, but Hawthorne had already written it up and released the news to Gates's papers."

Richard Cromwell looked over to the door leading into the reception room of the White House, where a mob of senators and congressmen were gathering to be seen and photographed with the first heroes of the Kazan War. Other knots of officers and enlisted personnel nervously walked about the room: nearly all the surviving Goliath pilots, a sergeant with the 9th Cavalry who had led an action similar to Abe's, and Rear Admiral Petronius, now admiral of the fleet.

"Look, Abe," Richard motioned to the door. "This is the reality of it. The Republic needs heroes for this war. Sure, we turned back the first wave, but this is only the beginning. The Kazan's industrial capability is far beyond us. Their lost battleships can be replaced in months, while it will still take us years. That's why we're here in this room today, waiting to get served up."

He put his hand on Abe's shoulder.

"I know how you feel and agree. Sergeant Togo should be here, I saw your report on him. I had a copilot," and he paused for a moment, "well, we all had friends who paid the price for all our mistakes."

"You of all people, though, should be wearing this," Abe replied, and he pointed to the Medal of Honor pinned to his left breast. "You were the one who warned us and led that suicidal attack that cleared the way here for Rosovich to do his strike."

Rosovich nodded in agreement.

"Bearers of bad tidings rarely get medals, Abe," Richard said, and forced a smile. "There's still a lot of questions about how I got out, about Hazin," and the smile disappeared, "about Sean."

"What was said in Gates's is absurd," Adam snapped.

Cromwell stiffened slightly.

"Freedom of the press, my friend."

"Freedom to print lies," Abe replied forcefully. "Whoever said you abandoned him—"

Richard extended his hand, indicating that Abe should lower his voice.

"Let it rest, Abe. Let it rest."

Richard looked past Abe and stiffened slightly as Admiral Petronius approached.

Again the ritual of saluting Abe first, and again Abe reddened.

"The Republic's first father and son team of Medal of Honor winners. A worthy decision, young man."

"Thank you, sir."

Petronius's harsh scan swept the three and his features softened.

"Mr. Rosovich, the Gold Star for Valor looks good on you," Petronius said, "and you, too, Mr. Cromwell."

"Thank you, sir," Rosovich replied, a bit embarrassed. "And congratulations on your promotion."

Petronius shook his head.

"A damn poor way to get it. Bullfinch was the creator of our service, its traditions. A good death, but I would have preferred that stout old man to still be with us." He sighed. "I just wish this foolishness was over, I want to get back to our command. They're still out there."

The battle of Constantine had actually gone into a second day, with the aerosteamer carriers launching a second attack after the retreating battleships were spotted with dozens of transports. But another storm was rolling in, contact was lost after the destruction of two transports and one more hit on a battleship. The carriers had retired back to Constantine where, in the half-destroyed wreckage of the yard, thousands of laborers were swarming over the three precious, remaining ships, refitting them under the direction of Theodor Theodorovich.

The door that Abe had come through opened again, everyone in the room stiffening as the president entered,

Kathleen beside him. There was the snapping of salutes and Andrew smiled, offering one in return.

The president's attention fixed on Petronius, and he headed straight for him. Abe, Richard, and Adam started to respectfully withdraw, but Andrew motioned for them to stay.

"You boys might as well hear this as well. Admiral, I want you to head back to Constantine within the hour, I'll have an express waiting to take you. Mr. Cromwell, you'll go with him and take over command of the air groups."

Adam shifted uncomfortably, wanting to speak, but afraid to do so.

Andrew looked over at the diminutive pilot and smiled.

"Sorry, son. You're grounded."

"Grounded, sir?"

"Personal request from Varinnia Ferguson. You're part of her damn team now."

"Damn Theodor," Adam whispered, then seeing that Kathleen had overheard, he reddened.

"My apologies, ma'am."

She laughed softly and put a reassuring hand on his shoulder.

"I've heard a lot worse from the president, Adam."

"Mr. Cromwell, my son expressed his feelings to me, quite forcefully I should add, about you receiving the Medal of Honor. I agree with him. I think you understand the reasoning. There're concerns, some lingering questions in spite of your correct and heroic service."

"I understand," Cromwell said quietly.

"I believe in you, Cromwell, I want you to know that."

Cromwell nodded, saying nothing.

Andrew's features hardened.

"You boys might as well hear this, as well. Admiral, a flyer located part of the Bantag Horde this morning and spotted the Golden Yurt of Jurak on the coast."

"The enemy fleet?"

Andrew nodded.

"Report of fifty or more transports off-loading troops and supplies. I want you to sortie and try and intercept. Any lingering questions about this war are gone. The Kazan have joined with the Bantag."

"I pity Jurak," Abe said.

Andrew looked over at him.

"He'll get more than he bargained for."

Andrew nodded.

"You gentlemen head in, I want a moment with Petronius."

The three comrades turned and, as the doors to the reception room opened, went in together, side by side.

Andrew, smiling sadly, watched them go, then looked back to Petronius.

"Keep your ships alive, Admiral. It'll be a year or more before we can bring anything new into this fight."

"I know."

"And Cromwell. He's a good man, try to keep him alive. I think we'll hear a lot more from him."

Petronius did not reply.

"Good luck out there."

The two shook hands, and Petronius followed the crowd into the reception hall.

Andrew looked over at Kathleen as she slipped her hand into his.

"Proud of our boy?" he asked.

"He's changed. Quiet, far too stern, with a look in his eyes that wasn't there before."

"War does that," Andrew sighed.

"Damn all war."

"Yes, damn all war. But we're stuck with it."

"Andrew, can't you keep him back, the way you did with the Rosovich boy?"

"He must take the same risks I'd ask of anyone else. I'm president, my dear, I can no longer think as his father."

"God bless Vincent Hawthorne, at least he ignored you for once and sent those extra planes out to look for him."

He smiled.

"I'm glad he did. Now let's go do our jobs."

Hazin stood at the railing of his ship, watching as landing ships surged in to shore. The dark mass of thousands of the Shiv were already forming up on the beach, beginning to move up into the hills. By the end of the day the last of them would be ashore, followed by the umen of land cruisers, and then he could withdraw.

He looked back out to sea. Three battleships lay off the

bay, the rest of the fleet beyond. Admiral Vasa, now commander of the fleet, was compliant enough in terms of keeping the fleet with him. He wisely knew what might happen otherwise. Three of the surviving cousins had died as well, one of them from quite natural causes, shot by a strafing enemy airship.

Vasa knew and understood. The Shiv under General Zhan would do their job well while he returned home to properly protect the unborn emperor or empress.

He looked over at O'Donald, who stood by the bow, gaze locked on the ships steaming in, carrying with them the terrifying striking arm of the Shiv. He would go with them, ready to be used at the proper moment.

All things were now possible, Hazin thought with a smile.